PRAISE FOR

"*Doon*, by Carey Corp and Lorie Langdon, is a YA retelling of *Brigadoon* that is fresh and enchanting."

— *USA Today*'s Happily Ever After blog

"*Oz* meets *Once Upon a Time*."

— City Book Review

"… An imaginative reboot of the classic *Brigadoon*."

— *School Library Journal*

"Musical-theater fans will rejoice … Give this romance to fans who can't get enough of 'Will they? Won't they?' plot twists."

— *Booklist*

"The perfect mix of mystery, magic, and romance; be prepared to get lost in another world!"

— Maria V. Snyder, author of the *New York Times* bestselling Poison Study series

Destined for Doon

Other books in the Doon series:

Doon

Destined for Doon

Carey Corp and Lorie Langdon

BLINK

BLINK

Destined for Doon
Copyright © 2014 by Carey Corp and Lorie Moeggenberg

This title is also available as a Blink ebook.
Visit www.zondervan.com/ebooks.

Requests for information should be addressed to:

Blink, 3900 *Sparks Drive SE, Grand Rapids, Michigan 49546*

This edition: ISBN 978-0-310-74240-1 (softcover)

Library of Congress Cataloging-in-Publication Data

Corp, Carey, author.
    Destined for Doon / by Carey Corp and Lorie Langdon.
        pages cm. — (A Doon novel)
    Summary: Kenna realizes she made a mistake in leaving Doon behind forever
    and now she has received her Calling — proof she and Duncan are meant to
    be — then Duncan informs Kenna Doon needs her, but even if she can save the
    enchanted kingdom, her happy ending is far from assured.
        ISBN 978-0-310-74233-3 (hardback)
        ISBN 978-0-310-74240-1 (softcover)
        ISBN 978-0-310-74234-0 (epub)
        [1. Fairy tales. 2. Love — Fiction.] I. Langdon, Lorie, author. II. Title.
    PZ8.C816De 2014
    [Fic] — dc23   2014026659

Thank you to the Alan Jay Lerner Estate and the Frederick Loewe Foundation for
use of the *Brigadoon* premise.

Cover design and photography: Mike Heath/Magnus Creative
Cover direction: Cindy Davis
Interior design and composition: Greg Johnson/Textbook Perfect

Printed in the United States of America

15 16 17 18 19 20 21 /DCI/ 20 19 18 17 16 15 14 13 12 11 10 9 8 7 6 5 4 3 2 1

Dedication

For the prodigals of the world,
the lost and those who've found the courage to go home:
You are so much more than your mistakes.

ChAPTER 1

Mackenna

I glided down the backstage hallway with the sort of stealth that would've made my best friend proud. Unfortunately my ninja-like skills didn't last for long, as I stumbled over my own feet and careened shoulder first against the wall. Before I could recover, Jeanie waved at me from the doorway of the adjacent green room.

"Outstanding show tonight, Kenna."

"Thanks." I flashed my fellow intern a dazzling smile meant to overshadow my clumsy moment. "I'm really grateful for your support."

I gave her a quick hug before slipping into the sanctuary of my private dressing room. The familiar aroma of roasting greasepaint and lilies, so pungent I could actually taste it, greeted me. Rather than turn on the sizzling, artificial lights that would transform the windowless room into a life-size Easy-Bake Oven, I lit a candle.

Adrenaline Theatre interns didn't usually get the royal treatment. But none had ever stepped into the leading role hours before opening night and then been proclaimed "a fresh and stunning revelation" by the *Chicago Tribune*. After a six-week run and forty-eight performances, I was no longer just an intern. I was the actress who saved *Little Jimmy: The Margaret Mitchell Musical*, an up-and-coming talent with invitations to audition for a handful of Broadway shows and national tours.

Even Adrenaline's artistic director, Weston Ballard, wanted a piece of me — in more ways than one. He'd announced a new musical for the following season, written exclusively with me in mind. In typical Wes fashion, he'd commissioned the work without even asking if I wanted the role. I guess since he felt like he "discovered" me, he assumed he owned me as well. I wasn't doing his show, but I *was* avoiding the part where I informed him of my decision — at least until after closing night.

Just in case he decided to pay me a visit, I locked the door before kicking off my tap shoes and getting out of costume. As much as I'd wished for house elves to magically tidy up after me, my street clothes were still lying in a heap behind my folding screen. Padding over to the changing area, I shimmied out of my constricting 1940s dress and girdle, my hips sighing in relief as I eased on my favorite jeans.

Since the first time I heard "Hard Knock Life," I'd dreamed of stage life in vivid detail, from the dressing room to the curtain call. But not once did I ever picture being on stage without my bestie applauding me from the first row. And now, thanks to my misadventures in Doon, other dear but improbable faces joined her in my ultimate theater fantasy. Some nights I caught myself scanning the audience as I dared to hope for the impossible — that I could celebrate my success with the people I loved.

"Hello, Mackenna."

Holy Hammerstein! The voice stopped me cold.

I hastily pulled on a sweater and then peeked around the

screen to see Duncan MacCrae leaning against the edge of my dressing table holding a duffel bag. But I knew from experience it wasn't really him. It was a Calling delusion, a manifestation of my subconscious longing for my one true love — a boy who was literally a world away.

Like every other time he'd appeared in my visions, he was ridiculously gorgeous — even in faded jeans and a white button-down shirt. Which was odd ... The many times I'd conjured him, he'd always worn Doonian clothes — breeches, tunics, the occasional kilt, and often a sword strapped to his side. I'd never pictured him in anything close to modern before.

Something about his unexpected attire caused my heart to wrench. He looked so natural, as if he belonged in this place — this life. Which was inconceivable! He was a Scottish prince, complete with a castle and kingdom.

Stepping out from the screen, I skirted a pile of discarded clothes to grab my bag. Similar occurrences had taught me that Duncan's apparition could linger stubbornly for hours. But if I left, he wouldn't follow.

"Mackenna." His soft, deep brogue tempted me to reconsider. But I'd already played that role — talking back to his image, begging him to stay ... He never did. He'd fade away and I'd be an emotional basket case for days.

"I'm too tired for this," I pleaded. "Please go away."

When I brushed past the imaginary Duncan, he grabbed my arm. Warm, solid fingers produced little electric tremors on my skin as the clean scent of sunshine and leather saddles enveloped me.

While I wouldn't have ordinarily believed my eyes — or ears, or any other sense as far as Duncan was concerned, my soul stirred in recognition as a voice in my head cried out that the impossible had come true. "You're real?"

"Aye." His velvety brown eyes, with the golden flecks that reminded me of melting caramel, fastened to mine. "And so are you."

Giddy with shock, I whispered, "What are you doing here?"

I waited for words of love, a confession that he couldn't exist without me any more than I could live without him, reassurance that he realized my leaving him on the Brig o' Doon had been at the expense of my own heart, and the promise that we would never be apart again.

Instead, Duncan let his hand drop from my arm. His posture stiffened as his gaze refocused in the vicinity of my right earlobe. "The queen has tasked me with bringing ye back to Doon."

The queen? The absence of his touch left me feeling ice-cold. Goosebumps covered my arms as I crossed them over my chest. "You mean Vee? *My best friend?*"

"Aye. She has need of you."

She needed me? And the unspoken truth — he didn't. He was here only because those were the orders he'd been given. The hope that'd been welling up inside of me froze. "What's going on? Is she okay?"

Shadows from the flickering candle shifted across his face, making it impossible to read. "She's well. She requires your assistance is all. I'll explain when we're underway."

It was probably a best friend thing. She wanted a confidante or someone to keep her grounded despite her recent ascension to royalty. The reason didn't really matter because if she needed me, I would go. However, since Prince MacCrae was *only* following orders, I didn't have to make this easy for him.

"Now's not really the best time." I let my shoulders rise and fall with my words. "I've got a lot of stuff going on."

Duncan stepped closer so that I had to lean backward ever so slightly to see his face. Through tightened lips, he said, "It's not a request. I'll throw you over my shoulder and drag ye back if I have to."

"You came all this way to threaten me?" I took a cautious step back and flicked the switch near the door. The overhead lights hummed to life.

He clamped his eyes shut and sighed. "No."

When he looked at me a moment later under the unforgiving lights of the dressing room, he appeared older. Deep worry lines formed creases above the bridge of his nose and at the corners of his mouth. Purplish crescents accentuated the baggy skin under his eyes making me wonder when he'd last slept. Most noticeably, the easy grin that seemed to be an integral part of his persona was gone, and I couldn't help but wonder if he'd left it on the bridge next to my heart.

Threading his fingers through his dark hair, he said plainly, "Look, I dinna like it any more than you. Do ye think I'd be here if I could've avoided it?"

The question was obviously rhetorical. Everything from the deep frown he wore to his awkward posture indicated he could barely stand being in the same room with me. Not that I could blame him. I promised him that we could be together in the modern world and then tricked him into returning to Doon alone. At the time, I believed it was the right thing to do.

Almost like he'd been eavesdropping in my head, he said, "Ye made your choice and I swore to respect it. I *promise* as soon as we get things sorted out, I'll return you to your life and you'll never have to see me again. My queen says I'm to beg you, if need be."

I wouldn't make him beg — he'd been humiliated enough. My best friend wanted me to come so nothing would keep me away. Not even the animosity of the prince who was once mine. "Okay."

Duncan hoisted his duffel over his shoulder. "Good, then. We'll leave right away."

"No." I stepped to my dressing table to tidy my things. "I've got one more performance tomorrow afternoon and then I'm free."

From the reflection in the mirror, I watched the corners of his mouth pinch downward, hardening his face. I braced myself for an argument, but rather than fight me, he agreed with a single nod.

Before I could fully absorb the implications of our arrangement, the knob on the dressing room door rattled, shattering our awkward truce. Duncan's hand instinctively reached for his sword, and when it came up empty, he clenched it into a fist.

The rattling quickly escalated into pounding. Each reverberation caused Duncan to tense a bit more — like a windup jack-in-the-box. If I didn't intervene, he would likely spring forward, rip the door from its hinges, and use it to pummel the person on the other side.

Dreading what was about to unfold, I hurried to the door and twisted the knob to release the lock. Bracing it with my body, I edged it open. Through the gap, I saw Weston's salon-perfect blond locks and his narrow eyes with their faint traces of guy-liner. When he realized I wasn't alone, he quickly replaced his scowl with an overly wide smile that revealed high-end veneers. He leaned against the door, forcing me to give way.

"There's my diva!" Weston glanced from me to Duncan. His expensive smile never faltered as he sauntered into the room and snaked his arm around my hip. "Who's this, babe?"

My heart pounded against my ribcage as Duncan coiled into what I recognized as his Highland warrior stance. For a moment I worried he would clobber Wes like an opponent in the coliseum ring back in Doon. Fortunately, he seemed to reconsider. Raising himself to his full height — a full head above his adversary — he stepped forward with regal grace. "I am Duncan Rhys Finnean MacCrae, Third Earl of Lanarkshire. You may call me *Lord* MacCrae. And you are?"

"I'm Weston Ballard, lord and artistic director of this theatre. And Kenna's boyfriend."

Boyfriend? That was *so* not true. Well, maybe a little bit. After a couple of miserable dates, during which the company started referring to us as *Keston*, I broke it off. Dating Wes had been a mistake, a pathetic attempt to get over Duncan after months of agony. But I quickly found I had no stomach for being wooed — at least not by him.

At the B-word, Duncan's smile froze. He blinked at Weston while he absorbed that little relationship bomb. I'd heard Wes do this multiple times — especially where other guys were involved. He loved to exaggerate circumstances to make himself appear important.

Wes pulled me closer so that our hip bones jabbed against one another. "Who *is* this guy, babe?"

"Just an old friend from Scotland." My heart hitched in my chest. As if Duncan could be "just" anything.

Duncan's smile warmed slightly. "Not *that* old." It was an obvious dig at the fact that Wes was in his twenties — practically an old creeper compared to the eighteen-year-old prince.

Wes bared his freakishly white teeth. "That's right. You're barely out of diapers."

Before things could get any more testosterone-y, I stepped between them. I just needed to keep the peace with Wes for one more show. Was that really so much to ask?

Flashing Duncan a threatening smile, I explained to Wes, "He came to surprise me."

Weston's free hand captured my face. In a deceptively gentle-looking caress, he dug his index finger into the flesh under my chin and forced my head to turn until we faced each other. "Is that so?"

If it hadn't been for Duncan's presence, I would've broken Wes's hand. He was being a jerk on purpose and his actions bordered on abuse. Out of the corner of my eye, I observed Duncan's murderous scowl. Obviously, he'd noticed the inappropriate behavior as well. He took a fraction of a step forward, his smooth Scottish brogue heavy with subtext. "Aye. We go *way* back."

Since childhood ... which I hadn't realized until recently.

Releasing my face, Wes leaned toward me and nuzzled my neck like Snuffleupagus. With an affected and no doubt rehearsed nonchalance, he asked, "Where are you staying tonight, mate?"

That was a good question. All too aware of the way Duncan's hands clenched into fists, I subtly twisted away from Wes's face. Under the pretext of straightening up, I slipped his grasp to pick up a sock lying at my feet.

Considering the question with an elegant tilt of his head, Duncan mused, "I suppose I'll stay at the local inn."

"Duncan is staying at my place." It tumbled from my mouth before the thought had finished forming. He didn't know this world, and even if he hated me now, it was my job to protect him until I could get him home. I wasn't about to let him out of my sight, not even to sleep.

Wes grabbed my arm and spun me around so that we faced the corner with our backs to my newly declared houseguest. Leaning in, he hissed in my ear, "Babe, you haven't even let *me* spend the night, and *this guy's* gonna sleep over?"

"Wes" — it took every ounce of effort not to glance toward Duncan to see if he overheard and had a reaction to Weston's innuendo — "he doesn't know Chicago. I'm not letting him stay in some random motel — "

"So put him up at the Hilton," Wes shot back, showering my neck in spittle.

"No. I didn't ask him to come, but now that he's here, I feel responsible for him."

"Okay." Wes's fingers dug into my arm, to hurt me or brand me, or maybe a bit of both. "But I'm coming too."

Keeping the discomfort my "boyfriend" was inflicting from coloring the casual tone of my voice, I replied, "Duncan and I will be talking old times. You'd be bored."

The pain increased. A muscle in Wes's cheek ticked as he said through gritted teeth, "I'm not letting you go without me."

I felt Duncan's heat at my back as he stepped closer. His scent filled my senses, flooding me with a sense of safety in spite of the present situation. In a lethal voice, Duncan growled, "Tha's exactly what's going to happen, *mate*. Mackenna and I are going to her flat and you can go wherever the devil it pleases you. As long as it's no' with us. Now unhand the lass."

With one last pinch, Wes let go. As he stepped back, he had the audacity to look hurt. But I wouldn't waste one speck of empathy on his smoke and mirrors. I was *so* done with him.

However, in case I had any illusions about what the future held with a certain Scottish prince, Duncan lifted his hands and said, "You need not worry for your girlfriend's sake, mate. I wouldna so much as lay a hand on her."

chapter 2

Mackenna

If Sondheim is to be believed, and I see no reason why he shouldn't be, size matters — at least when telling lies. Letting Duncan believe I was Weston's girlfriend seemed harmless enough for the moment ... or at least better than the alternative — confessing that I was still crazy in love with the boy from the bridge and getting shot down because he hated my guts. As soon as I found the right time, I would tell him the truth.

With unsteady fingers, I fumbled to unlock my studio apartment. When the bolt finally cooperated, I opened the door with a flourish, followed immediately by a sense of panic. Little molehills of clothes were strewn about the floor, exactly where I'd shed them before collapsing into bed. I hurried inside, scooping up jeans, undies, and bras while making a joke about it being the maid's day off, then flipped on the desk lamp. Low lighting seemed better than the overhead considering the state of my humble abode.

Duncan stepped into the room, set his duffel by the door, and surveyed the area the way a lieutenant inspects his new quarters. I knew from my extended stay in his kingdom that he kept his chambers tidy. My style tended to be clutter bordering on chaos. Dirty clothes erupted from the hamper in the corner. Makeup and hair stuff littered my desk/dressing/dining room table. Dishes were stacked in the shallow sink next to the tiny fridge and second-hand microwave that perpetually smelled of burritos. Next to the kitchenette, there was a small bathroom that I'd thankfully cleaned the previous morning. At the opposite end of the room, an unmade full-size bed, dresser, and freestanding wardrobe took up the majority of the space.

It took Duncan all of about five seconds to take the grand tour. "This is your home?" His flat tone gave me no clue how he felt. Or if he even cared at all.

I glanced around the room feeling slightly defensive about my dwelling of the past ten months. It wasn't paradise, but it was — Who was I kidding? Even by Eliza Doolittle standards it wasn't loverly or anything that could be fixed with an enormous chair. It was merely where I crashed. Not home. I didn't even have a TV. Not that I'd gone medieval or anything, but there'd been an ill-timed resurgence of fairy tales on television, both scripted and reality shows. You couldn't channel surf these days without bumping into a freakin' prince.

An old tissue stained with red lipstick lay in a crumpled ball on the floor next to the wastebasket. I snatched it up and threw it away. "I'm not here very much."

Duncan paused to inspect the small shelf above the desk/dressing/dining room table. That particular spot housed my new obsession, little replicas and postcards of Scottish castles. Although I still enjoyed my theater memorabilia — posters and playbills of *Wicked*, *Into the Woods*, *RENT*, and other faves — my shelf of Scotland made me feel most alive. When I looked at it, I felt the misty breeze with its faint hint of heather, transporting the melody of bagpipes from across the ocean.

I watched uneasily as Duncan picked up a replica that looked suspiciously like Castle MacCrae. It wasn't an exact match, but close enough. Before he could read too much into it, I offered, "That makes me think of Vee. I can hardly believe she's a queen."

Then, desperate to change the subject, I said, "Seriously, Duncan. Lord MacCrae, Third Earl of Lanarkshire — what was that about?"

He shrugged, his dark eyes lacking the wry spark I associated with him. "I didn't lie. Veronica cautioned me about using the title of prince, so I used one of the other ones."

"You're a prince and an earl?"

"Among other things."

And I was the girl who'd discarded him like one of my lipstick-blotted tissues. Hopefully returning to Doon would give me the opportunity to make up for that mistake. If I could prove to him how sorry I was, maybe he would forgive me. And then ... I wouldn't allow myself to dream about what came after — at least not yet. "Are you hungry?"

He shook his head and set the miniature castle back in its spot. "Nay."

Under other circumstances, I'd have dragged him halfway across town for the best — make that second-best — pizza on the planet. Over dinner I would've asked a million questions about his journey over the bridge, what he thought of the modern world, and helped him decide what to do and see while he was here. But it was late. I was exhausted and secretly thankful that there was no reason to prolong the awkward evening.

"Since you came all this way to get me, don't you think you should tell me what's going on?"

"Later, once we're on the road. Right now ye need to pack. Tomorrow, we'll go directly from the theater to the airport."

"Okay. Let me just text the box office and get them to hold a ticket for you."

"There's no need. I shall wait in your dressing room."

He didn't want to see me perform? My stomach sank. Even though I had no right to be offended, I could feel the disappointment stinging my eyes. Dissing my show hurt like he'd dumped a bucket of water on my spirit — my soul was melting. Wasn't he the least bit curious about what I'd chosen to do with my life?

Grateful for something to do, I grabbed my oversized pink canvas bag and set it on the floor in front of my makeshift closet. As I sifted through the haphazard drawers, I was aware of Duncan crossing to his duffle, producing a book, and returning to my desk/dressing/dining room table, where he seated himself in my only chair.

I packed in silence, unable to concentrate on the task and, therefore, erring on the side of excess. I didn't know how long I'd be gone, what the weather would be like on the journey, or what I'd be facing — so the kitchen sink approach seemed best. In addition to jeans and tops, I threw in an umbrella, a heavy jacket, snow boots, some earrings for Vee, and a few protein bars.

Opening my underwear drawer, I surveyed the jumble of sensible striped cotton and impractical scraps of red and black lace. What to pack ... practical or something that made me feel pretty? I glanced at Duncan, who appeared engrossed in whatever he was reading — some massive book with dragons on the cover. Although I couldn't see his eyes, his expression was intense — the corners of his mouth turned down and pinched, his brow severe, not a laugh line in sight. He reminded me of a babysitter enduring a distasteful assignment.

Granny panties it was.

Shoving all my girly matching sets to the back of the drawer, I grabbed two handfuls of soft, mismatched underwear and dropped them into my bag. If Duncan was determined to treat me like an outcast, then I'd endure my exile in comfort.

Keeping with the soccer mom theme, I grabbed my most comfy sleep pants and a giant *Company* T-shirt and stepped into the bathroom. Now that packing was done, I could no longer avoid the final portion of the evening, sleeping arrangements. And what Duncan wore when he slept.

The one night we had spent together in Doon — rather, I should say, occupying the same space — he slept in his tunic and the Doonian equivalent of flannel pajama bottoms. But I suspected that if I hadn't been there, the shirt would've come off. Thinking about Duncan in my bed, bare-chested and despising me, caused my vision to swim again.

Determined not to cry, I turned on the faucet. The night-time ritual — washing my face, moisturizing, brushing my teeth — had a calming effect. After a couple of minutes, I felt ready to face Duncan again.

The last things I needed were over at my desk, so I reluctantly approached, waiting for him to acknowledge me. He didn't. The way his body tensed told me that he was every bit as aware of me as I was of him, but he wouldn't do me the courtesy of looking up. Fine. I could be curt too. "Can you please hand me my makeup bag? It's the plaid one next to the lamp."

Eyes never leaving the page, he grabbed the bag and handed it to me. As I reached for it, our fingers brushed. Electricity crackled up my arm to my startled chest. It was the first contact since he touched my arm in the dressing room. Like the previous instance, the connection was nearly unbearable, but the minute it was gone I grieved its absence.

I stood, makeup bag in hand, feeling oddly numb. "Do you need a toothbrush?"

"No, thank you." He squeezed his hand into a fist and released like he was trying to work out a cramp as he nodded toward his duffle. "I've everything I need."

Considering myself royally dismissed, I crossed to my makeshift suitcase and let the bag fall with a soft plop. Only then did I address the final act of the night. "Since you're the guest, you can take the bed and I'll sleep on the fl —"

"Dinna be daft." His interruption bordered on rude. "Sleep in your own bed."

Being the chivalrous knight, I knew he'd never budge. With a stiff "Good night," he clicked off the light at the desk, effectively ending the discussion.

While I wondered what to do next, he got up and headed into the bathroom. Light blazed from the adjoining room, narrowing to a crack as the door closed between us. I could hear him going through his own nighttime ritual, and then ... *Sweet Baby Sondheim!* The shower turned on. Duncan MacCrae, the boy I thought I'd never see again, was showering just a few feet away.

Climbing into bed, I began mentally rehearsing my repertoire of Broadway's most depressing musical numbers. Anything that would distract from the wet, naked guy in the next room. Not that I was a prude, but the cruel universe seemed to be dangling what I couldn't have on a cosmic string in front of me — which called for *Parade, Blood Brothers, Side Show,* and *Next to Normal.*

After seven morose ballads, the water stopped, and I turned to face the wall. A few minutes later I heard Duncan settle into my desk/dressing/dining room table chair. That he would sit in my chair and ruin my sleep while I lay a few feet away, aware and alone, held some sort of poetic irony.

I clamped my eyes shut, trying not to thrash about too much and give away my pretense at sleep. Sometime around midnight my phone buzzed. Snatching it off my nightstand, I scanned the text from Weston: *I'm not home, so don't bother stopping by.*

As if I'd just show up in the middle of the night! In the whole time we'd known each other, I'd never been to his place. I couldn't even say where it was. Another buzz.

Don't worry about coming in for the matinee. Letting Jeanie have the final performance. She's VERY persuasive! She says hi.

Ewww! I didn't even want to think about Jeanie's persuasive talents. I waited for the grief of losing the final performance, essentially being fired, to kick in ... but all I felt was relief. No forced smiles as I greeted patrons and thanked staff, no awkward exchanges between the boy who owned my heart and the guy who thought he owned me, no more pretending to be someone I wasn't. In that perverse way that life imitates art, my whole existence had become a performance, one I was glad to leave behind.

From the darkness, Duncan asked, "What is it, Mackenna?"

Although he hadn't moved, I should've guessed he was wide awake. He probably wouldn't sleep at all. But whether he was watching over me or just watching to ensure I didn't run away again was anyone's guess.

Despite being free of my performance obligations, I would never escape the shackles of betraying the sweetest, most gentle boy I'd ever met. Forcing brightness into my tone, I replied, "Good news. Wes got Jeanie to cover the final show. So I can go anytime you want."

It was quiet for a beat, then in a voice that sounded a hundred miles away, he declared, "We leave at first light."

Traveling with Duncan was surprisingly uneventful ... until the flight. We used the same taxi service that had delivered him to the theater the previous day. At the airport, Duncan produced a wad of cash to pay the fare, including a generous tip. Then he'd charmed the lady at the ticket counter to book us on an earlier flight — which I totally attributed to his swoon-inducing Scottish accent. Although I was curious how he'd assimilated into his contemporary surroundings so thoroughly in just a few days, his unwillingness to engage in conversation and my lack of adequate caffeination caused me to hold my tongue.

Once we finally boarded the plane — after a quick trip to Starbucks and a shop that sold electronics — I was ready for some answers. Duncan waited for me to stow my bags in the overhead bin before offering me the window seat. As I struggled with my seatbelt, he folded himself into the aisle seat with his usual elegance. I watched him fasten his belt as if he'd flown a thousand times and marveled yet again at his ease in my world.

"How do you know to fly first class?"

He offered me a small smile, the first spontaneous one since our unexpected reunion, and said, "Veronica."

Of course. She'd want nothing but the best for Duncan while traveling abroad. Before I had a chance to ask him to elaborate, he pulled out a small brown leather diary from his back pocket. "She made me a journal for the journey. It covers everything ... garments, transportation, lodging, colloquialisms, even music."

I settled into the luxurious cabin for our nine hour flight appreciating Vee's style. I'd never gone anywhere in first class. Which led to my next question. "What about money?"

"The treasuries of Doon are well stocked with gold and jewels. Your aunt Gracie referenced in her writing a firm of great discretion that she and your uncle Cameron engaged to keep their affairs. While they don't know all the details of Doon, they knew enough to accept me as a distant relative of the Lockharts. They extended to me a line of credit, half the amount of what they expect my treasures will fetch at auction."

"Which is . . ."

"Thirty million dollars."

"Shut up! So you have fifteen million dollars?"

"Not on me." His devilish grin indicated he understood and enjoyed his Daddy Warbucks status. "I do have a couple thousand for incidentals. They also gave me a plastic card that debits the account when used. Quite an ingenious concept, really."

"And you know what to do with it?" He nodded earnestly, but I didn't need him to elaborate. Obviously Vee would have included a section on credit cards, modern currency, and shopping. She was meticulous that way.

But even her freaky knack for details couldn't account for some obstacles, like international travel. Passports took like thirty days and a boatload of documentation to issue. And I was pretty sure neither Aunt Grace nor my bestie had the first notion of how to get a fake I.D. "What about a passport?"

"Ah. That was most fortuitous. One of the Destined — " He paused. His eyes widening and then dropping to his lap as he awkwardly cleared his throat. The Destined were those called to Doon when it appeared once every hundred years. Like me, they had a choice to accept their destiny or leave. Unlike me, almost all of them chose to stay. Regret balled in my chest as I motioned for him to get on with the story.

"One of the Destined, a lass named Analisa, is quite skilled in making paper copies. Although Doon didn't have everything she required, she was able to make a mock-up that her associates in London used to produce the real thing." He pulled his passport from his pocket and waved it at me.

For the love of Lerner and Loewe! He might as well have been shouting his illegal status through a megaphone. I batted his hand down, and that same electric zing of energy crackled through me. "Put that away! You let some girl who makes forgeries into Doon."

Duncan shook his head. "It is not for us to decide who enters our kingdom. Our Protector leads those who are meant to be."

"So you're saying the Protector of Doon called a criminal to your land?"

"We had need of her skills, didn't we?"

Whatever I'd been about to reply died on my tongue as the bubbly flight attendant appeared. Duncan smoothly slipped his fake document back into his pocket as he returned the attendant's smile in greater measure. The middle-aged woman blinked like she was on the verge of sunstroke before continuing down the aisle. Not that I could blame her; Duncan looked the part of privileged, modern-day royalty, from his dark, tousled hair, to his moss green designer button-down and khakis, to his — *Be still my showtune-lovin' heart!* He was sporting black-and-white high-tops.

Was that Vee's doing? Did she remember that my inner Goth girl couldn't resist a boy in Chucks? Curiosity burned through me as I pointed to Duncan's new shoes. "Did Vee tell you to buy those?"

He shook his head. "Nay. She recommended something called a Nike, but I rather liked the look of these."

That Duncan had chosen Converse high-tops out of every other shoe in the universe incited girly flutters that rippled all the way to my toes. I started to say more, but he'd already opened his book. Not ready for him to shut me out just yet, I switched to the one topic he couldn't ignore.

"Does this count as the road?"

He let the book drop slightly so that he could stare at me with puzzlement and the slightest bit of suspicion. "This is an airplane, as ye well know."

"Geez, I know where we are ... but you said you'd tell me what was up with Vee once we were on the road. Which is now, right?"

Duncan's lips thinned and his dark eyes turned distant, as if recalling some troubling memory. After what felt like an eternity he said, "The northern borders are under attack. We think ..." He took a deep breath and refocused on me. "It's almost impossible to discern — like there's an invisible barrier. The view beyond seems hazy, similar to how the bright sun distorts the horizon. But it's easy to miss."

"Then how do you know for sure that something's wrong?"

"At first we didn't. One of the outlying farms reported a herd of cattle gone missing. Then half their sheep. Once we determined the livestock had been in a secured paddock and couldna wander off, my brother and I accompanied Veronica to make a personal inspection of the disappearance. It was there we first noticed the flowers."

From his tone, I knew exactly what type of flowers he meant. When Vee and I first came to Doon, black petunias started to grow on the barren land surrounding the abandoned witches' cottage. According to Doonian legends, they were the harbingers of evil — which proved to be true in our case. We'd unwittingly transported a cursed journal into Doon, making the kingdom vulnerable for the first time in centuries to an old hag with a revenge fixation.

"Jamie threw a rock over the threshold and it immediately disappeared from sight, although we could hear it rolling through the underbrush. And then ..."

He shook his head back and forth, his face tightening. "One

of the farmer's hounds took off after the rock — before we could stop it. The dog charged passed the petunias and vanished. We could hear it running. All of a sudden, it began to yip, an' the yips became shrieks — high, keening yelps that animals make when they're in agony.... and then after a few minutes, it went silent."

Chills clenched my spine. I didn't know which was creepier: the sounds of an animal being tortured by something unseen or the unnerving silence that followed. While Duncan shook off the memory, I reached under my seat for a blanket.

After a moment, he continued, "Veronica and Fiona found a reference in the castle library to a similar occurrence when Doon was under siege. The witches cast a spell that encircled the kingdom like a snake. The villagers called it an *Eldritch Limbus*, which means 'strange limbo.' Everything in its path — villagers, animals, nature — decomposed instantly."

"You mean died?"

"Nay. They rotted alive, from the outside in. But they didn't die, they became enslaved to the witches in a suspended state of undeath."

Zombies! I'd had an irrational fear of them since Vee and I snuck into an R-rated movie when we were twelve — at my insistence, of course. We'd lasted all of three minutes. Just long enough to see some creature in a prom dress eat her date's face off. In retrospect, it was one of my less-than-fabulous schemes.

"So. You guys think this limbus thingy is happening again?"

Duncan frowned. "We're no' sure. There are some similarities ... but whatever this is seems to be contained to the Northern Borders. We need more information."

"How do I fit in?"

Vee was a one-woman research facility and Fiona had sight into the supernatural realms — together they were a problem-

solving dream team. I failed to see how I could contribute ...
unless they needed someone to headline a half-time show.

"A couple o' days after the farm, Veronica had a vision of
you standing near the border surrounded by a green light.
Fiona thinks that the light symbolizes the Ring of Aontacht.
She believes that you're meant to come back to Doon to assist
in whatever we're facing."

The plane began to taxi. "What do you think?"

"Doesna matter. I do as my queen bids me." Pressing his lips
together, he gripped his armrests and stared at the seat in front
of him. When the plane picked up speed, I covered his hand
with mine. His warmth comforted me as we shot into the sky.
As soon as the plane leveled off Duncan lifted my hand and
placed it in my lap without making a big deal. But the message was loud and clear. Regardless of what Doon or her Queen
needed, he didn't want anything to do with me.

Reclining his seat, he opened his book and began to read.
"It's a long flight. Ye best try and get some rest."

I was reminded, yet again, that I had a lot to atone for.
Duncan had certainly made it clear that coming to get me
wasn't his choice ... but maybe with time, we could go back to
before. If I could help Vee save his kingdom maybe he would
see me as someone worthy of a second chance.

CHAPTER 3

Veronica

Fairy tales made it look so easy. The girl finds her prince, they fall in love, a crown is placed on her head, and *voila!* A new queen is born! The stories never mention the killer learning curve: court politics, indigenous customs, royal protocol, and hundreds of years of history to memorize. And don't even get me started on all the names. If I met one more Ewan, I'd have to start sticking color-coded name tags on people just to keep track of which Ewan belonged to which clan.

It was hard work, but as I stared out at the grand throne room — the crisscrossing vaults of the three-story ceiling, the colorful tapestries bringing Doonian history to life, and the long plaid carpet leading to the dais I now sat on — my destiny had never been clearer. More than anything I wanted to prove that I could be the queen Doon needed — that I'd been Called here for this specific purpose.

However, there was a fine line between leadership and conformity, and some antiquated traditions were meant to be broken.

"Is this really necessary?" I wiggled beneath the royal blue cloak and searched its heavy folds for an opening. The eighty-five degree heat combined with my frazzled nerves made the velvet cape feel like a pressure cooker. I made a mental note to commission a modern antiperspirant research team. The baking soda I'd patted under my arms that morning was long gone.

"Yes, 'tis necessary, and so is this." Fiona opened an intricately carved wooden box and removed the most ornate crown I'd ever seen in real life. Golden peaks of alternating heights flashed with green and blue jewels the size of my thumb. "The hearing of the grievances is quite a serious matter in Doon. These implements are all about the perception of authority."

"What about the *perception* of a queen who faints upon the throne because she's drowning in her own cloak?" I hissed, not wanting the guards stationed around the room to hear me. My fingers finally found a gap in the layers of fabric, and, inhaling with a sharp gasp, I swept the bejeweled material over one shoulder.

So far, Fiona had been a God-send. I'd congratulated myself on the brilliance of making the wiser-than-her-years girl my chief advisor, but as she placed the weighty diadem on my head, I was forced to rethink that decision.

Fiona tsked under her breath and closed the robe, covering the strap of my maxi-dress. After much debate, she'd agreed to have a wardrobe of modern clothes made for me as long as I promised to keep them covered while in court.

I glanced at Fiona's pretty freckled face as she leaned over me adjusting my hair, her hazel gaze sparkling with amusement. "The color of the robe is lovely with yer eyes, Yer Highness."

"Shut up," I muttered as the gold-and-jewel-encrusted crown slid over and caught on the delicate skin of my ear. My judicious advisor giggled. She had a mischievous streak as wide as her ginormous fiancé.

As if in response to my thoughts, Fergus entered the throne room and aimed an enigmatic half grin at Fiona before he turned to me, his expression becoming stoic. My personal guard bent in a curt bow. The weapons strapped to his belt clanged against one another as he straightened and announced the first complainant. "Mr. Ewan Murdoch seeks an audience with Her Majesty."

Another Ewan?

The Doonian entered the hall with a sheep in tow, and I visualized the family trees I'd been studying the night before. *Ewan Murdoch, unmarried, son of Alan and Martha Murdoch.* Martha was Called to Doon from Wales. Alan's family had been here for generations.

Satisfied that I'd placed the man, I shifted forward so that my feet actually touched the floor. Being vertically challenged wasn't so bad during a pyramid cheer formation, or when trying to find a prom date who was tall enough that I could wear heels, but when working to gain the respect of an ancient civilization it became an epic adversity.

As the farmer made the long walk across the room, Fiona positioned herself beside the throne, and I was forced to retract the hateful thoughts I'd had toward her just moments before. I'd never been more grateful for her steadying presence by my side. But as appreciative as I was for her wisdom, I longed for another — the boy who fulfilled my dreams.

My co-ruler-to-be, Jamie MacCrae, was preoccupied with preparing the royal army to protect the kingdom against something more physical than disappearing livestock and eerie supernatural flowers — something he could fight. In Duncan's absence, he had sunk his teeth into the role of captain of the guard with a tenacity that was admirable, if not a tad bit scary. Being raised since birth to rule the kingdom — which in Jamie's case encompassed his entire world — meant he was one of the most driven, goal-oriented people I'd ever met. So, even though I hadn't seen much of him lately, I was happy he'd found an outlet for his indomitable energy.

As much as I missed him though, I had to admit, conducting this first hearing on my own was for the best. I could imagine how hard it must be for him to relinquish the throne to his girlfriend. But every time I went to him with a question or point of discussion, he sprang into action, took control, and solved the issue for me. It wasn't that I didn't want his help, but I'd never earn the people's respect if they still saw Jamie as their leader.

I forced my attention into the present as the scowling Ewan stopped before me. He jerked in an awkward bow and then straightened, keeping his eyes pinned to the floor.

Waiting... for me. This was my show to run, and yet with a flash of panic I realized I had no idea where to begin, how to act, what words to speak. Why hadn't I asked Fiona to walk me through the steps of the process? Maybe make up some note cards?

Silence covered the room. Fiona shifted beside me.

I glanced at my folded hands, searching for inspiration, and recalled being sent to the principal's office for fighting — Kenna and I'd finally had enough from a group of fourth-grade bullies. Afterward, Kenna had talked the principal out of giving us a week of detention by holding her chin high and using a clipped British accent. Whenever my BFF was intimidated by a situation she pretended to be someone else, a character who embodied the qualities she wanted to convey.

And that's exactly what I needed to do... *But who?* I didn't think Mary Poppins would cut it this time. Then, thanks to my dad's obsession with all things *Star Wars*, an image of a young ruler with a painted face popped into my mind. Channeling the young Queen Amidala, I lowered the tone of my voice and spoke without inflection. "Mr. Murdoch, please state your grievance."

"Yer Highness, when I awoke to tend my flock this morn, I discovered half their wool shaved from their bodies." He glanced up at me, and I could read the hurt and anger swirling in his gaze. "No' all their wool, mind ye. Half! As ye can see here." He tugged the sheep in front of him.

A giggle bubbled up in my chest as I caught sight of the animal for the first time. The poor thing looked like a poodle styled for a dog show. Poofs of white fluff dotted its back, and its sides were shaved in a checkerboard pattern.

With effort, I reigned in my amusement and asked in a monotone, "Do you know who did this, Mr. Murdoch?"

"I dinna have proof, but I can tell ye precisely who it was." He lifted his chin and puckered his lips under his bulbous, sunburned nose.

"And that would be?" I arched my eyebrows, wondering why he hesitated.

"Them wild Rosetti twins." He sighed with a shake of his head.

Rosetti twins? Mario and Sharron Rosetti were two of the most gracious people I'd met in Doon. They ran the pizza tavern in the village and had a gaggle of kids, including their two beautiful daughters, Sofia and Gabby, but I had yet to meet their other children. I searched my memory, but realized I hadn't gotten to their family tree yet.

Fortunately, Fiona sensed my confusion and leaned down to whisper in my ear, "He's referring to Fabrizio and Luciano, the fourteen-year-old Rosetti brothers. They've been known ta cause a bit o' harmless trouble."

I peeked back at the farmer and his pitiful sheep. "Why do you believe these boys shaved — " A laugh choked off my words as I imagined the rest of the flock milling about like something out of *Edward Scissorhands*. So much for my ultra-controlled Queen Amidala routine. Kenna would rip my thespian card to bits. I swallowed hard and my cheeks quivered with the effort not to smile. "My apologies, sir."

A small grin appeared on the man's weathered face. "Tha's quite all right, Yer Majesty. 'Tis humorous to behold." He chuckled as he patted the animal's head. "But ye see, 'tis almost shearing season, and I rely upon that wool for income."

"I see," I replied, sobering instantly. "What makes you think it was the Rosetti boys?"

"Last week, I found them playing polo with some friends on my south field. I ran them off on account of their horses' hooves tearin' up the ground. But I can tell ye, they were none too happy about it. Threatened ta make me pay, they did."

Based on my experience with fourteen-year-old boys, Mr. Murdoch's story seemed plausible, but I knew I couldn't make a ruling without hearing both sides. "Fergus, please send for Fabrizio and Luciano Rosetti, and make sure at least one of their parents accompanies them."

"Aye, Yer Majesty." Fergus nodded and then exited into the outer corridor.

I turned my attention to the farmer. "Thank you, Mr. Murdoch. I will investigate further, and I assure you that if the boys are found guilty, you will find that you have two extra hands around your farm in the coming months."

The man's grin told me he approved. With a quick bow, and a thank you, he stuffed his hat back on his head and made his exit. Stylishly shaved sheep in tow.

Heartened by Mr. Murdoch's reaction, I lifted the solid gold crown off my head, placed it in my lap, and opened both sides of my cloak with a sigh. The auld laird told me once that authority was exhausting. I had to agree, but at least I was beginning to get the hang of it. As I rolled the tension out of my neck, Fergus returned from outside the chamber door, his alert posture signaling the next petitioner.

Fiona squeezed my shoulder. "Ye did a fine job, Veronica. Now do tha' a few more times, and we can be done for the day."

When I closed my robe and placed the crown back on my head, the weight pressed into my skull, giving me an instant headache. I straightened my spine and ignored the pain. One down, and "a few" more to go. I could do this.

Fergus bowed deeply, but when he straightened an impish smile curled his lips. "Laird Jamie MacCrae seeks an audience with Her Majesty."

I sucked in a breath and my prince stepped through the door, bringing the light of the sun with him. As he strode toward me, I soaked in his powerful form, from his fitted leather pants tucked into tall boots to his forest-green tunic stretched across broad shoulders. All the time he'd spent training outdoors looked good on him. When he reached the dais, he shoved the strands of honey-blond hair off his forehead and flashed a dimpled grin, the white of his teeth in stark contrast to the golden tan of his skin. My heart mamboed a quick rhythm in my chest.

Jamie swept into a low bow, a leather bag tucked underneath his arm. "Queen Verranica, I come bearing gifts."

"What? No grievance, my lord?" I teased.

"Only that Her Majesty doesna have enough time for her favorite subject." His dark eyes twinkled, one corner of his mouth tilting. "But I've come to remedy that travesty with an offering."

Although we'd officially been a couple for several months, after everything we'd struggled through to be together I was still astonished that Jamie MacCrae was mine. Maybe that explained the acrobatics going on in my belly, and why every one of my nerve endings strained toward him. But he was still Jamie, the boy with a bit too much confidence for his own good. So I tilted my chin and gave him a superior smirk. "Who says I have a favorite subject? I vow to remain supremely objective, no matter what bribery you offer, sir."

"We shall see about that." His warm brown eyes danced with a mixture of humor and devilry. "A little birdy told me … or perhaps no' such a little birdy." Jamie threw a glance over his shoulder at Fergus, then turned back to me and winked. "Told me ye were a bit uncomfortable in your royal regalia."

As if to punctuate his sentence, the enormous crown on my head toppled to the side and caught on the skin of my ear still raw from the last fall. I winced. Fiona took the torturous piece of metal and placed it in its velvet-lined box before curtsying to Jamie. "My laird."

"Fiona." Jamie bent in a cursory bow as Fiona glided past him and out of the room. At her gesture, Fergus and the remaining guards followed her, leaving us blessedly alone.

A true grin, the first one I'd felt in days, broke across my face as I swept the cumbersome cloak off my shoulders and flew into Jamie's arms. He squeezed me against the hard expanse of his chest, my feet lifting off the floor. I nuzzled into the warmth of his neck where it sloped into his shoulder, breathing in his distinct scent of the air before a storm. "I've missed you," I whispered as he put me down and cradled my cheek in his palm.

"And I, you." His gaze swept down the length of my aqua blue dress, and then back up to my face. "Lovely dress. Is that new?"

I nodded as I rose on my toes and brushed my lips against his, the room spinning around me as I lingered, my fingertips skimming the firm, silky stubble on his cheek.

People are waiting for me, right? Yes, I'm the queen now ... responsibilities and all that.

With great effort, I pulled away, but the moment I did Jamie's hand cupped the back of my neck. He lowered his mouth to mine, his lips and tongue performing a seductive dance that washed every thought from my head. Both his hands tangled in my hair as he deepened the kiss. I stood on my toes, pressing against the strong, solid heat of him, wishing I could get closer.

"Arrrhmm."

With agonizing reluctance, I slid my lips from Jamie's. I must have looked as off balance as I felt, because he smiled into my eyes and kept an arm around me as we turned to see Fergus leaning into the room around the half-open door.

The giant's cheeks were a kaleidoscope of pink and red. "Excuse me ... er ... my laird. Yer Majesty, ye have several people awaitin' an audience."

"Give us five minutes, Fergus," Jamie replied before I could respond.

With a quick nod, Fergus pulled back and shut the door.

"Now, where were we?" Jamie growled.

"No way." I ducked out from under his arm and skipped away. I glanced pointedly at the leather bag that had fallen at his feet. "Didn't you say something about a gift?"

He snatched up the sack and quirked a mysterious grin. "Tha' I did."

He untied the cord on the leather satchel, and what he removed made me gasp in wonder. It was a circlet of silver, so delicate it looked as if it could easily snap in his large fingers. But when he held it out, I could see by the intricate weave of silvery branches that the construction was solid. Leaves, dotted with tiny green jewels and what appeared to be amethyst and topaz flowers, caught and reflected the light.

"Oh, Jamie, it's exquisite!" He set it lightly in my hands. "Where did you get it?" As far as I knew, the ceremonial crown I'd worn that day was what the queen had worn for generations.

"T'was my mother's favorite. She couldna stand that beast of a crown either." The light seemed to leave his face, his gaze fixated beyond me to somewhere in the past. "Before she passed, she gave it to me, to give to *my* queen someday."

When he focused back on me, the temporary grief was replaced by something as hopeful as a summer sky. "May I put it on you?"

"Please." I handed it back to him. "I wish I had gotten the chance to know her." A little tear opened inside me. If Jamie's mother were still here, I could have had a role model to help groom and prepare me for what was ahead — instead of being thrust head first into a duty I was so pitifully unprepared to face. And just maybe I could have shown her that I was worthy of her son, and her kingdom.

Jamie set the circlet upon my head and it settled on with comfortable ease, as if it had some magical property that made it mold to each queen who wore it. I stood a little straighter, held my head a little higher, feeling connected to the woman whose shoes I was trying so desperately to fill.

My prince brushed a length of hair behind my shoulder, his hand lingering on my back as he searched my eyes. "She's here with you in spirit, Verranica. Dinna ever doubt — "

A crash, followed by shouts, sounded from the outer corridor. Jamie spun and pushed me behind him just as the door slammed open.

"Where is she?" a ragged voice bellowed.

"Gregory, what's happened?" Jamie's voice was like smooth-edged steel.

A horrific groan echoed through the chamber. My curiosity propelled me around the protective barrier of my knight's body, and my jaw almost hit the floor. A man staggered toward us, his right hand thrust out before him. Like something straight out of a horror movie, gory bits of flesh hung in ragged shreds off of the exposed bones of his fingers. Dark red spattered his clothes and soaked the remaining fabric of his sleeve. I choked back a gag. Two sword-wielding guards followed behind the man with wide, terrified eyes, clearly afraid the grotesque degeneration of the man's arm might be catching.

"It ... it took my brother!"

Bile rose in my throat at the agony in the man's voice and the implication in his words. I prayed he wasn't saying what I thought he was saying.

"It's her, I tell ye! This dark magic is all her doing!" His eyes swiveled in his head like a wild horse before locking in on my face. "Yer nothing but a queen of the damned!"

"Guards, seize him!" Jamie commanded. The guards glanced at each other and shook their heads.

Jamie edged over to block me from view, but as much as I wanted to, I couldn't hide behind his strength. I moved around him and took several steps toward the injured man.

Keeping my attention away from the melting flesh of his arm, I begged, "Sir, *please* tell us what happened so we can help you." I stopped and reached an open palm in his direction to show I was unafraid. The man hesitated, his frantic gaze shifting from me to Jamie, who poised at my side like a tiger ready to spring.

Gregory's posture seemed to wilt as he reached a shaking arm across his body to clutch the bicep of his injured limb.

Green eyes spilling over with tears, he began to speak. "Drew and I were choppin' trees by the northern border ... and ... carrying them to the river ta be sent to the mill, but ... but ..." He trembled so hard every word was a struggle. "But his end dropped and ... and he was just gone, sucked into ... nothing. I went to the spot where he disappeared. I could see his shadow and I reached out, but ... it hurt so terribly, the very air eating the flesh from my arm." He paused and his entire body began to convulse, his voice catching on a sob. "He was screaming som-somethin' terr-rrible, but I pull-lled back. I ... I couldna ss-save him."

Jamie stepped forward just as the man collapsed, catching him before he hit the stone floor. He cradled the man's head against his bent knee and ordered the guards to send for Doc Benoir. Both men rushed from the room and several Doonians spilled through the door followed by Fergus. Blood streamed from his temple, and Fiona attempted to prop the giant up with her shoulder.

I met Jamie's somber gaze and saw my own horror reflected on his face. What we'd feared most had happened — the erosion of the borders had taken its first human life.

My only hope was that together, my BFF and I could pull off another miracle.

Oh God, I prayed, *please let Kenna get here soon!*

chapter 4

Mackenna

I stood off to one side as Duncan tipped the Alloway driver generously. Since his first "horseless carriage" ten months ago, he'd become an expert at traveling by taxi. Despite the late hour, we'd decided to skip my aunt's cottage and go straight to the bridge. My companion was anxious to get back to his kingdom ... and away from me. He'd made that much as clear as the Phantom of the Opera's high-pitched tenor.

As the taxi's taillights disappeared into the night, he turned to me. "Ready?"

When I nodded, he reached into his pocket and produced a pair of rings. Not just any rings, but the ones that would open the bridge portal between my world and his so that we could cross into the Kingdom of Doon. He slipped the gold and ruby one onto the tip of his pinky finger as far as it would go. According to Fiona Fairshaw, who had special insight into the supernatural realms, the Rings of Aontacht chose their owners and not the other way around. If that were true, the gold and ruby one had chosen my best friend Veronica. And my uncle Cameron's silver and emerald one had chosen me.

Duncan offered me Cameron's ring, and for an instant my treacherous heart imagined he was going to drop on bended knee. Thankfully he did not assume the proposal position, but extended his hand with the ring cradled in his palm. Doing my best Chuck from *Pushing Daisies* impression, I gingerly picked up the ring while avoiding any actual skin-to-skin contact.

An awkward moment followed. Given the colossal importance of what we were about to do, it would have been natural to hold hands. Heck, it might even be necessary to activate the rings like the Wonder Twins ... *form of a hostile Scottish prince, shape of a girl who's blown her shot at happily ever after.*

Before handholding became too tempting an option, I started across the bridge — alone. The minute I stepped onto the cobbled stones, an unbearable stench assaulted me — like rotting meat, decomposing plants, stagnant swamp, and sun-baked garbage all rolled into one odor straight from the pits of hell. Nose burning, eyes watering, I backpedaled, bumping into Duncan in my efforts to get away from the stink.

The prince's arms encircled me as I tried to get off the bridge. Thrashing out of his grasp, I stumbled off of the stone path and collapsed into the cool grass of the riverbank. My throat burned as I gulped in ragged breaths of fresh air. My body shuddered as my stomach dredged up my afternoon venti mocha.

Suddenly Duncan was kneeling beside me. With one hand he held back my hair while the other kept me from collapsing in my own puke. After an indeterminable bout of dry heaving, I rolled away from the mess and flopped onto my back, shivering.

Duncan's scowling face loomed over me. "What happened?"

"I don't know." My voice sounded raw, so weak it was hard to hear over the whooshing sound of the blood in my ears. "Something's wrong with the bridge. There's an awful stench, like — "

"Like what?"

"Death." My teeth chattered as another bout of shivers racked my body. "I know it doesn't make any sense, but it reminded me of death."

Duncan stood and walked to where the grass bordered the ancient stones of the bridge. He glanced at the ring on his pinky, as if assuring himself that he still wore it, before scanning our surroundings. Streetlamps illuminated both sides of the riverbank at precise intervals with golden spheres of light. Only the center of the bridge remained in shadow. "I dinna see anything."

I struggled into a sitting position. My body complained, like it'd been steamrollered by sumo wrestlers. "Do you smell anything?"

"Nay." He cautiously took a step on the Brig o' Doon as I cried out a warning. But he only shook his head. "I don't sense anything."

"I'm not lying about this."

"I dinna say you were." He continued to stare at the opposite riverbank, but with his back to me I couldn't read his face.

I forced myself to my feet. Lightning fast, Duncan turned and was by my side helping me up. The temptation to sag against him, if only for a moment of reassurance, was strong. But before I could act, he let go.

He crossed to the edge of the grass and I followed, careful not to come in contact with the stone pathway. The riverbank on the opposite end of the Brig o' Doon looked normal. The air was fresh, and I felt none of the terror that had gripped me moments before. Perhaps I had hallucinated it? Like an extreme stress reaction or something ...

Indicating the opposite side of the river, Duncan asked, "Do ye smell anything now?"

"No." For a long moment he studied me. Under his scrutiny I felt like a puzzle that was missing important pieces. When I could bear it no longer, I asked, "None of you saw anything like this at the northern border, not even Vee?"

"No." Duncan shook his head. "The Queen was right to send for you. You can see things that the rest of us cannot. I hate to ask this, but I need to know what's on the other side. Do ye think you could step back onto the bridge?"

My entire being screamed in protest, but Duncan was right. He needed what only I could provide. I wouldn't fail him again.

Using my scarf as a mask, I held it over my nose and stepped forward. The glowing emerald of my ring washed the bridge in a sickly green color. The stink returned, but now that I was braced for it, it wasn't completely overpowering.

Duncan's mammoth hands fastened to my hips. He held me gently, yet firmly, from behind becoming a physical anchor to safety. His smooth brogue penetrated my fear as he spoke quietly into my ear. "Do you smell it?"

When I nodded, he said, "Let me know if it becomes too much to bear. Now, what do you see?"

I tried to block out the stench and focus on the horizon. Fuchsia and orange streaks lit the indigo sky as I glimpsed a world that was not my own. "It's dawn." The words were muffled by the scarf. "I can see the castle in the distance."

"What else?"

I pulled my gaze back, focusing on the land between us and Castle MacCrae. The woods looked just as I remembered, except they were slightly off on one side, like a see-through scrim separated the setting from the audience. Looking closer, it seemed that a catastrophic event had destroyed most of the natural life. I could see skeletal branches and some kind of slimy black fungus that had inserted its dominance in the aftermath. "The forest looks wrecked. All the plants are decaying and moldy."

"Where?"

"On the right side of the Brig o' Doon."

"How far?"

"Starting at the riverbank. As far as I can see."

The more I focused on the rotten land, the more the smell threatened to overpower me. My eyes began to burn. Fighting the urge to step back to safety, I tried to absorb more details. From out of nowhere a crow swooped across the riverbank.

Maybe it was because I was somehow holding the portal open, but the bird flew from my world straight across the river and into the devastation as if it could sense no threat. The instant it reached the other side, it let out a bloodcurdling squawk, followed by a shriek as it dropped to the forest floor. It flopped for a moment, then unsteadily stood on broken, twisted legs. Most of its feathers littered the ground and the flesh of the creature fell away in chunks, exposing the bones underneath. Making low, guttural noises, the crow lurched away deeper into the putrefied woods.

"Enough!" I gasped.

Duncan's hands guided me as I stepped back and dropped the scarf. Dragging clean air through my nose to my lungs, I took several calming breaths before addressing his questions. Same as the farmer's hound, he'd seen the crow disappear, but he'd only heard what came next. I filled in the gaps, recounting in as much detail as I could recall, including the transformation of the zombie crow. As I described the bird lurching away into the slimy undergrowth, one other significant detail surfaced. "The ground—" I stated. "The edge of the riverbank was covered with black petunias."

Duncan shivered. "So the northern and eastern borders of Doon, from the bridge to the high farmlands, are compromised by the Eldritch Limbus. How about if we stay south once we cross the bridge?"

Panic seized my chest. The stench, the undead animals—death was on the other side of the Brig o' Doon. I couldn't cross the bridge—I wouldn't. My head shook from side to side and I heard myself babbling the word no. Was this what it felt like to be hysterical?

"Relax." Duncan led me a short distance away from the path. "I'll not risk your safety. If the way is not sure, we'll try for the mountains in the morning."

The mountain pass was the back door into Doon. It was steep and long, but if it kept us far away from zombie crows, I'd take it. Even better that we were going to rest first. Relieved, I staggered over to a nearby park bench and slumped down. I might've curled up right there to sleep, except Duncan inspected me with narrowed eyes and asked, "Shall I carry ye to Dunbrae Cottage?"

There was no teasing in his tone, but no tenderness either. If I said yes, he'd scoop me up and cradle me against the warmth of his chest. His steady heart would beat a rhythmic lullaby and I would drift into a safe, dreamless sleep in the shelter of his arms ... and wake up to the harsh reality that he'd merely been obeying orders.

"I can make it on my own." Summoning the last of my strength, I got to my feet. The world began to tilt and I took another deep breath to steady it. Fighting vertigo, I walked away from Duncan's tempting offer. It was time to leave the woods.

Dunbrae Cottage, just a short walk from the bridge, was as quiet as when I'd left it ten months ago. Except the key was missing from its hiding spot. I flipped over a couple more rocks, my brain swirling with scenarios that involved the return of Adelaide Blackmore Cadell, the witch bent on the destruction of Doon.

"Lookin' for this?" Duncan, who'd been following a few paces behind, held up the key.

The swirl of worst case scenarios going through my head caused me to snap. "Where did you get that?"

Duncan seemed suddenly unsure. "Veronica said ye wouldna mind if I stayed while I got my travel affairs in order."

I snatched the key from his hand and busied myself with unlocking the door. After a couple of failed attempts, I fit the key into the lock and turned. Duncan followed me into the foyer. After carefully locking the door behind us, he asked, "Can I get ye anything?"

The pragmatic tone of his voice made me want to lash out. Couldn't he understand that I needed more right now? I needed Duncan the boyfriend, not the duty-bound knight on a quest. With effort, I reminded myself that it wasn't his fault that I had unrealistic expectations — if anything the fault was mine for messing things up in the first place.

"I just need sleep." And perhaps a time out.

Duncan nodded. "I'll carry your bag up to your room." Only then did I notice my canvas tote slung over his shoulder. I'd dropped it on the bridge and never given it a second thought. He must've gone back for it after I started toward the cottage.

Shamed, I followed Duncan up the stairs to the room I'd claimed as my own. I watched from the doorway as he flipped on the light by the nightstand and set the bag next to my bed.

Before turning to leave, he scanned the room, going so far as to peek under the bed. Satisfied there were no witches or monsters to torment my sleep, he crossed to the door. Instead of leaving, he paused and studied me again.

It was impossible to decipher the thoughts flowing across the canvas of his eyes. Good thoughts? Negative ones? I had no clue. What struck me most was how the absence of his trademark twinkle altered him. Where was the laidback boy with the quick, wry humor? Was he this somber all the time now? Or only around me? When we got to Doon, I would ask Vee.

Clearing his throat, Duncan said, "You should get some rest. The journey tomorrow won't be an easy one."

Of course not. I suspected nothing would be easy for us ever again. "Thank you. Take any room you like."

My attempt at civility sounded oddly hollow. But if Duncan noticed, he chose not to react. Evenly, he announced, "We leave at —"

"First light." By now, I knew the drill.

Without another word, he left, closing the door behind him. Instead of retreating to another bedroom, however, I could hear him hovering just outside. From the sound, I guessed that he was setting up camp in the hallway. With only a door separating us, it would be so easy to use the horrors of the bridge as an excuse to invite him in. If I begged, he would hold me through the night. He was too much of a gentleman to say no.

With a heavy heart, I turned off the light and crawled into bed. If his nearness got to be too much, I'd count zombie crows. After everything I'd done, I owed it to Duncan to protect him — especially from myself.

CHAPTER 5

Mackenna

A smooth expanse of white sand, recently washed clean by the tide, stretched before us. Too early for sun-bathers and boogie boarders, Ayr Beach was blessedly deserted. Ribbons of rose and tangerine streaked through the lightening sky, reminding me that I had no business being up at the butt crack of dawn for the second morning in a row.

I glanced at Duncan, whose singular focus seemed to be getting back to Doon. His intense, haggard expression only increased his hotness, and as usual my heart swooned a tiny bit. To our right, down the shoreline and invisible to the modern eye, waited the steep cliffs that would be our passage into his world ... assuming it wasn't overrun by the zombie fungus.

Maybe it was the lack of caffeine and that I'd slept very little the night before, or the fact that all sane people were still drooling on their pillows, but I was suddenly overcome with urges I couldn't control. I wanted to dig my toes into the wet sand, feel the cold waves against my legs, and savor the salty air. For one brief moment, I wanted to be fully present on this beautiful beach. Then I would follow the prince who used to love me into the uncertain future.

Blocking Duncan's path, I nodded toward a nearby bench. "It's more fun to walk along the beach barefoot."

Anxiously, I watched him sit and begin unlacing his Chucks. I settled beside him, removing my sneakers and socks in silence and stuffing them into my bag. Side by side, Duncan and I rolled up our jeans. When finished, we both stared at the colorful horizon over the softly rolling surf. Maybe I wasn't the only one not in a hurry to face the horrifying unknown.

Keeping my eyes on the view, I asked, "Can you guarantee that we'll make it to Doon alive?"

For several beats he stared at the vast ocean, his face as unchanging as a marble statue.. Finally he shook his head. "Nay ... And I'm sorry I had to ask this of you. I would've preferred to let you be rather than disrupt the life ye chose, but I didna have a choice."

"I know." It was easier to talk when we weren't facing one another. "Can I ask a favor?"

"Aye." Duncan inhaled sharply, and I wondered what was going through his mind.

"Can I have a few minutes? I want to walk along the ocean one last time."

I glanced at him out of the corner of my eye. His face hardened as he waged some internal battle, but all he said was another, "Aye."

I knew it would be asking too much of him to join me — and I had no right — so I walked down to the water alone. The cool sand clumped beneath my toes, shifting with each step. My psyche felt equally unstable where Duncan was concerned. I missed that solid foundation where I didn't over analyze every interaction and second-guess my instincts.

At the shoreline, I waited for the tide to /
Cold, briny waves lapped at my toes, tuggi'
receded. They seemed to be pulling me a/
the world: egomaniacal directors, diffident p.
curses. For a moment, I empathized with Ophelia a...
of surrendering to the water for all of eternity. Not that I w.
suicidal or anything, just tired ... of a long journey that hadn't
really even started.

"It pulls at you." Duncan's wonder-filled voice settled over
me like a Scottish life preserver tethering me to the beach. I
turned to see him ankle deep in the surf, studying the receding tide. "I've seen the ocean my whole life, but never been able
to touch it. So I've tried verra hard not to wonder what I was
missing."

The borders of Doon ended at the top of the cliffs overlooking the Atlantic. The only other time he'd been on the beach
was on the way to rescue his brother, Jamie. Then, we'd been
so focused on saving Doon's young king that we'd never come
close to the water.

Another wave tumbled over our feet, and Duncan's dark
eyes lit up with delight — I'd missed that spark. Finally I
glimpsed the boy I remembered, the young nobleman dancing through life with carefree abandon. As the water ebbed,
he readjusted his footing with a laugh. "The sea's a force ta be
reckoned with," he declared.

His twinkling eyes met mine, giving me the boldness to say,
"For the next fifteen minutes, there's no future or past. Only
this." *Only us ...*

He nodded and flashed me an easy lopsided grin — the first
one since our awkward reunion. That smile was like the perfect spring day after a seemingly endless winter. My tension
drained away with the hope that he was finally warming to me.

Look!" he exclaimed, pointing as a half dozen reddish abs scurrying along the shore. Duncan jogged to one and bent over it in fascination. "When Jamie and I were wee boys, my ma used to make believe the Loch o' Doon held all the mysteries of the Atlantic. We'd pretend to find sea creatures and mermaids and the like. It probably sounds daft, but it was one of my favorite games."

Before I could comment, he was on to the next treasure — a jagged outcropping of rock housing a small tide pool. The miniature microcosm contained pale anemone, tiny fish, and purple starfish clinging to the mossy sides of the rocks. Duncan sank to his knees and reached into the clear water. He stroked one of the starfish, speaking to it affectionately. Had he been part of my world, he might have been a marine biologist.

After a few moments, he gestured toward me. "Mackenna, come see this bonnie specimen. She's a right beauty, she is. I wish I could take her home with me."

Boy, did he need a puppy!

Duncan's enthusiasm for such an impractical pet made me recall the time Vee and I tried to keep a butterfly with a damaged wing. Vee snuck it into her room and kept it in an old shoebox. But by the next morning, poor Flutter was dead.

I knelt beside Duncan and asked teasingly, "What are you going to call her? I'm thinking Stella or Starla."

He shook his head. "Nay. She's Maureen."

"Why Maureen?"

He favored me with his uneven smile and a mischievous shrug. Clearly there was more to the name than he was willing to say. Beyond our tide pool, I spied a section of beach littered with shells. With a little luck I'd find a washed-up starfish among the debris — Maureen's twin sister, one that had already given its life and would make the trip back to Doon. "Seems like you two could use some alone time. I'm going to head down the beach a bit."

He nodded absently—too busy bonding with Maureen to acknowledge me. I picked my way through the sand to a cluster of shells that'd been left high and dry by the tide. Poking out of the sand was exactly the thing I was looking for.

I hastily picked up the little mummified starfish and slipped it into my pocket just as Duncan called out, "What're ye doing?" Later when we were in Doon, I would surprise him with it.

To cover my tracks I answered, "I want to gather a few shells for Vee." I stopped just short of blurting out, "Since she's never gonna get to the ocean again."

As with anything in life, living in a secret Scottish kingdom was a trade-off. I knew Vee would happily forsake the ocean to live with her prince in a world where she belonged and was loved—what girl wouldn't?

Duncan walked toward me in the surf. "Great idea."

My heart hitched. It took me a moment to realize he was responding to the thing I'd said about collecting shells for Vee and not my musings about love.

With a small exclamation, he bent over, scooped something into his hand and then straightened again, holding his treasure triumphantly in the air for me to see. As Duncan held up the white scalloped shell, his smile radiated from his mouth into the depths of his brown eyes, causing them to shine as he ran his fingers through his dark hair to form chaotic peaks. My heart seized. It was the very same gesture I remembered from when we were kids and he used to play with me on the Brig o' Doon.

Back then he was my imaginary friend Finn. And I had no idea his appearance was some form of what the Doonians referred to as the Calling—soul mates reaching toward one another across time and place.

Unable to resist, I drifted toward him. The ocean swirled around my toes as I worked next to him gathering shells. Without warning the receding tide ripped the sand from beneath me, and I crashed onto the beach, landing on my hip. Duncan collapsed next to me. As I caught my breath, I looked at the boy sprawled at my side, whose surprise mirrored my own. Suddenly, we were laughing.

In unison, we flopped onto our backs and howled. Despite the cold, wet sand, Duncan was a furnace. Even from a few feet away, his warmth washed over me. Scooting closer, I turned my head to catch him staring at me. Down the beach, a crab scurried along the surf, its claws clicking a hollow melody that sounded suspiciously like "Kiss the Girl."

Feeling like a mermaid with a brand new set of legs, I contemplated Duncan's very tempting lips and his mouth froze in a half smile. He inhaled deeply, his nostrils flaring as his eyes pulled me into the fathomless depths of his soul.

My pulse pounded in the base of my throat. It overrode rational thought as I murmured, "Kiss."

Duncan answered with a nearly imperceptible shake of his head, and then rolled onto his elbow so that he hovered over me. Afraid the tiniest movement would break the spell, I froze as his gaze lingered on my lips before leaping to my eyes.

With an agonizing slowness, he lowered his face to mine. I could sense his minty breath against my skin. When his lips were close enough to taste, I let my eyes drift shut and ... *Holy Schwartz!*

A giant wave surged over my head.

Salty water pummeled my face, clogging my nose and mouth as the mighty ocean forced us apart. Sputtering, we scrambled out of its reach. By the time the evil wave receded, Duncan was on his feet, laughing as he dripped from head to toe. He reached for me, and I slid my hands into his and let him pull me up. His velvet smooth expression caused a wild rumpus in my chest. My mouth went dry as my heartbeat grew manic with giddy pleasure. But as much as I wanted to smush myself against him and never let go, my head shouted that I needed to come clean.

"I have to tell you about Weston."

The smile that I craved more than oxygen vanished, the spark between us doused not by the wave — but by my inner Jiminy Cricket. Stupid conscience!

Duncan dropped my hand. "No, ye don't."

He headed back up the beach to the spot where we left our shoes and bags. I followed after him, trying to figure out what I'd done. The truth was supposed to set us free, wasn't it? "Wait."

By the time I reached the bench, Duncan had his shoes back on. I collapsed next to him. "Look," I pleaded. "I'm sorry."

He regarded me unapologetically. "Believe me. 'Tis I who's sorry. I shouldna have let myself get carried away." Standing, he shouldered our bags and fixed his gaze on the horizon. "Time's up, Mackenna. Let's go."

Without another word he slipped Vee's ring onto his finger and turned toward the invisible cliffs that would lead us to Doon.

The hike up the treacherous mountainside to the northwestern border was a nightmare in wet clothes. My jeans chaffed. My shirt clung to my torso like a wetsuit, and my gritty undergarments scraped with every step. Several spots on my skin had been rubbed so raw that my outer irritation nearly matched the irritation I felt on the inside. Partially at Duncan. But mostly toward myself for not clearing up the whole Weston thing right away.

For the better part of the morning, I slogged miserably behind the boy of my dreams humming the music to *Bring it On: the Musical*. In Vee's withdrawal from the modern world, she'd missed the show about singing, dancing cheerleaders. The movies had been one of our guilty pleasures, so the least I could do when I arrived was reenact for her the highlights from the national tour.

Just as I was building to the big number at the end of act one, Duncan slowed his pace. Ahead of him, I spied a clearing that I recognized as Muir Lea, Doon's Eden-like meadow high in the northern mountains. If I hadn't been so chaffed, I'd have done a happy dance — complete with jazz hands.

The lush grassy space, dotted with wildflowers and lazy butterflies, looked just as I remembered. Of course on my last visit, my biggest concern was whether or not Prince Duncan would try to kiss me ... and if I wanted to kiss him back. (He hadn't and I did.) This time I was stressed about real things, like salvaging our relationship, saving the kingdom from the zombie fungus, and surviving the rest of our journey in my hateful clothes.

A dozen steps into the lea, Duncan set down our bags — which he'd insisted on carrying up the mountain. Before you could say Sweet Baby Sondheim, he pulled off his shirt.

"What're you doing?" I demanded, my voice cracking like a thirteen-year-old boy's.

"Changing out o' these wet clothes."

It was like trying not to stare into the sun. Even if I'd wanted to, I couldn't look away from his half-nakedness. The curse of the ginger prickled up my neck to my cheeks as I sputtered, "Geez! Warn a girl first."

A familiar twinkle lit his eyes as he reached for his belt. "Just so ye know, I'll be takin' my trousers off now."

The air I so desperately needed fumbled in my throat as my face went from warm to volcanic. He was going to make me swoon — literally! Any second I would face-plant into the grass. Fisting my nails into my palms, I focused on the pain as I took a deep breath.

When I finally found the strength to look away, he teased, "I didna know you were so afflicted with modesty."

Had he just called me a prude?

"I'm not!" I spat, glancing at him and getting an eyeful of checkered boxers before looking away again. "It's just — just that, I mean — ."

"Your boyfriend Wheaton wouldn't approve." All traces of humor vanished from his voice.

"Weston." I corrected half-heartedly. "Can we just talk about him? Please."

"I'd rather not."

"But he's — "

"I said I'd rather not discuss the bloke."

Fine! At least I tried to tell him the truth. As I listened to Duncan pulling on his boots, I wondered what I would've said to explain about Wes. He was a jerk, and my director — and against my better judgment, I'd dated him, which was complicated enough. But the real confusing part was how being with him made me feel achingly bereft. When I was with Wes, my life became a two-dimensional farce.

"Finished." Duncan's soft growl drew me back to the present. When I swung around, he averted my gaze as he said, "Let's get on, then."

So much for resting. Duncan had changed out of his jeans and Chucks into typical Doonian clothes: sturdy leather boots, dark breeches, and a soft-looking, cream-colored tunic. He looked so warm and comfortable that I determined not to take another step until I changed into something equally as comfy.

Duncan hoisted my bag onto his shoulder just as I made a desperate grab at it. "Wait. I need to change too."

He let my bag gently drop and I began rummaging around for a suitable outfit. I hadn't thought to pack sweats — because, well, that would imply I intended on exercising.

Unfortunately, I hadn't packed any of my rehearsal clothes either. The only soft pants I had were for sleeping. So I was declaring this day — whatever day it happened to be on the Doonian calendar — Doon's official pajama day.

I grabbed pink flannel bottoms that went with my Evolution of Acting top. Duncan crossed his arms and waited, his face pinched into a frown. Whether the expression was annoyance with me or disapproval over Wes, I was afraid to guess. "Turn around and don't peek."

He immediately complied. "Trust me, ye have naught to worry about. I promised your beau not to lay a hand on you, and I wouldna go back on my word."

"But you already did," I said as I stripped off my wet shirt and quickly shimmied into my jammie top. "You touched me at the bridge, when I saw the limbus." *And on the beach when we almost kissed.*

"That was an extreme situation," he replied softly. With my back to him, I could barely make out his words. "I had ta make an exception."

Next, the tricky part. After a quick glance confirmed Duncan was not looking, I wrestled free of my jeans. I quickly swapped my soggy grannie panties for clean ones and stepped into my flannel bottoms ... *Ahhhh, cotton.*

Fully clothed again, I switched socks and wriggled back into my athletic shoes. All the other footwear I'd packed were open-toed sandals or flip-flops. And while I'd been sadly deficient in my choices of practical clothing, I had had the presence of mind to pack at least a dozen different colors of nail polish.

I tossed my wet things into my bag. As an afterthought, I grabbed my damp jeans and fished Uncle Cameron's ring from the pocket. "Done," I announced.

Duncan turned around and pieced me with a cold glare. "I'm sorry I broke my promise. It will not happen again."

The air between us felt so charged, I couldn't seem to hold my tongue. "Good."

Duncan snatched up our bags while I slipped the Ring of Aontacht onto my finger. Holy Schwartz! The instant I put the ring on, Muir Lea changed. The ungodly stench of rot slammed into me so that I pinched my nose with my fingers. My eyes stung, and I swiped at them with my other hand, trying to clear my vision.

The woods on the far side of Muir Lea were ravaged by the zombie fungus. It was just beginning to ooze into the meadow. And Duncan was headed right toward it.

"Stop!"

He looked back at me, his confusion quickly turning to alarm as I hunched over, breathing heavily through my mouth. He searched the meadow, looking for signs of distortion that indicated the presence of the limbus. As he squinted toward the opposite end, a small patch of yellow flowers withered. They collapsed into a slimy brown pile as black petunias blossomed in their place.

"It's reached Muir Lea, hasn't it?" he exclaimed. He didn't even try to mask the fear in his eyes. "Soon the northern pass will be cut off. And if it continues to work its way around the borders, we'll be trapped."

Imprisoned within a ring of zombie-producing rot — I couldn't think of a worse way to die. Or in this case, not die. I just hoped when we reached Castle MacCrae, Vee had some solution in mind to save the world ... again.

CHAPTER 6

Veronica

The comforting aroma of tangy tomato sauce and rising pizza dough made the Rosetti Tavern the ideal setting for my meeting with the small group of Destined who'd managed to cross the Brig o' Doon during the last chaotic Centennial. The familiarity of the place seemed to put all of us at ease. *Pizza: the great equalizer.*

But at that moment, even the anticipatory growl of my stomach couldn't hold my attention. After last night's lengthy discussion with my advisors about the border hazards and the recent disappearances, not to mention Jamie and me fighting about what we should tell the kingdom, the voices at the table droned into a lullaby. I sat up straighter and rubbed the tiredness from my eyes.

While Jamie and I both agreed the limbus had Addie's name written all over it, the stubborn boy insisted we shouldn't tell the people. I'd wanted to disclose everything to the Doonians even before Duncan left, but Jamie had argued against telling them until we knew more. My prince had been born a leader, he was brilliant and charismatic, just a few of the reasons I'd fallen so hard for him, but those same qualities made him extremely hard to oppose when he set his mind to something. So it was no surprise that my advisors had agreed with Jamie to keep things quiet.

At least for now the limbus appeared to be isolated, and we'd stationed a few trusted guards around the area, so I needed to focus on the task at hand. I desperately wanted to help the individuals before me assimilate and come to love Doon as much as I did. Becoming queen and even accepting my Calling hadn't been a leisurely afternoon at the mall. Like everything in my life, I'd had to fight tooth and nail for both. But I hoped to make their transition a bit smoother.

My gaze wandered over the handful of Destined at the table. A few of the individuals, like the environmental scientist from Dublin and the Australian inventor beside him, wouldn't need much guidance. Both men carried themselves with a confidence born of knowing their place in the world, not unlike my BFF.

A part of me used to envy Kenna that insight. The girl had practically tap danced from the womb singing "All That Jazz," her dream to act hardwired into her DNA. Now I realized that knowing your purpose — even being born with it — didn't make your path easy. All it did was illuminate the obstacles and motivate you to traverse them with a fiercer determination. But everyone needed to learn that firsthand, including the individuals before me. The most I could do was guide them in the right direction.

With a solid clunk, a frost-coated mug appeared before me, and I was startled into alertness, my ears tuning back into the conversation.

"... it's quite clear you lot were Called here for some brilliant purpose or epic love story. But what use could Doon have for a vagabond, document forger, d'you think?" Analisa Morimoto tucked the silky curtain of her asymmetrical bob behind one ear and searched the table, her dark, probing gaze settling on me.

The sixteen-year-old was fresh off the streets of London. From what I'd gathered, her home life had been plagued with absentee parents lost to drug addiction and prison. She'd barely survived by counterfeiting various documents. If anybody needed a clean start, it was this girl.

So I pushed off my exhaustion and attempted a trick I'd learned in college-prep psychology. "So you're looking for your purpose beyond helping Duncan that one time, and you aren't sure where you fit in."

"Right." Analisa let out a slow breath. It was like watching the liquid leak out of a water balloon as the tension left her body and she slumped back in her seat.

I hadn't given the girl a single solution, and yet her relief was almost palpable, simply because she felt understood. Maybe all those extra courses hadn't been a waste of time after all, even if I'd never set foot in a college now.

"Analisa should report to the printing press first thing in the mornin'." Jamie's deep voice traveled over me from behind as his warm hands settled on my shoulders. Residual anger from the night before made me stiffen. Our "discussion" had ended with us stalking to our rooms on opposite ends of the castle.

As his thumbs found the knots in my neck and began to rotate with just the right amount of pressure, I could feel the apology in his touch melting away my irritation. He continued to speak to Analisa. "The MacGowans could use a bit o' updatin' in their process."

Analisa's exotic looks transformed into true beauty as she beamed a smile at the boy standing behind me. "Thank you, Prince MacCrae. Will they welcome help from me, d'you think?"

Although I knew Jamie was trying to be helpful, I had hoped to get Analisa to come to this conclusion on her own. If it was her idea, she'd be more committed to it. The comforting weight of Jamie's hands left my shoulders, and he pulled a straight-backed chair over from another table, flipped it around, and straddled it, so close his knee touched my thigh.

"If they don't welcome your assistance, let me know, eh?"

Analisa nodded eagerly as two steaming pizzas were delivered to our table. The group dug into the pies and Jamie leaned over to me, whispering, "I'm sorry."

"You're sorry you were absolutely wrong," I blinked at him with a syrupy-sweet smile. "Or you're sorry you're such a mule-headed jerk?"

"Er ... both?" One of his brows arched as the same side of his mouth kicked up in a dopy, optimistic smile.

I giggled. His goofy sense of humor, a side of his personality that he only seemed to let show when we were together, melted me every time.

"I'll take that to mean I'm forgiven."

I reached over, clasping his large fingers in mine, and nodded, wondering if there was anything this boy could do that I wouldn't forgive if he asked. As he tugged on my hand, moving my chair so our legs were flush, I noticed he'd left his weapons belt behind for once — hopefully anticipating a peaceful dinner. The group at the table laughed at a joke the inventor was telling about a wallaby and a croc, but as I looked around at their smiling faces, I couldn't forget that we were missing one.

I leaned into Jamie and whispered, "Have you seen Emily Roosevelt? I haven't spoken with her since I had to break the news about Drew's ... er ... disappearance." Emily was a shy young woman who'd been Called to Doon via dreams of Drew Forrester. Drew's brother was still in the hospital in a medically induced coma, leaving everyone with the impression Drew had died in a milling accident. But our story didn't change the fact that Emily's sole reason for coming to Doon had been sucked into the evil abyss. The thought that *somehow* that wicked witch, Addie, was still hurting us even after I'd stripped her of her powers, made a boiling heat race through my soul.

"Thas why I'm late, actually. I found Emily sitting outside the tavern cryin'." Jamie's dark eyes clouded with concern as he shoved a hand through the burnished waves of his hair.

"What did you say to her?"

"I dinna rightly know." His mouth curled in a self-deprecating smile. "Some gibberish about helping her carve out a new life here. Ye know I canna handle tears."

"I recall you handling mine quite well." Memories of his lips on my eyes and cheeks, kissing away my grief after I realized I might never see Kenna again, sent a warm flush over my skin.

Jamie drifted closer, his eyelids growing heavy as he lifted a dark curl from my shoulder and wrapped it around his fingers. "Yer the exception, love."

"Ex-excuse me." Emily stood on the other side of the table wringing her hands. "May I join you?"

"Of course!" I jerked away from Jamie with a squeak.

"Certainly." Jamie rose, spun his chair around for the girl, grabbed another, and moved to sit on the other side of the table.

Emily dropped heavily into the seat beside me, brushed her light-brown bangs out of her puffy eyes, and grabbed a napkin off the table. She blew her nose with several loud honks. I took a couple of plates and set them in front of us while I waited for her to compose herself. All I could think to say was, "Ah ... would you like some pizza?"

"No-no, thank you." She stuttered through the hiccups shaking her chest.

I slid a slice of pepperoni onto my plate and just stared at it. "Well, I'm here if you want to talk." I couldn't even imagine what she must be feeling. If I'd crossed the Brig o' Doon only to have my reason for coming here ripped away — Jamie gone forever — there would be no words that could lessen my pain.

Emily grew still beside me, her next words pouring out in a rush. "How could your Protector lead me here and then take my soul mate from me? It isn't fair. I have nothing now. Nothing!" She buried her head in her hands, sobs shaking her shoulders.

I swallowed the lump in my throat as I reached over to rub her back in slow circles. She was right. It wasn't fair. But the deadly limbus had nothing to do with Doon's Protector. I said a quick prayer for guidance and reached my arm around her plump shoulders. "You're not alone, Emily. In fact, I was wondering if you'd be interested in moving into the castle."

She stopped crying, and a hazel eye peeked at me through her fingers. "Really?" came her muffled reply.

I gave her a small smile. "Absolutely. There's a role I've been trying to fill on my staff, but I haven't found the right person. I think a fellow American would be perfect. Would you like to be my personal assistant?" It was true. I'd realized there was just too much to do in a given day for me to handle, even with Fiona's help.

Emily straightened and lowered her hands. "I would love that."

A quiet warning pinged in the back of my mind telling me I had no clue as to her qualifications for the role or even if we would get along, but when I saw the stark gratitude shining from her face, I pushed aside my doubts. "Then the job is yours."

"Oh, thank you, Queen Veronica!" Emily threw her arms around me in a tight hug. "I promise I won't let you down."

She released me with a tearful sniffle, and I noticed Jamie hovering behind us. His posture ridged, his expression like granite. Not a good sign.

"We have to go." He took the back of my chair and slid it out. "Now."

Startled, I shot to my feet. "What — ?"

Sharron Rosetti, one of the owners of the tavern, rushed over to us. "They seem ta be content to loiter outside. Fer now."

"Who?" I demanded. "Will someone tell me what's going on?"

Jamie ignored me. "Where's Mario?"

Sharron's normally rosy cheeks were washed of color as she whispered, "He's out there with some of my boys and Gideon, tryin' ta reason with them."

My gaze flew to Jamie. "Gideon?" The former captain of the guard had been doing everything within his power to prove his loyalty to the crown after being released from the witch's power, but I wasn't yet sure if I could trust him.

"Aye. He's trying to talk them down."

I glanced toward the front of the tavern. Jerky, agitated bodies milled about in front of the windows. As the room hushed and people peered outside, the sound of their raised voices resounded in the tavern. My stomach tightened. They were chanting, "Not our queen!"

"What can I do?" The Australian shot to his feet. Judging from his wiry muscles and dark tan, he hadn't spent his entire life indoors fiddling with his inventions. Analisa stood beside him, her narrowed eyes flashing like a jungle cat's. "Come on. We'll sort them out." She punched him on the arm as they headed toward the door.

"Wait!" My two would-be-defenders stopped and turned at the sound of my voice. "I'll go speak to them."

"No." Jamie's voice was as unyielding as stone as he stepped in front of me, his eyes turbulent. "I'm sorry, Verranica, but I canna allow you to go out there. These are some of the same men who attacked us outside this verra tavern not three months past. And they're drunk and wantin' trouble."

"How many are there?"

"A half dozen, but —"

"I'm their queen. It doesn't matter if there are six or six hundred. They'll never respect me if I run away." I gripped Jamie's arm. "I *need* to face them."

"Then I'll have my men round them up and bring them to your throne room in chains."

"That wouldn't do any good at all! If I talk to them, I know I can make them see that I only want what's best for Doon." How could I get through to this bullheaded boy? He was only trying to protect me. But protection was not what I needed. "If you arrest them it would just prove their point."

"And I'd prove mine. They canna get away with this fool-hardy behavior," Jamie practically snarled.

"You can go with me." I tilted my head with a slow smile and stepped toward him while looking up into his eyes. "They won't hurt me if *you're* there."

As soon as the words left my mouth, I wished I could take them back. My mom had a history of changing for the various men in her life. Like a chameleon, she would become whatever her current boyfriend needed — from instant vegan to NASCAR fan to marathon runner. But when Janet really wanted something, she'd manipulate them with a cute smile and a bat of her eyelashes. Exactly what I'd just done.

I watched in horror as Jamie's face softened and his shoulders relaxed in response to my flirtation. But it only took a moment before he snapped back to attention and took my arm.

"Right. And what if I'm no' in the right place to take a blow to the head for you this time? We're leaving. Now." He reached down in the blink of an eye and pulled a wicked-looking dagger from his boot. So much for my delusions that he'd come to our dinner party in peace.

Jamie addressed the table, "All of you, stay here until things die down and then get straight to your rooms. Sharron, give me five minutes, then let Mario and your boys know we've gone."

He turned toward the back of the restaurant towing me behind him, but I dug in my heels, my pulse pounding so hard I could feel it in my fingertips. He was doing it again — taking control. Had he only been playing at me being queen? Letting me be the figurehead while he still made all the decisions? I stabbed my fingernails into his muscled forearm, causing him to stop and turn around. "I'm not going."

"Aye, you are."

I set my jaw and met his blazing stare. I refused to cave to Jamie's will like some stage-four clinger. Like Janet. "Last time I checked, I was the ruler of Doon. Not. You."

He dropped my arm and blanched like I'd punched him in the gut. I pushed aside a sudden wave of guilt and plowed ahead. "I'm ordering you, as your queen, to allow me to speak to these men. You've earned their trust, now it's my turn." Something in Jamie's face shifted with understanding or maybe respect. I pressed on, "If you wish to accompany me, that's fine. But I *have* to do this."

I spun on my heel and got about three steps before I was jerked around and swept off my feet.

Jamie hoisted me onto his shoulder like a sack of flour, the air leaving my diaphragm with a *whoosh*. "We may not be married yet, but when you chose me as your future co-ruler, you relinquished any authority over me," he hissed, his arms clamped around my thighs like iron bars. "We're in this together, whether you like it or no'."

It certainly didn't feel like we were in this *together.* "Let me go you ... you brainless Neanderthal!" I pounded my fists against the solid wall of his back, but he didn't even slow. "I'm not a child!" Despite my statement, tears of helplessness and anger burned in my eyes as he carried me through the steamy kitchen.

"Act like a baby and I'll treat ye like one. There will be a time and place for you to address your opposition. But not if you're dead."

The still-functioning part of my brain found the warped logic in that statement, and I stopped fighting him, which made the hard shoulder digging into my stomach marginally less uncomfortable. As we passed the huge stone ovens, whoops and cheers from the kitchen staff made it clear they thought we were off on some lovers tryst. Perpetuating their assumptions, Jamie raised his free arm in a fist pump of male solidarity.

The blood that had rushed to my face burned even hotter. *Obnoxious git.* Using all my strength, I worked my legs against his torso, trying to give him a good kick-ball-change. But his hold was too tight.

We pushed through the back door, and the angry chants reached us through the cool night air. From the sound of it, the small group had grown into a mob. I felt the thump of Jamie's heart escalating against the palm I had pressed to his back. "Not our queen!" "Down wit' the American!" "She's brought evil here!"

A hard shiver racked through me, causing Jamie to grasp me tighter and quicken his steps. These men didn't even know about the deteriorating borders.

Hearing the dissention and even fear in the protestor's voices, I had to wonder what they would do when the truth came to light. Storm the castle and remove me from the throne? Tie me to a pole and dunk me in the loch to see if I would drown?

The musky scent of horses mixed with sweet hay told me we'd reached the stables. Jamie stepped into the dim interior, and I could feel his indecision.

"You can put me down now. I won't go back."

He hesitated.

"I promise."

Slowly, he guided my body down the length of his until my feet touched the ground. I pushed the riotous waves of hair out of my face and rubbed a palm against my aching stomach muscles as I backed away from him. "Don't ever do that to me again."

Jamie's face was set in hard, determined lines, the torch light casting shadows beneath his cheekbones, making them appear white against his skin. He crossed his arms and spread his feet, clearly preparing for a fight.

Our gazes locked. Then a trace of remorse lightened his eyes and his shoulders slumped.

"Vee, I'm sorry. I'm no' sorry I protected you, but back in the kitchen …" He raked a hand through his hair. "I dinna want them to know we were fighting."

So he cared more about people's perceptions than my feelings? An icy wave of detachment swept through me, leaving me empty. I was too tired for his Heathcliff routine tonight. What I needed from him was comfort and support, things he couldn't seem to give me. Turning my back, I found the beautiful mare he'd gifted to me what seemed like years ago. I reached up to stroke the white diamond of silky fur on Snow's head, and she nuzzled into my hand. My chest ached as I slipped inside the stall and pressed my face into her warm neck. Jamie was so close that I could hear him saddling his horse beside us, but it felt as if we were worlds apart.

Begrudgingly, I admitted that even if he was a cretinous jackwagon, he'd been right — at least about *one* thing. It was best to keep the limbus a secret, for now. At least until Kenna and Duncan arrived, and we could find some answers. The thought of Kenna made me want to collapse in a heap of tears.

If Duncan hadn't run into any snags, they should've been back by now. I wouldn't allow myself to believe Kenna had refused to return. I needed her desperately, not only because in my vision she had a role to play in protecting the kingdom, but because she was my best friend — my strength.

And I didn't know if I could do this without her.

Chapter 7

Mackenna

Back in my choir days we sang an old Scottish song that debates taking the high road versus the low one — like there's always a choice. Maybe in a world without zombie fungus that was true ... but not in Doon.

The path to the high road had been overrun by the limbus. And when I suggested taking the low road, Duncan pointed out it was not parallel but clear on the other side of the kingdom — so nice of the composer to leave that part out! Which meant our only option was *off*-road, and that turned out to be far worse than it sounded.

We picked our way down the wooded mountainside on an improvised trail that was barely fit for cliff goats. Duncan kept mostly to himself as he led the way. Occasionally he pointed out a particularly helpful foothold or a patch of loose rock to avoid. Even when he held back branches, he was careful not to make any physical contact.

At least we seemed to be making good progress — until Duncan stopped in his tracks. Directly in front of him a deep ravine cut through the hillside. He stared at it in equal parts shock and frustration. "This shouldna be here."

"Are you sure? I mean, how well do you know these mountains?"

"Well enough not to lead you inta a dead end." His irritation came out in a sharp huff. "Jamie and I have played capture the flag all throughout this area. I can assure ye that this ravine wasn't here."

"But that was a long time ago, when you were kids, right?"

"Nay. We were on this range just a fortnight ago."

I couldn't quite keep the sarcasm from my voice. "Playing capture the flag?"

"It's a practical application exercise in strategy for the troops. It's also good to learn terrain, in case of ..."

"In case of what?"

"Just because we're protected from the witch under a divine blessing, that doesn't mean we shouldna be prepared. We honor our Protector by remaining vigilant."

To me it sounded like an excuse for grown men to smear mud on their faces and play war games. "So what do we do now?"

Duncan looked to the south. The ravine got wider in that direction. To the north it began to narrow, but we'd be heading back toward the zombie fungus. Duncan nodded in the direction of the latter. "Perhaps we can find a way to traverse the chasm if we head that way."

"Toward the limbus?"

"Aye. Unless you want to turn around and climb back up to Muir Lea?"

Both options sucked. Now would be the perfect time to have Glinda the Good Witch's skill set. Travel by bubble the rest of the way and gently float into the courtyard of the Castle

MacCrae. *Ta-da!* When I hesitated, Duncan regarded me with somber, brown eyes. "I vowed I would get ye back to Chicago, and I mean to keep my promise."

For the love of Lerner and Loewe! Did he have to remind me at every opportunity that he couldn't wait to get rid of me? Still, his determination to deliver me back to the modern world gave me an ironclad confidence that he'd keep me safe — but I was not about to underestimate the limbus either. I'd witnessed the devastation it could cause. All things considered, with my chaffed skin and aching muscles, the option of hiking back uphill held even less appeal than being zombified.

Decision made, I gave him a small nod. "Lead the way."

We continued downward, tightly following the ravine as we angled back toward the limbus. Even using my scarf to cover the lower part of my face, the stench of decay burned through my nostrils. My eyes watered, making it hard to focus on the treacherous ground. And if that wasn't bad enough, the darkening skies started to drizzle.

Grateful I had thought to pack my favorite umbrella, I called for Duncan to wait. When I caught up to him, I rummaged in my bag until I found what I needed. Just as the rain picked up, I popped it open.

Duncan quirked his eyebrow at my umbrella and then at me. "Wicked?"

"It's the name of the play," I explained. The umbrella had alternating panels, two depicting Elphaba and Glinda separated by the name of the musical. I'd bought it with my allowance after seeing the show for the first time. "It's about the witch from the *Wizard of Oz*, and it has all these great songs in it. It's one of my favorite shows."

Duncan nodded curtly and resumed hiking. I followed along behind, suddenly seeing things through Doonian eyes.

The last time I'd visited his kingdom, I'd been accused of being in league with the witch trying to destroy their world. Of course, it didn't help that Vee and I had brought a cursed journal into Doon and nearly destroyed the land ourselves. Now I was returning with a statement umbrella that proclaimed me as "Wicked."

I envisioned trying to explain to the Doonians a story that had a misunderstood witch as the main heroine — that would go over well. I might as well wear a matching raincoat with "Please burn me at the stake" printed on the back.

On impulse I collapsed the umbrella and tossed it into the ravine.

The commotion drew Duncan's attention. He turned just in time to see my favorite accessory go tumbling down the side of the chasm. Water flowed down his face in little rivulets and he swiped his eyes, before demanding, "What'd ye do that for?"

What could I say? The umbrella was a mistake, just like bringing the journal into Doon ... and abandoning him on the bridge. Instead, I shrugged. "I just didn't want it anymore."

Duncan looked at me critically. After a moment he shook his head. "I fear I shall never understand you."

"Then don't try."

"As you wish." With that, he turned to continue our descent. But after two emotionally charged steps, he spun back around. "Why did you leave me?"

"I couldn't bear the thought of you in my world."

His eyes widened. In the heat of the moment, my hurried words had come out all wrong. I'd meant that he belonged in Doon. Even if he came to Chicago willingly, I couldn't allow him to leave the kingdom he loved behind. But before I could clarify, he crossed his arms over his chest and asked, "Was it because of him?"

Although the timing wasn't ideal, I needed to set the record straight about my director. "No. Wes and I did date a bit. I was trying to move on with my life. After you and I broke up — "

"*We* broke up? We didna break up; you broke — everything."

"I'm sorry. If you'd just let me — "

"Tell me this. After you left me on the bridge, did you go to him straight away? Or did ye have the decency to wait a week?"

That wasn't fair. I'd never have dated Wes if I hadn't been desperately trying to get over the boy I actually loved. But if Duncan thought so little of me, why did I even care? A sob clogged my throat, but before I could fight my way through it, Duncan's expression hardened.

When he spoke, his icy brogue bordered on haughty. "Thank you for clarifying your position. I shall make every effort to deliver you to Castle MacCrae posthaste so you will not have to endure me a moment longer than necessary." This time as he turned away, I suspected it would be for good.

As Duncan launched himself forward, the ground crumbled beneath his feet. One moment he was there, the next gone. I rushed forward in time to see him sliding feet-first down the side of the steep canyon. His hands grasped at the wet, muddy ground, desperately seeking anything they could cling to.

Inside, I was screaming, my soul plummeting alongside him. On the outside, I seemed to be frozen, helpless to do anything other than watch him plunge to his death.

About twenty feet below, just before the ravine went vertical into darkness, Duncan hit a small ledge. His duffel strap snagged on a rock and stopped. But Duncan was sliding too fast. He arched over the side, only managing to grab a root at the last second.

Duncan's dirty hands, clinging to the plant root, were clearly visible, but the rest of him disappeared over the side.

How far down did the chasm go? Would that lone root continue to support his weight or give way? And how could I help him before it did?

After a couple of false starts, I managed to find my voice. "Duncan?"

"Aye. I'm here, woman." His grunted response was strangled by the exertion of holding on to something the size of an iPod cord, but other than that he sounded okay.

The rain intensified as I sank to my knees and crawled to the edge of the landslide. "Hold on. I'm coming to get you."

"Nay! It's not safe." His hands wobbled, and I assumed he was scrambling with his feet for a foothold. The root that was his lifeline started to come free from the earth, and I screamed at him to stop. Thankfully he listened for once and his hands stilled.

I rolled to my stomach and scooted backward until my feet dangled over the edge. The descent to the ledge was at a steep angle. I would have to go slow, try not to gain momentum. My heart jackhammered against my chest, and I felt like I needed to barf. Pushing my fear aside, I began to make my way down the mud-slicked canyon at a turtle's pace.

For the first time in my life, I was grateful for high school phys. ed. and the rotation on rock climbing. Clinging to the tiny bit of skill I had gleaned in those weeks on the wall, I managed to find footholds that allowed me to descend with some control. About a third of the way down, I called out, "I'm on my way."

Duncan groaned before bellowing, "I said no! Stay where you are. Thas an order!"

"You're not the boss of me, you stupid ogre!"

What did he think, that I'd just watch him die? I was supernaturally stubborn when I wanted something. Right now I wanted Duncan MacCrae to live. Otherwise, what would have been the point of all this? Of abandoning him so that he didn't have to choose between me and the kingdom he loved. If he didn't go on to build a life rich with love and purpose, then all this agony would be for nothing.

I continued to pick my way downhill. Mud oozed between my fingers, around my ankles, and seeped into the rips in my pajamas. Tiny rivers rushed down the ravine, washing the ground out from under me. And to make matters worse, the stench of death grew as I descended.

Finally, I felt the solid ledge beneath my feet. Easing my canvas bag to the ground, I rolled from my stomach to my back so I could get a better look at the situation. The rock shelf appeared thick and sturdy, about four feet long but only two feet wide. The plant root that supported Duncan protruded just above the ledge on the far right. Most of it had been pulled free of its earthly tether and the rest was in danger of giving way at any moment.

Sinking into a seated position, I shimmied forward onto my stomach so that my head faced where Duncan's hands clung to the makeshift rope. Reaching out, I grabbed his wrists and scooted forward to look down at him. "I'm here."

Rather than gratitude, he glared up at me. "I told ye not to come."

"And I didn't listen."

"When do ye ever?" he grumbled.

Cold rain pelted my back as the canyon water flowed uncomfortably around me. "We can fight, or, since I'm here, I can save your sorry butt. Your choice."

Blinking the rain from my eyes, I surveyed the ground below. A thin crevasse bottomed out about five feet below Duncan—which would've been good news except it was covered in dark slime. I tracked the zombie fungus up both sides of the ravine. As I watched, a clump of grass level with Duncan's abdomen withered and black blossoms sprouted in their place.

"Don't move," I cautioned. "The limbus is all around you."

Duncan let loose a curse — one of the only times I'd ever heard him do so. "I can see the flowers, but naught else."

"Just stay still. I'm going to pull you up."

"Nay, Mackenna, 'tis impossi — "

"Shut up and let me try!" I'd had it with his noble knight routine. The only way we would survive this would be to work together. I stretched forward, trying to get a better grip on his wrists, but the mud caking my hands made it impossible to improve my hold. "I need to clean my hands off. Don't move."

The minute I let go, the root gave way with a sharp crack. His fingers slid through mine as I reached for him. Then he was gone.

I couldn't breathe, couldn't think ... until I heard an agonized shout. Tears stung my eyes as I wriggled toward the edge. Just below the rock ledge was another root. Duncan's right hand grabbed it as his body smashed against the side of the ravine and into the limbus. A nightmarish shriek echoed from his mouth as the zombie fungus wrapped around his lower half. My own screams mingled with his as I scrambled forward until my torso hung over the ledge.

I grabbed for his hand again and again, straining against the distance between us until my fingers grasped his free hand. The instant I touched him, my uncle Cameron's ring began to glow green. In answer, the ring on Duncan's pinky flashed a brilliant red. The ruby light surrounded him like a spotlight causing the zombie fungus to wither away and his inhuman howling to stop.

Terrified to see what the limbus had done to him, I focused on his hand in mine. He let go of the root and clung to me with his whole being, which was much heavier than I'd realized. My arms felt as if they were being pulled from their sockets but I was determined to hold on.

Dangling halfway over the ledge, I had no leverage and no way to hoist him to safety. His weight began to pull me over. As I slipped forward, my lower half scrambled for some sort of way to brace myself.

His pale, stoic face told me he understood the situation. He showed no pain, or terror, just a soft expression that caused my heart to ache. "You have to let me go," he said calmly.

"No!"

Despite my obstinate refusal, I couldn't hold on much longer ... and we both knew it. His eyes were huge and warm as he nodded. "Let me go, woman."

My eyes began to sting, and I furiously blinked back tears. If the Protector of Doon had a purpose for us, he wouldn't let this be the end of Duncan MacCrae. And if this was it, I wouldn't let him face the zombie fungus alone. I'd go with him.

"Please!" Not sure who I was begging, the universe or the Protector, or any other cosmic being within earshot, I pleaded, "Please. Help us."

The space around us began to swirl with green and red rays of light. The colors merged, bathing the canyon in brilliance. As the light surrounded me, I felt hands fasten around my ankles. A glance toward my feet confirmed I was still alone — yet not alone. I suddenly felt stronger and less afraid. Those invisible hands anchored me to the rock while other hands surrounded mine, shouldering the burden of Duncan's weight. Glorious bodies of light lay on both sides of me to help pull the prince to safety.

With minimal effort, I hoisted Duncan onto the rock ledge where he collapsed on top of me. As soon as he was out of danger, the sensation of unseen help vanished. For the longest, time we didn't move. We were both filthy and exhausted, but alive.

Duncan's forehead rested against my dirty flannel pants on the curve of my calf. His hands wrapped around my leg as if he would never let go. Perhaps he wouldn't. My face nestled into the muddy, tattered fabric covering his thigh. Below the knee, he looked as if he'd been through an explosion. The leather of his boots had been shredded. His socks and trousers hung in rotting scraps, but the exposed skin underneath appeared miraculously unharmed.

After an indeterminable length of time, Duncan asked, "How did ye do that?" His reverent voice caused chills to tremble up my wet back.

"I — don't know."

Something supernatural had happened, just like it had when Vee and I first crossed the Brig o' Doon. But I couldn't begin to explain it beyond that.

Duncan sat up and I followed. This was the point where he would take me in his arms and forgive me. Then I could confess Weston meant nothing and I was still crazy in love with him. I would tell him how I remembered everything about our Calling and how I wouldn't let go because I couldn't live without him.

Instead of declarations of love, his expression hardened as he became a soldier once again. "You should have obeyed me."

"You mean I should have let you die ... or zombify ... or whatever happens when the limbus gets you?" He clearly had a head injury if he thought I'd walk away because he told me to.

Duncan raked his hand through his muddy hair to create chaos. "What I mean is, you shouldna have risked your life for mine. Doon still has need of you."

Ignoring the sharp pain in my chest, I countered by saying, "Maybe Doon still has need of *you*. Did you ever think of that?"

"Regardless of my life, we need to get you across the ravine and away from the limbus." He stood and nodded to the edge of our perch, where black petunias were sprouting.

There was apparently no rest for the angsty. Duncan reached out to help me to my feet, but I batted his hands away. If he wanted it to be every man — or drama diva — for themselves, then so be it.

The zombie fungus had encroached at least six inches in the time that we'd been recuperating. Soon it would overtake our little ledge. "Got any bright ideas?"

He pointed across the chasm. The other side didn't look nearly as steep. Rocks jutted out at regular intervals to create a natural staircase. "See that outcropping on the other side? It's about five feet away. I think we can jump across. From there, the climb up to the top should be easy."

"You want to jump over the limbus?"

He was delusional. There was no way I could make that leap. When I told him so, he stated, "I can. We'll leap together."

"I can't."

Towering over me like a drill sergeant, Duncan barked, "Ye can and ye shall. You just lifted a lad more than twice your size. You can do this."

While I silently debated my options, another patch of petunias sprouted at the far end of the ledge. We certainly couldn't stay where we were. With no choice and no other options, I agreed with a nod. "How are we going to do this?"

Duncan pointed to the flower-infested end of our little shelf. "We start there. Run diagonally across the ledge and launch ourselves off the edge. That should enable us to reach the other side."

"Okay. Let's do this before I lose my nerve." I'd had enough of these *Fear Factor* stunts — and I was beyond anxious to get this final one over with. I moved to the far end, careful not to step on the flowers while Duncan slung both our bags over one shoulder.

When he joined me, he started to curl his arm around my back and then hesitated. "May I make another exception?"

Geez! I grabbed his hand and slipped it around my back. Then I wrapped my arm tightly around his waist. "This time I touched you. Now come on."

He peered into my eyes. "Go on three."

I nodded and he began to count. "One ... two ... three."

We dashed across the outcropping, and just before we hit dead air Duncan pushed off from the edge. In half a second, I knew we would reach the other side. As soon as we did, Duncan lost his footing. I slipped from his grasp and stumbled forward, smashing my head into a boulder. Pain burst through my skull at the same instant that Duncan shouted my name. I ricocheted off the rock and fell backward. An instant after I felt myself toppling toward the bottom of the limbus-covered ravine, steady arms grabbed me.

Duncan's shocked face filled my vision, but the world surrounding him grew fuzzy around the edges. Like in a dream, I sensed his hand touch my temple. Then I surrendered to spinning blackness, and as I did, I could've swore I'd heard him say, "I'll be making another exception."

chapter 8

Mackenna

Cradled against Duncan's chest, I listened to the soothing percussion of his heart. *Ba-boom, ba-boom.* All the difficulties of the journey, all the tension in our relationship, seemed far away. When he stopped and gently lowered me into soft blankets, I clutched his shirt, pulling him down. My head felt pretty jacked up, my right temple throbbing with each breath. But despite the pain, my senses were achingly aware of the boy reclining at my side — his amazing scent, the delicious warmth of his skin, the confident yet vulnerable expression in his huge brown eyes as he hovered over me.

My eyelids fluttered closed as he eliminated the distance between us. Without a word, he pressed his lips to mine. His tongue caressed my lips in a kiss that was surprisingly . . . *juicy*?

I blinked against the shifting light. Rays of amber sunshine, thick with floating dust motes, cut diagonally above my head. I rubbed my eyes and peered into the gloom, trying to figure out exactly where I was.

As I struggled to focus, the variant angles of light and darkness reformed into the heavy crossbeams and wooden supports of a hayloft. In confirmation of my assumption, a cow lowed. I arched my neck to look behind me as a giant tongue swiped my nose and cheek.

Ewww! I was being kissed by a bovine with no sense of boundaries. Pushing Elsie the Amorous Cow out of the way, I sat up and searched for Duncan.

Next to me, the hay vibrated in a deep, rumbling snore that caused the previous night to come back in a montage of images. I'd hit my head against a rock when we'd jumped the ravine — that much I remembered. Then I'd drifted in and out of consciousness in Duncan's arms as he'd carried me out of the mountains. The last thing I thought I recalled was him lowering me onto a blanket — presumably in this barn. I could have sworn he kissed my temple as he whispered, "Sleep, my beloved."

But my memories might've been compromised by the pervy cow. Confirming my suspicions, Elsie snuffled my hair and tongued my ear. I sooo didn't swing that way but lacked bovine vocab to tell her so. Scooting away, I hissed, "Get off."

Duncan sat upright, instantly alert, his posture rigid as he went into warrior mode. His dark eyes scanned the interior of the barn, taking in our surroundings in the span of a heartbeat. With no enemy in sight, he visibly relaxed. "Are ye all right, Mackenna?"

"I'm fine."

"I thought I heard something."

I glanced at Elsie, who batted her lashes innocently. Her large brown eyes looked suspiciously like the ones from my dream. Not about to admit I'd gotten action from a brazen beast, I mumbled, "The cow mooed."

Duncan took a deep breath as if trying to untether his mind from the nocturnal world. "I was havin' a dream. I was a wee lad waitin' on the ..." With a troubled glance in my direction, he trailed off.

I knew better than to try and force more than he was willing to share. But I couldn't help the feeling that the dream had something to do with me. Rather than dwell on what he'd not said, I asked the obvious. "Why are we in this stinky barn?"

"You were injured. It was pourin' rain, and we needed shelter. Don't ye remember?"

My memories of the previous evening were jumbled, mixed with vague, crazy dreams and all-too-real barn animals. I shook my head, which was a big mistake. My right temple protested with agonizing throbs that crescendoed into nausea. Shutting my eyes, I steadied my woozy head between both hands.

After a moment, another set of hands gingerly joined mine. "You took a nasty blow to the head. Does it hurt badly?"

"A bit," I confessed.

"Try not to move more than necessary." Although he was doing his best to appear authoritative, bits of hay poked out of his disheveled hair at every imaginable angle. It was the most adorable thing I'd ever seen.

Curious about my own hair, I ran my fingers though the length and a rain of straw bits fell around me. Immediately, I sneezed. Not a high-pitched, girly sneeze, but a long, deep one — way too much *AH* followed by a head-rattling *CHOOO*. The violent backlash of the sneeze caused me to see stars. Bile filled my mouth with foulness, and I gagged.

Duncan rummaged in his knapsack and then handed me a green, downy leaf. "Here. Chew on this."

I picked it up, and held it dead-fish-style between two fingers. "What is it?"

His eyebrows shot up toward his hairline in disbelief that I would question his offering. "'Tis mint."

"Really?" I popped it into my mouth, and instantly savored the burst of spicy goodness that exploded over my taste buds, obliterating the lingering impression of Elsie. "Mmmm."

"I'm glad ye approve," Duncan said before chewing on his own leaf.

I didn't just approve of the Doonian equivalent of gum; I heartily, emphatically *lauded* it — yes, that was the Doon-appropriate word — I *lauded* it with every cell in my body. Mouth open wide, I pursed my lips in a perfect O-shape and exhaled at Duncan.

He watched me — or more accurately, my mouth, with a slight frown. For a moment, his index finger brushed absently across his lower lip as he blinked at me. Then with a playful glint in his eyes, he exhaled back. I met his unspoken challenge by blasting him with another burst of minty air. Suddenly we were mere inches apart and laughing. Then abruptly as it started, the laughter stopped.

For a tiny eternity, we considered one another. I could sense the exact moment he started closing off, and grabbed his arm. "Last night is a little jumbled. Did you carry me here?"

Duncan quirked his lips into something half smile, half grimace. "Aye."

"Up out of the ravine?"

"Yes."

I glanced at Elsie, who despite outward appearances was most likely as shocked as I was. "And down the side of a mountain."

He nodded.

"Was I unconscious?"

"You were in and out. You hit your head pretty hard."

That I remembered. "Did I say anything?"

He snickered. "You mumbled a fair bit."

In addition to the nausea, I now had a sinking feeling. "What did I say?"

"You kept saying some lass named Mimi needed Roger and asking if we could jump over the moon." He glanced away, a faint redness washing over his cheeks. "You also said Marius was an idiot. That he should've loved Eponine while he had the chance."

Of course he'd pick up on my barely coherent *Les Mis* reference. If I remembered correctly, he kept a first edition written in French among his personal collection. "Well, he should have."

Duncan leveled his gaze on me. "Marius had given his heart away. 'Twas impossible to have affection for some other lass, even if he wanted to."

"Agree to disagree." Of course he'd pick pretty, perfect Cosette's side. 'Ponine was a work in progress, full of passion and life. She deserved more than to die in the rain in the arms of someone who could never be hers. "He fell in love with the wrong girl in the first place."

His face was an inscrutable mask as he conceded, "Perhaps."

He started to get up, and I stood alongside of him. "You saved my life last night. But I also saved yours." Before he could remind me that he'd ordered me not to, I added, "In some cultures, we'd be bound to one another for life."

Duncan opened his mouth, most likely to protest, but I cut him off. "What I'm saying is I owe you but you owe me too. So how about we call a truce?"

His eyebrows lifted, questioning my point and giving me the courage to continue. "I'd really like to put the past behind us and be friends."

"Friends?" He tried the word on like he'd never heard it before. The soft rustle of barn animals filled the void as I waited Duncan out. Finally, he smiled. "Aye, Mackenna. We can be friends."

Acting on pure instinct, I hugged him. My hands slid around his chest like they were going home and I pulled him close. Instead of hugging me back, his hands stayed at his side. But he didn't push me away either, which was progress. Baby steps, I reminded myself. Repairing the damage I'd caused would be a slow process. Unfortunately, patience had never been one of my virtues.

When I finally let go, Duncan began to gather our things. Amazingly, in all the chaos of the previous evening he'd managed to hang on to our bags. I bit back the need to apologize to him for having to heft me and my overstuffed luggage down the side of a mountain. Instead, I wondered aloud, "What time is it?"

"'Tis after noon." His voice was still a little husky with sleep. "We should eat and get going."

"Eat what? Hay? Or is there a farm nearby?" A farm would be fantastic. I could already smell the bacon. My mouth began to salivate anticipating fresh-baked bread, fried eggs, and coffee.

Duncan flashed me a self-satisfied grin. "This barn has a store of food, weapons, and useful sundries. We've got provisions stashed in stables all over Doon."

"Because of your war games?"

"Training exercises," he corrected as he walked to a long wooden chest built into the side of the barn and opened it. He reached inside and grabbed a sword, which he set on the hay bale next to the trunk, followed by a foot-long dagger, a smaller knife, a water pouch, and a green apple.

He also produced a new set of boots, and what looked like fresh clothes. When he was finished, he took the knife and began to slice the apple into quarters.

"Think you got enough weapons there?"

Nonplussed, he paused mid-slice. "Just three ... A dagger, a sword, and this wee knife."

"Oh, is that all?" I reached for the water pouch and masked my smirk by taking a long drink.

"Aye." He looked at me plainly. "Do ye think I should carry more?"

"More?" I wasn't sure what else he could possibly want — an Uzi or submachine gun maybe. But I was pretty sure those weapons weren't all that easy to get a hold of — unless a Navy SEAL had crossed over with the new crop of Destined.

He lowered his face to finish cutting and then handed me a piece of apple. "Jamie also carries a hunting bow. 'Tis handy for bears."

Bears — oh my. I knew Vee'd encountered one, but I chalked it up to Doon trying to stop her from crossing the borders and breaking the Covenant. I never considered there might be more roaming around. "Does Doon have a lot of bears?"

"Nay. And they're mostly in the highlands. I dinna expect to encounter any this low."

"What about lions and tigers?"

A deep scowl crossed his face, as if I'd noticed something essential that he'd missed.

"Relax." I bit into the tangy green apple, finding it better than expected. Usually I hated green, but this wasn't the time to be picky. "I was just teasing you."

"Oh." Duncan popped a slice into his mouth and chewed it thoughtfully. "I guess I'm a little out of practice, friend."

We ate in silence. When we finished, Duncan carefully wiped his knife and placed it alongside the dagger. Taking the pile of fresh clothes, he announced his intention to step outside and change. As he crossed to the door, I noted that his pants ended in tattered ruins like a shipwrecked castaway. His feet were cut and caked with dirt, like he'd walked down the mountain barefoot. Which I guess he had ...

I was really going to have to make it up to him.

Just before he slipped through the barn doors, Duncan flashed me a mischievous grin. "This is always dangerous territory for a lad, but you might want to freshen up a bit too. We wouldn't want to scare the townsfolk, would we?" With a wink, he was gone.

I looked down and discovered new depths of mortification. My pink pajama shirt was the color of dung. Several large holes in the fabric exposed my filthy sports bra. My bottoms were equally ragged. And I didn't even want to think about my face or hair.

I crossed to my bag and pulled out the only other soft clothes I'd thought to pack, another set of jammies. This sleep shirt was black with teal lettering that said "Make musicals, not war." Quickly, I replaced my destroyed top with the clean one. Then I stepped out of my pink flannel bottoms and into fresh black-and-teal-striped ones. Movement outside a barn window caught my eye, and I looked out just in time to see Duncan strip off his shirt. I caught a glimpse of belly button and smooth, tan abdominal muscles. Holy Marvin Hamlisch and the cast of *A Chorus Line*, he was an inny—something I'd failed to notice back at Muir Lea.

As much as I wanted to gawk, I forced my gaze away before I got caught looking. Friends don't ogle other friends. I was fairly certain on this. And I definitely didn't want him spying on me—at least not in my current state. A moment later, Duncan reentered the barn, fully dressed except his bare feet. For the first time since Muir Lea, his face was alight with expectant energy. "I just need to get on my boots and weapons, then we can depart."

"Sure." The sight of Duncan's stomach — even clothed — caused my skin to feel supercharged and tight. The insides of my knees tingled with little bursts of electric current. I swayed unsteadily, and Duncan's hand shot out, hovering just under my elbow in case I needed support. He waited as I regained my balance and then stepped away.

I watched in silence as he finished dressing. After slipping on his boots, he sheathed his sword on his left side and strapped the foot-long dagger to his right. Then he slipped the three-inch knife he'd been using to slice apples into his boot.

There were so many things I wanted to apologize for. But I settled on the one I could vocalize without becoming an emotional basket case. "I'm sorry about your feet."

"'Tis nothing," he said with a shrug. "I've sustained much worse than this from playing my war games."

I laughed, liking the easiness between us. Being friends was good. It felt like a positive step toward repairing our relationship. Duncan hefted both our bags, clearly eager to get home. "Ready?"

With a parting nod to Elsie, I headed for the door. Halfway there Duncan stepped in my way. "Mackenna, there's something I have to tell you."

Pushing away thoughts of love declarations, I tried to anticipate what one friend would say to another. "Okay. Shoot."

"No one in Doon knows that I came for you except for the queen, my brother, Fergus, Fiona, and Analisa, who helped with my papers. But even she dinna get the entire story. For now we're keeping the limbus quiet. There's enough discord in the kingdom — some of the citizens oppose Veronica being our ruler. Jamie thinks if those people hear that the witch is cursing the land, they might become violent."

A chill crept up my spine. I remembered all too well the

angry mob that we'd faced the last time. "So where do the people think you are?"

This time there was no trace of humor lightening Duncan's eyes, no sardonic quirk of his lips as he answered, "Training exercise."

That explained his absence, but my sudden arrival? Even if the hazardous trip had been the opposite of traveling by bubble, the effect might be the same. If I magically appeared in Doon without a good cover story, I might as well be carrying a *Wicked* umbrella.

CHAPTER 9

Mackenna

Castle MacCrae flickered ahead in the darkness like a beacon. Vee and I had talked every day since kindergarten, even the days after my mom died and her dad went MIA. Even when my dad uprooted me to Arkansas right before senior year.

We'd shared every high and low — the day I got the lead in *Once Upon a Mattress*; the first time the Fighting Badgers quarterback, Eric Russo, asked her out; me being pursued by Greg the stage tech; her making the cheerleading squad despite Stephanie Heartford's best efforts to cheerblock her. These past ten months had been dismal without her to start and end my day.

"We're nearly there." Duncan's soft voice urged me on. "We'll enter through the kitchens, which should be nearly deserted this time of morning."

Which led to a good question. "What time is it, do you think?" My phone stopped telling time the second we crossed into Doon.

Duncan scanned the starry sky. This was the first break

in the clouds we'd had since I arrived. Fiona had explained a bit about the connection the protected kingdom had with the weather. When Doon was most vulnerable, it experienced turbulent storms. The funeral of the previous king had been accompanied with torrential rains. And when Vee had tried to breech the borders to get rid of my aunt's cursed journal, she'd instigated a blizzard.

Duncan pointed to a clump of stars. "Based on Ursa Major, I'd say 'tis between three and four."

We'd been walking forever. I felt like that hobbit from the *Lord of the Rings* movies Vee'd tortured me with on multiple occasions after I'd flat-out refused to read the books. In my opinion, that series would've seriously benefitted from some Bollywood-esque musical numbers.

The road we'd been following forked. Duncan pointed down the smaller cart path toward a stone wall on the back end of the castle. "We go through there."

"The first thing I'm going to do after I see Vee is soak in that giant tub of yours." Ever since the barn, I'd been fantasizing about the Jacuzzi-sized tub in Duncan's private bathroom. I'd even packed a bubble bath for every occasion: Coco-Lime Cocktail, Bashful Blossom, Enchanted Midnight, Extraordinary Orchid, and Lavender Dreams. I also had a bottle of Vee's personal fav, Grapefruit Crush.

Duncan reached the gate first. He flipped the latch and held the heavy door open for me to pass. Following me inside, he refastened the door and chuckled. His eyes twinkled as he offered me a contrite smile. "Now that we're here, I guess I should tell ye ... Veronica's no longer staying in my chambers. She has quarters of her own, including a guest suite for you."

I'd just assumed since Vee and I crashed in Duncan's rooms during our first visit that Vee was still there. It made perfect sense that Doon's new queen would vacate her boyfriend's brother's rooms in favor of her own space. Part of me felt disappointed that I wouldn't be surrounded by Duncan's things. But the other part of me was mortified that he'd let me go on and on about the things I wanted to do in his bath.

"You stupid ogre!" I backhanded him across his bicep. "Since the barn, you've let me blabber on about taking a swim in your tub. Couldn't you have managed to tell me sooner about the guest suite?"

He shrugged innocently. "Mackenna, if ye wish to use my tub, you may. My friends are always welcome to share my bath." The last sentence was punctuated by tiny guffaws that were so reminiscent of the old Duncan, my irritation melted away.

I refused to dwell on his flirty innuendo when I was so close to reuniting with my best friend. With a playful tap on his arm, I suggested, "How about you take me to Vee!"

In all the imaginings of my reunion with my bestie, not once did I picture the short, bushy guard blocking Vee's chamber. The man's craggy face seemed to be more mutton chops than skin surface. The caterpillar mustache that concealed his top lip muffled his brogue and made it nearly impossible to comprehend a word he uttered. The only thing I understood for sure was that he refused to budge.

"For the last time, open the door."

"Nay. I'll no' do it. Her Highness's sleeping."

"I don't care if Her Highness has a fatal case of bedhead —
I'm going in."

Duncan stood off to one side, leaning against the wall with his feet crossed at the ankles. He watched the exchange with a sardonic quirk to his lips. It was tempting to appeal to him as the prince to intervene, but since I'd been adamant about not needing his help, I was determined to do this on my own. After all, it was only one bushy guard.

One of the first things you learn in acting is that every person has a motivation and a weakness. Everyone is exploitable under the right circumstances. I just had to figure out what motivated Mutton Chops. I decided to start with the obvious.

"Just listen. I'm the queen's closest friend, which makes me the royal bestie. If you let me pass, I'll see you're rewarded with a bag of ducats."

The guard widened his stance, crossed his arms over his chest, and set his shaggy jaw. The hairy little fellow barely came up to my shoulder, but as always seemed to be the way with the vertically challenged, what he lacked in stature he made up for in determination.

"Nay." Yep, he was compensating big time.

Channeling my inner Mimi, I pouted my lips and batted my eyelashes. "Come on. She's gonna be so happy to see me. She'll probably give you a medal or something for letting me in."

When he didn't answer, I added, "Pleeeeeese?"

The hairy man had to be a robot. Bribing my way past him had been a dud, ditto for flirting. And my secret weapon, the whiny voice, had shockingly failed me. So there was only one course of action left.

"Hey," I said, seeming contrite. "I understand you're doing your job. So I'll just wait here until the queen wakes up."

As I spoke, I took miniscule steps forward until the guard was close enough to kiss. "Thank you for taking such good care of her."

Without warning, I brought my heel down on Mutton Chops' foot. He doubled over as I grabbed his backside and shoved. When he went sprawling, I launched myself at Vee's door.

I staggered into Vee's dimly lit sitting room, scanning for the bedroom door. Mutton Chops came scrambling after me on his hands and knees. Like a tenacious badger, he sprang to his feet hissing, "Halt!"

Faking left before going right, I scurried around an ottoman. Mutton Chops tried to cut me off, so I climbed up and over a couch — and crashed into an accent table. Knocked to my knees, I scrambled for a basket of pillows and began lobbing them at Mutton Chops like fuzzy missiles. When I was out of ammo, I leapt to my feet and flung myself at the door which I hoped led to Vee's sleeping area.

"In the name of Her Majesty Queen Veronica, I order ye to halt!"

Mutton Chops grabbed the back of my shirt with both fists, and I jerked to a halt. As he tried to pull me backward, I planted my feet and strained to move forward. For a second I toyed with the idea of shedding my top, but the sports bra I'd been wearing since the stinky cow barn was currently tucked into the waistband on my PJs. I'd removed the uncomfortable, disgusting thing when Duncan's back was turned. Although I had an admittedly low inhibition threshold, I wasn't about to go au naturel it on my first day back in Doon.

Instead, I strained to take another step. "Let. Me. Go."

"Nay." Mutton Chops tugged me back with a grunt. "Halt. Now."

From the next room, a muffled, lovely voice said, "It's okay. I'm up."

"Let her be, Eòran." Duncan lounged in the entryway looking thoroughly entertained, like a circus spectator minus the peanuts. When the guard seemed reluctant to release me, Duncan stepped into the sitting room with my canvas bag.

Addressing Mutton Chops, he gently ordered, "Back to your post, man."

The guard hesitated for a fraction of a second. "Yes, m'laird."

As Mutton Chops let go, I grabbed my bag and pivoted to face him. "I told you she'd want to see me." I couldn't help but stick my tongue out in triumph before escaping into the chamber beyond.

Vee stood barefoot next to her bed wearing a blue-and-green flannel robe over her nightgown. "You're here!" she exclaimed, opening her arms for one of her famous bear hugs. "What happened to you?"

Now that I clung to my best friend, all the emotions of the past year churned to the surface, threatening to bubble over. Using my excess adrenaline to keep the weepies at bay, I babbled, "It's nothing. Except I nearly died and got kissed by a cow, but I'm here, finally."

When Vee eased up on her death grip, I perched on the edge of the bed, pulling her down next to me. "I want to hear about you. What's it like being a queen? What kind of cool perks do you get?"

She frowned at me in the lamplight. "Ken, it's not like I dress up all fancy and walk around greeting people like a Disneyland character. I'm running a country."

"And I bet you rock at it!"

"That remains to be seen — but I want to know why you're wearing pajamas and look like a refugee from an Aldous Huxley novel." She touched my face, wiping at what was likely a smudge with the pad of her thumb. "I'm not buying that dirty dystopian is the latest trend in beauty."

I didn't get what boring high school literature had to do with my filthy PJs, but I'm sure Vee had some logical connection. "The Brig o' Doon was out," I explained. "So we had to enter Doon through the mountains — but then Muir Lea was out, so we had to improvise by going off-road, which was nearly impossible because of the zombie fungus."

"Zombie fungus?"

"Yeah."

"What's that?"

"You know, the limbus."

"No, I don't know. You're talking in circles. Take a slow, deep breath and tell me about the limbus."

Inhale, hold ... and exhale. "I don't really want to talk about the limbus right now. Duncan's got that covered. He's preparing a full report. Did you know he hates me? At least he did, but after I saved his life from the zombie fungus he owed it to me, so we made a truce."

Vee rubbed sleep from her eyes. "Wait, I thought you said *you* almost died?"

It was like she wasn't even listening! "I did. Saving Duncan's life. Now, since we're indentured to one another, we decided to be friends."

"You're still talking a mile a minute." Vee winced and rubbed at her ear. "How about you take a shower while I order tea. Then we can try this again?"

"Sure. But could you make mine a latte?" Based on her inability to follow the conversation, she obviously needed to caffeinate her brain. Normally Vee didn't need a schematic to keep up — maybe we were just out of rhythm from being apart for so long.

Regardless, a shower sounded fantabulous. "And do you have something I could wear? Something comfy — because after that never-ending trek, I'm chaffed in places I didn't even know were places."

Vee flashed me a luminous smile. "I have something I think you'll like. I'll set it out for you."

"Thanks." I grabbed my dirty canvas bag and headed into Vee's royal powder room ... which made Duncan's bathroom look like a primitive port-a-potty. There was a huge walk-in shower and a giant tub on a raised dais in the corner that was surrounded by ornate, floor-to-ceiling windows looking out over the Scottish countryside. The entire room was tiled in cream with blue and green accents and the MacCrae lion crest.

One of the most pleasant discoveries during my first trip to Doon was the indoor plumbing. I took my time in the shower, letting the hot water cleanse me of all the drama from the last year. I envisioned the water washing away my past, carrying it down the drain and out to sea until I felt clean. A half hour later, I stepped from the bathroom a new person and wearing the cutest lavender maxi dress, which, other than being a smidge tight in the hips and chest, fit me perfectly.

I passed through Vee's bedroom and into the fully lit living space — which my bestie had definitely made her own. The room was primarily white with purple and crystal accents. I suspected that when the sun hit the space just right, it lit up like Narnia in winter. She looked up from her book as I entered, and I did a slow twirl for her. "Love this!"

Vee beamed at me. "I thought you might. Later we can head to the boutique in the village and pick some up in your size."

"There's a boutique in Doon? How did I miss that?"

"It's new. I found a very talented seamstress who can make anything I describe to her. I had her design a few items, and the next thing I know, all the young girls in the kingdom were copying my style. I feel like Jackie Kennedy."

"Didn't she wear old retro styles, like dress suits and pearls and stuff?" I flounced the skirt of my strappy dress, which looked nothing like the 60s. "This looks totally modern."

Vee rolled her eyes at me. "Anyway, the seamstress got so many requests that she opened a shop."

"What's it called? Vee's Vestments?"

For the first time, a note of chagrin tainted her pride. "Close. Royal Regalia."

"You trendsetter. Remember that outfit you wore for sixth grade pictures? Within a week, every girl in middle school was wearing a long shirt belted high on the waist with leggings."

"Thanks for reminding me." Vee set her book on the coffee table and handed me a steaming mug of java before picking up her own cup. "Let's try this again."

"Sure. Where do you want to start?"

She took a sip of tea as the wheels in her beautiful brain turned. "Why don't you start at the beginning?"

"Okay. After we defeated the witch, I went back home. Then I had about a week to pack and find an apartment before my internship started. You wouldn't believe how hard it is to find a decent place to live in Chicago. Oh, my dad is dating someone and he brought her to see my show. I thought it would be weird, but she's really nice."

Vee tilted her head. "Where does your dad think you are now?"

"Aunt Gracie's cottage." I blew into my mug. "He knows I'm with a boy, so I doubt he'll worry if he doesn't hear from me for a while. Speaking of boys, thanks for coaching Duncan on all things modern — even if he only came to get me because he was following your orders, I appreciated the first class."

As I swallowed a mouthful of coffee, Vee looked at me quizzically. "I gave Duncan lots of suggestions, but only one order, not to take no for an answer. I didn't force him to go get you. He volunteered."

"Oh." There were many reasons a guy would volunteer for

an unpleasant task — especially if evil seemed to be spreading across his kingdom. It didn't necessarily mean he wanted to see me again. "Sorry. What were we talking about?"

"You were going to tell me about your trip."

"Right." I told Vee about the Brig o' Doon with the zombie crow and going through the mountains in my pajamas. I described Duncan nearly dying and how unseen hands had come to my aid when I had risked my life to save him. I explained about the barn and Elsie's unwanted adoration. And I finished with the part about Duncan and me calling a truce.

Vee poured herself another cup of tea, carefully adding milk and sugar as she asked, "Do you think Duncan's really okay with you guys being friends?"

After a moment's thought, I nodded. "Yes. And I'll take it. When he first showed up in my dressing room — he was so not himself. Distant and cold. And the whole boyfriend thing only made it worse, ya know?"

"No, I don't know. You're talking in Kenna circles again."

In my haste to tell her about the fungus, I neglected to fill her in about Duncan's and my reunion in Chicago. "Sorry. He thinks I have a boyfriend."

"Who?"

"Duncan."

"No. Who does Duncan think is your boyfriend?"

"Weston Ballard, the director — "

"The hottie from your internship?"

"Turns out, he's not so hot." Memories of him wrenching my arm caused my stomach to sour. "Or a nice guy. In fact, he's a total creeper."

"So why would Duncan think that Weston is your boyfriend?"

My coffee, which had stopped agreeing with me, suddenly

threatened to come back up. I set my half-full mug on the table. "Maybe because Wes introduced himself as my boyfriend."

"And why would Weston do that?"

"Because ... we were kinda dating."

"Kenna!"

"Don't 'Kenna' me. I went out with him to get over Duncan, but it didn't work — and then I was stuck playing Wes's girl-friend so I could keep my lead in the show. Which I lost anyway once Duncan appeared."

"So why didn't you tell Duncan that?"

"Don't you think I tried? He won't let me explain."

"You hurt him, Ken." Her brows pinched apologetically. "He's going to need time to get over it."

"For the Love of Lerner and Loewe, it's been almost a year."

She shook her ponytail at me. "It's been two-and-a-half months here."

"Two-and-a-half months?" I wouldn't have been more stunned if she said Doon had been attacked by flying monkeys. "I completely forgot about the time difference between the real world and this one ... Argh! I'm an idiot."

I remembered the third month after the bridge incident. I'd buried my grief in tearful ballads and Ben & Jerry's Cherry Garcia — and consequently spent months four and five in the gym, hating my life in a whole new way. "It's only been two-and-a half months here?"

Vee nodded.

When I opened my mouth to ask her what she'd been up to during that time, a giant yawn popped out. Suddenly, I was exhausted. Blinking to regain focus, I regarded my bestie unsteadily. "I want to hear about you."

"We can talk about me later. There's actually not a lot to tell. I mean, what could go wrong in two months? ... Other than the limbus, which is enough." Vee stood, reached for my hands, and pulled me to my feet. "Let me show you your rooms. They're just across the hall."

Mutton Chops joined us in the corridor to unlock the guest suite. Despite my warm reception from the queen, the guard continued to give me the evil eye as I stepped past him into a slightly smaller version of Vee's rooms awash in sunflower yellow.

I expected Vee to follow but she paused in the doorway to address her personal guard.

"Eòran, will you ask Emily to set up a meeting for early this afternoon?"

"'Tis already arranged, Your Majesty."

"By whom?" Although she was doing her best not to react, I could hear her surprise.

"Prince Jamie hisself. By your orders, m'am."

"I see. And did he give you the particulars of my orders, such as what time I requested and who needed to attend?"

To his credit Mutton Chops didn't judge — or if he did the expression was lost under all his facial hair. Blandly, he replied, "Aye. One o'clock with hisself, Fergus, Fiona, Prince Duncan, the vexing American lass, and you, Your Highness, in Her Majesty's privy chambers."

"Thank you, Eòran. That will be all."

As she shut the door, Vee chewed her lower lip. Before turning around, she inhaled — her whole body rising with the controlled breath — and exhaled slowly. Calm restored, she clapped her hands together as she pivoted to face me. "Ready for the grand tour?"

Although I'd been gone for nearly a year, we still shared a brain. I knew that Jamie hadn't been acting on any order from his queen. Which meant two months had been enough time for things to go wrong. The trillion dollar question was, how wrong?

CHAPTER 10

Veronica

Kenna's melodious snores filled the air as I backed out of the door and locked it behind me. She would be safe in the Princess Tower, but after everything she'd been through, I wasn't taking any chances.

I practically skipped around the circular hallway, passing another empty room. The tower was one of the largest in the castle, designed for the queen-to-be and her female relatives. Being there alone had somehow felt wrong. I slipped into my suite and leaned against the door, the joy inside me spreading across my face. No more Rapunzel locked away in her tower. My family was here!

I crossed the sitting room, picked up pillows, righted toppled books, and gathered the pieces of a broken candle holder. Kenna was like a mini tornado, chaos following her everywhere she went. But having her here was worth any mess.

Too hyped up to rest, I grabbed my copy of *Persuasion* and took the three stairs to my favorite part of the suite — a turret that jutted off the main tower, creating a hexagonal sunroom. I curled up on the plush window seat, opened the book in my lap, and stared at the words blindly. Not even the great Jane Austen could hold my attention tonight.

Setting the book down, I unlatched a window and pushed it open. The chilled breeze brushed against my face, bringing the scent of pine and a hint of early autumn frost. I stared into the inky-black night. It was that in-between time when the stars were fading, the moon had set, and the sun was yet to rise. Too late for sleep and too early for the day to begin. Even in my happiness, I couldn't relax — couldn't forget my duties as queen. I wished I could celebrate my best friend's return with abandon, without fears and worries crowding out my joy. But those carefree days were no longer my reality.

I rose on my knees and leaned out the window. The kingdom was cloaked in pre-dawn shadow, and I strained to see any sign of the zombie fungus — as Kenna had so eloquently named it. I searched for any denser blackness or crows flying into nothingness, but I saw only the same shrouded hills and valleys, the same indigo waters of the loch that I saw every night. I slumped back onto my heels.

How had my best friend been able to see it? I'd been wearing the ring when we'd inspected the Northern Border where Drew Forrester had disappeared. The creep factor was off the scale — the forest projecting a foreboding that would put the black gates of Mordor to shame. But outside of the ebony petunias, I'd seen *nothing*. No pulsating void or ravaged trees. No zombified birds. Nothing like what Kenna described. Shouldn't the queen of Doon be able to see when her kingdom was in danger? Why would the Protector grant that power to another?

Then it hit me. This was why Kenna had to come back — the reason for my vision. Just like when we'd defeated the witch, we were stronger together.

Suddenly, the protesting villagers, my problems with Jamie, and even the cursed borders were no longer insurmountable obstacles.

I jumped down from the window seat and was halfway to the door before I remembered Kenna was exhausted and sleep deprived. Creating our master plan to save the kingdom would have to wait. Instead, I jogged into the bedroom, yanked my nightgown over my head, and slipped on my running clothes. I did my best thinking when I was moving.

After a brief confrontation with Eòran, I raced down the endless spiral stairs and catapulted out the door. I lengthened my stride and pushed myself faster as I crossed the courtyard, anxious to get out of the castle and away from my ricocheting thoughts. I'd promised Eòran to stay on the grounds. But with the misty morning stretched before me and my Nikes slapping against the cobbles in rhythm with my breath, I wasn't sure I could keep that promise.

I crossed the drawbridge and turned down a path that curved behind the castle. Never having taken this trail before, I was unprepared for the unevenness of the terrain and almost tripped over the shadowy rocks. I was too focused on the questions that had begun to bombard me to pay close attention to my feet. Now that Kenna was here, was defeating the limbus as simple as touching our rings together and calling out some magical spell. No, something told me it would never be as simple as that.

But I still had no idea where we should start. We didn't even know what was *causing* the limbus. We suspected Addie had something to do with it, but if I'd stripped all her power, how could she have activated it?

A low shape loomed out of the darkness. Before I could dodge it, I was flat on my face. Lying still for several seconds, I determined that I had no serious injuries and then pushed up on my elbows. Eye level with a flat, rectangular stone, I stared at the broken writing carved into its face: *Here lies Lynnette ...*

Here lies?

I was in a freaking graveyard!

My vision dimmed as I tried to get my legs under me, but they were stuck. Something held my feet! I kicked and squirmed until a ripping sound stopped the blood in my veins. I whipped my head around, anticipating a hunched, drooling ghoul tearing my shoes from my ankles. But instead, I found my laces tangled in a knee-high wrought iron fence. A chuckle of relief, and shame at my own stupidity, gushed out as I turned to free my feet from the metal.

After retying my shredded laces, I stood. The golden glow of the sky in the east illuminated lines of crooked stones and life-size statues. The stained-glass windows of the royal chapel behind me, the ground covered with tributes to dead kings and queens — I'd stumbled upon the MacCrae family cemetery.

Remembering how the auld laird's body had been burned on a pyre in the loch, I wondered if these stones were for memorial purposes only. I squatted in front of the marker I'd started to read and wiped the grime from the pitted stone.

Here lies Lynnette Elizabeth Campbell MacCrae.

Mo ..., Wife, Sist ... and Queen.

May ye reign fo ... ver in ... hearts.

I plucked out stalks of overgrown grass at the foot of the stone. Chunks had fallen from the base, rendering the set of dates illegible. But I didn't need to see them to know I'd found the grave of one of the early queens of Doon — the very queen who'd passed on during the witch's first attack. I scrubbed dirt from a faded carving of a face above the inscription. I traced the lines of her hair and cheeks with my finger, unable to make out the overall picture. Swallowing a lump that tasted like grief, I whispered, "How would *you* save the kingdom, Lynnette?"

Not hearing an answer — not that I expected to — I rose and made my way to the other end of the yard where newer, shinier stones resided. I approached a headstone covered in fresh heather and bluebells. *Maureen Elise McPherson MacCrae.* Jamie's mother.

A series of rhythmic clangs echoed through the air. My chest seized as I spun around. The sound continued unabated for several minutes. I moved toward it, down the hill and around an expanse of moss-coated castle wall. The noise grew louder, vibrating against my ribs, a powerful clash of metal against metal.

I rounded a corner and came upon an arched doorway set into the lowest level of the castle. Light emanated from the space, drawing me closer. The clanging stopped. I crept forward and paused inside the entrance of a cavernous room, the ceiling at least two stories high. There were wood and metal contraptions all over the space: a wide wooden ladder with no rungs, just a row of metal brackets cradling a single bar; something that looked like a narrow set of uneven bars; and a workbench covered with medieval tools. Swords, claymores, daggers, bows, and wicked-looking arrows in all shapes and colors covered the walls.

Had I stumbled upon some kind of primitive torture chamber?

The ring of metal began again, accompanied by grunts and the shifting of feet on dusty stone. Spotting movement toward the back of the vast room, I tiptoed toward it and passed a row of painted targets and burlap dummies hanging like faceless scarecrows. Ahead, a man moved through a vertical maze of metal bars while hefting a broadsword, the dark coils of a Celtic tattoo covering one shoulder. He slammed the sword into the pipes in a controlled sequence, sweat glistening over his muscled arms and back. His catlike grace sparked a familiarity in my gut. I took a step closer as he spun into a pool of light, the blade swinging over his blond head.

"Jamie!"

His eyes widened only fractionally before he lowered the sword, left the maze, and bent at the waist in a quick bow. "The one and only. Yer Majesty."

"When did you get that tattoo?" It was an inane question considering I'd just found him working out in a dungeon straight out of a Stephen King novel. But I was curious all the same.

He shoved drenched strands of hair off his forehead. "A few weeks past. Wanted one when I turned sixteen, but my ma threatened to skin me. Said it was 'marrin' God's perfect creation.'"

Fascinated, I approached and circled him to get a better view of the tattoo stretching around his shoulder. The loops converged in the middle, creating a trinity symbol entwined with a heart. On the front and back of his arm the design arched into two roaring lions in profile. I traced the intricate swirls that ended in dagger-like points on his slick bicep. He shivered, sending a jolt of awareness pulsing through me. I dropped my hand and stepped back.

"What does it mean?" I whispered.

Jamie didn't speak for several beats. Tension hung almost visible in the air as he turned to me, his dark eyes unreadable. "The Triquetra denotes fealty to the Protector. The lions symbolize ferocity and courage, and the blades, an oath to defend Doon with my life. Yer Highness," he added with a slight bob of his head before he turned and walked over to set his sword in a metal rack.

His formal tone grated against my already frayed nerves. We'd never discussed our argument at the Roselli Tavern since that night, but clearly he was still angry. And by being here, I was going against the one thing he'd asked me not to do — leave the castle alone. As he busied himself straightening his perfectly aligned weapons, I felt awkward, like I'd invaded his personal space. Taking a few steps back, I called, "I'll just be going —"

"Why?" He turned and stalked toward me, his brows hunched over his eyes. "Why do ye insist on putting yerself in danger at ever' turn?"

I backed into a solid object and stopped. "I ... er ... just needed some air." *Wait.* I was the queen of Doon. And if I wanted to go for a run, I was going to do it! I straightened my spine and lifted my chin as Jamie advanced on me. "You can't expect me to stay cooped up in that stale castle all day like some dried-up old prune. I won't do it."

"At the verra least, take a guard —" He stopped before me as comprehension dawned, and his face turned stormy. "What kind of fool ... I'll beat that blasted Eòran to a bloody pulp!" He slammed his fist into his palm.

Looking at him now, all broad, glistening muscle, I had little doubt he could do it.

"Don't be too hard on him." I couldn't help the smirk that slid across my face. "In order to stop me, he would've had to go against a direct order from his queen."

Jamie stilled and met my gaze. "I see."

Was that appreciation I saw in the slight crinkling of his eyes?

"Well, ye dinna look like much of a queen in that getup." He tugged on the tip of my ponytail and looked over my tank top and yoga pants.

Time for a change of subject. I walked over to the uneven bar contraption and ran my hand along the metal frame. On a far wall there was a type of scoreboard with Jamie and Duncan's names written at the top and rows of hash marks underneath. "What is this place, anyway?"

"Duncan and I found this grotto when we were wee ones and claimed it as our own. We've kept addin' to it over the years. It's our private training room and weapons store." I could hear him moving closer as he spoke.

I turned and threw him a teasing look. "Kinda like a medieval man cave."

Jamie looked thoughtful for a moment and then said, "More like a brother cave."

"That's perfect." I laughed, and then realized he would've been as worried about his brother as I'd been about Kenna. I reached for his hand. "You must be happy to have him back."

"Mayhaps." He pressed his lips together, trying not to smile, and then gave into a dimpled grin that lit his entire face. "But dinna tell him tha'. Or I'll never hear the end of it."

I stepped toward him, drawn like a magnet to steel. His expression went neutral, a furrow appearing over his left brow as his dark eyes searched mine. I moved closer and rose onto my toes. He stepped back, withdrawing his hand.

"I've much to do before meeting with Duncan and Mackenna." He ambled over to where his shirt lay draped over the back of a chair, grabbed it, and pulled it over his head.

I tried to ignore the rejection burning in my gut. Had I ruined things between us already? Did he not want me anymore? Destroying relationships seemed to be my superpower. "Um … okay." I cleared my throat as I rotated on my heel and headed for the door. "I'll see you in a few hours then."

"Verranica."

He'd said my name, not, *"Yer Highness."* I stopped in my tracks.

"If ye insist on leavin' the castle in *that* — " I turned to see his eyes pause on my lycra-clad backside. "Come and get me first, aye?"

From the inscrutable look on his face, I couldn't tell if he wanted to accompany me on my runs or talk me out of wearing these clothes. But either way, that bit of protectiveness gave me hope that he hadn't given up on us yet. I swept into a deep curtsy. "Aye, my laird."

Silence followed Jamie's words, and the five other people sitting around my dining table appeared as dumbstruck as I felt.

"Well I, for one, think it's a horrendous idea." Kenna slouched in her chair and crossed her arms under her chest.

"I concur," I said into the unnatural quiet. And it wasn't just because it was Jamie's suggestion. Or that he and I had just gone ten rounds over whether or not to tell the kingdom what Kenna had seen inside the limbus. Duncan and Kenna pretending she had returned to Doon to accept her Calling with the younger prince had "tragic ending" written all over it. She hadn't given any indication she was staying once we averted Doonmageddon. Her word, not mine. I didn't believe we were at DEFCON 1 quite yet.

"Vee! I thought you would at least agree with me," Kenna huffed, hitting me with wounded puppy-dog eyes.

"Ken, I concur with you." She arched a fiery brow in my direction, forcing me to clarify. "I *agree* with you."

"Oh, good. Because three against one is totally unfair."

"Make tha' four against two." Fiona glanced at Fergus, who nodded his head in agreement. Fiona turned back to Kenna. "If we aren't going ta tell the people about the limbus as yet, then why else would ye have returned, Mackenna?"

I shot Jamie a glare across the table. I couldn't believe that even after Kenna and Duncan had relayed their horrific story of Muir Lea's disintegration, he wouldn't budge on telling the kingdom. He met my gaze steadily and offered a small smile. I turned away. How much longer could we keep it a secret? I shuddered at the thought of the people's reaction if they found out from someone other than their queen. Wasn't I supposed to have their best interests at heart? The temptation to call a general assembly that very afternoon was almost overwhelming, but I'd agreed to give Jamie time to survey the borders to determine the rate at which the limbus was growing. In the meantime, I'd be spending every waking hour making sure the people steered clear of the infected areas, and the time I should be sleeping searching for answers.

Tuning back in to the conversation, I heard my BFF spout something about alien babies and flying monkeys.

Jamie cut her off mid-rant. "Mackenna, ye be a fair actress. If anyone can —"

"Why" — Duncan leaned forward splaying his large hands on the table — "has no one asked *me* if I'll go along with this plan?"

Jamie raised his eyebrows in surprise. Every head in the room focused on the younger prince as he continued, "'Tis a lie." His gaze flicked to Kenna and he swallowed hard before turning back to Jamie. "And I'll no' be a party to it."

Jamie's spine went ridged and he challenged, "Even for the greater good, brother? Isna that why we're hiding the truth about the limbus?"

Duncan shoved his chair back with a loud screech. "This is not the same and ye know it!"

"Oh no, here we go again," Fiona muttered, scooting closer to Fergus.

I grabbed my new purple ceramic vase from the center of the table, clutching the delicate white tulips to my chest.

But for once, Jamie didn't take the bait. He leaned back, stretched his legs out in front of him, and linked his fingers over his abdomen. "Tha's fine. You're just afraid you can't pull it off. I understand." He lifted one shoulder in a lazy shrug. "We'll think of something else."

The moment he said it, it was as if the cloud of my own stubbornness lifted from my eyes and I could see the perfection of his plan. I set the vase back on the table. If we could get Kenna and Duncan to act out the feelings we all knew they were hiding from each other, then *maybe* they would eventually accept they were meant to be together. And Kenna would stay.

Kenna stared out a nearby window. If she sunk any lower in her chair, she'd disappear under the table. I opened my mouth, not even sure what I would say, but before I could speak, Duncan grunted, "Nay." He'd been watching the girl beside me as well.

His focus shifted to the opposite end of the table. "Jamie, your plan makes the most sense." Then, with a crooked half smile, he turned back to my friend. "Mackenna, I'm willin' if you are."

"Fine." She met his gaze, her cheeks glowing crimson, but she brazened it out with a lift of her chin. "Just leave the acting to me."

Duncan's grin faded as he arched a brow. "Is that so?" An enigmatic look passed between him and his brother, prompting Jamie to shake his head and roll his eyes, the corner of his mouth tilting.

Duncan stood and cleared his throat, drawing the attention

of everyone in the room. Striking a pose, he opened his hands as if beseeching and he began to speak. "O, she doth teach the torches to burn bright!"

Each word forceful and deep, he moved around the table toward Mackenna as he continued his impassioned rendition of Romeo's speech to Juliet.

"It seems she hangs upon the cheek of night." Duncan lowered to one knee, taking her limp hand in his, dark eyes intent upon her face. "Like a rich jewel in an Ethiope's ear; Beauty too rich for use, for earth too dear!"

After several beats of silence, Duncan sprung to his feet with a wide grin and swept into a bow.

I burst into applause. One glance at my best friend, who sat like a parody of a statue with her mouth unhinged, and I blurted the first thing that popped into my head. "Wow, Duncan. If I'd known acting could be like that, I would've raced to join the drama club!" I fanned my face with my hand and winked at him, doing my best to draw his attention until Kenna could gain control.

"Thank you, my lovely queen." Duncan inclined his head in my direction and took his seat, looking like he'd just hit a grand slam in the bottom of the ninth. Which, judging by Kenna's stunned expression, he had.

"He doth nothing but talk of his horse," Jamie mumbled with a shake of his head.

Something resembling a croak escaped my throat as I tried to cover my laugh with a cough. I recalled the quote from a reading we'd done in Advanced Lit of *The Merchant of Venice*. The MacCrae brothers sure knew their Shakespeare.

"That may be, brother. I have missed Mable somethin' fierce." Duncan wiggled his brows, his eyes full of mischief. "But me thinks I've proven I can handle a wee bit of acting."

Kenna rose from her seat, pink cheeked but composed. "I *concur*." She shot Duncan a fleeting glance, and then turned to me. "If this meeting's over, I'd like to return to my room."

At my nod, she turned on her heel and headed for the door. Maybe this ruse wasn't such a great idea after all.

CHAPTER 11

Mackenna

Whoever said knowledge is power obviously had no other marketable skills ... and no Wikipedia. As a member of the digital generation, I struggled to see any merit in wandering through shelves of dusty tomes in hopes of finding a literary needle in a haystack.

During my last visit to Doon, I'd successfully managed to avoid the library, mostly by staying in the dungeon. As I entered the stadium-sized room, I debated which — the library or the dungeon — was more enjoyable. I hated the way knowledge smelled; dusty with a faint tinge of mildew. Not that I didn't enjoy learning, I was constantly expanding my audition song repertoire. But books seemed flat and impersonal ... and hard to finish. That's why I always opted for the movie version if available.

At least the space was airy, with large windows and high ceilings. Cozy little nooks of overstuffed chairs and divans, perfect for napping, existed in every corner. Which would be tempting, if I wasn't actively trying not to think about my farce with Duncan.

It was my very own messed-up version of *Victor Victoria*, a silly, pointless musical that had never held much appeal for me. I was faking being in love with a boy that I was pretending not to be in love with, but was really head-over-heels crazy about.

I worried over what this little stunt would do to our truce. Duncan was finally starting to act like himself again. Faking a Calling would be a painful reminder of my betrayal and all the reasons he had to doubt me. Maybe this was fate's way of telling me I didn't deserve another chance.

Footsteps echoed across the marble floor. I turned toward them, intending to chide Vee for being late, but she wasn't there. A curvy girl with dark bangs, a sad-yet-determined smile, and a clipboard strode toward me wearing a sky blue maxi dress. "Her Majesty's running late."

Who? It took me a moment to realize we were talking about Vee. "Oh, okay. I'm —"

"Mackenna. Yes, I know. I'm the queen's personal assistant, Emily Roosevelt." She held out her hand and I gave it a shake.

So this was the girl whose future had been destroyed by the zombie fungus? Her nose was a little larger than I'd pictured, but for the most part she was exactly as my bestie had described her — a lost soul in need of a project. Looking at the poor girl, I decided I could forgive her air of self-importance under the circumstances. She'd lost her other half. Even if she did move on with her life, she would forever be incomplete. Something I understood all too well.

"The queen will be here shortly. In the meantime, she's requested that I bring you and Analisa up to speed on the project. Shall we get started?"

"It seems to me we're a person short." Despite Vee's assurances that Analisa wasn't "too bad," I didn't relish spending the afternoon with a felon. Hope blossomed that the forger's absence meant she'd be a no show. "Maybe Analisa can't make it."

"Or maybe she's already here and sitting right under your noses."

Holy Hammerstein!

Clutching at my chest, I stepped back from the clipped London accent coming from the furniture directly in front of me. The voice seemed to emanate from thin air, but on closer inspection I detected the motionless form of a girl molded into one of the high-backed chairs.

Taking her sweet time, the girl rose to her feet in one fluid, feline motion. Unless she'd just materialized, Analisa had gotten to the library before me. She'd seen me enter. But instead of identifying herself, she sneakily intruded on what I thought was a moment alone. Had she heard me muttering to myself about Duncan? I hoped not.

Analisa tucked the long side of her platinum-over-jet-black bob behind her ear and crossed the floor with the smooth, lanky strides of a supermodel. Her Vee-inspired dress swirled bewitchingly around her legs as she approached. I disliked her more with each step. Girls that looked like her tended to think the rules of mere mortals didn't apply to them.

As she joined us, she gave me the once-over with a perfectly arched brow. "So you're the actress from Chicago. Funny, I thought you'd be ..." She trailed off, and I couldn't help picking up where she left off. *Thought I'd be ... what? Prettier, more petite, older, thinner ... Please don't let it be thinner.*

Analisa's cat-like eyes blinked as she shrugged. "Never mind. You are what you are." By way of dismissal, she turned to Emily. "Shall we get started then?"

Emily, who'd been studying the notes on her clipboard, nodded. "Yes. Her Majesty wants to compile a complete history of Queen Lynnette Elizabeth Campbell MacCrae. She was married to the king who invoked the blessing, but didn't live to see her kingdom delivered. She passed away while Doon was still under attack."

I knew all this. We'd discussed it as the cover story to research the previous limbus, but I nodded along like I was hearing it for the first time. As Emily continued to speak, pointing out the organizational flow of the library, I studied the girl who'd gambled everything on true love and lost. Her stick-straight brown hair accentuated dark, wounded eyes. More than her physical appearance, she radiated an inner fragility that clung to the structure of her task causing her to wield her clipboard like protective armor. Unlike Analisa, this girl I could be friends with.

After the official tour, we split up. Relieved to go separate ways, I wandered toward the back of the library, marveling at the sheer volume of books. Who knew so many books had been written prior to the Renaissance? But what we were looking for were older volumes. Doon had vanished off the map right before the 1600s, and we needed firsthand accounts leading up to that event.

In an alcove at the back of the library, I discovered another inviting space arranged around a roaring fireplace. Above the mantle hung a portrait of a young woman wearing a crown. An unruly mass of auburn curls framed her lovely face. Her expression was equal parts mischievous and determined. The inscription read *Queen Lynnette, founder and patron of this esteemed place of learning.*

This was the girl who'd been queen when Doon had been attacked? The one who'd died from illness at the height of the siege? She looked like a teenager, but at the same time she possessed a poise that transcended age. In truth, she reminded me of Vee — not in looks, but in bearing.

"I adore that painting."

Vee's voice startled me out of my musings. Standing behind me in one of her patented maxi dresses with a delicate crown entangled in her dark hair, she looked more like a fairy princess than a queen, except for the tightness around her eyes. The weariness in her face spoke of the weight she carried for her people. Had we been in a musical, now would've been the perfect time for an expository duet about the challenges of governing a kingdom.

Instead of warbling in beguiling soprano, Vee flopped into a chair. "Queen Lynnette was my age when the portrait was painted. The Master Archivist told me she'd just had a baby."

"Really?" I looked again at the girl for signs of baby weight. Nothing. Then again, portraits were the original form of airbrushing. Heaven help the artist who captured nobility as they truly were rather than how they wanted to be seen.

"I often come here when I need a source of inspiration." Vee inhaled softly and stood a little straighter. "Queen Lynnette gives me strength. She was a great visionary and a champion of the people. It's because of her that this library exists. She had books brought in from all over the world. Languages, science, history, religion. Anyone could come to the library at Castle MacCrae and learn. At every Centennial, there's a group of Doonians dedicated to continuing her legacy by collecting new books, both fiction and nonfiction."

"Except this past one." My words caused Vee to flinch. This last Centennial had been pandemonium. The bridge had been impassible due to a spell cast by the witch, Jamie nearly died, and Vee had ended up in charge of the Doonians. Which reminded me ... "How did Analisa, Emily, and the others get here if the Brig o' Doon wasn't working?"

"A couple of the guys came through the mountains. The

rest were gathered at the bridge. When it opened, they took the scenic route around the lake — just like we did the first time. When we crossed at midnight, we went the opposite way, so we didn't find them until the next morning." Vee gingerly rolled her head from side to side. "We'd better get started. We're looking for anything that mentions the limbus. Fiona will join us after her dress fitting."

Heading to the right of the portrait, she pulled a stack of books from a section labeled local history and piled them on the end table between two leather chairs. As she settled into research mode, I wandered among the stacks in the alcove waiting for inspiration and humming the music to *Beauty and the Beast*.

Despite the overabundance of books, the library had killer acoustics. I wondered if anyone had ever thought to stage a concert here. I was just about to ask Vee when she set aside her book with a thump. "You *do* realize we'd accomplish more if you looked in the books and not just at them?" she huffed.

Doubtful. I don't think I'd ever researched anything without either Cliffs notes or a Veronica Welling cheat sheet. I continued my perusal, unaffected by her impatience. "I'm searching for something specific."

"What?"

"Books that look really old."

"Kenna — you can't just eyeball spines and tell the age of a book."

"Why not?" I shrugged. "People do it with wine all the time."

She glared at me like I'd spoken pig Latin. "What?"

"Wine. One sip and they can tell how old it is. Scotch too, I think. So I'm going off first impressions. Looking for something ... like this." Tucked between two large volumes that'd tipped toward each other was a thin leather-bound book. Easy to overlook if one wasn't really paying attention.

Vee shook her head while I eased the book from the shelf. As I opened the cover she said, "Just because it's an old book doesn't mean it's applicable — "

I cut her off with a wave of my hand. "A Complete History of Queen Lynnette Elizabeth Campbell MacCrae, Autobiographical."

I'd discovered the Holy Grail. Vee leapt from the chair to get to the book. "May I see that?"

Rather than surrender it, I silently arched an eyebrow and waited until she said, "Fine. I'm so sorry. Your Jedi-like skills are far superior to my traditional research techniques. May I please have it now?"

I placed the book gently in her hand. "Was that so hard?"

Instead of answering, Vee checked the date in the front and then skimmed through the entries to the back. "Her entire life seems to be documented in here, in her own words ... except for the end. And there's chapter titles."

She crossed back to the sitting area with her nose buried in the pages of Queen Lynnette's life. I followed, looking over her shoulder at the uniform words. "If it's told in her own hand, why is it typed? They didn't have typewriters back in the medieval ages." At least I didn't think they did.

"No, but printing presses were common by the early fifteen hundreds. Someone must've printed this after she died."

As Vee reclaimed the chair she'd previously occupied, I grabbed the notebook and pen I'd thought to bring from the modern world and sat opposite her. "I'll take notes." I might not have been a Master Jedi when it came to the heavy lifting part of research, but I was the Anakin Skywalker of bullet points — minus the whole dark-side thing.

My mind started to wander down the Star Wars Saga as a musical path. Like *Children of Eden* but with lightsabers and Darth Vader. Every once in a while Vee would read out a fact for me to capture. Age. Birthdate. Marriage. Philanthropy — Vee's word, not mine. Most of it was not nearly as exciting as my vision of singing Ewoks.

We'd yet to unearth any mention of the witches' siege, or the limbus that plagued the kingdom four hundred years before, when Fiona appeared. Her forceful stride made the petite girl seem taller than five two. As she approached, her strawberry blonde curls bobbed around her agitated face.

Vee set the book aside in favor of our friend. "What's wrong?"

"It's my mum." She huffed to a stop in front of us and then began to pace as she elaborated. "I wanted a simple dress. Elegant and flowin' like a mermaid. Or a glen fairy. With a garland of wildflowers. But Mum, she told the dressmaker *lace*. Yards and yards of stiff, itchy lace. An' she's got the milliner creating this abomination of a veil. I'm going ta look like a giant cumulous cloud!" She paused her movement on the last statement for emphasis.

In tandem, Vee and I stood to comfort our friend. "I'm sure it's not so bad," I said as I patted her arm.

From her other side, Vee added, "And lace is really — "

"Veronica Welling," Fiona interrupted. "Do you know what happens ta queens who lie? They roast in the fiery pit. So think carefully before ye finish that sentence. Lace is really *what*?"

Vee blanched and then replied tentatively, "We'll love you anyway, even if you do look like a giant cloud." She glanced at me, transferring the mental image of Fiona decked in miles of lace to my brain. We both began to snicker despite our distraught friend.

Like wildfire, the snickering became full-blown giggles. After a tense moment, Fiona caved, her agitation dissolving into maniacal laughter. We clung to each other until tears leaked from our eyes. As the hilarity ebbed, Fiona moaned, "What am I ta do?"

Sharing a brain, Vee and I said without hesitation, "Bachelorette party!"

"Who's having a bachelorette party?" Analisa's ghetto-British accent cut through the moment as she rounded the corner with Emily.

Before I could say ix-nay on the bachelorette arty-pay, Vee answered, "We are. For Fiona."

Analisa rubbed her hands together. "We're in."

Fiona blinked at us curiously. "What's a bachelorette party? A modern custom?"

Before I could explain, Analisa flashed her a wicked smile. "Oh, you'll see." Then she turned to Emily. "Could we get that oldest Rosetti boy to do the entertainment, do you think?"

Emily began to make notes on her clipboard when Vee interjected, "We are *not* getting anyone to do *that* kind of entertainment, as tempting as your suggestion is ..." She shook her head to dispel the image. "I'd already planned on throwing a bridal shower. We'll have the bachelorette party after. Strictly no boys allowed!"

"But we could do karaoke," I suggested. "Show tunes!"

"Yes." Vee nodded and pointed to Emily's clipboard. "That one you can write down."

Emily made a note and then turned to her queen. "Did you find any books mentioning Queen Lynnette? We found a couple of mentions, but nothing we didn't already know."

Vee shared a glance with Fiona and me before answering, "I did find a couple interesting accounts, but I'd like the chance to read them through before we go any further. So, for the time being, can you and Analisa plan the shower and party? Oh, and the second wedding-night ball?"

Fiona paled. "You're throwing me a ball for the second night?"

"Yep." Before I could ask, Vee explained, "It's tradition to have two wedding receptions. One after the ceremony and one the following day. Usually the second night reception is informal, but I recently learned that when royalty gets married in Doon, the second night is traditionally a ball held at the palace. So I was thinking that would be a nice tradition to start for all marriages in the kingdom. And ... I think Emily and Analisa are the ones to organize it."

Vee tilted her head ever-so-slightly as her eyes widened, meaning planning the second-night ball was a great way to get them out of the way while the Scooby gang focused on how to save Doon.

"I agree." I smiled at the two newcomers. "They're perfect for the job."

It was a fabulous idea. A ball would be an excellent distraction for the whole kingdom. Plus, it would centralize the Doonians in one central and safe place, far away from the zombie fungus. Leave it to my bestie to face down the latest Doon apocalypse in style — any excuse for a party.

CHAPTER 12

Mackenna

This party was a terrible idea!

Vee tugged at my hair, wrapping the medieval curling iron around a misbehaving strand. The sitting area of my rooms resembled the aftermath of a strip mall leveled by a tornado. Clothes and open-toed shoes were strewn across the couch. Cosmetics littered the table. But no matter how I tried to pretend Vee and I were getting ready for Winter Formal, little touches of Doonian culture reminded me that we weren't in Kansas anymore.

On the eve before their Sabbath, the kingdom gathered at the castle for a feast and dancing. This would be Duncan's and my first outing as a fake couple. Since he'd left for the borders shortly after our little powwow, we hadn't had a chance to work out our characters yet. I prayed he would get back in plenty of time to rehearse.

Riding my wavelength, Vee said, "Jamie and Duncan are going to be late."

"How do you know? Did they send a carrier pigeon or something?"

She rolled her eyes at me. "They sent a messenger."

"So that's how they texted in the Dark Ages. Nice."

"We're not in the Dark Ages. There. All finished." She fluffed my hair. And then handed me a silver hand mirror.

Under Vee's expert care, my waves looked more like the Little Mermaid than Ronald McDonald. The temptation to belt out "Part of Your World" lodged in my gut. But I couldn't afford to want to be part of this world, at least not now.

Afraid Vee would read my thoughts, I said, "You look gorgeous!"

Despite Vee's fashion-forward influence, she'd insisted we dress more traditionally for the weekly dinner-dance. We both wore peasant blouses, calf-length skirts, and cute lace-up vests — emerald green for me and lavender for Vee. But my bestie also had a tiara adorning her dark curls and the Doonian plaid draped across her torso like a sash. "You're like a Scottish prom queen."

A shadow flickered across her eyes. "Kenna, this is the second time you've referred to me like I'm playing dress up. Being queen of prom and queen of a country are totally different things. As my best friend, I would expect you of all people to understand how difficult this is. I'm on the outside trying to learn the rules and customs. The people don't respect my authority — not that I really have the opportunity to establish any with Jamie constantly stepping in, and worst of all, I never get to shed the crown and be a normal teenager. Ever again."

Whoa — hold up, Hal Prince! She was definitely going through more than I'd realized. Unfortunately, she'd made the transition look so easy that I hadn't noticed how much she struggled. But as her best friend, I should've seen it ... Maybe I would have if I hadn't been so self-absorbed.

"I'm sorry." I stood and wrapped my arms around her. "You're really doing a great job."

"It's just so hard." Her voice hitched, causing my throat to clog along with it. "This isn't like some fairy tale where you win the prince, become royalty, and live happily ever after. This is real life. *My life*. Every day brings a new challenge that only I can solve. Some are as trivial as vandalized sheep, but I've also got to face angry mobs who don't want a foreign queen —"

"You're not foreign — you're American." She pulled away just enough to level me with an incredulous look. "Sorry. Continue."

"Well, you saw what the limbus is doing. Sometimes ... I feel completely and utterly alone."

I may not have understood all the intricacies of politics but I was an expert in friendship. Pulling her back into a tight hug, I said, "You're not. I'm here. And I'm sorry. Plus you've got Jamie — not to mention Duncan, Fergus, Fiona, and a whole lot of other folks."

She squeezed back for a couple of moments and then let me go to check her makeup in the mirror. While Doon had pencils, powders, and rouges, I'd supplied mascara courtesy of my local drugstore. Too bad I hadn't brought the waterproof kind.

Rummaging through my bag, I grabbed a tube of Vee's most favorite gloss and handed it to her. "Here. Jamie MacCrae will have no idea what hit him."

"Oh, Mango-granate, how I've missed you!" Vee hugged the tube to her chest. "Thanks, Ken. I am so glad you're here — and not just because of the limbus. I've really needed you."

"I've needed you too." As Vee applied her gloss, I grabbed my preferred flavor, Strawberry-colada-tini, and did the same. With a smack of my lips, I declared, "Ready."

With Eòran on our strappy heels, we descended the tower and then wound our way through the castle to the Great Hall. Dancing had already begun. A dozen young couples stepped across the gleaming walnut floor in an intricate reel. I recognized Analisa's willowy form as she glided by in the arms of the Rosettis' oldest son.

Banquet tables for dining, and later for playing cards, were at the opposite end of the room. Uttering something about lavender cream puffs, Vee pointed toward the buffet feast laid out along the interior wall. I knew from my previous visit to Doon that this party was a casual affair so people could eat — or not eat — as it suited them. I definitely fell into the latter group. The idea of pretending to be in love with Duncan was making me nauseous. How long before everyone guessed that I was wearing my true feelings as a mask?

What I needed was to lock my emotions in a box. Although I suspected I would find no peace of mind in pretending, I would make-believe each word from my lips did not betray my heart.

Fiona and Fergus had leaked the news that I'd returned, so no one seemed surprised at my sudden appearance as the queen's plucky sidekick. As Vee wandered through the hall greeting her people, many offered me their heartfelt congratulations. Maybe it was my imagination, but the crowd seemed smaller than the last time I was here.

When we reached the far corner, a young boy perched on a low, wooden stool peered at us with hopeful caramel-colored eyes. Grabbing Vee's arm to get her attention, I pointed to the boy who, in turn, frowned at me. "Who's that little guy?"

"That's Lachlan. And I'm sure he's out of sorts because Jamie isn't here." As if sensing he was the topic of our discussion, the boy crossed his arms. His lower lip jutted out defiantly, prompting her to say, "I'll go talk to him."

I nodded, barely hearing her words as a distant memory surfaced. A boy of seven — my imaginary friend, Finn, — sat Indian-style on the Brig o' Doon, his arms crossed, his lips puckered and downcast. I recalled skipping up to the bridge and asking him what was wrong.

"I'm supposed to be at a dance. But I don't want to be there," *he said belligerently before standing up. "I want to be here* *with you."*

My heart fluttered as if I'd eaten butterflies. The strange *little tremors made me feel both happy and anxious. It was my* *first summer in Alloway, a lonely one until I happened on Finn* *the day before. "I'm glad you came back."*

"I promised ye I would. Jamie told me you aren't real, and I *need to stop making up stories. But I dinna believe him." Finn* *glanced over his shoulder. "They're looking for me. I canna stay."*

I distinctly remembered the warmth of his hand as I grabbed it. *"Promise me you'll come back tomorrow."*

"I'll always return for you. Tha's a promise."

And he had, day after day, summer after summer. In the end, it was I who'd eventually broken faith and stopped coming.

Finn faded away along with the memory. Had he really mentioned his brother, Jamie, to me all those years ago, or was I misremembering? Maybe the whole imaginary Finn really being Duncan thing was wishful thinking on behalf of my subconscious.

Vee would recall if I'd ever mentioned that conversation with Finn. When we were growing up, I told her everything about him. Unfortunately, Vee was too busy being the dutiful monarch to notice I'd taken a stroll down memory lane. And if I asked for her confirmation, I'd have to confess what I suspected, that my Calling to Duncan had been going on for over a decade. Then she'd start pressuring me to stay. It would be cruel to get her hopes up, when I didn't even know what I wanted ... Aside from Duncan's forgiveness.

"He's not budging." I looked to Vee for context, afraid she was sharing my brain again, when she gestured to the boy. "Lachlan says he's waiting for Jamie."

She took my arm and continued to make nice with the villagers. Just as we were finishing our first lap, Gabriella and Sofia Rosetti waved us over. Vee smiled at them and pivoted on the balls of her feet, but I grabbed her elbow before she could move. "Wait, I thought we hated them?"

Speaking through her frozen smile, she replied, "I'm the queen, remember. It's my job to like everyone. Besides, we were wrong about the Rosetti sisters. Gabby is very sweet once you get to know her, and Sofia has become a good friend."

Before we could cross the floor, Gabriella rushed at me, dragging her older sister by the sleeve. The younger of the Rosetti sisters was even lovelier than the last time I'd seen her. Her gangly limbs had developed subtle curves. And her golden hair seemed longer and flowier than before. A hint of makeup accentuated her emerald eyes. Her green maxi dress, complements of the Queen Vee summer line, matched her perfectly and belled around her as she approached.

"I heard you came back. Your Calling to Duncan must've been too strong to stay apart. That's so romantic." Even with a Scottish brogue, she rolled her Rs like a true Italian. The effect would've been charming if she didn't bristle with excitement like a puppy about to happy tinkle.

Sofia stood off to one side. While Gabby was the spitting image of their Scottish mother, Sofia favored her dad's fiery, Italian roots. But this girl was a mere ghost of the Sicilian bombshell I remembered. Purplish crescents appeared just below her ebony eyes, and her dark curls looked like they hadn't been tamed in weeks. Her traditional Doonian skirt and blouse seemed too large on her thin frame, as if she'd recently lost weight. And I couldn't help noticing the way she flinched when her sister trilled "rrromantic" — like she'd been slapped.

Gabby continued to talk a mile a minute, oblivious to her sister's discomfort. "You must tell me all about it. When did you first realize that you and Duncan shared a true Calling? And what did Prince Duncan say when he met you at the bridge? Are you engaged?"

She grabbed my hand and I hastily jerked it back. I opened my mouth, at a loss over which question to answer first, when Sofia said, "She only just arrived, Gabby. Of course she's not yet engaged."

With a nod, Gabby accepted the answer and moved on. "How did your Calling first manifest?"

"What?" "Excuse me." Sofia and I spoke over one another, and then the petite Italian hurried away.

Vee glanced at us, her eyes rounded in concern. "I'll go after her." She followed in Sofia's wake, leaving me trapped.

Gabby continued to — well, gab as if her sister's behavior was nothing out of the ordinary.

"Each Calling shows itself differently as the souls connect across the bridge." She nodded toward Vee. "Queen Veronica had visions of Jamie while she was still in Indiana. And Prince Jamie had dreams of being in her world."

She paused for a moment, clearly proud she'd been privy to the private details of Vee and Jamie's love life. "So how did Duncan appear to you?"

To my horrification, I spouted out the memory that was freshly in my mind. "First as a little boy."

Holy Schwartz! I hadn't meant to say that. I glanced at Vee, who was talking in a low, animated voice with Sofia and gave no indication of overhearing my confession. Leaning in to the younger Rosetti sister, I adopted a tone that indicated my next statement was just between us. "He used to appear as my imaginary friend when we were little."

Before Gabby could follow up with a million questions, Sofia abruptly ran toward the exit. With a hasty apology, Gabriella followed. As I watched the sisters' retreat, I couldn't help but feel sorry for the girl who had once nearly been betrothed to Jamie.

"What was that about?" I asked Vee as she returned to my side.

"Sofia had a Calling before the Centennial. But the boy from her dreams didn't cross the Brig o' Doon with the Destined. She's been confused and heartsick."

Make that very sorry. If life wasn't cruel enough, why not add a cast of happy couples to torment her. "Did she elaborate on her Calling? Like how it was manifesting?"

Vee's eyes narrowed slightly. "No. Why?"

"For character research. Gabby said something about each experience being unique."

Vee continued to consider me, and I swear I could see the gears turning behind her shrewd eyes. While I groped for a safe change of subject, Analisa whirled by, still in the arms of the oldest Rosetti boy. Which made me wonder where the other girl with the unfortunate Calling had disappeared to ...

"Where's Emily?"

Vee shrugged. "She usually skips these feasts. They're too difficult in her current emotional state."

I nodded, watching Analisa and her dance partner cross over to the table of ale. She was leading the boy around like a prize bull. Before I could check myself, I blurted, "Could she be any more shallow — parading her arm candy around the room like some supermodel?"

Vee followed the direction of my gaze. "What's your issue with Analisa?"

"She's a criminal."

Using her low, "serious" voice as she pulled me toward an unoccupied space near the buffet tables, she said, "She's not a criminal here. She's one of the Destined — led to this kingdom for a purpose. We need her gifts."

"I still don't like her. She has squinty eyes."

Vee jabbed my ribcage with her stiletto-like elbow. "Kenna, she's half Japanese!"

"Ow! What's her ethnicity got to do with anything? I'm talking about her shiftiness."

Vee groaned. "Is this about Duncan? Because they're just friends."

My gut clenched like I'd been punched. "That girl and Duncan are friends? What kind of friends?"

"Never mind. Forget I said anything." Vee turned toward the nearest pastry table, a sure-fire sign she was trying to avoid telling me something.

I grabbed her arm to keep her from fleeing. "How much time have they spent together? What kind of things do they do when they're together?"

"I don't know. It's not like I have them followed." But as queen she could have ... Before I had a chance to argue the point, she continued. "You left him, Ken. When he first came home — "

I cut her off with a hand gesture. I didn't need to hear how messed up he was when he got back, or how it was all my fault. I already carried epic guilt over what I'd done, even if I'd had the best of intentions. What I wanted was to understand the nature of their relationship. Was she the reason that every time

Duncan seemed to thaw, he immediately pulled away? "Are they dating?"

"Not that I've seen. That's the truth." Vee paused. "Mostly they just … talk."

"Talk a little or a lot?"

"Does it really matter?" *So a lot.*

A million thoughts swirled in my head. What were his feelings toward her? How did she feel about him? And what about the oldest Rosetti boy? Was he a ploy to make Duncan jealous or was the obnoxious Londoner a fickle shrew as well as a felon?

I glanced at Analisa cupping her boy toy's bicep and whispering conspiratorially into his ear. Both their lips quirked in a half-suppressed secret smile, their eyes gleaming from some inside joke. If Duncan did care for her, she'd undoubtedly wreck him.

"Ken? Maybe you should talk to Duncan. Just ask."

And what if he confirmed he'd moved on? Luckily, Fiona's arrival spared me from having to respond. Her hazel eyes blazed as she gestured toward the doors that led outside before crossing the room. With Vee and me following at a discrete distance, the three of us slipped into the night.

The battlement formed a balcony along the entire side of the castle facing the lake at one end and the mountains at the other. With the party not yet in full swing, we had the space to ourselves.

Without any sort of prelude, Fiona stated, "The lads are back."

Vee opened her mouth, but before she could get her question out Fiona added, "They're all fine. Just getting cleaned up. I expect they'll be here anon. Although Fergus Lockhart can perish on the moors for all I care at the moment."

Vee made a sympathetic noise somewhere between a cluck and a whimper. "What's wrong?"

"He wants ta move the wedding up — to a week from tomorrow!" She began to pace, her hips twitching like an agitated housecat's. "My mum's already enough of a terror. If we move up the date, I'll never hear the end of it!"

I exchanged a helpless glance with Vee. Although I considered Fiona a true friend, we didn't share any bestie psychic connection. "Did he say why?"

"Nay. He just said it'd be a mistake to wait." Fiona pivoted and blanched. "Speakin' of the devil — here he comes."

CHAPTER 13

Mackenna

Looking like they just stepped off the pages of warriors gone wild, Duncan, Jamie, and Fergus strode into the Great Hall. White tunics and clan kilts showcased the movement of their sculpted bodies. Despite the award-winning smiles they projected into the room, there was something reckless — desperate and almost dangerous about them, as if they'd been to hell and back and couldn't quite regain their bearings.

Fresh from the shower, Duncan surveyed the room. His dark, wet hair was slicked back from his tanned face and his cheeks retained the slight pink flush caused by hot, hot water. With feral grace, he circled his way through the crowd and out of my line of sight.

Jamie made it halfway through the room when Lachlan intercepted him. The little boy's eyes danced with excitement as he handed the butt end of a sword to the prince. Jamie reached for it and then seemed to change his mind. Using the sword to pull the child closer, Jamie scooped him up into a tight hug. The boy immediately started to squirm.

Murmuring "Be right back," Vee headed in their direction. When she reached them, Jamie released Lachlan, who scampered just out of reach, and wrapped his arms around my bestie. She sighed, her body relaxing against him as if her world were finally right again.

Averting my gaze from their intimate moment, I caught Analisa waving Duncan over. As he approached, her hand fell away from the Rosetti boy. She reached for Duncan and pulled him into an embrace so she could whisper against his ear, the way a confidante or lover would.

Duncan's severe expression lifted into a crooked smile over whatever Analisa was saying. Was he just being kind, or was there more to them? Did she secretly burn bright in his thoughts the way he did in mine? I would lose my mind wondering about it, so I forced myself to look away.

This time I settled on Fergus. The big guy stood in the doorway of the battlement. His large pale blue eyes glistened like a chastised puppy's. "Fee," he implored. "Canna we talk this out?"

With a huff, Fiona turned her back on him and marched through the nearest open door. Fergus emitted a ragged sigh as he watched her go. With a nod to me, he swiped at his eyes before chasing after the girl he loved more than life.

I tracked his movements through the crowd until a different scene caught my attention. Jamie had moved a banquet table and was now battling Lachlan with toy swords. Nearby, Vee lounged on a bench, her eyes glued to his every move. Judging by the adoration on her face, their squabbles had been put on hold for the moment.

From a distance that might as well have been a million miles away, I watched as my friends fought and made up. Sure, their love lives weren't perfect, but they were living. Risking. And I was doing the one thing I was truly good at … pretending.

Pretending I wasn't in love with a prince who might have feelings for a thief. Pretending I didn't have a real Calling so that I could fake one. Pretending I didn't want to stay, even if it were possible.

Little goose bumps prickled over my skin from the breeze as I walked away from the party. But I welcomed the emotion-numbing cold. At the corner of the battlement I tipped my face toward the starry sky. *Help me*, I prayed just in case anyone or anything out there was listening. *Help me get through this.*

"Meditating on the inconstant moon; that monthly changes in her circled orb?"

Holy Hammerstein! Duncan's soft voice tumbled from thin air. Deep in shadow, he blended into the night.

Narrowing my eyes, I stared into the darkness at the approximation of Duncan's shadow self. "Are you spying on me?"

"Nay." I heard him push off the wall before his ridiculously gorgeous face emerged from the gloom. "Come. We've parts to perform."

"Not until you tell me what you were doing out here."

"Seeing you."

The statement wasn't flirty or coy. No smile quirked his lips into a lopsided grin. There was just Duncan with his luminous eyes staring gravely through me. His scrutiny made my skin feel uncomfortably tight.

Refusing to let him *see* how he was affecting me, I replied, "We haven't had a whole lot of time to prepare. How do you want to do this?"

"I figured you could follow my lead." He offered me his hand, palm up so that I could see the calluses on the pads.

Instead of complying, I demanded, "Meaning?"

His trademark grin broke forth in the face of my skepticism. "You'll just have to trust me. Isna that what your director boyfriend would say? Ye've got to trust your scene partner."

The mention of Wes was like throwing down a gauntlet. He was goading me. Looking pointedly at his outstretched hand, I countered, "Wes would also say you promised not to lay a hand on me, but you seem to be making a lot of exceptions."

"Right. Sorry about that." He bent his arm, offering it to me like an escort at Winter Formal. "See, no hands involved."

Arranging my game face, I slipped my hand into the crook of his elbow and said, "Lead the way, actor boy."

A slow waltz underscored our steps as we wove our way through dancing couples. Since he was determined to keep his hands to himself, I assumed we were headed toward the food, when all of a sudden he paused in the middle of the Great Hall. "I reckon I'll need to ask for another exception."

"No." I let go of his arm, resting my hands on my hips. "No more exceptions. If we're going to do this, we've got to be natural around each other. You can't be asking for exceptions all the time. So I'm now giving you permission — touch me as much and as often as you like."

Just as that last part flowed from my mouth, the music stopped so that my overly loud voice ricocheted through the cavernous space. The couples on the dance floor turned to stare. After a moment of silence, the room became an inescapable symphony of whispers as hundreds of curious eyes dissected us and our first public outing as a Called couple.

And still the music didn't start.

Duncan's expression faltered as if he was suddenly at a loss as to what came next. For an eternity, he just stared at me. The more he gawked, the more the gossip seemed to spread. The curse of the ginger heated my cheeks. If I didn't do something quick, I would soon be blushing lobster red.

"Touch me already!" I hissed.

He continued to stare as if he were deaf. His noncompliant arms hung awkwardly at his sides with no acknowledgement that I'd begged for his touch.

Our cover story would never work if we didn't do something quick. Impulsively, I wrapped my arms around his neck and pulled him down as I rose up. It was just supposed to be a hug, but my lips decided to ad lib.

Before I could stop myself, I pressed my lips to his. At first his mouth didn't move. Then after a tiny twitch, it opened. As quick as a lightning strike, his massive arms clasped my body tightly against him. A split second later we were a tangle of tongues and limbs. His touch — the one I'd just demanded — was everywhere at once, scorching my skin as my insides threatened to go nuclear.

A voice in the back of my brain mumbled that it was all an act — that he was just playing along because I hadn't been able to keep my hormones in check, but I ignored it. I'd waited forever to kiss him again — and make-believe or not, I was going to seize the moment.

As suddenly as the music stopped, it started up again. And just as abruptly, the kiss was over. Duncan wrenched his mouth away, tilting his face so that his forehead rested against mine. In the aftermath of our kiss, I shook. Or maybe that was him … trembling?

Wait, he was trembling? Did that mean he felt something too? After a lot of resistance, he seemed to have warmed up to our fake Calling. My heart fluttered, but the tiny wings of hope were too fragile to risk more crushing rejection. Instead, I whispered, "Way to sell it, actor boy."

Duncan pulled back. His eyes shone like stars as he captured my gaze. The confident, charming boy I'd loved my whole life had returned. "If what you were really after all this time was a thorough kissing, you might've just asked. I seek to serve."

I raised my arm to backhand his bicep, but the warrior in him preempted my strike by capturing my hand in his. He raised it to his lips for a perfect, chaste kiss that sent shockwaves all the way to my core. "Let's give the good people o' Doon a show they'll remember through the ages. Dance with me."

Oh h-e-double hockey sticks no! Not after that little show of PDA. I would not be able to pull off this charade if I had to spend the evening in this boy's arms. He might look all puppy-dog sweet but his kisses were as deadly as a viper. It seemed, however, I was already infected because when he flashed me his irresistible grin and said, "And dinna give me any line about having two left feet. I know you to be a right fine dancer," I totally caved.

"Okay."

"All right then." He raked his fingers through his hair to form those darned chaotic peaks. Grabbing my hand, Duncan pulled me into the melee of Scotsmen, and women, as they twirled with abandon. It was a jig with wailing bagpipes and pounding, animalistic drums — like a primitive Celtic rave.

This was Vee's forte, not mine. My bestie could *Riverdance* with the best of 'em. But I was too self-conscious to lose myself in the rhythm. I needed to break down the steps, analyze each one, and practice before I could execute them.

As if sensing my hesitance, Duncan whispered, "Relax. Jus' let go." Before I could argue, he grabbed my hips and pulled me in close. Much to my astonishment, he started to slow dance. Right in the middle of the whirling crowd.

Convinced people would start staring again, I whispered, "You're not fast enough."

Duncan's left hand slid up to the small of my back, pressing me even closer, urging me to sway like it was the last dance on prom night. "I think we should take it slow. Just relax. We're supposed to have a Calling, remember. It doesna matter how we move, only that we move as one."

Right. I could do this. I could slow dance with him — it's not like it was the first time.

I tucked my chin into the crook of his neck. He smelled clean, like fresh soap and new leather, and I could feel his pulse thrumming against my cheek. The frenetic music faded away as I let go, falling into his rhythm. Somehow this discordant-yet-harmonious act felt more intimate than being lip-locked. Desperate to maintain my grip on reality, I asked, "Are you sure Analisa doesn't mind?"

"Ana's fine. She knows we have a story to keep up." Sure enough, when I took a quick glance about the room, I spied her watching us with a Mona Lisa smile.

I wrenched myself out of his embrace and took a step back. "She knows? You told her?"

"Aye." Duncan nodded innocently.

"When?"

"Before I headed back to Muir Lea."

So she was the last girl he'd seen before he left as well as the first one he sought out when he got back? Part of me was desperate to know if it was serious, but another part wanted to close my eyes, stick my fingers in my ears and go "La la la." While yet another part berated the other fragments for their childishness. *"You left him — not the other way around,"* the grown-up part chided. *"He has every right to move on, so make your peace and snap out of it!"*

"Mackenna, are ye all right?"

"Yes." I blinked up at him, doing my best to mean it. "It's

just … I'm surprised. I thought she was into the oldest Rosetti brother."

Duncan chucked. "Are you jealous, woman?"

"Me?" *Heck yeah!* "No. I'm just concerned — as a *friend*. Be careful. She seems like the kind of girl who breaks hearts."

If Vee had been within hearing range, she totally would've called me out saying something about pots and kettles. I braced, expecting Duncan to fling my statement back in my face. Instead, he became pensive. "Maybe I don't have a heart to break."

I placed my palm against the thin fabric of his shirt. My fingers registered a steady beat, which began to accelerate under my touch.

"You do. Trust me." And any girl who dared break it didn't deserve him.

"So say you."

His hand covered mine so that it was trapped over his heart. His other hand reclaimed possession of my hip, and we took up slow dancing where we'd left off. The next several songs passed in a delicious blur.

When we finally came up for air, I did a quick check for my friends. At the other end of the hall, Fiona was ripping her fiancé a new one. Head downcast and slump-shouldered, Fergus appeared even more miserable than earlier, if such a thing were possible. Fiona had the big guy practically cowering in the corner as she punctuated her heated words with her small, shaking fist. But hey, at least they were talking.

In the opposite corner, Vee and Jamie were arguing around staged smiles. From my vantage point Vee appeared to be almost pleading. As I watched, an elderly couple approached their queen, and as she turned to greet them, Jamie's smile froze. His eyes darted away as he angled himself ever so slightly toward the wall. For the next several seconds the smile dissolved from his face as he stared at nothing.

When the couple showed signs of moving on, he rolled his shoulders, fixed his grin, and swiveled back toward the conversation. By the time they left, Jamie was beaming down at Vee as if he'd never disconnected. He opened his mouth, but whatever he'd been about to say was lost to the spectacle of Fiona pulling Fergus toward the small dais with the musicians.

Without a moment's hesitation, Fiona stepped onto the platform and demanded that the musicians stop. Gripping Fergus's hand like she was the hulk and he barely bigger than a child, Fiona squared her shoulders and faced the curious crowd.

"I just wanted to tell ye all that Fergus and I have news." She glanced at the boy by her side, who nodded, his puppy-dog eyes shimmering with adoration. "We've decided we canna wait any longer to be husband and wife. So we'll be getting married a week from tomorrow. Everyone who seeks to wish us well is welcome to join us."

With those words tears began to stream down her face. Faster than you could sing, "Get me to the Church on Time," she flung herself into Fergus's arms.

In my peripheral vision, I saw Vee poke Jamie in the middle of his chest. She leaned in and hissed something, her head bobbing toward Fergus and Fiona. Jamie shrugged, doing his best to play the part of a maligned, bewildered boyfriend, but he wasn't half the actor that his brother was. His I-have-no-idea-what's-going-on face was as flimsy as a Halloween mask. And twice as fake.

Duncan, on the other hand, hadn't batted an eye over Fiona's abrupt change of heart. He might've been a better thespian than his big brother, but something told me that he had beans to spill. Taking his hand, I gave it a gentle tug. "Let's go get some air."

His eyes devoured mine in a familiar way that made my insides shout "Huzzah!" I wasn't sure whether the look was real or staged, but before I could figure it out he replied, "You're wish is my command."

As we headed back toward the darkness of the battlement, Gabriela Rosetti intercepted our path. "You two look so perfect when you're dancing together," she trilled.

"Thank you." Nice to know the act was working.

I started to excuse us, when Gabby said to Duncan, "Mackenna told me about your Calling. How as children you used to meet on the Brig o' Doon."

"Did she?" He peered at me, and even though we were in a fully lit room, a shadow crossed his face. "I met her on that bridge every day of every summer she spent in Alloway. Those were the happiest days o' my boyhood."

Was he speaking the truth? When I'd first shown up in Doon, had he known me from our lifetime of summers? If so, why hadn't he said anything?

My neck felt hot. I rubbed it with ice-cold fingers as the room began to tilt. "Sorry," I mumbled, pressing past Gabby. "I really need air."

I staggered into the night, not stopping until I reached the wall at the far side of the battlement. Unlike the other end, which opened onto the gardens and lake, this side faced the mountains of Doon and ended in a wall overlooking a thirty-foot drop onto jagged rocks.

Leaning far over the ledge, I gasped in mouthfuls of crisp air. The wind tore at my hair, turning my curls into miniature whips that lashed my face. It hurt, but in that good takes-your-mind-off-other-pain way. Already, the icy onslaught was making me feel calmer.

Just when I thought I knew where Duncan stood, he mixed it up. One moment, he hardly wanted anything to do with me, and the next he kissed me like he meant it. He showered me with compliments that felt sincere, but it was an act. He looked at me like I was the one, and then whispered confidences in another girl's ear. Now it seemed that he knew we shared a Calling as children but never said one word about it.

I sensed Duncan's presence before he spoke. He surrounded me. I felt his warmth to my right, my left, up my back — everywhere at once. He sheltered without embracing me, and I began to shiver.

"Dinna jump." His husky whisper tickled against my ear.

Unable to face him, I continued to stare out toward the desolate terrain. "Why did you say those things to Gabby … about us?"

He angled his face toward mine to compensate for the howling wind. "I was just following your lead. Improvising."

My heart caved. I wanted to look into his eyes, but was afraid I'd see nothing more than his shadow self. Either it really was a crappy coincidence, or he didn't want me to know he remembered because it was no longer relevant. "You're better than I thought."

"Thank you." Duncan backed off the tiniest bit so that the wind rippled between our bodies. The resulting chill felt shocking. "Mackenna, we're friends, right?"

Right. Friends. I nodded, unable to say the words out loud.

His large hand gently turned me around to face him. Despite the tiny bit of space between us, he filled my senses, leaving room for nothing else. "Then tell me — is something wrong?"

"I suddenly didn't feel so good. The heat maybe, or something I ate."

He shook his head. "But you didn't eat. At least not since I arrived."

Our close proximity made it difficult for casual chitchat. "You're right. I forgot to eat ... that's probably it."

"Tell me, as your friend, how can I make you feel better?"

If he wasn't going to talk about us, I could at least get other answers. "Explain to me what just happened with Fergus and Fiona. And don't tell me you don't know, because I know you do."

Duncan stilled and looked over my shoulder at the black mountains. After what felt like an eternity, he sighed, shedding part of his shadows. "I'm guessing that Fergus told her."

"Told her what?"

His low voice was barely discernible over the windstorm. "The truth about the limbus."

"Which is?"

He cocked his head to the side in an effort to gauge my reaction. "It's attacking our borders. Soon, we'll be completely surrounded."

"How can you know?"

"Because we took one of the Destined with us — a lad named Adam who studied environmental science at Oxford. He's setting up a temporary base of operations at the hunting lodge. Based on the limited data, Adam estimates the Eldritch Limbus will encircle Doon in less than a fortnight."

That was bad, sure — but the way Fiona and Fergus were acting you'd think we were on the verge of another Doon apocalypse. Duncan knew me well enough to sense where I was headed, because he said, "Tha's not the worst of it ... The

154

limbus is also expanding. If it keeps up, it'll overrun the whole kingdom in less than a month. And then ..."

The final curtain call.

A short while after Duncan escorted me back to my suite and left without so much as a peck on the cheek, Vee came knocking. Wearing flannel pajama bottoms and a tank top, she looked like her old self. Once again, I was reminded of how incomplete life was without her.

Of course I ruined the moment by telling her about the limbus first thing. Although she listened without interruption as I recounted my conversation with Duncan, I could sense her growing agitation. When I got to the part about the final curtain, she pounded her fist into the comforter.

"The moment I saw Jamie, I knew something was wrong!" she exclaimed. "The way he hugged Lachlan — I adore the jerk, but emotional availability is not one of his selling points."

She grabbed the brush from my dressing table, returned to the foot of my bed, and attacked her hair like it was a proxy for her boyfriend. "I begged him to tell me what was wrong and he just replied, 'Nothing ye need ta worry about right this moment.' Arrrrgh!"

Her Scottish accent had gotten really good — but this was definitely not the moment to point that out. Instead, I reached for the brush, hoping she would surrender it peaceably while she still had some hair left. "Don't you have maids or henchwomen to do this? What kind of queen are you?"

"The kind who comes from Bainbridge, Indiana and is completely self-reliant." She placed the brush in my hand and then shimmied forward so that I could scoot behind her. We'd done this countless times during sleepovers. "When I was back home, I couldn't even afford to get my hair done. I'd save up for months only to have Janet give me some sob story about how we were on the verge of being evicted."

I laughed softly, but not because the memory was funny. "Then your mom would spend the money on box wine and Cheetos for Bob the Slob."

"Did you talk to her — you know, Janet — when you got back?"

"Uh, yeah. I told her you met someone in Scotland and decided to stay for a while."

I noted the tiny hitch in Vee's breath. "And what did she say?"

"That the timing was perfect because Bob the Slob's brother needed a place to stay." Her mom had prefaced that statement by stating how she'd always known her daughter would turn out like her no-good daddy — but Vee didn't need any more baggage from her train wreck of a parent. "On the bright side, she got rid of most of your stuff, so you don't have to worry about Bob's brother fondling your delicates."

Vee emitted a halfhearted laugh and then fell silent for a bit. I continued to stroke her hair, getting it smooth and glossy in a way I could never achieve with mine. Eventually she relaxed and admitted the truth. "Sometimes I think Jamie keeps things from me because he knows I'm a fraud. I'm not a queen — I'm a cheerleader."

"Shut up." I tugged her hair just enough to get her attention. "You are the strongest, most stubborn person I know. If something is threatening Doon, you'll find a way to save this place or die trying."

"This time the whole kingdom might pay for my stubbornness."

I touched her shoulder and swiveled her around to face me.

"Anyone who knows you can see this is what you were born to do."

Her eyes dropped to the vicinity of the bedspread. "Except Jamie."

"Nonsense. More likely he was trying to protect you. Put yourself in his shoes. You're the ruler — the fate of the kingdom rests on your shoulders, and if the natives get restless, it's your head on the chopping block. He probably feels pretty powerless when it comes to you."

She looked up, tears trembling in the corners of her eyes. "I don't need him to protect me!"

"Wouldn't you — haven't you — done the same? It's human nature to need to protect those we love. Not respecting that need is the same as negating your love."

Vee rubbed her face. "Is that what you were doing with Duncan when you abandoned him on the bridge, protecting him?"

"In a way. Anyone with half a brain can see how much he loves his kingdom and people. Until I came, he never thought about what lies beyond."

"Still, don't you think it was his choice to make?"

I stood and tossed the brush on the dressing table. Keeping my back to my best friend, I busied myself with straightening bottles of nail polish. "Here he has friends and family. In Chicago, he'd have been alone and miserable."

"How can you be sure?"

I shrugged, placing a bottle of Peachy Keen polish between Ruby Red and Sunset Glow. "I'm not ... but it doesn't matter now. I made my decision and I have to live with the consequences."

As I arranged Passion Plum next to Luscious Lavender, I heard Vee stand and braced for what I knew was coming.

"Kenna," she urged. "Look at me."

Adjusting the final bottle, Licorice Lust, I retreated deep within — to that place where actors lock their true selves away — and turned to face the person most likely to see through my act.

Her turquoise eyes bore into mine. "No one would fault you if you decided you made a mistake. You know, if you've changed your mind about staying."

If I told her that I regretted my choice from the instant I walked away from the Brig o' Doon and every day since, I would only get her hopes up. As much as I wanted a do-over, the dance had proven I couldn't stay in Doon. I couldn't watch Duncan be with someone else. Not even for the sake of my best friend.

I met her gaze with what I hoped would appear to be a confident, straightforward smile. "Thanks, but I'm happy with my life."

And the Tony Award for the most miserable liar goes to ... Mackenna Reid.

CHAPTER 14

Veronica

Authority, I'd found, did not make one a queen. I closed the book, but the line from Queen Lynnette's memoirs continued to play in my mind. I wished she'd been able to expound on that statement, but according to the timeline I'd constructed, it was likely the last she ever wrote.

I'd stayed up half the night searching for some way that we could do things differently and stop the limbus before it got out of control, but what I'd found had me more confused than ever. I rubbed the heels of my hands against my stinging eyes. Honestly, perhaps a tiny part of me had waited up for a knock on my door — for a certain blond prince to share what he knew about the increasing disintegration of the borders. Clearly, my wait had been in vain.

"Why doesn't my suite have one of these?" Kenna asked as she plopped down on the window seat beside me and pressed her face to the diamond-paned glass. "You can see the entire kingdom from here."

"Because yer not the queen, tha's why." Fiona set a plate of assorted scones beside the tea and coffee that had already been brought up, and slumped into the seat across from us.

Kenna leaned away from the view and pinned our friend with a withering stare. "So glad you cleared that up, but not even a turret that looks like the inside of a genie lamp would make me want that staggering responsibility." She reached for a cup and the pitcher of coffee. "No offense, Vee."

"None taken." *Staggering* was actually a perfect word for it.

Fiona leaned forward on her elbows. "I'm sorry, Mackenna!" she blurted, big tears swimming in her hazel eyes. "I dinna seem ta be quite myself these days. With the bans being announced this mornin' ... I ... I love Fergus wit' all my heart, but ... I never pictured my wedding—" *Being held as a last-ditch effort to distract the kingdom from its impending doom*, I finished for her in my head.

Fiona buried her face in her hands, and Kenna rushed over, hugging the girl's shaking shoulders. "Hey, don't worry about me. You've got enough on your mind right now. I can take a little sarcasm. Plus, we all know I would make a craptastic queen." She threw a helpless glance in my direction.

"Yeah. Can you imagine her first decree?" Improvising, I stood and cupped my hands around my mouth. "Attention, Doonians: Every third Tuesday shall forevermore be Show Tune Day! All communication shall be expressed only through song and dance!"

"You mean my first decree *after* I outlawed the color orange," Kenna added as she released Fiona's shoulders and reached for a scone. "It really does nothing for my complexion."

Wet giggles bubbled from Fiona like a soda fountain.

"And," Kenna persisted, "my third, and most important decree would require proper costuming for Show Tune day. All men would wear plaid knickers and buckled tap shoes."

"Can you imagine Fergus?" I demanded through my laughter.

"We'd make a special costume to match his favorite tam." Kenna nodded in decision.

The thought of the giant tap-dancing in head-to-toe yellow plaid like some ginormous leprechaun was too much to take. The drink of tea I'd just taken spewed out of my nose in a decidedly un-majestic display. Fiona leaned back and clutched her stomach as tears of glee now rolled down her cheeks.

After the burning in my sinuses subsided, and the much needed laughter had cleared the tension from the air, I got us back on task. "Thanks for meeting with me before services, girls. I read something rather interesting last night, but I'm not quite sure how it can help us." Setting my plate aside, I picked up Queen Lynnette's book and began to read the passage I'd marked:

> With the limbus creeping ever closer and the army yet to return, I have devised a plan. I shall utilize my previous acquaintance with the coven. When I was but a baker's daughter and before I knew Adelaide and her sisters to be evil, I would often trade with them on market day — baked goods and bread for herbal remedies and such. Perhaps it is naïve, but I believe I can appeal to whatever good nature is left in them.

I paused and looked up from the text. Fiona and Kenna sat across from me in identical poses, leaning forward with their elbows propped on their knees while clutching their mugs. Satisfied I had their attention, I opened to the next slip of parchment I'd used as a bookmark. "Here's where it gets interesting.

> Under the cover of darkness, and without the king's knowledge, I traversed the dark forest to the witch's cottage. They welcomed me with open arms and listened

respectfully to my proposal. The coven have agreed to a bargain. No more lives shall be lost to this heinous war, but we must leave Doon within a fortnight. Never to return. I've given Addie and her sisters the throne.

I only hope Angus can one day forgive me."

The old leather spine creaked as I closed the book and pasted an expectant look on my face. These passages left me unsettled, a deep-seeded worry niggling at the back of my mind.

"What happened?" Kenna prompted, waiting for me to wrap everything up with a neat little bow.

"I don't know, because then she died."

"She died?" Kenna slumped back against the pillows. "But she gave Addie what she wanted, right?"

"I think that's what she believed." A chill stole across my skin, and I pulled a blanket over my lap. "But according to the legend of the Miracle, the coven had already made a bargain with the Great Deceiver, and he didn't just want the land, he wanted the souls of the people as well."

"She didna have faith," Fiona whispered. "She took matters inta her own hands, and she failed."

"So we're supposed to just sit back, have faith, and *poof* . . . the limbus will disappear?" Kenna demanded.

"Nay, but acting outside o' the Protector's will" — Fiona's gaze drilled into mine — "is pure folly."

I cleared my throat. "Ah . . . there are a few more pages here, but they're increasingly cryptic. It's pretty clear that Lynnette realized she'd been duped before she passed on. I have some more books to read through," I finished lamely, and stared at my folded hands.

Queen Lynnette had done everything I would've done. She'd put the people above her own life, but it hadn't been enough.

Wasn't self-sacrifice honorable? How was what Lynnette did different than me trading places with Jamie to save him from the same witch? I swallowed a gulp of tepid tea along with the lump in my throat.

Fiona stood and began to tidy the table, and Kenna rose saying she needed to get ready for church. But I couldn't move. The weight of my responsibility pressed me to the spot. Kenna glanced at me as she walked by, her eyes filled with questions. Attempting to reassure her, I shook my head and rummaged up a small smile. I didn't want to talk through what was bothering me. For once, I didn't think she'd understand.

After my friends had gone, I couldn't deny the questions burning inside me. What would the Protector want me to do? *Me.* A girl-queen with a handful of months on the throne. I'd lectured Jamie once about his lack of faith, about putting his own selfish desires above those of his kingdom and his Protector. But in fact, I knew nothing of the Protector's will.

I'd waited all day. Jamie'd been by my side through services, a stilted luncheon with my advisors, and our weekly calls on the infirm, and still he'd told me nothing about the ticking time bomb of the limbus. I'd spent the remainder of the evening scouring every book that had anything to do with the original curse on Doon and felt no closer to discerning the Protector's will for me, or for the kingdom. And now, at the end of a very long day, I stood in the middle of my beautiful tower suite, my gut coiling like a python around a rabbit, squeezing tighter with every breath.

Jamie's lack of confidence in me only solidified that I was a figurehead—a queen in name only. I tugged at the tiara he'd given me, my scalp screaming in protest as the hair twisted around the edges fought to hold it in place. With a vicious yank, I pulled it off my head, and blinked back tears as a few strands of hair went with it. I held it out and stared at the intricate design; regal jeweled flowers entwined in a simple setting of silvery leaves, anchored by sturdy branches. In my heart, it represented everything I wanted to be — noble, humble, and strong. Everything I knew I *could* be, if only the boy who claimed to love me recognized it too.

But if Jamie didn't see it, how could I expect the people to? How could I be the queen they needed? The queen the Protector needed? I dropped the crown onto the table with a clink.

I had to *move*.

Sprinting into my bedroom, I stripped out of my dress and threw on my running clothes. I was halfway to the door when I remembered Kenna's gift to me that morning — a solar battery pack. It was the sole thing I would've asked her to bring me from the modern world. But I hadn't needed to ask. One advantage of sharing a brain.

After clearing a space in the middle of the room, I jogged over to the window seat and cheered. The tiny light on the box had turned green, indicating a full charge. I grabbed my cell phone, plucked out the small, flat battery, and replaced it with the charged one. The screen lit up with an electronic pixie jingle. As expected, the bars at the top of the display indicated zero connection, but I wasn't trying to make a call. My fingers trembled as I plugged in the earphones Kenna thought to include and tapped the *Play Music* icon. I hit shuffle, and the first strains of a Justin Timberlake remix hit my ears and shot through my nerve endings.

God bless solar power!

Head bobbing, hips swaying, my chest throbbed with the beat. The deep bass line slammed into my brain, and then there was nothing but the music. Pieces of an old hip-hop routine flowed into pirouettes and leaps. Time had no meaning as every ounce of my being was consumed by the current of movement, the dance washing away every worry and fear. I twirled and let the ebb and flow of the rhythm guide me. Feeling like I could fly, I jumped, extending my legs into a jeté and then landed with a whirl, the weight of the world spun off my shoulders.

As the beat built to a crescendo, I swiveled, tipped back, and extended my leg to the ceiling. Upside down, I caught a glimpse of tanned legs topped by a blue and green kilt. I straightened and pivoted so fast, I toppled to the side, barely catching myself on my other foot. Heat, which had nothing to do with the sweat coating my skin, prickled up my neck.

Jamie lolled against the doorjamb, taking up most of the arched entryway. His time leading the guard had thickened his already muscled frame, causing his shirts to stretch across his chest and shoulders like an actor in a superhero movie. My heart hammered against my ribs as he shrugged off the wall and in a few smooth strides closed the distance between us.

Less than a breath of space between us, he stopped, and I caught a hint of his scent — clean and stormy like the rain-washed sky. He glanced down at me, a slow grin spreading across his face, white teeth flashing in the setting sun. Then his lips moved, but I couldn't hear. I plucked out one of my earbuds. "What?"

He lifted a finger and drew a line through the sweat on my upper arm. "I said, when you move, 'tis like silent poetry."

A warm rush of pleasure buzzed through me. Jamie MacCrae had his ways of being charming, but banal flattery was not one of them. When he said something, you could be sure he meant it. I smiled into his dark eyes and replied, "Not so silent." As a new song began, I stepped closer, took my other earbud and raised it toward his head. But before I got far, a hard bass line blared and he tilted his head away. His brows lowered as he turned to glare at the miniature speaker, like a lion irritated by a new species of fly.

Giggling, I lowered my hand. "Hold on."

I scrolled through my songs and selected one with a slower tempo. But when I lifted the speaker, he stepped back and shook his head. "Nay."

"Just try it, okay? I want you to hear *my* kind of music."

After a moment's hesitation, he nodded and stepped forward. I rose on my toes, brushed back his hair, and slipped the tiny bud into his ear. Jamie's eyes widened as the song swirled around us, Christina Aguilera's bluesy voice filling both our heads. I guided his hand to my hip and began to move with the languorous tempo. The tension eased out of him, and he relaxed against me, the hint of a smile tugging at his lips.

Lost in the music, I closed my eyes and raised my arms. The notes swept through me, blocking every worry and transporting me to a place where I was not queen and no lives depended on my decisions. A place where the only thing that mattered was this moment with my ridiculously hot boyfriend.

Placing one hand on my ear to keep the bud in place, I swiveled to the slow beat and then wrapped my arms around Jamie's neck. He began to move with me, our bodies synchronized like we were dancing together in a club. But when I opened my eyes, Jamie's gaze was anything but serene. He gripped my arms, backed me into the table, and smashed his mouth against mine.

The music pulsing in both our ears, he cradled the sides of my head in his palms and slowed the kiss. With the smooth slide of his lips, I melted against him, digging my fingers into his rounded shoulders. As soon as he touched me, every rational thought flew out of my head. He was like an addiction, and I didn't think I'd ever get enough.

Jamie deepened the kiss as one hand cupped my neck, and the other wandered down my back, his thumb tracing my spine. Hot and cold tingles shot all the way to my toes, and the world spun out of control. Dizzy, I grabbed a fistful of his shirt. He flattened his palm against the indentation of my waist, pressing me tighter against him. Then, low and deep, he spoke something unintelligible against my lips as he lifted me and set me on the tabletop. With a powerful shiver, I broke the kiss, startled by the urgency building between us.

Jamie lifted his head, both of us breathing hard. His eyes blazed into mine as he wrapped his other arm around my waist, and gently set me on my feet. I tucked my head into that perfect spot beneath his chin and listened to the rapid beat of his heart.

"I like your music." He paused. "It's no bagpipes and fiddle, o' course."

He chuckled and I savored the vibration of the rare sound against my ear.

"I've missed you, Verranica," he whispered into my hair and tightened his embrace. "Missed this."

I'd missed him too. Desperately. But his words reminded me of all the things that stood between us. Physical attraction had never been one of our problems. I breathed him in, pressed my lips to the warm, firm skin of his neck, and then let him go. I separated our limbs and took the speaker from each of our ears, before winding the cords around my phone. Reaching across the table, I set it inside the circle of my tiara.

Unable to believe I'd let his freaking amazing kisses distract me, I kicked the throw rug, unfurling it back into place. Was I just like Janet? Swayed by whatever man showed me affection? Changing to suit his whims? I could feel the weight of Jamie's gaze on me, but I ignored him and picked up an end table.

"Let me do that," he said, trying to take it out of my hands.

"No, I can do it." I jerked the table away from him, and carried it to its spot beside the sofa.

Jamie picked up a dining chair in each hand.

"Stop." I took one of the chairs from him. "I've got this."

"Why won't you let me help you?"

I set the chair down and whirled on him. "Why don't you trust me?"

"O' course I trust you." His brows scrunched over his eyes. "Though I dinna think you're referrin' to your ability to move furniture. What *are* you talkin' about?"

"I've been waiting for an entire day." I stalked toward him. "Twenty-four whole hours for you to tell me what you learned while surveying the borders. But you've said nothing!"

Jamie widened his stance and crossed his massive arms in front of his chest, but his intimidation tactics wouldn't work on me.

"The moment I saw your face at the dance, I knew you'd learned something terrible. If it hadn't been for Kenna, who was told by Duncan … who isn't even technically with Kenna … I would've had to guess what was happening."

"I wanted to — "

"No! No lame excuses. We have an accepted Calling! That's practically like being engaged. How could you keep this from me, Jamie?"

A muscle twitched in his jaw, and his expression shut down.

I jabbed a finger into his chest, and demanded, "Am I the queen or aren't I? If I don't know what's going on, how am I supposed to protect my people?"

He stared down at the floor so long, I began to notice the ticking of the clock that hung over the mantel. Finally, his shoulders slumped and he raised his head, his eyes dark with anguish. "You *are* the queen, Vee. But they're *our* people. Ye were never meant to do this alone — that's what the Completing is about. A partnership where two individuals balance each other's strengths and weaknesses."

He sighed and focused on something behind my head. "I dinna want to be your consort."

"My what?" I squeaked, my eyes flaring wide.

"Paramour, consort … ye know." He raised his hands and made awkward air quotes. "Yer *boy toy*."

"What the — Where did you hear *that*?"

"Duncan may have mentioned …" He suddenly became enraptured by the toe of his boot as he mumbled, "Tha's what they call it in the modern world when a boy is so in love with a girl, he does everythin' she tells him to do."

I could just see Duncan taunting his brother about being *whipped*. It made me want to give the younger prince a high kick to his fat head. Or better yet, put him in the stocks for a day. That would teach the jerk a lesson. "Jamie, you could never be — "

His eyes locked on mine, and I was silenced by the intensity of his gaze. "I couldna bring myself to tell you about the limbus, because I felt like I'd let ye down. I was waitin' until I could provide some ray of hope, a possible solution. But it's what I came up here tonight to tell you … I received word from Adam. He believes the limbus is growing not just around Doon, but inward as well. With every acre it destroys, it seems to be gaining speed."

I sunk into a nearby chair and dropped my head into my hands. What if my detractors were right, and all I'd done was open the kingdom to evil? Maybe if I stepped down from the throne, it would stop.

"Vee, love?" Jamie knelt in front of me. When I raised my head, he brushed my hair out of my face. "Dinna worry. We'll figure something out."

"A queen has never before been Called to Doon, right?"

He searched my face and then nodded. "Tha's true."

"Well, I want to give you back your throne." I reached behind me, picked up my crown, and shoved it toward him. "Take it. I don't want it anymore."

"No." He rolled back on his haunches and stood.

"Don't you see?" I shot to my feet, the crown still in my hand as I gestured wildly. "This could all be my fault for bringing the cursed journal here in the first place. You are the rightful ruler, Jamie. I became queen by default. All I wanted to do was save you — "

"Nay, that isna true. You sacrificed everything to save Doon. You could've died! I've never seen a more courageous act in my life." He took the crown from my fist and tossed it onto the sofa. "You've always been part of the Protector's plan. I knew that from the moment I saw you in my dreams."

I stared up into his face, breathing hard. "Right. And then you were convinced those dreams were actually nightmares." A shadow passed across his eyes before he could hide it. "See? You'd be better off without me. You all would." I turned on my heel, intent on storming to my bedroom for a good cry, but Jamie took my arm and spun me back around to face him.

"Vee, don't you understand? You *own* me." He clutched a fist and brought it to his chest, his eyes slicing into my soul. "Everything I do is for you. I'm doing my best to support you and protect you, but I couldna be king without you. I wouldna want to. We're meant to rule side by side. To *live* side by side."

In the space of a heartbeat, I was in his arms. Afraid I was about to go into the ugly cry, I buried my face in his shoulder. How could I have been so wrong? About *him*. About *us*. My chest expanded with light until I thought I might burst with it. He *did* believe in me. I'd just been too blinded by my own insecurity to see it. There was a massive difference between what Janet did and what was between Jamie and me — he'd never expected me to change for him.

I sniffled and wiped the moisture from under my eyes.

"We can do this, love. We'll find a way to lead the kingdom together." He leaned back and tipped my chin up. "If ye stop being so blasted stubborn and let me help you."

"Only if you promise to stop being so bossy." I fought the grin that was trying to break out across my face.

"Promise." He nodded solemnly.

"And stop being so crazy protective."

Jamie rolled his eyes to the ceiling and shook his head. "All right, I'll try. But …" He put me at arm's length and glanced down with a wicked smirk. "Only if ye stop wearin' these wee, skin-tight trousers. Otherwise, we might need to get someone to protect you from me."

"Sorry, I can't make that promise." I tilted my head, my eyes meeting his in challenge. "I like to keep you on your toes."

"Oh, ye do, aye?" With a quick grin, he reached beneath my knees and scooped me up into his arms. It felt right. Like I'd regained a piece of myself that'd been missing. And then I realized that part of the Protector's will for me was gazing into my eyes that very moment.

Perhaps one right step at a time was enough.

CHAPTER 15

Mackenna

I wandered through the darkness of royal gardens looking for a quiet spot to decompress. Today had been *a lot ...*

I'd woken up this morning with my stomach in knots at the idea of going to church. For Doonians, especially those like Duncan, faith was integral to their culture. Each Sunday they came together in the Auld Kirk to thank their Protector. Last time around, Vee and I had both been on the outside looking in. This time she was their leader, and I was the odd American out.

I spectated from the back row next to Emily and Analisa. Vee'd invited me to sit with her, but I'd assumed that would mean sitting next to Duncan in front of the whole kingdom — awkwardly on display again.

Turned out that I'd worried for nothing. The younger prince was noticeably MIA. I assumed he'd taken the first shift of "training exercises" along the border until Analisa made a snarky comment about him not being much of a churchgoer — which proved she didn't know him as well as she thought. If

Doon chose a poster boy for their beliefs, it would be Duncan. Or so I thought.

But once the service ended and I followed the crowd outside, Duncan materialized from the ether. With a wink to Analisa, he slipped into the receiving line next to his brother as if he'd been there the whole time.

Before I could get to the bottom of his holy hooky, Vee whisked me away to a boring luncheon and then an afternoon of social calls — with more grub at every stop. After the obligatory sampling of savory pies, Scotch eggs, sausage rolls, bridies, bangers and mash, shortbread, and half a dozen puddings, I felt like Little Red after a bakery binge. When stars began appearing in the indigo sky and we finally returned to the castle, we were each eager to go our separate way. To my immense relief, there'd been no talk of supper.

Rejecting the temptation to laze about like an overstuffed Garfield, I decided to go for a walk hoping the outdoors wouldn't be too crowded. Castle MacCrae housed nearly half the people it employed, especially the young ones — which made total sense. Who would want to live with their parents when they could have a condo-like setup with all the castle amenities — including an awesome green space? But it made getting some alone time a bit more challenging.

Torches lit gray graveled paths that wound through acres of unique gardens containing everything from perfectly sculpted lawns with large hedgerows to chaotic patches of overgrown wildflowers. Couples occupied the occasional bench or strolled languidly down the widest of the lanes. A guy I vaguely recognized as one of the Destined jogged by, saluting me as he passed.

On the great lawn, a small but boisterous group had commenced an impromptu karaoke night — apparently it was a grand night for singing. Although their tune was unfamiliar, it had the distinct meter of a drinking song. Apropos since to counteract the nip in the air, they were passing around a bottle.

Thankful I had thought to grab a shawl, I draped it over my shoulders and set off in the opposite direction of the revels in search of something more private ... my own little secret garden. After a couple of twists and turns, I discovered a perfect, secluded spot lit by flickering torches.

The duality of the new Duncan weighed heavily on me. Did I really know him as well as I thought? Perhaps Analisa now held the distinction of knowing him best ... because he was as open and honest with her as he'd once been with me?

As much as I wanted to believe there was a chance for us, I wasn't sure my wounded heart would survive the wishing.

Ever since middle school, I'd worked through tangled emotional knots by singing. Vee called it "musical processing." Back in Chicago during the month of Ben & Jerry's, I clung to a weepy rendition of "Without You" as my signature song. That seemed like the obvious place to start now. Taking a deep, controlled breath, I let my eyes drift shut and focused on enunciating as I immersed myself in the first verse. The night absorbed my voice so that I had to make tiny adjustments for pitch and volume. But by the refrain, I'd become one with my instrument.

Song followed song, one after another. I rooted my feet into the earthen stage and let the melodies flow, spending myself in the dynamic emotions of requited and unrequited love until I felt empty — not like a bad void of nothing, but empty of turmoil. Cathartic empty. Ready to fill my vessel with something fresh and positive.

For my big finish, I ended with one of my all-time favorites from *A Chorus Line*. New understanding filled my consciousness as I belted out an unapologetic version of "What I Did for

Love." Focused solely on the song, the words, my voice soared higher and louder with each note, building into a mighty crescendo that vibrated through every pore. In the roaring silence that followed, I giddily swiped at my face with trembling hands.

My pulse thundered in my ears so loudly that I almost missed the slow, deliberate clap of an uninvited audience. I whirled toward the sound as a deep voice said, "I'd nearly forgotten what a lovely singing voice you have."

Holy Hammerstein!

Duncan lounged in a heavily shadowed patch of grass. Propped up on his elbows, his legs were prone, as if he'd recently been staring up at the stars. He sat forward just enough that I could see traces of stardust sparkling in his eyes.

My heart pounded even harder as I realized that he'd been watching me in the dark. Half of me wanted to yell at him for being an eavesdropping creeper while the other half — the part that yearned for his approval like oxygen — was desperate to hear what he thought. Another glance into his glittering eyes and the battle was over.

I crossed to a wide stone bench near his feet and perched on the end. "I didn't know you'd ever heard me sing."

"Aye, a time or two." He leaned back, letting the shadows overtake him. Despite not being able to see his face, my skin prickled with the awareness of his scrutiny. "Like when the queen brought on the blizzard that nearly destroyed us. You sang half the night away."

"I remember." It was a dark, tempestuous night in every way possible. After Duncan had been put in his place by his older brother and ordered to babysit me, he'd brooded while I wandered the confines of his turret chamber, warbling show tunes. Tons of them. But as far as I could recall, I'd mostly hummed them under my breath.

I scooted forward, trying to find his face in the night. "When else have you heard me sing?"

"You sing every chance you get. Half the time I don't think you're even aware of it." While that sure sounded like me, I couldn't help feeling like he was dodging the question. After the long day, the last thing I wanted was to trade banter with a boy who couldn't give me a straight answer.

Rising to my feet, I dropped into a deep bow. "Glad I could entertain." Then I turned my back on him and headed toward Castle MacCrae.

I hadn't managed more than a half dozen steps when he said softly, "Chicago ... I saw your show in Chicago."

I froze.

"You were luminescent. Like the sun rising in the east. If I had any doubt as to where you belonged, seeing you on that stage ... You were created for that world."

I turned, and when I did, I saw that Duncan was sitting up. Although no longer in shadow, he still appeared haunted.

"But you said you didn't — why would you lie?"

Rather than answer, he looked away. Even if he'd seen me perform and possibly understood why I made certain choices, it didn't change the fact that I'd hurt him. "Fine," I said. "You don't want to talk about it. How 'bout you answer me this ... Why don't you go to church anymore?"

He shrugged, his face half hidden. "It doesna matter."

If he was determined to shut me out there was really no reason to stand around. "I'll see you later."

Abruptly, he sprang to his feet. "Usually I'd be inclined to escort you back, but I'm late to meet Ana. I trust ye can find your way."

All the tumultuous emotion I'd worked so hard to purge re-formed, like a tornado. I marched right up to him and stared

176

into his ridiculously gorgeous face — that I really wanted to slap. I could feel my nostrils flaring as I sucked in bursts of air. "As you might have noticed in Chicago, I've managed just fine on my own. So go on. You don't want to keep your little thief waiting."

He tilted his head, his lips quirked with amusement. "So you *are* jealous."

"Of her? No."

I made a scoffing noise meant to sound dismissive, but it came out more like a sob. Duncan's dark eyes bore into mine. He took my hand, holding it so that his thumb lightly brushed across the back. "Do you remember the last time we were alone in this garden?"

I did. It was during the ball. He'd begged me to take him to Chicago and, under the spell of the moon and his lips, I'd foolishly agreed. Fireflies stirred in my chest as I tried to remain stoic.

With his free hand, Duncan grabbed my waist and pulled me against him. He lowered his face to mine and said, "You wrecked me."

Without warning, he let go and I stumbled backward. Before I could recover, he retreated into the shadows. His tone revealed nothing further as he said, "Good-bye, Mackenna."

Then he turned and walked away . . . to her.

For the longest time, I stood rooted to my spot, feeling the fireflies die off one by one. Gradually, the mournful sounds of the night penetrated my consciousness. In the distance, an owl screeched. The wind howled like an old woman, and the revelers on the lawn waned to a single melancholy tenor who began to sing in a tender, slightly slurred voice:

In the gloaming, oh my darling
When the lights are soft and low

And the quiet shadows, falling
Softly come and softly go
When the trees are sobbing faintly
With a gentle unknown woe
Will you think of me and love me
As you did once, long ago?

I shook my head, desperate to break the spell Duncan had cast by leaving. A gust of icy wind tore at my hair, and I pulled the shawl tighter around my shoulders as I marched down the path that would take me back to the castle.

In the gloaming, oh my darling
Think not bitterly of me
Though I passed away in silence
Left you lonely, set you free.

Had Duncan paid them to sing that dreadful song? Desperate to escape, I jogged past the group surrounding the tenor. The lyrics of his song nipped at my heels like hellhounds as I sprinted the rest of the way to my room.

For my heart was tossed with longing
What had been could never be
It was best to leave you thus, dear
Best for you, and best for me.

But it hadn't been best for me ... or, as far as I could tell, for the sweet prince who had worn his faith and his heart on his sleeve.

"You wrecked me."

The truth of his words slammed through me. I hadn't just left him, I'd caused him irreparable damage. His duality, the loss of his beliefs, his association with Analisa — all my fault. I didn't deserve a second chance to stay in Doon or with the prince that was once destined to be my soul mate. I wasn't worthy.

Chapter 16

Mackenna

The queen of Doon and her royal hottie clung to one another in the doorway to her chambers. Their good-bye kiss rivaled a gum commercial. If the world wasn't about to end and the boys didn't have to check in with the border patrols, Jamie and Vee might have made it last all day.

Duncan and I stood awkwardly on the sidelines, staring at our shoes while we waited out the PDA. Our conversation in the garden had caused us to take a step backward. His guard was up, which made being in close proximity unbearable. From opposite sides of the room, our occasional glances would meet only to shift away as quickly as possible.

He'd accompanied his brother to say good-bye before heading out for "training exercises." While this was clearly Jamie's last stop, I couldn't help but wonder if Duncan had yet to visit Analisa. And if she would be sad to see him go, or simply fill the space on her dance card with the Rosetti boy.

After an eternity, the Dentyne Duo came up for air. While common decency kept my vision focused on the purple wallpaper, Jamie's murmured endearments made my cheeks feel hot.

"Time to save the world. We're depending on you." He reluctantly released Vee and took a step back. "Both of you."

Vee nodded. "We'll find something. When will you be back?"

"Midday tomorrow if all goes well. We'll spend the night at the hunting lodge, see if Adam's found anything new."

Vee closed the gap between them to give Jamie a peck. "Be safe."

Before they could commence PDA part deux, Duncan placed a hand on his brother's bicep and said, "Time to go, man." With a final halfhearted nod in my direction, he slipped through the doorway. Jamie captured one more kiss from his lady love before following his little brother.

Shutting the door, Vee leaned against it with her eyelids at half-mast. With her mussed hair, swollen lips, and glassy gaze, she could've been posing for the cover of a romance novel. But if we were going to figure out how to stop the limbus, she needed to stop swooning and bring her A-game. "Do you need to take a cold shower before we start?"

She blinked at me, her cheeks turning deep red as she got my meaning. "Sorry. Duncan was awfully quiet. Everything okay?"

"Things are fine." Last night when I returned from the garden, she was sound asleep. I'd planned to fill her in over breakfast, but the princes had interrupted us. And now that I'd seen Duncan again, I didn't feel like talking. Desperate to change the subject, I parked myself on her settee and started organizing the dozen or so books on her coffee table into piles by color. "Find anything useful?"

"Not yet. But I've only gotten through half of these so far."

Scouring old, moldy books for the key to saving the kingdom had about as much appeal as skydiving naked, but it's not like I had any better ideas. I couldn't exactly tap dance my way to answers. So I picked up a brown-leather hardback and offered, "How about I skim for keywords and you tackle the heavy lifting?"

Side by side, we passed the day in research mode. Whenever the words started to blur, I'd take a break for refreshments and a musical intermission. By early afternoon, our progress could be measured in cold cups of tea, half-eaten plates of food, and my repertoire of iconic Patti LuPone songs. But we still had a big fat nothing regarding the limbus.

Vee closed yet another book with a thwack. When I glanced at her, I noted she was resisting the urge to pick it up and hurl it across the room. Time to acknowledge the giant pooka in the room. "What if we can't do it?"

She stood and methodically rolled the kinks from her shoulders. "Failure is not an option."

"But it's a definite possibility." I hated to be the one to say it, but we'd scoured every relevant book in the royal library. "Research isn't getting us anywhere. We need to think outside of the box. Try something more radical."

"Like what?"

"How should I know? You're the brains. I'm just the talent."

Vee sighed. "What we need is a miracle."

The outer door opened and Fiona hustled inside. She was one of the few people who didn't get screened by Eòran. Emily, Jamie, and I were the others. Although not a divine phenomenon, she was a most welcome addition.

"Sorry I'm late." Our friend removed her shawl with a bright smile. "Figure out how ta save the world yet?"

"Nope." Who was this cheerful creature and what did she do with Fiona?

"I've no doubt ye'll figure it out." Out of habit, she began tidying the dirty dishes while humming a lively tune. "After all, the Protector o' Doon called the both of ye here. There's a purpose in all o' this."

"Beyond getting zombified and dying when Doon comes to an end?"

"Kenna!" Vee's pointy elbow speared my ribs.

"Sorry, but we're all thinking it."

Fiona made a *pffttt* sound as she retrieved a cup I'd left on top of a music box on the bookshelf. "No need to be so pessimistic, Mackenna. Life is good."

Said the girl who'd spent the last week in perpetual waterworks. All in all, I think I liked teary Fiona better than this sunshine-and-rainbows version. Giving voice to my thoughts, Vee stated, "You seem pretty cheerful. If you've got good news, please share. We could use some right about now."

"I've jus' come from the dressmakers. There's no way that lace monstrosity will be ready by Saturday, so I'm getting my mermaid dress after all." Fiona placed the cup on the tray of dishes and rang the service bell. "Mum's so forlorn, she's taken ta her bed."

Okay, that was a small win, but getting her dream gown didn't change the fact she was on the barrel end of the universe's shotgun wedding. "You do realize the world is still coming to an end unless we find a way to stop it?"

"You will."

"How can you be so sure that there's a divine purpose here?"

"Because, Mackenna, you've the gift of sight. You're the only one that can see the true nature of the limbus. Do you think that's a coincidence?"

When I shrugged, Fiona took my hand. Her earnest hazel eyes trespassed into places I didn't want her to go. "Because of Veronica's fate, I fear ye've dismissed your role in this too easily. This isn't just her story, it's yours too. The Rings of Aontacht chose the both of you. Whether you want to accept it or no', you were destined for Doon."

An efficient knock sounded at the door, followed by Eòran entering the room. Grateful for the interruption, I moved away from the girl who saw too much. Even if Fiona was right, I rejected the notion that I didn't have a say in the matter. After all, it'd been my choice to leave Duncan at the bridge. The universe had nothing to do with it.

Eòran looked from Vee to Fiona, who indicated the tray of dishes. Mutton Chops cleared his throat. "Shall I have these cleared, m'lady?"

"Yes, please." Vee lifted her mouth into a forced grin and indicated a stack of books next to the coffee table. "And would you arrange to have these returned to the library?"

"Certainly, m'lady." The guard held out his hand to offer Vee a tiny green leather-bound volume. "The Master Archivist sent this over. He said you left it behind the other day."

A tiny frown furrowed Vee's forehead as she took the book and politely waited for her personal guard to retreat with the tray of dirty dishes. As soon as the door closed, she turned to Fiona and me. "I didn't leave a book behind."

I opened my mouth to challenge her, but she cut me off. "Kenna, you've known me forever. Does that sound like me?"

She could be dreamy, but she was practically OCD when it came to double-checking her surroundings. A byproduct of having a mom who would pawn anything of value that happened to be lying around. "No." Half in jest, I said, "Maybe it's that miracle you wanted."

"Aye," Fiona replied in earnest.

Vee opened the book. Her frown deepened to craggy proportions. "It looks like English — all the right letters are there — but it doesn't make sense."

Fiona and I approached Vee from opposite sides to read over her shoulders. Sure enough, some of the words were perfectly understandable English while other were gibberish.

Fiona pointed to the text. "Tha's Scots."

Vee turned the page and then glanced at our friend. "Can you read it?"

"Aye. And write it."

"That's a crazy coincidence," I interjected with a chuckle.

"Not really," Fiona replied. "Most of the village can read and write Scots."

"Well, it's our good fortune you're here," Vee added diplomatically. She turned the next several pages, which were mostly pictures with captions. Rectangles with one rounded end — like the shape of a tombstone — filled the book. Each one was filled with swirling designs and hieroglyphics that reminded me of Celtic tattoos.

When I spoke my observation aloud, Fiona said, "Not Celtic. Pictish."

Glancing from Fiona to me, Vee said, "Of course. Those drawings are Pictish stones."

Since my two friends seemed to be on the same nerd wavelength, I had to ask, "What's Pictish? Anything like Pictionary?"

Vee looked at me with feverish eyes that I recognized as her knowledge-is-power expression. "Remember World History freshman year — that unit on Celts?"

"Vaguely. There was a boatload of drama going on. The cast had just been announced for *Children of Eden*. Everyone thought I would get Eve because I nailed my audition. But then

Suzi Klein got it just because she was a senior, even though she sang 'Memory' at tryouts and I sang 'Children Will Listen.' I mean, Sondheim trumps Andrew Lloyd Webber every single time, am I right?"

Vee's eyes narrowed, so I added, "I do remember the unit on ancient Mesopotamia — it came in handy for my character's backstory as the marked servant girl."

"*That* you remember?" When I shrugged, she said, "You wrote a paper about Stonehenge."

Something tickled in the back of my brain. Giant rocks, extraterrestrial theories, and a C minus for effort. "So Pictish is an alien language?"

"No. Pictish originates from Scotland, not outer space. But it's an ancient, dead language. Nobody reads or writes it anymore. And as far as people can tell, nobody ever spoke it."

Fiona cleared her throat. "Except the Picts."

"Yes, except the Picts," she replied with a half-roll of her eyes. "But they're extinct."

Fiona fidgeted. "Mostly."

"What does mostly mean?"

"At one time Doon had a family who was directly descendent from the Picts. They kept all the old arts alive. They even taught their ways to some o' the other womenfolk in town."

"Are any of them still around?"

"They all perished, except one."

I had a sinking feeling in my stomach that I knew where this was going. Apparently, so did Vee. She paled as she asked, "Which family was it?"

With deep, grave eyes, Fiona replied, "The Blackmores."

Vee and I spoke over one another. "As in Adelaide Blackmore Cadell?" "The Witch of Doon?"

"Aye. The Blackmores had a growing coven — at least until

the church began to speak out against them. The legends say that Adaira Blackmore married Gowan Cadell, a boy from a respectable farming family, ta quiet the opposition. Shortly after their union, the lad died. Rumors began that Adaira had murdered the boy — sacrificed him to her dark lord. Nine months later she bore triplet girls. Villagers were convinced that the babies were not the issue o' Gowan but o' the dark lord hisself."

As if just speaking of the dark lord made her susceptible to evil, Fiona crossed herself before continuing. "One night, a mob descended on their cottage demanding that Adaira hand over her babes. They took the infants to the lake, planning ta drown them, but the queen, being a mother herself, took pity on Adaira. She interceded with the king, gettin' him ta promise to protect the children until they were of age. His guards rescued the babes, and they were restored to Adaira with the caveat that she give up witchcraft for good."

A rude noise burst from my lips, one that would've been embarrassing if boys had been present. "Which she obviously didn't."

Tendrils of strawberry blonde hair bobbed around Fiona's shoulders as she shook her head. "Nay. On the surface, the Blackmore Cadells were a picture o' propriety."

Fiona walked to one of the wingback chairs and perched on the edge. Vee and I settled on the couch as she continued. "They nursed the village sick back ta health and went to church on Sundays. The triplets grew into intelligent, lovely girls that seemed to be the embodiment of goodness. But secretly, they all practiced the dark arts."

After a small dramatic pause, she continued. "No one in Doon saw the pattern at the time. Most o' the males they nursed died, while the females thrived. Several o' the women they healed joined them in their pagan worship.

"When the king fell sick, Adaira and her daughters were called to attend him. Whether they killed him or merely failed to cure him is a mystery but when he died the throne passed to his only son, Prince Angus Andrew Kellan MacCrae. Angus was a handsome and just lad. Before becoming king, he surprised everyone by naming Adaira's daughter Adelaide Blackmore Cadell as his queen-to-be. This was how the Blackmores were ta get their revenge, by ruling Doon."

I'd gotten a glimpse of all the junk that plagued Doon's new queen on a daily basis. Her life of royalty seemed to be one mind-numbing blur of diplomacy and politics. No thank you. "That sounds like the stupidest revenge plan ever."

"Not really," Vee countered. "A ruler can regulate their country's religion. They can force their subjects to comply with their beliefs or face execution. Continue."

Fiona nodded. "Exactly. Addie would've murdered her bridegroom and then forced all o' Doon to worship the dark lord. But the queen, whose suspicion had grown since her husband's death, figured out the pattern — that the Blackmore Cadells were draining the life force out o' the men they were supposed ta be healing. Unfortunately, before she could officially oppose her son's choice o' bride, she died."

"Obviously of foul play," I interjected.

"But it was never ta be proved. Adaira, who was the last person to see the queen alive, claimed the queen took her own life out o' grief over her husband's death. With the queen out o' the way, there was nothing to stop the Blackmores from merging their line with Doonian royalty.

"At Prince Angus's coronation, he performed the Completing by recording the name of his queen-to-be. That night at the coronation ball, Angus revealed that his parents had appeared ta him in a dream. They had come on behalf of the Protector of Doon to intercede for the welfare o' the kingdom. Next, he revealed that his choice o' bride as written on the paper was not Adelaide but a pious girl from the village."

A thought flickered across Vee's face, and she gasped. "It was Lynnette Elizabeth Campbell, wasn't it?"

"Aye." Fiona's wide, rounded eyes dominated her grave face. "Then right in the middle o' the ballroom, Adaira tried to curse Lynnette. The witches were seized. Adelaide and her sisters pleaded for their lives, claiming their innocence — that they, too, were victims o' their mother's evil deceit. The young king believed and pardoned them. However, as a warning, he made the triplets bear witness ta their mother's execution. And as Adaira's body burned away, her girls began plotting their revenge, an unholy campaign that would eventually bring about the Great Miracle."

The miracle she referred to led to Doon being enchanted — or blessed, whatever you called it. The Protector of Doon hid the kingdom from Addie and the rest of the world, so that it only appeared for one day every hundred years. But even when the portal on the Brig o' Doon opened, the enchantment made it so the powerful witch couldn't enter.

Vee twisted her hair until it was gathered into a knot, a sure sign the gears in her brain were churning. "How do you know all this?"

Fiona smiled. "My granny used ta tell it to me as a bedtime story. Scared the mischief outta me, it did."

While I like a good campfire tale as much as the next girl, I failed to see how Fiona's spooky soliloquy related to the little green book. Sure, we now had an origins story on evil Addie, but the bottom line was our best shot at deciphering the images in the book resided with the person trying to kill us.

Vee, who'd been cradling the book during Addie's backstory, held it out to Fiona. "Can you translate the part that's in Scots?"

Taking the book, Fiona sank back into her chair. Vee and I remained on the sofa, fidgeting as she read the first two pages. Three quarters of the way through, Fiona made an excited breathy noise, flipped ahead to one of the Pictish drawings and then back to the text. She scanned the last bit and then looked at us with bright eyes.

"This book pertains to the kind o' witchcraft practiced by the Blackmores." She held the book open to us like some twisted kindergarten story time. "The Pictish stones are spells ... and the text below contains instructions ta break the spell."

Vee leaned in. "So it tells us how to defeat the limbus?"

"I believe it does, but whoever created this book assumed tha' the reader could decipher the Pictish symbols. I canna tell which o' these is the spell responsible for the limbus."

Indicating the stacks of books littering the floor next to the couch, Vee murmured, "Maybe there's something in one of these others."

"Nay. The only source I can think of would be the witches' book o' spells."

"And where is that?"

Fiona frowned. "I presume it's still in their cottage."

Vee bounced to her feet. "So let's go get it."

As she passed, Fiona stood and grabbed her arm. "Nay, my queen. That cottage is the source o' the witches' evil. Granny said it was intentionally built over an ancient Pictish site of human sacrifice, and that every time the Blackmores slaughtered another innocent on the grounds, the dark lord hisself gave them a spell for their collection writ in their victims' blood."

The day's snackage congealed in my stomach. We weren't

dealing with some Scooby-Doo hoodoo; this was pure and terrifying evil at its worst.

Maintaining her death grip on Vee's arm, Fiona explained, "There's a reason that cottage is not protected by the Great Miracle — it's a foul, unholy place. After Doon was saved, King Angus decreed it forbidden ta set foot inside the malevolent boundaries o' the witches' cottage. Breaking this law is an act o' treason."

Pulling away from Fiona, Vee crossed her arms. "I have to do what's best for my people, even if it breaks the law."

"There are those in Doon who would like nothing better than ta see you stripped of your crown and thrown inta the dungeons ... or worse. If you're found guilty of breaking that decree, Jamie or anyone else who defends you will be punished as well. What's best for the people is for you to adhere ta the law."

As Vee opened her mouth, Fiona added, "Your actions save or condemn us all. Promise me you won't go after the witches' spell book. Please."

"Fine. I promise."

"Thank you. Now, if ye have no objections, I'll be taking my leave to tell Fergus the good news about my dress." Fiona set the book on the coffee table and gathered her shawl. "We'll find what we need. I do believe that. We just have to be patient."

As soon as the door shut in Fiona's wake, Vee grumbled, "I *believe* we already know what we need."

For all Vee's intelligence, she could be frustratingly shortsighted when she set her mind to something. "You heard Fiona. It's against the law to trespass on the witches' unholy ground. If you disobey, the villagers will chop off your head and burn you at the stake."

Vee rolled her eyes. "I'm their queen. They're not going to kill me."

"Um, history would beg to differ. It's full of royal heads that have been severed from their royal necks."

Her brow lifted. "History? Really, Kenna? Would you care to elaborate?"

"Fine. HBO would beg to differ." Before she could comment, I added, "I'll go get it."

"Stop. I'm not letting you go alone."

"You have to. Don't you get it? I'm the talent. I'm not under Doonian law, and I can see the limbus. This is probably what I'm here to do. So let me do it."

"Fine. But I'm going too — at least to the borders." She approached the large bay window, staring at the deepening twilight. "It's too late to go now."

She was right. By the time we got to the cottage, it would be pitch black. We wouldn't be able to see a thing and we couldn't risk using torches. Not that I was all that keen to go sleuthing around in the middle of the night anyway. "Let's go at first light."

"Perfect. I usually go for an early jog, so you can join me."

Great. Not only was I intentionally going into the zombie fungus to some cursed cottage that may or may not contain a spell book dictated by Satan himself, but now there was jogging involved. Elphaba was right when she said no good deed went unpunished.

chapter 17

Mackenna

NARRATOR
"Once upon a time—"

MACKENNA REID
"I hope ..."

NARRATOR
"in a kingdom outside of time and place—"

MACKENNA REID
"More than Broadway ..."

NARRATOR
"lived a colossally stupid maiden,"

MACKENNA REID
"More than London's West End ..."

NARRATOR
"an equally idiotic queen,"

MACKENNA REID
"and a—"

"Kenna, enough with the prologue!" Vee hissed at me over her shoulder without breaking her stride. "We're trying to be stealthy, remember."

Of course I remembered. Stealthy had been my word. Inconspicuous had been hers, but there was nothing inconspicuous about two Midwestern girls — one of them a newly appointed queen — jogging through Doon at the butt crack of dawn.

"To be continued ..."

She shot me another dirty look. I gestured to my closed lips, and Vee returned her attention to the winding, overgrown path. "If you can't help yourself, then sing in your head."

Vee knew I was trying to keep my mind off the reason for our little journey through the woods. I wasn't sure if I bought Fiona's granny's story about the witches' cottage existing over a Hellmouth, but facing the zombie fungus again was terrifying enough. This time I would go through it alone. Would I be as brave when the life of the boy I loved wasn't on the line?

MACKENNA REID
"I hope ..."

An unhappily familiar stench warned me that the limbus was close. I rounded the bend and collided with my bestie's royal backside. Vee stumbled forward but managed to stay on her feet. As soon as she regained her balance, she hopped in reverse. As she backpedaled, I caught sight of the obstacle in her path. If she'd fallen, Vee would have face-planted in a patch of black petunias.

Like every other time I'd encountered the limbus, the putrid smell threatened to drop me to my knees. The forest, which I remembered as skeletal from my previous visit, was overrun with black, slimy moss. Vee'd had the forethought to rub a pair of scarves with lavender. I pulled mine over my nose to ease the stench.

Vee watched me and then stepped forward right to the edge of the limbus. "Does it smell bad?"

I nodded and managed to croak out, "What do you see?"

Vee shrugged. "The same old creepy forest as usual. Bare except for the flowers." The Ring of Aontacht blazed bright on her hand as she reached toward the nearest putrefied tree.

"Wait." I batted her arm away. "Aunt Gracie's ring didn't protect Duncan."

"I know, but the limbus didn't hurt you. So we can't draw any conclusions without more tests."

"Tests? This isn't an AP science fieldtrip. If you end up with a zombie limb, Prince Overprotective is going to kill me ... and then you ... and then me again ... and then the world's gonna end."

"The world's ending anyway, Kenna. Besides, Jamie and I have a new understanding. We're playing to each other's strengths. While he protects the kingdom, my job is research." She reached tentatively forward. "This is just investigating a research theory."

My hand hovered alongside Vee's, ready to pull her back at the first shriek of pain. She reached into the limbus and then withdrew. "See? I'm fine."

"Sure — if fine means that your sleeve is rotting from your wrist."

Vee looked calmly at the disintegrated cuff of her hoodie. When she wanted, the girl could be as rational as a Vulcan. "We should have brought an extra set of clothes."

"I hope you're speaking in the royal we — as in, 'We should've brought extra clothes for Kenna,' because that's the only 'we' here. This is as far as you go, Queenie."

"But — "

In no mood to argue, I grabbed her newly exposed wrist. Before I could reach toward the limbus again, Vee began to gag. Her free hand covered her mouth as she pulled away from me.

When I let go, her panic disappeared. She blinked at the forest, trying to make sense of her own perceptions.

"What just happened?" she asked in a low voice.

"I tested my own theory. You saw what I see, didn't you?" Sharing my sight had been totally accidental — I'd meant to pull her back out of harm's way. But if it changed her mind about coming with, I planned to use the fluke to my advantage.

She faced me. "I didn't realize ... I mean, I knew it was bad, but I couldn't see, or smell ... Oh boy."

"Now you understand what we're dealing with."

"But Duncan couldn't see the true nature of the limbus when you touched him?" I shook my head back and forth, and she said, "What made you think that I could?"

I held out my hand with my uncle Cam's glowing emerald ring. "Fiona said the rings weren't done with us, remember?"

Her eyes narrowed. "But you had no idea that was going to happen when you grabbed me."

I should've known she'd call my bluff. "None whatsoever."

Vee pulled her scented scarf up to her nose and then lifted her ringed hand to mine. "Let's see what happens if we actually reach in together."

She clutched my fingers.

As we reached toward the limbus, the green glow of Uncle Cameron's ring merged with the red light of Gracie's to become dazzling white. The black flowers sprouting along the border shriveled, just as they had when Duncan hung over the crevasse. Wherever the light shone, the zombie fungus skittered away, leaving a bare and slime-free path. We swept our hands in a half-circle while watching the phenomenon. But as soon as the light moved on, darkness and decay crept back in with the promise of death.

Like a perverse game of hokeypokey, we pulled our hands

out and let go of one another with a little shake. I hadn't noticed at the start, but the power of the combined rings gave off a charge of energy, like an electric current.

The border of the limbus, which had been bare a second ago, was now overflowing with petunias once more. Vee's eyes sparkled with discovery as her gaze leapt from the flowers to Aunt Gracie's ring. "That was interesting."

"Little bit." Prolonged exposure to the limbus made my throat feel scratchy, like I was on the verge of a cold. I coughed to clear it.

Vee rotated her wrist back and forth. "No clothing damage that time. And did you notice the smell?"

"No, I didn't notice the smell. I was a bit preoccupied watching the limbus skitter away from the light like cockroaches ... Wait, I *didn't* noticed the smell."

Grinning, she said, "Exactly. When the light of the rings turned white, the smell was barely noticeable."

"Great, but so what?"

"Don't you see, we're both supposed to do this." She grabbed my hand. "The rings of unity. Together, the rings provide a small bubble of protection."

She did have a point. I wasn't terribly keen on going into the limbus — with the horrible stench and the decomposing clothes — by myself. But I needed to look out for her the same way she protected me. "Are you sure you're ready to commit treason?"

"I never wanted you to face this alone. But this clinches things. We're not even talking about the greater good here. This" — she shook our hands — "is a sign. The rings will help us defeat the limbus, but only if we work as a team. Besides, I've seen you search for things ... Do you really want the fate of the kingdom resting on your Nancy Drew skills?"

I didn't need the ninety-minute sales pitch to know she was right. "If *we* are about to break Doonian law, then let's be quick about it."

Using our intertwined hands as an anti-evil Mag light, we stepped into the limbus. Off in the distance, just to the left of the oozing path, I caught a glimpse of a crumbling stone structure. The dilapidated remains of the Blackmore cottage. If Fiona was right, the key to stopping the limbus was in a book somewhere in that ruin.

The white light kept the limbus at bay just enough to keep the clothes from rotting off our bodies. After a short, blessedly uneventful walk, we arrived at another heavy patch of petunias surrounding the neglected fence of the cottage. Pointing to the flowers, Vee announced, "If the limbus is attacking the border of Doon, then this should be where it ends. Do you see any sign of it around the cottage?"

I scanned for the black blossoms that heralded the zombie fungus. "No."

Wrenching open the dilapidated, iron gate with my free hand, Vee and I stepped across the threshold. As soon as our feet touched the other side, the bright white light faded so that the rings were once again glowing green and red.

Vee let go of my hand and let out a slow yoga breath before she nodded toward the cottage. "Okay. Let's go find that spell book."

Up close, the cottage reminded me of those ancient tourist attractions. After five centuries of neglect, it just barely resembled a building. The walls were crumbling and in a few places had collapsed entirely. Parts of the roof had caved, the long wooden crossbeams resting across the rotting floor and dirty furniture like skeletal remains. The only thing that seemed unaffected by time was the heavy wooden door at the front.

Cautiously, Vee and I circled around to our left until we found a space wide enough to enter the remains of the witches' evil lair.

"Watch the floorboards," Vee warned as she stepped inside. "We can't afford for you to have one of your clumsy moments right now."

As much as I wanted to take offense, she spoke truth. I slipped carefully in after her, feeling a bit overwhelmed by the task ahead. Vee was right; I didn't want the fate of Doon resting on my inner sleuth. Now, if we needed someone to sing a magical aria that would reveal the hiding place of the book, I would be all over that. But creating order out of abandoned chaos was beyond me.

Doing a slow three-sixty, I surveyed our surroundings. In the not-so-far distance, a garbled animal groan pierced the silence. I'd witnessed what the limbus had done to the crow, so I could only imagine what it would do to a raccoon or opossum. Zombie opossums of unusual size stampeded across my imagination, causing the hairs on my arms to stand on end.

Vee must've been imagining her own zombie Jumanji, because when her gaze met mine with a reassuring smile, I noted fear around the edges. "There are only two rooms," she said. "Why don't we split up? You take the back one while I search in here."

"'Kay." It was fine with me. The sooner we found the spell book, the sooner we could get the heck out of Zombie Dodge.

Picking my way across the large main room, I approached the second room like a guest-starring detective on a New York procedural drama. Flush with the wall, my index fingers pressed together like a fake weapon, I pivoted and peeked into the back room. Resisting the urge to shout "Clear!" I stepped through the doorway.

The back room was smaller than the main part of the cottage, but equally as devastated. With a section of the roof missing, the elements had taken their toll on the few pieces of furniture: a giant bed with a moldy mattress, a decaying nightstand off to one side, and a huge water-stained chest at the foot. Wishing I had a set of rubber gloves like a proper crime inspector, I walked over to the chest. Using the edge of my scarf as a protective barrier, I lifted the top.

A plump brown spider scurried out, and I jumped back, barely managing to swallow the scream erupting from my throat. I forced a breath deep into my lungs and exhaled slowly. No need to alarm Vee over a creepy crawly. Prying up a broken floorboard, I used it to probe the contents of the chest — clothes, mostly. I stirred the fabrics around until I was satisfied that there was no book inside.

Crossing to the nightstand, I nudged the door open with my foot to reveal a whole lot of nothing inside. Next, I shoved the nasty mattress off the bedframe to look underneath. Through the discolored rope supports crisscrossing the wooden frame, I could see the empty floor below. So far my inner Nancy Drew was O for three.

Out of places to check, I tried to think like a desperate, wicked witch. She'd want the book close to her while she slept. And she wouldn't use any place as obvious as the chest. Which left hiding it in plain sight by means of a spell or concealing it in a secret space. If it was in plain sight but cloaked, we were out of luck. So I decided to focus on potential secret spots in the room.

I'd checked the chest and nightstand, and I didn't believe either one contained a false back or bottom. The stone walls were too solid to conceal nooks or crannies. The mattress was too thin, plus the possibility of mold would make it a lousy hiding spot for something consisting of leather and paper. In fact, any places where the elements could get at it were out. If this were a TV show, the book would be in a waterproof box under the floorboards. But real life was never as convenient as fiction … or was it?

Getting on my hands and knees, I crawled over to the spot where I'd pried up the plank of wood. The three-inch gap between the rotting wooden floor and the bare dirt underneath was dark. Wrenching up the surrounding boards, I peered into the gloomy space. Underneath the floor, below the chest, I caught a glimpse of something solid.

The odds that it was the spell book were astronomical. But that didn't squelch the excited feeling in my chest as I pried up the floor. With a little luck, the mysterious something beneath the floor would disprove Oscar Wilde. Sometimes, when it mattered most, art did indeed imitate life.

CHAPTER 18

Veronica

After the off-the-charts spine-chiller we'd just walked through, the witch's cottage was a bit of a disappointment. Nothing like the creepy-chic abode from *Hocus Pocus,* or the frightful towers of *Sleeping Beauty*'s Maleficent. There was nothing at all terrible or awe-inspiring about this crumpled old ruin. Beyond the aesthetics, though, I'd hoped to get a sense of Addie, some clues to what made her tick. But whatever pieces of her life she left behind had disintegrated along with the furniture. I only hoped that didn't include her book of spells.

Rolling up the one ragged sleeve and one intact sleeve of my hoodie, I began to search the perimeter of the main room, looking for any chinks in the stone large enough to hide a book. But everything seemed to be in plain sight. What I didn't see was a kitchen. I knew from many of the houses in the village that the kitchen was often in a separate area to lessen the risk of losing the entire house to fire. As I ran my hands over the walls, and around the mantel, I encountered an indentation — a door I hadn't noticed before.

"Ken, I found another room!"

Without waiting for a response, I turned the knob and pushed the door open with a whoosh.

It was a small space, and much better preserved than the rest of the cottage, indicating it had been built more recently. The majority of the roof was still intact, and the walls were only crumbling in one corner. I swiped at cobwebs and descended five steps into the room. A round table with three chairs, storage cupboards, and a huge cast-iron pot hanging in the fireplace indicated I'd found the kitchen.

I stepped toward the cooking hearth, and a chill raised goose bumps on my arms. Was this a bubble, bubble, toil and trouble type caldron, or did they merely use it for soup? Rubbing the trepidation from my skin, I dispelled images of Addie and her sisters hunched over the blackened pot, brewing foul potions.

On the other side of the room, I ran my finger through a thick layer of dust coating a potbelly stove, and then stopped in front of an odd-looking, three-legged cabinet. Using my sleeve, I wiped the grime from its face. The drawers were covered in coarse carvings — multiple pentagrams, a three-headed dog, a gryphon, and a flock of ravens. From my research of Celtic symbols, I knew the animals represented multiple themes, but they all had one meaning in common — protection.

Bracing myself to find jars of eyeballs or lines of severed rat tails, I took a steadying breath and pulled open the first drawer. Loose sticks and balls of twine rattled around the almost empty space. *Strange.* A bit braver now, I opened the second drawer to find scraps of material in various patterns, and needles stuck in an apple-shaped pin cushion. Everything was strangely well preserved. I rummaged around and found a few spools of thread and some cotton batting, confirming my theory that I'd found the witch's sewing cabinet. But why bother with all the symbols of protection for something so mundane?

I yanked open the next drawer and stumbled back. A neat row of dolls made of sticks and twine, and wearing tiny clothes, stared back at me with drawn-on expressions of horror. One with brown yarn for hair and a lavender dress had a clump of needles piercing her abdomen. The one beside it was smaller, with short hair and trousers, a pin stabbed into both of its eyes. A child?

"Ken, I think we should go," I called in a surprisingly steady tone.

"One more minute," came the muffled reply. "I think I found something."

I stared at the cabinet for several seconds before slamming the drawer closed with two fingers. As I was ready to turn away, an irregular shadow beneath the cabinet caught my eye. I squatted down and reached underneath it. Trying to ignore the sticky cobwebs and bug carcasses, I patted the floor until I felt a solid shape.

Cautiously, I pulled out a small box. The exterior was plain oak and an iron key rested in a lock on the front. I swiped a hand across the top. There were no symbols carved into the wood, just the letters *L.E.C.M.* I turned the key and felt the mechanism pop. Sweat trickled down my neck as I lifted the lid, half afraid I'd find more voodoo dolls, or worse. But nestled in a lining of purple velvet sat a silver pendant in the shape of a luckenbooth. The heart, topped by a crown and inset with tiny multi-colored jewels, was identical to the one Queen Lynnette wore in her portrait. The initials carved into the lid had to be hers — Lynnette Elizabeth Campbell MacCrae.

If the pendant was the queen's, what was it doing in this cursed place? I plucked it out of the box, and a long silver chain came with it. The metal felt solid and warm in my hand as I closed my fingers around it. Ken and I had agreed the spell book was the only thing we would take from the cottage — less evidence that we'd been here. But with deep conviction, I knew Lynnette would not want her prized possession left to rot in this evil place. And for some reason, just holding it made me feel connected to the past queens. Like I was meant to have it.

As I heard Kenna approach, I stood and slipped the chain over my head, tucking the pendant beneath my shirt. I slid the empty box back under the cabinet with my toe and turned around.

"This has to be it." Kenna descended the stairs and entered the kitchen carrying a large book covered in withered brown leather. "I found it hidden in a box under the floor. What does it say, do you think?" She held out the ancient text. The cover was engraved with a row of symbols I couldn't read, but recognized as Pictish.

"I don't know." I cracked open the cover and leafed through the tissue-thin pages. Similar to the green book we'd found before, the contents appeared to be written in pictures and Scots. "But I know someone who will."

"Fiona," we said at the same time. As if in response to the name, or perhaps to the book itself, the wind picked up and whistled through the broken eaves above us.

Kenna's unsettled gaze met mine. "Let's get out of here before this place falls on us."

I nodded and headed up the stairs. I'd gotten what I came for. And found something I didn't know I'd been missing. In the main room, I stepped over a scattering of broken pottery. "I thought houses only fell on wicked witches."

"Do you really want to stick around and find out?"

I shook my head and kept moving.

Outside, the forest felt heavy. Even worse than on our way into the cottage. Despite the warm breeze, it took an effort to pull air into my lungs, and my steps felt sluggish, like I was in a dream. Almost as if something didn't want us to return to the safety of Doon's boundaries. "Do you feel that?"

Kenna slipped her scarf over her nose and pulled in a deep breath. "Yes. Let's hurry."

She reached out, and I stared at her fingers. Feeling the limbus was bad enough, but seeing it ... I knew I'd never get the images out of my head as long as I lived. But it was our only way out. So I took her hand, and watched the rings light up like glow sticks on Halloween night.

We stepped through the gate and into a Tim Burton nightmare. The trees withered as if in agony, branches bent in on themselves, their leaves black as coal. The very air tinged to a putrid yellow-gray, like it had been charred. I began to jog, pulling Kenna with me. Red eyes peeked from behind a nearby bush, but I wasn't about to wait around to see whatever it was step into the light, its fur melting from its bones, blood staining its teeth.

Force field or not, I wanted to get out of there. I kicked into a run. The wind howled and pushed against us, whipping our hair into wild torrents and forcing us to lean into it as we ran. We'd almost reached the outer perimeter of black petunias when a vision of their vines bursting from the ground and lashing around our legs made me stumble. Kenna yanked on my arm, keeping me from face-planting into the swampy ground. I had no idea if what I'd seen was prophecy or imagination, but I wasn't taking any chances. I righted myself and yelled over the wind, "Jump over the flowers!"

She stared at me for half a second before she readjusted her grip on the spell book and pulled me back a few steps. "Okay. Ready?"

I nodded, and we took off at a sprint, heading for the narrowest section of flowers. It was still several feet wide, and as we approached my heart beat faster yet. Just before our shoes hit the black carpet, I shouted, "Now!" With a mighty leap, we flew over the abyss and into the sunshine-dappled forests of Doon.

When we landed, Kenna tripped forward with her momentum. We crashed through a stand of trees and into a small clearing. Before I could let go of her hand, she fell and pulled us both to the ground.

I rolled onto my back, post-traumatic laughter shaking my entire body. I'd never been so happy to see clear air and blue sky. Lolling my head to the side, I glanced at my BFF sprawled out beside me. "You okay?"

She hesitated, and after several slow breaths turned to look at me. "Sure. But next time you decide to perform a jeté, I hope I'm sitting in the audience. I think I pulled a hammy or something." She bent her legs and rubbed the backs of her thighs with a grimace.

I sat up and leaned on my hands. "That's it. I'm starting you on a yoga regimen first thing tomorrow."

"No way." Kenna pushed herself up and hoisted the spell book into her lap, wiping bits of grass from the cover.

"Why not?"

"You know what my granny used to say."

When I shook my head, her face went slack and she lowered her voice to a quiver. "Yoga's nothing but young girls twistin' themselves into pretzels and prayin' to the devil." Then in her regular voice she said, "No thanks."

I swallowed my laughter. I *so* did not want to encourage her drama. "You're the one holding the witches' spell book."

"Speaking of." Kenna rose to her feet, looking a bit like her granny as she clutched her lower back. "Let's get a move on. I don't want to be responsible for this thing one second longer than I have to."

I sprang up, and we made our way to the overgrown path. After a few minutes of walking in silence, I commented, "Yoga isn't evil, you know. The breathing and the movement just helps clear my head."

"I know. Like when I sing — "

The snap of a stick silenced her, and we both froze. Quick footsteps echoed through the trees. Kenna's eyes were huge as she held the massive book in front of her. There was nowhere to tuck it away where it wouldn't be seen. "Duck behind that bush." I pointed to an overgrown bramble just off the trail. "And I'll see who it is."

"Sure, stick Robin behind a thorny hedge while Batgirl runs off to save the day," she hissed, but she rushed into the forest anyway. "I see where I rank."

"Not sure if you've noticed, but there's nothing about you that reads sidekick." The bush shook violently in reply. With a grin, I took off at a jog. But I hadn't gotten three steps when my prince stepped into the path, brows lowered, his hand gripping the hilt of his sword.

"Jamie, you're back!" I took a running leap and threw myself into his arms. It was a calculated distraction, but also fun because I knew he would catch me. "I didn't expect you until later tonight."

I wrapped my legs around his waist and buried my face in his neck, soaking in his familiar scent. His skin against my cheek felt like the breeze off the ocean, a rainy Saturday morning, and Christmas Eve all rolled into one amazing place that only existed when we were together.

Jamie breathed in the scent of my hair and then pulled back. "Aye, Duncan and I had to see to a few things for the festivities."

He gave me a final squeeze and kissed my forehead before lowering me to the ground. "Who were you talking to?"

I met his steady gaze with my best doe-eyed stare. "No one."

"Odd, I could ha' sworn I heard voices." He let go of my arms and gave me a head-to-toe once over. "Were you running ... alone?"

"Er ... yes. I know you asked me to stay on the castle grounds, but it was too crowded up there, and I figured no one would be out this close to the witch's cottage."

"Aye, and for good reason. What if — " Jamie clenched his jaw and ran a hand over the back of his head as he looked into the sky, apparently searching for strength to deal with his obstinate girlfriend/co-ruler.

"Hey." I took his large, calloused hand in mine and he lowered his chin. Curling one side of my mouth, I winked. "At least I didn't wear the wee, skin-tight trousers."

He returned my grin with one of his own and spun me around by the shoulders to get a better look at my red cutoff sweats. He stopped and held me still with my back to him.

"Och, lass! What is that written across yer bum?"

I'd forgotten these particular sweats sported the word *Juicy* in white, cursive letters across the back. I glanced over my shoulder to see his broad cheekbones drained of all color, his eyes wide — totally adorable. I turned all the way around and his arms dropped to his sides. "Jamie, it's just a name brand."

He blinked and focused back on my face. "A brand, like on a cow?"

I swallowed a giggle. "Kind of. It's the name of the company who made these pants." His brows shot up. "Er ... trousers."

Before he could answer, a loud rustling announced the arrival of Duncan, who was carrying a huge basket in both arms. "Hey there, I got everythin' for tonight's merriments. Did ye order the pine tar?" The younger prince wore a grin, the first real one I'd seen on him in months. "Oh, hello, Yer Majesty. I didna see you there."

He set down the basket with a groan, and I could see it was full to the brim with rocks. *Rocks and pine tar?* What were these two up to?

Duncan straightened, his eyes glued to me with a mischievous sparkle. "Don't ye look fetching in those ... er ... red trousers." He took my hand and bent to give it a quick kiss.

I laughed, wishing he could be his old charming self all the time. But Jamie didn't seem to share my sentiment. As soon as his brother stood and stepped back from me, Jamie put both hands on Duncan's chest and shoved. Caught off guard, Duncan stumbled back as Jamie growled, "Is that how you speak to your queen? Cave. Ten minutes. I've a mind to teach ye some manners."

The smile gone from Duncan's face, he regained his balance and stepped into Jamie. "Gladly. But we'll see who teaches whom."

"Oh, you mean the Brother Cave?" The words rushed out of me in an attempt to alleviate the tension.

Two sets of hot, dark eyes swiveled in my direction, and I resisted the urge to turn tail and run.

"The what?" Duncan demanded.

"Ah ... you know ... the cave where you guys work out ... and stuff." By the way Jamie was shaking his head, I could tell he hadn't told Duncan that I knew about their hideout.

"You told her!" Duncan's voice sounded equal parts outraged and hurt as he turned back to Jamie.

"Nay, brother." Jamie took a step back. "She found me doing drills there one morn' while she was running. We christened it 'the Brother Cave.'" He thrust his hands into his jacket pockets, ducked his head, and shrugged. "I kinda like it."

It seemed I'd betrayed some sort of brotherly pact. "Um ... I'm sorry."

Jamie tilted his head in my direction, his hair falling across one eye as he shot me a sweet, forgiving smile. Unable to stay away, I moved to his side, and he linked his fingers through mine. Instantly, all the tension drained from my body. The boy was seriously like a drug.

Duncan glanced between the two of us. "I guess I like it too."

I grinned.

"But that doesna mean you're invited to join us," Duncan added.

"To work out in an icky dungeon? No thanks. And don't worry. Your secret's safe with me." Except for the someone who was hearing this entire conversation, I added in my head as I saw the bush quiver out of the corner of my eye.

"Thank you, Yer Majesty." Duncan bowed his head with a tiny smile.

Jamie cleared his throat. "Better, but I'm still itchin' to teach you a lesson, little brother. Are we on?"

Duncan's expression took on a blank quality, something I still had a hard time getting used to seeing on him. "I'll meet you there in an hour. I promised Ana a visit as soon as I returned." He squatted and picked up the heavy basket.

Jamie squeezed my fingers and I met his dark, gold-flecked eyes. "I'll walk ye back to the castle, love."

It took me several seconds to shake off the spell of his gaze to answer. "Thanks, but I'll finish my run."

"We need to talk. I'd like to give you an update."

"Me too." Knowing he would freak, I couldn't yet tell him about the spell book, but I did want to discuss everything else

I'd learned, and hear about the patrol. There was also the matter of Gregory Forrester waking from his coma to address. I'd convinced the miller to keep his brother's disappearance into the limbus a secret ... for now. "Meet me for lunch in my suite?"

"Aye." He hesitated, but then pressed his lips to mine in a quick kiss. "Be careful," he whispered before stepping away from me.

"I always am," I called as he and Duncan set off to the main road.

As they rounded the bend I overheard Jamie say, "Here, I'll carry that for a while." Followed by a grunt, and then a strangled, "Saints! Did you get enough, do ye think?"

Duncan's laughter echoed back through the trees.

I turned to find a slightly disheveled Kenna beside me.

"You shouldn't frown like that. It'll give you wrinkles," I said as I pulled twigs from her bright hair.

"Like I care what I'm going to look like in ten years. Seriously, what does it matter ..." She trailed off and began walking down the forest path.

Clearly, she was upset, and I was pretty sure I knew why.

Catching up to her, I prompted, "Do you remember when I thought Jamie wanted to be with Sofia?"

"Yeah ..."

"I'd not only convinced myself that Jamie loved her, but that he was meant to be with her instead of me." I kicked a pebble with the toe of my shoe and watched it roll into the underbrush. "That she was meant to be his queen.

"Even though I loved Doon with every fiber of my being, I refused to consider the possibility of staying. I couldn't stand the thought of living the rest of my life pining after Jamie and watching him with someone else."

"Thanks for the stroll down memory lane. We should go." Kenna picked up her pace.

The stretch of her long legs forced me to jog to keep up with her. "Stop, okay?"

She paused and turned toward me, gripping the enormous spell book to her chest like a shield.

"Duncan and Ana are friends. That's it."

"Vee, I don't care. That oaf can do whatever he wants with whomever he wants."

Before she spun on her heel and stalked away, I caught a shimmer in her eyes. She was using Duncan's relationship with Ana to convince herself she didn't care. But I knew better. We shared a brain, after all.

CHAPTER 19

Mackenna

Doing my best human Ping-Pong ball impersonation, I volleyed between Vee and Fiona, deciphering the big bad book of spells in my rooms, and the bridal shower preparations heavily underway in Vee's chambers. Emily and Analisa were decorating Vee's sitting room in pink hearts of all shapes and sizes. Since Doon, despite all its progressiveness, was still apart from the modern world, there was no logical place to hold a bachelorette party that wouldn't send the older citizens into culture shock, no matter how tame. Vee's chambers seemed the most private place to party.

At the end of the room near the fireplace sat a small tin tub in front of a comfy wingback chair. Vee had learned that the washing of the bride's feet was an ancient Scottish wedding tradition. Giving the custom our own spin, the adjacent table held everything needed for mani-pedis, including nine different shades of nail polish.

A mirrored ball hung from the center of the room, waiting for the sun to go down. Apparently, Emily had it custom made by the local glass cutter. I'd no doubt that by next market day there'd be a dozen more for sale … a royal disco ball for every home, just in time for the end of the world.

"Tell Queen Veronica we're nearly done." Emily finished wrapping a heart garland around a pillar and then stepped back to survey her handiwork with a wide smile. In the brief time I'd known the girl, this was the happiest I'd ever seen her.

Analisa was her same shifty self. Twice she snuck away to do who-knew-what with who-knew-whom. I could only guess that Duncan was involved, but I refused to speculate as to what they actually did when they were together. My heart couldn't handle the truth.

Walking back to my own rooms, I nodded at Eòran as I passed. Mutton Chops was growing on me. He was loyal to a fault and never asked questions above his pay grade. Beyond that, he would die to protect his Midwestern Queen. That kind of devotion was rare.

As I stepped inside, Vee motioned me to the table. "Fiona found it." She pointed to the Pictish symbol on the open page of the spell book. Above the graphic, the word *LIMBUS* was written in slanting script.

Next to Vee, Fiona was bent over the spell-breaker book, writing furiously. She didn't even look up as Vee continued. "According to the description in the spell book, this is the same limbus that plagued King Angus just before the miracle. It was dormant, and something the witch did reactivated it."

The memory of Addie as I'd last seen her, shriveled and cackling, caused goose pimples to crawl across my skin. "So this was like her getting the last laugh?"

Vee frowned. "Hopefully. You said she was gone when you returned to the cottage — so as much as we want to assume she's just a powerless old woman, we can't be sure."

Although she didn't mean to accuse me, guilt settled squarely on my shoulders. "It never even occurred to me to figure out where she went. I was just glad she was gone."

"No one's blaming you, Ken. My point is when it comes to Addie, we can't be sure of anything."

"Aye." Fiona spoke and we both refocused on her. "I'm done with the translation. It seems the limbus will go inta a suspended state like a hibernation if the witch who cast the spell dies. But anyone from that bloodline can reactivate it."

Vee nodded. "So that explains what happened at the Miracle. One of Addie's sisters must've cast the spell. When she died, it went dormant."

"Aye, until Adelaide restarted it."

There was a dot I was failing to connect. "But if we don't know where Addie is, how do we stop the limbus now?"

Pointing to the text under the spell-breaker book, Fiona replied, "By destroying the original spell for good. All we need is an axe blessed by God and tested in righteous battle."

"Is that all?" She might as well have said we needed a golden unicorn horn from over the rainbow.

Vee cast her a sly glance. "I don't suppose Doon just happens to have one lying around?"

"Well, if my gram is to be believed, tucked away somewhere in the catacombs under the castle is the Arm o' the Bruce."

While I didn't doubt there were tons of body parts in the MacCrae catacombs, and I was pretty sure she didn't mean a literal arm, I couldn't help but crack wise. "What about the rest of Bruce?"

Fiona rolled her eyes and Vee grimaced apologetically as the former explained, "The Arm o' the Bruce is the battle axe of the great king of Scotland, Robert the Bruce. He used it in Scotland's war of independence from England."

"And it's just laying around in the castle basement?"

She nodded. "Yea, that and other things, if the stories are true."

Before Vee could question her to specify what "other things," shouts sounded from the courtyard. Judging from the sheer volume of noise, the entire kingdom had their panties in a twist about something.

Vee leapt to her feet and raced to the door. She flung it open and barely escaped the knock of Eòran's knuckles against her forehead. As Vee jerked back, Mutton Chops stilled his hand and sputtered apologies.

"What's going on, Eòran?"

"There's a group of lads requesting an audience, m'lady."

"With me?" Her eyes grew huge, no doubt picturing the mobs that had been occasionally gathering to oppose her rule.

"Nay, with Miss Fiona."

Confirming this news, I heard the unmistakable voices of Jamie and Duncan calling to Fiona, followed by uproarious laughter.

Suddenly, Fiona shoved me to the side. "Those MacCrae brothers better not have laid a finger on my fiancé!" Shouldering Vee out of the way, the petite girl charged into the hall muttering, "Princes or no', I will end them."

Lured by the commotion, Emily and Analisa stepped from Vee's suite, and the four of us tripped down the stairs in Fiona's wake. At the bottom of the tower, we curved right and out a side door into the rowdy courtyard.

The diminutive bride-to-be faced down several dozen guys. Doonians who worked at the castle and locals from the village clustered around the fringes watching the spectacle unfold.

The boisterous crowd grew expectantly quiet as they faced us with wide grins and subdued chuckles. I recognized the oldest Rosetti boy along with some of his brothers as they exchanged conspiratorial glances with the princes. After a moment, the sea parted to reveal a black-and-white chicken man hunched over with a bushel of rocks on his back. Shirtless, his entire body was covered with an oozing dark substance and a haphazard layer of downy white feathers. Straining under the weight of his burden, the Chicken Man turned doleful pale blue eyes our direction and moaned, "Give us a kiss, Fee."

Fiona planted her hands on her hips. "Over my dead body, Fergus Lockhart."

The male population of the crowd — presumably the same ones responsible for Fergus's current state — howled in response. Fiona glared at the group before turning her fury back to her fiancé. "You're nearly twice the size of most o' these lads. How could you let them do this ta you?"

The giant seemed to wither under her reproachful stare. "Don't be like that. The lads are just havin' a bit o' fun."

"I can see that."

Behind Fergus, jovial whispers were exchanged along with some coins. A dark jug was being passed around. As far as bachelor celebrations went, Doon seemed to have its share of gambling and booze — and we'd been worried about our little party.

Fergus shifted the basket of rocks and rolled his massive shoulders back. From the way he strained, I guessed he'd been doubled over the whole way from the village. "Now, about that kiss."

In regards to his request, Fiona and Fergus seemed to be at an impasse. She shook her head back and forth as he continued to silently implore her to end his misery. Taking pity on the big Chicken Man, I shouted, "Just kiss him already."

Vee echoed the sentiment, and soon the entire crowd was chanting "Kiss! Kiss! Kiss!"

With a huff, Fiona stepped forward. Fergus had the sense to look contrite as she hastily touched her lips to his cheek. When she retreated, her mouth was coated with black grime and sprouting a feather. More laughter ensued as she swiped at her lips.

Several of the guys helped to rid Fergus of the basket — it was saying something that it took half a dozen men to lift it. With a grateful sigh, Fergus straightened up.

Fiona pointed a tiny finger at Jamie and Duncan. "I'm holding the two of you personally responsible. When next I see my betrothed, he better be as pink as the day he came inta this world, or I'm going to treacle and feather you."

"No worries, Fiona," Jamie said between bursts of laugher. "Our next stop is Loch Doon."

"We'll see tha — " Duncan clutched his brother's arm in an attempt to straighten up enough to talk. "We'll see — that he gets washed up — right proper."

"You better." With those words, Fiona pivoted on her heels and charged back into the castle. As soon as she left, the crowd began to disperse. Emily and several other girls who'd been invited to the bachelorette party headed inside. Fergus went the opposite way — lamenting something about the temperature of the lake — with most of the instigators cheerfully following.

Jamie sauntered over to Vee, grinning smoothly as he said, "Give us a kiss, my queen." Vee giggled, and a second later they were enacting the sequel to their gum commercial.

Not eager to witness another marathon make-out session, I turned to go when large hands grabbed my waist. Duncan spun me around so that I was pressed against him. He stared down at me with his wide, lopsided smile and murmured, "We're supposed to be in love, you and I."

Although I couldn't see her, I could sense Analisa lurking

around the fringes. She was probably waiting out the necessary PDA to set up another clandestine meeting with my fake boyfriend.

Suddenly, it all felt like too much. Double lives, covert trips to the witches' epicenter of evil, trying to save a world that didn't know it was on the brink of extinction — the lies were everywhere. Actress or not, how in the midst of everything going on could I just cut loose and have a good time? How could Duncan?

Careful not to make a scene, I whispered, "How can you just act like everything is normal? I'm busting my butt to try and save your kingdom and you're busy — what, hazing Fergus? Do you even care?"

His smile vanished. "I care, Mackenna. Probably more than ye can even comprehend. But the minute I start acting like my world is coming to an end is the moment our enemy wins. I recently realized that if I were to die, I would have two major regrets. One of them is not truly living each and every moment when I had the chance."

"What's the other?"

The tips of his fingers brushed my hair as they tucked a wayward curl behind my ear. "I'll tell ye that after you save Doon." He closed the distance between us to press his warm, cidery lips briefly to mine. "In the meantime, do what you can, and when you canna do any more, pause to honor the people in your life that make it worth living." Then he let me go to rejoin his merry band of troublemakers.

Duncan was right. I was eighteen and might only have a week or two left. Tonight, I couldn't stop the limbus, but I could be present with the people I cared about. I could celebrate their lives and my own while I had the chance.

As I climbed the stairs to the turret, I hummed along to the

Broadway radio in my head. Kim and Conrad were right, I had a lot of living to do. I wouldn't hide in a corner wasting what little time I might have left.

Foot washing, mani-pedis, and presents out of the way, the evening transitioned from wedding shower to bachelorette party. We'd danced half the night away, the fairest single ladies in the land undulating under the improvised disco ball to music from the tiny speaker of Vee's solar-charged iPhone. In the wee hours of the morning, Jamie crashed the party, instantly turning it from a girl-power rave into prom night.

Analisa ducked out as soon as our little soiree turned coed but I refused to think about where she'd gone. The rest of the guests then left in clusters, with Gabriella Rosetti bringing up the rear. Which left me to assume cleanup duty with Fiona while Vee and Jamie slow danced in the corner. Not that I was jealous or anything — Vee deserved to be with the one she loved.

Fiona wiggled her violet fingernails at me. "I quite fancy this Twilight Orchid." Her voice had that overly loud, post-clubbing quality. Even with our primitive resources, she'd partied like a twenty-first century rock star. After the Chicken Man hijinks and her mom's hijacking of the wedding plans, the girl deserved to blow off a little steam.

I cleared the manicure station, trashing little blobs of wool and placing bottles of polish in a small basket. About halfway through my task, Duncan, shouting from somewhere outside the tower, shattered the early morning calm. He called my name at the top of his lungs.

Everyone froze. When he called out again, Fiona made a *tsking* sound and she crossed to the window overlooking the courtyard. "Not again."

Jamie followed, crowding the windowsill so that my only view was the back of his head. "I warned him about knowing his limit. He clearly didna listen."

Vee, who'd started nervously tidying up her surroundings, looked everywhere but at me as she added, "Does he ever?"

The way they spoke — it was like Duncan was some lost cause in need of an intervention, not a caring, loyal prince who'd do just about anything for anyone. I raised myself up on tiptoe, but it wasn't enough to see out. "Is he okay?"

Jamie turned away from the window, his expression guarded. "He's fine. Just soused is all."

As in drunk? To prove his brother's point, Duncan bellowed my name again. With Jamie gone, I rushed forward. Fiona moved out of the way, and I looked down to see Duncan standing in the middle of the courtyard with his face lifted toward the sky.

Scotland's legal drinking age was eighteen. And in Doon, which was more medieval than modern, to drink one only needed to be "of age" ... Whatever that meant. Even though Duncan could legally drink by both standards, I knew he didn't approve of drunkenness. At least, the boy I used to know didn't.

While I watched, he threw his head back and yelled my name with so much force that he was thrown off balance. After staggering a couple of steps, he recovered and bellowed again.

I'd seen enough. Turning back, I frowned at my friends. "Has he done this before? Gotten drunk and shouted some girl's name at the top of his lungs?"

Fiona shrugged. "Once or twice. But the last time was weeks ago, so we thought the worst was over."

"And not some random girl's name." Vee paused to look at me apologetically. "Just yours."

"Mackenna!"

"My brother's an idiot," Jamie grumbled to himself before addressing Vee. "I'll go talk some sense inta him."

"No. I should go." I hurried to beat Jamie to the door, but my best friend stepped in my path.

Vee's large eyes shone with pity. "I don't think that's the best idea. Why don't you let Jamie — "

"But he's not asking for Jamie, is he? This is my mess to fix — I'll go."

As I passed Jamie, he grabbed my arm. "Is that what my brother is to you, a mess? This is all your doing, ye know. He's not the same boy you abandoned on the bridge. Have ye not figured that out yet?"

"Jamie!"

Vee's reprimand briefly redirected his anger toward her. "Well, 'tis the truth, and someone should tell it to her." And then back to me. "You broke his heart."

"I know."

It was all I could think of to say. Ever since I'd experienced my first Calling delusion with Duncan in Chicago, a million thoughts had run through my head, from excuses to apologies. But in that moment words failed to convey the depths of my regret. So rather than answer, I stared at Jamie MacCrae's hand until he let go. Then I strode out the door to face my music.

chapter 20

Mackenna

I descended the stairs with my heart thrumming in my ears. My chest felt like it had been trampled by giants. As I stepped into the courtyard to face the consequence of my actions, the full weight of my guilt settled in an ache above my eyes.

Duncan stood with his back to me in the middle of the torch-lit courtyard. As I approached he flung his arms wide and bellowed my name to the heavens. Swaying ever so slightly, he continued to face the stars, waiting for answers. Finally, he dropped his head in resignation and my heart could take no more.

"I'm here."

He spun around, his torso moving more loosely and quickly than his legs so that he had to stagger to remain upright. After pausing for a moment to ensure his balance would hold, he blinked at me as if he didn't trust his own eyes. "'Tis really you?"

"In the flesh."

"An' what beautiful flesh it is." He lurched toward me, and I rushed forward to intercept him before he fell down. His large hands pawed at my face while I struggled to get his arm around my shoulder for support. "You came back. I never stopped looking for ye."

"I'm here." There was no way I'd be able to keep him upright if he stumbled again. In the absence of benches, I pointed to the wide steps leading to the formal entrance of Castle MacCrae. "How about we go sit on the steps over there?"

"Aye." Duncan staggered across the courtyard, his momentum propelling me along with him. A foot from our destination, we went sprawling. One moment I was careering toward the stone steps, the next I was lying on top of the prince of my dreams in a tangle of arms and legs.

For a moment we stared at one another in surprise. Pressed against his chest, I could feel his heart beating out an adrenaline-fueled rhythm that matched mine. It was like that moment in a movie where the action morphs into slow motion.

Duncan lifted his head, his perfect lips parting in a silent invitation. Without consciously deciding what to do next, my mouth answered. The moment our lips touched the universe unraveled and re-formed so that it revolved around our kiss. Nothing else existed or mattered.

Gradually, my consciousness extended outward — his tongue moving in counter-rhythm to mine; his hands reacquainting themselves with the contours of my back and neck; to the small noise he made as he pulled me closer.

His mouth tasted sharp yet spicy, like ale and desperation. Clasping me in an impossibly tight bear hug, Duncan wrapped his solid legs around mine and rolled us in unison so that I was trapped beneath him. The freezing stairs dug into my back as he crushed me in a good way. His mouth moved to blanket my neck in sloppy, reckless kisses. He was drunk and I craved his touch — but how far would I let this go?

If the tables were turned, Duncan would never take advantage of me. He was not that kind of person. He was honorable and loyal and — suddenly this felt all wrong. I wanted him back, but not this way.

I couldn't help but feel in the sober light of day, this would be one more mistake to pile onto our long list of regrets.

"Stop." Lightly shoving, I pushed Duncan back enough to get his attention. His face darkened like he was waking from a dream — make that a nightmare, because he stared at me clearly horrified by his actions.

In one swift action, he rolled away. His momentum sent him crashing in the opposite direction and his shoulder smacked against the stone step. With a groan, he gingerly pulled himself to a sitting position and dropped his head into his hands.

"I'm so sorry, Mackenna," he moaned. "You have a boyfriend. Wretched, odious Wallace."

"Weston." I said numbly. Now that we'd separated, the night felt bitterly cold. My thin maxi dress, which was perfect for hours of dancing, offered no protection from the elements. "He lied. He's not my boyfriend."

"Have ye told that to him? He wanted you, Mackenna." Still leaning over his knees, his arm flew at me in a reckless gesture of emphasis. "I can tell when a lad fancies a lass."

Since we were getting to the truth of our relationships, I hesitantly asked, "The same way you fancy Analisa?"

His head bobbed in his hands. "Ana and I meet in secret. I tell her things I canna tell you."

The alcohol hindered his discretion; he wasn't intentionally trying to wound me. But his confession still hurt like crazy. "What kind of things?"

Angling his face to look at me, he said gravely, "I caused the limbus."

"What? How—"

"Over you. I wished for you ta come to Doon. I asked the Protector to bring you back to me. And I kept begging him for you, even after it was clear we weren't meant to be together."

He straightened up so that once again I could see only his shadowy profile. "Back in the barn, after I saved you—you said in some cultures we'd be bound for life. But the truth is we were bound long before that. I am bound to you ... and I canna ever be free, even if I wished it with all my might. And now my kingdom suffers for my weakness."

Despite his mixed signals, Duncan wished to be rid of me. Although I had suspected as much, to hear him confess it was more than I could endure. An invisible vise gripped my chest, making it difficult to breathe. My eyes started to sting. I wanted to run away, but I felt I had a responsibility to ease the mind of the guilt-ridden boy next to me.

Angling my body toward his until our knees brushed, I said, "The limbus isn't your fault. Things will look better in the morning. I promise."

He lurched toward me, bracing his hand on my shoulder to stop himself just before we collided. "You *promise*? You, Mackenna Reid, break your promises—just like you break hearts." His smooth, velvet brown eyes searched my face. "Why did ye leave me?"

Unable to bear his scrutiny a moment longer, I focused on the lights of the village in the distance. "Remember how when you saw me perform in Chicago you knew I belonged there?"

"Aye." He rested his head on my shoulder and snuggled close.

"You belong in Doon. This is where you're supposed to be— helping villagers mend fences and repair barns and watching out for your brother. You love Doon."

"Tha' I do."

"My turn," I said, savoring the feel of Duncan's face burrowed into my neck. "How come you didn't tell me you were Finn?"

After a weighty pause, his breath hitched as he let out a soft snore. Disappointment burned in my chest. I reclined against the stairs with Duncan curled against my side, sound asleep. Staring at the predawn light washing away the stars, I tried not to wonder how much of Duncan's conversation had been the ale talking ... And how much had been the truth.

One-hundred and seventeen steps — I paused at the top of the tower to knock on the heavy wooden door before letting myself in. Since my return to Doon, this was the first occasion I'd had to visit Duncan in his chambers. Afternoon sunlight cut through his floor-to-ceiling window, reminding me how much his rooms felt like home. Whenever I imagined living in Doon, this was the place I pictured inhabiting.

Duncan came from the bedroom, barefoot but otherwise dressed. In one hand he held a pair of riding boots. His other hand was pressed to his temple, shielding his squinting eyes from the light. Considering that I'd only recently crawled from bed myself — and I'd gone to sleep somberly sober — I was impressed he was even up. He had to be harboring one doozy of a hangover.

When he saw it was I who'd knocked, he frowned. "What are ye doing here?"

I shrugged, suddenly unsure of the wisdom of my decision. "Checking on you."

Although I knew it would be better to keep a deliberate distance, like a self-imposed restraining order, something in my heart needed reassurance that he was — or would be — okay.

Duncan sat down in one of the high-backed chairs with a wince. "Jamie already beat you to it. He stood over my bed ringing a bloody cow bell."

"Oh!"

He moaned in agreement. "Apparently, I got quite inebriated last night. It took four o' my brother's men to carry me up to my chambers."

I remembered. Shortly after Duncan fell asleep, Jamie appeared with four big Scotsmen. Under Jamie's direction, they hoisted the passed-out prince off of me. With no more than a good night, they headed in one direction while I slunk off the other way. "What do you remember?"

"Having pints at Rosetti's Tavern and then nothing ... until the cow bell. According to Jamie, I was passed out in the courtyard, and that's where he and his men came upon me."

"That's it?"

"Aye." He began pulling on his boots. "Did you hear any different?"

"Just that you were feeling a little melancholy." I pulled a wrapped present from my pocket.

He paused briefly. "Heard ... or did we happen to run inta each other last night? If we did, you shouldna heed anything I might've said, as I didn't mean it."

My instincts told me otherwise. I believed his confession on those cold stone steps. Duncan still resented me for breaking his heart and not allowing him to move on. He was still bound to the selfish shrew who'd ruined his life — which sucked for him.

While there were parts about the previous night I was glad he couldn't recall — like our make-out session — I was bummed he wouldn't remember what I said about Weston. No matter how many times I tried to set the record straight about me and Wes, the universe seemed determined to get in the way.

He returned to his boots with a grunt. "I don't condone drunkenness. I'm mightily sorry for whatever grief I might've caused due to my lack of judgment."

As he straightened up, I asked, "Where are you going?"

He stood and walked around me to retrieve his duffel bag. "There's been a development with the limbus. One o' the outlying farms has been swallowed up. It should've been evacuated, but we canna find the farmer or his wife."

"Oh."

Nodding to the gift, he asked, "What's that?"

"Nothing. I mean, just a little something ... to cheer you up." He extended his hand and I placed the present in his palm, careful to avoid direct contact. "You can open it when you return."

He flipped it over in his hands. "I've a moment now." Edging open the waxed paper, he stared at the dried starfish inside.

"So you could keep a little piece of the tidal pool with you," I explained. "I named her Maureen II."

Duncan favored me with a pained smile that made his eyes glisten. "Maureen means 'star of the sea.' It was my ma's name."

A lump lodged in my throat, making it difficult to do more than nod. I watched as Duncan crossed to his bookshelf and placed Maureen II next to his prized first editions of Shakespeare and Dickens. Then he returned to capture my hand. "Thank you," he murmured.

Never breaking eye contact, he bent over my hand and raised it to his mouth. The minute his lips touched my skin, his eyelids closed. Waves of heat radiated from his kiss to warm my whole body. After what seemed like an eternity, he let go with a sigh.

Now or never, Kenna. Butterflies started an impromptu kick line in my stomach as I cleared my throat. Duncan's eyes opened to regard me curiously as I sputtered, "I — uh, I never apologized for, you know, leaving you on the bridge. I'm sorry."

His body stiffened, and the emotion drained from his face until it was a stony mask. With cool detachment, he replied, "I know you are."

He grabbed his leather saddle bag. "Thank you again for the present. I'm late. Please forgive me for taking my leave. I trust ye can show yourself out." Then he was gone.

I stood in the entryway, listening to his footsteps on the stairs until the world fell silent. As I crossed to the door, a painting on the wall drew my attention. I remembered the oil color which I'd christened "Landscape with Bovine" from my very first trip to Duncan's rooms. I'd dismissed the pastoral scene as boring. What I'd failed to comprehend before now leapt out at me.

Behind the grazing cows and off to one side, a giant beanstalk ascended into the clouds. In the top corner, nearly off the canvas, was a pair of legs in mid-climb. This deceptively peaceful picture hinted at the difference between a cow and a bean for those who had eyes to see. And clearly I hadn't. It was too late to embrace an adventure with a handsome prince in a secret kingdom. I'd wasted my chance. The best thing I could do for Duncan now would be to save Doon, and then return to my boring, cow-filled world with as little collateral damage as possible.

CHAPTER 21

Mackenna

After the encounter with Duncan, I wandered aimlessly through the royal gardens. Eventually, I ended up under the wide stone arch. Although I hadn't consciously directed my footsteps, I realized it had been my destination all the same.

This was the site of our epic make-out session during my last visit. It was here where my heart had admitted what my head obstinately denied — that I was in love with a prince from a different world. Under this very arch, I'd voiced my concerns about staying.

"What if you experience a Calling? Then I'd be stuck here — "

"Shhh." Duncan's fingertip had brushed my lips. *"If you stay, I'll give you my heart and never ask for it back."*

I shook my head to clear the ghosts.

Duncan obviously remembered our childhood connection — little allusions he'd made during our previous time together made perfect sense now. With a simple confession, he could have rewritten our history. Why hadn't he told me the truth before it was too late?

A sob hitched in my throat. I didn't even realize I was crying until my hand came away from my face wet. Using my sleeve like a tissue, I blotted my leaky eyes.

For Duncan and me, there was no going back to before — I understood that now. Last night he'd confessed that we weren't meant to be together. Despite the twisted past that entangled us, he was trying to move on with Ana. The sooner I got out of his way, the better.

"There you are." Vee's voice preceded her down the path. I took one last swipe at my eyes and then turned around to face her with a soggy smile.

She pulled up short and inspected me with a critical eye. "Uh-oh. What's going on?"

I dug right down to the bottom of my soul … and stuffed my messy emotions away. "Nothing."

Closing the distance between us, she said conversationally, "I'm the queen, you know. One word and I can have whoever made you cry thrown in the stockade."

That would go over well — having her boyfriend's brother arrested. Besides, I was the one in the wrong. Even though Duncan had withheld critical information about our past, I hadn't remembered him — among other transgressions. "Does Doon even have stockades?"

She shrugged. "I'll have some built."

In silent agreement, we started strolling away from the arch toward the lake. After a couple dozen unhurried steps, Vee asked, "So is this about Duncan?"

"Like you didn't know that already?"

"I don't know the specifics. What happened?"

Rather than give her a straight answer, I shrugged off the question. "Nothing worth talking about. Are you ready to search the catacombs?"

She raised an eyebrow to indicate she'd caught my change of subject. "Jamie asked me not to go without a guide."

"What?" I stopped in my tracks, which prompted her to turn and face me. "You told him?"

"Chill!" She backtracked a couple of steps as she spoke so that she could keep her voice low. "I didn't tell him about the cottage or the books. Just that the tunnels under the castle were the one place we hadn't looked for answers."

"And?"

"And he agreed that it was a good idea. But apparently the catacombs are like a labyrinth, miles of tunnels and full of dead ends. They were created as secret passages for warfare. But since the Miracle, hardly anyone even goes down there."

Great. We needed to find a needle of an axe in a dusty, old abandoned maze of a haystack probably riddled with rats and spiders. Just let me write that on my bucket list — right below destroying the limbus and putting an alternate dimension between me and Duncan.

"He promised we'd figure it out as soon as he got back."

For a moment, I forgot what we were talking about. "Figure what out?"

"The catacombs ... What did you think we were talking about?"

Vee squinted at me — not her usual *I'm peering into your mind* squint but full on nearsighted old lady mistaking a rabid rodent for a Chihuahua. The pinched expression was an unfamiliar one.

"You okay?"

She lifted her hand to her brow, shielding herself from the slanting light of the afternoon sun. "Just missing my sunglasses. The sun's giving me a headache."

I chuckled. "I totally see an opportunity to extend the

Queen Vee fashion line. Panes of colored glass and wire frames. Very steampunk chic!"

My bestie smirked on top of the squint so that her eyes disappeared altogether. "That's not a half-bad idea."

"Take it," I quipped as I looped my arm through hers and steered us down a narrow offshoot of the main path heading away from the sun. "As long as I get half the profits."

When she stepped into the shade the tension melted away, allowing her face to open up. "Much better," she sighed. "So ... you still haven't told me what's going on with you."

I dropped her arm and picked up my pace. Vee followed. Waiting me out was one of her specialties, along with figuring out Doonian curses and executing the perfect handspring. After a couple dozen steps, I recognized the setting from my most recent garden encounter with Duncan. "Do you remember the imaginary friend I had when I was little?"

"How could I forget Finn?" Her forehead puckered, and I knew she was puzzling out what he had to do with my earlier waterworks.

"Turns out he was no six-foot, three-and-one-half-inch-tall pooka."

"A six-footed what?"

"A *pooka*, as in Harvey the imaginary rabbit ... Never mind. I called him Finn because he had a long name I could never remember." I paused, my words made difficult by the sinking feeling in my stomach. "I'm pretty sure his full name was Duncan Rhys *Finnean* MacCrae."

Vee stopped in her tracks to blink at me. "Duncan *appeared* to you when you were little?"

I nodded. "Every summer for six years."

Vee pointed to the lone bench in the enclosure. "Sit!" She

waited for me to comply and then sat beside me taking my hand in hers. "How come you didn't tell me?"

"I didn't remember until recently — well, when I was in Chicago. It all came back in a rush. Finn and Duncan and all the crazy dreams that — "

"What dreams?" Vee gripped my fingers painfully. When I yelped, she eased off, but just slightly. "Sorry — you never mentioned you were having any dreams."

I shrugged. "Throughout high school and then right before we left for Scotland. They weren't as clear as what you had with Jamie and I never saw a face, just a shadow — so I didn't really think much about them. Until Chicago, when Phantom Duncan started appearing in my day-to-day life like something from a Noel Coward play."

Vee regarded me with equal parts shock and amazement as she gently touched my arm. "You and Duncan have a Calling."

"It's worse than that. I'm pretty sure he remembers the time we shared as children. When you and I first stumbled into Doon, I had no clue — but I think he did. Looking back, he dropped all kinds of cryptic hints about our past. There were times he'd look at me so expectantly, as if he were waiting for me to have a revelation. But he never actually said anything. Why didn't he just tell me?"

I hunched forward, covering my face with my hands. Vee ran a soothing hand up and down my back, just as she had when I'd learned about my aunt's death. Although I'd never told anyone, I'd been mourning two losses ... because in losing Gracie I'd also lost my summers with Finn.

Vee continued to rub my back. "What did Duncan say when you asked him about it?" When I didn't answer, she said, "Kenna, you have to talk to him. Before it's too late."

"It's already too late," I moaned.

"Do you still love him?"

"Of course. I love him so much that every molecule in my body aches. But I blew my chance."

"Listen to me. You two share a divine gift. You're meant to be. Like Elizabeth Bennett and Mr. Darcy. Their relationship started out rocky, and they had to overcome some huge obstacles, like his pride and her prejudice, but it was worth it in the end."

At least she hadn't said Romeo and Juliet. "No. We've got too much baggage. He's trying to move on with Analisa and I've moved on with Wes —"

Her hand stilled as she said, "That's total bull. You don't care about Weston."

"Fine. I'm trying to move on without Duncan. So that he can be happy. He deserves that."

"What about you Kenna? What do you deserve?"

Nothing…

As soon as the thought sounded in my head, my resolve crumbled into great heaving sobs. A well of misery burst forth. As much as I wanted to blame Duncan for not speaking up about Finn, it was my mistakes that had cost us everything. It was all my fault. And the price of those selfish actions was any future involving my happily ever after.

Eventually, Vee led me back to my room and tucked me into bed. My throat ached something fierce, but I was too exhausted to ask for a glass of water. Grateful for the reprieve from my own pity party, I pulled the duvet over my throbbing head, curled into a ball, and willed sleep to suck me into oblivion.

CHAPTER 22

Veronica

The girl slept like the dead. If Kenna didn't answer my knocks in the next thirty seconds, I was going to have to hunt down Eóran and steal his keys. I knew from experience that denying one's true feelings was exhausting work, but it was nearly ten o'clock in the morning, and we had a kingdom to save. I raised my fist and hit the wood in quick succession.

While I was stunned that her imaginary friend, Finn, was actually Duncan, it didn't take a psychic to read the underlying currents of tension between them. It was almost painful to be in the same room with their fake smiles and clandestine glances. But Tristan and Isolde they were not — at least not if I had anything to say about it.

Tapping my foot, I counted to ten, and just as I turned to walk away, I heard footsteps and muttering from within.

The door flew open to reveal my sleep-mussed, squinty-eyed best friend. "What in the — "

"Get dressed. I found a guide for the catacombs." I pushed into the room and shut the door behind me.

"Okay, *Your Bossiness*, but not before my coffee."

"I've already sent for it." I marched into her bedroom in search of something sensible for her to wear while traversing subterranean tunnels, and stopped cold. "How do you find anything in this mess?" Articles of clothing covered every surface. The dress she'd worn the night before sat crumpled in a ball at the end of the bed.

Kenna shuffled into the room, and after a wide yawn answered, "I have a system."

"Oh yeah?" I arched a brow. "Then where might one find the leggings and tunic I had sent to you?"

"Oh, that ..." She wandered around the room kicking piles of cloths. "Oh! I've been looking for these!" She held out a pair of pink granny panties with Thursday written in glitter across the front.

Ignoring her antics, I walked over to the open wardrobe and searched through a multitude of autumn-colored maxi dresses until I found the forest green and brown outfit I was seeking pushed into the corner.

When I held it out, she took it and eyeballed my royal blue belted tunic and charcoal leggings tucked into sleek, knee-high black boots. "Next time we're dressing like Robin Hood's merry band, I'm going to need some of those boots."

"These were custom made for me." I pointed my toe to show off my new footwear. "The process takes almost a month from start to finish. Just say the word, and I'll take you to the cobbler for a fitting."

Silence.

Kenna pulled her PJ bottoms off, and I went back to straightening, trying not to read anything into her lack of response. Whether to stay or go was her decision, but that didn't mean I'd roll over and play dead either. A little BFF guidance was in order — when she was ready to hear it. I gathered the stack of folded clothes and reminded myself to fight one battle at a time.

"So who's our guide?" Kenna asked as she slipped the tunic over her head, the fabric muffling her words. "And please don't say the Crypt Keeper."

Tales from the Crypt DVDs, chocolate-covered Oreos, and my rainbow mani-pedi kit had been sleepover staples throughout middle school. Ironically, our guide wasn't too far off from the corpse-like Crypt Keeper puppet. "It's Gideon."

I placed the clothes in the dresser, closed the drawer, and turned to see Kenna frozen with one leg in her pants. "The maniac who accused us of witchcraft, murdered his own men, and tried to frame me for it? That Gideon?" Like a music box wound too tight, her voice grew higher and faster with every word.

"Gideon was under Addie's spell, Ken. He didn't know what he was doing." I sank into an overstuffed chair and massaged my throbbing temples. Just thinking about what Addie's spell did to the poor man had nausea rolling through my gut. "Have you seen him since you've been back?"

Kenna shook her head and pulled her leggings the rest of the way on.

"He looks horrible. Like a cancer patient or something." I closed my eyes and leaned my head back. "He's so remorseful, he's constantly trying to help me. To prove that he's not evil."

"Hey, are you okay?"

I squinted to find my friend leaning over me, her brow furrowed.

"Just tired, I think."

A knock echoed through the chamber.

"Coffee!" Kenna sang and rushed out of the room, looping her hair into a loose ponytail as she ran.

With a groan, I hoisted myself out of the chair and followed her into the sitting room. Caffeine sounded like heaven.

Kenna threw open the door to reveal princes bearing coffee and muffins. Damp-haired and smelling like soap, Jamie and Duncan filed into the room and set the breakfast items on a nearby table.

Kenna turned and shot me a scowl as she smoothed her hair. I shrugged. I didn't know the brothers were coming up here; they must have hijacked the maid bringing our breakfast.

Jamie stuffed half of a blueberry confection into his mouth and then said, "We're meetin' Gideon at the catacomb entrance in half an hour." The sight of my handsome prince dropping his veil of perfection never failed to warm my heart.

I hadn't told Jamie we were specifically searching for an axe blessed by God and tested in righteous battle. It was a tiny lie of omission, but if I told him, he'd want to see the source of my information. And I couldn't chance him being implicated for treason alongside me if the kingdom found out I'd traversed the forbidden ground to the witches' cottage.

"We'd best be going. We've a lot of ground to cover," Duncan said as he paused to examine the clock on the mantle. It was the first time he'd stopped moving since he'd entered the room.

Kenna stared at his back, her lips sloping into a frown.

The defeated set of her shoulders made me want to lock her and Duncan in a very small closet until they admitted their feelings to each other. For a brief moment, I considered it. There were a few dungeon cells I was familiar with that would work nicely … Or perhaps the hunting lodge … But knowing that stubborn pair, forcing them wouldn't do a bit of good.

Abandoning my daydreams, I took Kenna's arm and steered her toward the table. "We'll leave *after* our coffee."

"Ewww ... Why does it smell like Neptune's butt crack down here?" Kenna asked as we filed out of the staircase into a circular area with tunnels branching off in several directions. She yanked up the neckline of her tunic to cover her nose.

She was right. It smelled like a large fish had beached itself and died. Not a fan of seafood, the stench made me want to gag.

"Ye'll get used to it," Gideon commented as he cleared cobwebs from the mouth of a passageway with the broom he'd brought.

Jamie set one of his torches in a bracket at the bottom of the staircase. "'Tis rumored that these catacombs connect to a sea cave at the edge o' Doon. Duncan and I lost many hours searchin' for it when we were lads."

"That we did." Duncan, bringing up the rear, was the last to enter the room. "My brother must really love you, Veronica."

I met the younger prince's gaze. The torch he carried illuminated half of his puckish smirk, leaving the other side in deep shadow. "Why's that?"

"Duncan ..." Jamie warned, and as he turned I noticed his normally fluid movements were as jerky as a string-animated puppet.

"Oh, no reason," Duncan answered, but the glint of his eye told me I was about to find out. Abruptly, he poked his head down a passage, and let out a quick shout.

Jamie jolted and stumbled back, almost dropping his torch.

Grinning like a funhouse clown, Duncan's laughter reverberated around the room.

Kenna chuckled, but as soon as she realized she was sharing a joke with the younger prince, the smile dropped from her face and she began fiddling with the strings at the neckline of her tunic.

Jamie cursed under his breath. Tiny beads of sweat dotted

his forehead, and he was a whole shade paler than when we'd started down the stairs.

So my big, strong prince wasn't fearless after all. Ignoring his idiotic brother, I moved to Jamie's side.

He rubbed the back of his neck and gave me a rueful smile. "I hate this place."

Lacing my fingers through his, I bumped my shoulder against his bicep. "Don't worry, I'll protect you."

"Let's get moving." Gideon finished clearing the passage and retrieved his torch. The flames highlighted the tumorous growths on his skin and the cavernous hollows beneath his cheeks. My eyes jerked away from his ugliness as he continued. 'Tis purported there are hundreds o' miles o' tunnels, so we'll tour a small quadrant this morn' where I know some artifacts to be stashed."

I set my teeth and forced myself to meet his gaze, ashamed by my superficial revulsion. The witch was to blame, not this broken man who'd spent his life in service to the kingdom. "Thank you, Gideon. Please lead on."

His shoulders straightened with importance and he bobbed his head. "Aye, Yer Majesty. This way, please."

Hand in hand, Jamie and I followed Gideon into a darkness so deep it seemed to swallow our guide's light, cloaking him in shadow if we didn't stay right on his tail. The caverns carried an odd, almost reverent silence. The absence of sound, broken only by the echo of our footsteps, seemed intrusive. And unwelcome.

We reached a divide, and after a brief hesitation Gideon turned to the right. The tightness of the tunnel made it impossible to walk side by side. Jamie released my hand and gestured for me to precede him. But when I glanced back, I caught a furtive movement as he tucked something into his pocket. I turned fully and my lantern reflected on a white dash against the damp wall.

Not wanting to lose sight of Gideon, I kept walking, but asked, "What was that?"

"His security blanket." Duncan chuckled from behind us.

"Chalk," Jamie answered, his voice close and tight.

Relief mixed with admiration as I realized Jamie was marking our path. It wasn't that he didn't trust Gideon. This was just his way of keeping us all safe — even his dork of a brother.

"Jamie's been terrified of ol' Sawney Bean since we were boys," Duncan goaded.

Gideon took another turn, seemingly oblivious to the brother's bickering.

I heard the quick strike of the chalk as Jamie retorted, "Aye, and I'm goin' to fight him off with a wee piece o' chalk."

"Who's Sawney Bean?" Kenna asked.

"Sawney Bean captures humans and eats them alive." Duncan paused and then in a melodramatic tone whispered, "… one slow piece at a time. 'Tis rumored that between Sawney and his cannibal descendants, they've consumed thousands of Scotsmen. 'Tis why Jamie is afraid of the dark. Right, big brother?"

"Shut up." Jamie's reply held an iron edge as he marked another turn in the passage.

Despite Duncan's teasing, it was clear something had Jamie freaked — and it wasn't the Scottish Boogie Man. Was it the catacombs themselves or something more? Countless twists and turns later, I forgot all about Jamie's anxieties and began to battle my own. I was so disoriented, I felt like Alice following the white rabbit. Each tunnel took us deeper into the labyrinth until I knew even strategic chalk marks wouldn't help me find my way out.

We took a jog to the right, and the tunnel narrowed so much that the guys had to stoop to fit. Suddenly I became conscious of every breath. The very real fear that we could run out of oxygen dashed to the forefront of my thoughts. I was on the verge of hyperventilating when the tunnel opened up again. I rushed to follow Gideon into a large round chamber and sucked in a deep breath, relieved to note the air tasted cleaner here — or at least less like low tide on a hot day.

"This be the King's Cave." Gideon began to light torches around the room. Tunnels snaked off in every direction, but they were wider and taller than the one we'd come through. "'Tis where Robert the Bruce hid from his English enemies."

I exchanged a pointed glance with Kenna, and then turned back to our guide. "Where do all these passages lead?"

"Unlike the way we came in, these are antechambers. Each one is a dead end and, like this room, many contain historical items o' interest."

Walking the perimeter of the main chamber, I passed a full suit of armor, a set of archaic wooden tools, and other seemingly random items. In less than two minutes, I could see what we were searching for wasn't there. But a plan began to form in my mind.

Maybe I couldn't lock Kenna and Duncan in a closet together, but perhaps I could give them a bit of alone time. I addressed the group. "I suggest we split up in teams of two. We can each take a chamber. Jamie and I will start on the far left. Kenna and Duncan, you guys start on the right. Give a shout if you find anything interesting." I turned to see Gideon clearing the webs from the entrance I'd chosen.

"Gideon, do you mind exploring on your own?"

"Not at all, Yer Majesty."

I thanked him, took Jamie's hand, and we stepped into the darkness.

We followed the subtle curve of the hallway, our shadows lengthening ahead of us, and after a moment Jamie broke the silence. "I hate these caves. 'Tis too easy to get lost down here." He swiped at a low-hanging cobweb with the torch. "Duncan was right. But not about Sawney Bean. When I was a lad, I was afraid of the dark."

His steps slowed. I matched his pace and kept quiet, not daring to interrupt his rare moment of vulnerability.

"It was irrational, but I worried tha' if I couldna see what was tying me to the earth, I might float right off of it."

After a brief pause, Jamie went on in a soft tone. "My ma let me keep a candle burnin' in my room until I fell asleep ever' night." His fingers twitched in mine, his next words low. "But then my da found out."

He let out a heavy sigh and my breath caught at the shame etched on his face.

"My father was a firm believer that one should face their fears head on, so one evening he took me on a hunting trip deep into the forest, and when night fell, he left me there."

Not sure I understood correctly, I demanded, "He left you in the forest at night? By yourself?"

"Aye."

"How old were you?"

"Eleven and one half."

My heart thudded in my chest. "What did you do?"

"At first, I waited. Da left to gather fire wood, and even though I could no longer hear him rustlin' around, I figured he'd return shortly. But as the night deepened, something he'd said earlier came back to haunt me. He'd told me that as the future ruler o' Doon, even when I felt afraid, I dinna have the luxury of giving in to that fear. I had to learn to press on despite it."

We stopped by a stone bench and I faced my prince. The torch light cast the strong lines of his face in deep shadow, highlighting a furrow over his left brow. He looked anxious, like a part of him was still that scared little boy. I took the torch from his grasp, set it in a nearby wall bracket, and then tugged him down on the bench beside me.

"What happened then?" I prompted and took both his hands in mine.

He glanced away, his throat convulsing as he swallowed. "I slumped against a tree, hugged my knees to my chest, and cried like a babe. I'm no' sure how long I sat there rocking back and forth, listenin' to the animals scurry around me. But when I realized Da wasna comin' back, I wiped my tears and got up. At first I walked aimlessly, but then I found the first notch we'd made on a tree and everything he'd taught me about markin' my trail and followin' the clues in the sky clicked into place."

Jamie paused and stared down at our linked fingers before continuing. "'Twas nearly dawn when I found my way back to the castle. My da was waitin' for me at the gate. He said he knew I could do it. But he couldna hide the relief in his eyes." Jamie lifted his head and a corner of his mouth curled in an ironic smirk. "I no longer fear the dark."

I met his steady gaze and whispered, "What do you fear?"

He hesitated, the line of his jaw tensing before his dark eyes blazed into mine. "Not being the man my father believed I could be."

I realized then, an assumption I'd made that long-ago day we'd first arrived in Doon had been dead wrong — I'd seen how the king interacted with both his sons and presumed he favored Duncan. But it hadn't been derision I'd seen when he looked at his eldest son. It had been expectation.

I blinked the sudden tears off my lashes and gripped his

hands. "You, Jamie MacCrae, are all your father could've hoped for and more."

A slow grin spread across his face, bringing out the dimples in his cheeks. His smile faded as he reached out and brushed the moisture off my cheekbones. "What about you, my queen. What are you afraid of?"

I caught my lip between my teeth to keep from saying what popped into my head. That the thing I feared most was becoming like my messed up parents. That was a conversation for another day when we weren't sitting beneath thousands of tons of rock. So instead, I joked, "You mean besides wolf spiders and talking celery?"

His brows shot up on his forehead. "Er ... I can understand spiders, but why would ye think celery could talk?"

"Do you remember me telling you about cartoons?" I stood and pulled him to his feet.

"Aye, like moving drawings that tell a story." Jamie grabbed the torch and we continued down the passage. "I'd like to see that someday."

"Yeah ... well, when I was a kid there was this cartoon with talking vegetables. The characters danced around, drove cars, made dinner ... normal, everyday things, but they didn't have arms or legs. It completely defied logic." I shuddered. "And really creeped me out."

Jamie's laugh sounded amused and disturbed at the same time. "On second thought, perhaps I dinna want to see that."

We rounded a bend, and my hair stirred against my cheeks, blown by a breeze tinged with fresh air and foliage. "Do you smell that?"

"Aye." Jamie grasped my hand tighter and we rushed forward.

Until we hit a dead end.

Jamie raised the torch as we approached an intricate iron gate. The passage resumed on the other side, but when I pulled on the bars it held firm. I pressed my face against the chilled metal. What was the gate hiding? A valuable artifact? An exit?

"Did you hear something?" Jamie handed me the torch and walked a few steps back the way we came.

Standing on tiptoe, I strained to see farther inside. It appeared to open up again into a larger room, and there on the far wall my light reflected on rows of white lines — tally marks? But before I could figure it out, a shout sounded from the direction of the main cavern.

I turned and jogged to where Jamie stood alert. "That's Kenna." We both took off at a run. Visions of cave-dwelling celery monsters danced in my head as I hastily retraced my steps to the main grotto.

"Down here!" Kenna called again. "I found something cool!"

Gideon emerged from his tunnel and the three of us followed Kenna's voice down the far right passage. We rounded a corner and nearly bumped into Duncan's broad back. Kenna stood on his opposite side, grinning and pointing at a recessed alcove like a maniac. An axe was mounted in its center.

"Ye've found the ancient Arm o' the Bruce," Gideon panted.

Kenna turned, and our eyes locked. This was the artifact Fiona had instructed us to find. But not wanting to tip our hand, Kenna put on her best ditzy girl face and asked our guide, "What are those crazy-looking carvings on it?"

"The blade is covered in Pictish. I canna read tha'. But the writing on the handle is Gaelic." Gideon moved closer and tilted his head to read. "It says, 'Try, try again.'"

I'd heard the saying before, but had no clue it was Scottish in origin. "You're sure this is the battle axe of Robert the Bruce?" The handgrip was sturdy and well worn. The blade arched with a wicked-looking curve, and the counterbalance formed an equally lethal spike. I moved closer. It looked capable of breaking skulls or stone without discretion.

Gideon stepped to the side and bobbed his head. "Aye, my queen. 'Tis true."

I reached out to touch the handle, and the world spun away. In a flash, I was hovering over the packed ballroom of Castle MacCrae. In the center of the room, Fiona, in a shimmering white dress, danced in Fergus's arms. Drawing back, I flew away from the castle and over the trees. By the brilliant light of a full moon, the entirety of Doon stretched before me, and I could see the limbus encasing its borders. The hideous darkness no longer had a beginning or an end, but formed a complete circle of evil. At the mouth of the Brig o' Doon stood two girls, one red-haired, one brunette, in gowns of blue and silver. But as I moved closer, something about the bridge appeared off — a black carpet of petunias covered the stones, reaching toward the town of Alloway. The point of view flickered and I was beside Kenna, focused on an axe as she swung it above her head and then crashed the blade into the arch of a standing stone.

The tableau shattered, my vision returned, and I stumbled back against Jamie's chest.

"Hey, are you all right?" He clasped my upper arms.

"I'm fine." Actually, I was more than fine. We'd found the weapon that could destroy the limbus, and thanks to my divine revelation I knew we needed to do it during the second-day wedding ball. Unfortunately, we still had to figure out a way to get the axe out of the catacombs without raising suspicion. Navigating the labyrinth without Gideon's help would be impossible, but there was no way I could include him in our plans.

Jamie tipped my chin up and searched my face. "Are ye certain you're all right?"

"Sure. I just need to eat or something."

"'Tis gettin' late anyway," Gideon said. "Let's head back."

After snuffing the torches in the room, we all filed back into the entrance tunnel. My chest constricted tighter with every step we took away from the axe. What if I could never find my way back to the King's Cave? Was I making a grave mistake by leaving it behind?

If Robert the Bruce hid here, there had to be another way in. "Gideon, our passage ended in an iron gate. Do you know where it might lead?"

"Likely to a cave," he answered. "Many o' these old tunnels lead outside. They were meant as escape routes."

"Why is it locked?"

"The story goes that when the witch and her army o' undead attacked Doon, the caves were all gated and locked to keep them from gettin' in."

"Would anyone have a key?" I asked, trying to sound casual.

"Not that I'm aware."

If the gate led to an outside cave, we could come back in that way. But the entrance could be anywhere in Doon. As I tried to figure out a way to ask Gideon about its possible location without giving away my plan, I turned to check on the others and noticed Jamie worrying the leftover bit of chalk between his fingers.

Then, like a knock to the head, it hit me. The white hash marks, the burst of fresh air — I knew *exactly* what was on the other side of that gate, and how to reach it from the outside. Now all we needed was someone with a very specific and nefarious talent. Luckily, I knew just the thief for the job.

CHAPTER 23

Mackenna

The best plays always have a twist. You think the story is going one way, and then it does a one-eighty. Just when you've got the characters set in your mind — whom to root for and against — the all-powerful playwright mixes it up. You discover that giants can be the underdogs and witches the good guys. Individuals the main character trusts might betray them, or at the last moment an ally might come from an unlikely source.

"You want to do *what*?"

This had to be a case of a nightmare imitating art. Vee couldn't be standing in the middle of her sitting room informing me that she wanted to give Analisa the 411 on the Eldritch Limbus.

Except she was …

Vee dug her hands into her hips. "I know she's not your favorite person, Ken. But we need help to get the Arm o' the Bruce. And she has the right skill set."

"Favorite person? Try evil nemesis. She's the Ursula to my

Ariel; the Cha-Cha DiGregorio to my Sandy; the Elphaba to my Glinda."

"I thought Elphaba was the good one. Wasn't that the whole point — perspective?"

"Focus, Vee, we're talking about your harebrained scheme to spill the beans to Analisa, not musical theater." My bestie rolled her eyes, but I continued undeterred. "Speaking of *Wicked* — there's got to be another way to get that stupid axe."

"We don't have the luxury of another way." She advanced on me in one of those rare, stubborn moods that made her seem twice her normal size. "My kingdom is coming to an end. That trumps your petty rivalry, so suck it up and commit to Team Doon."

"I am committed," I grumbled.

"Good." Vee turned to straighten accent pillows rather than look at me. "Because she'll be here any minute."

Of course Vee had already sent for her. I should have guessed as much. For the sake of Doon, I could work with my archrival without having to change my opinion of her. "How much are you going to tell her?"

Vee reached under the couch and pulled out both the spell book and the spell-breaker book. She set them on the coffee table with a thump. "She already knows a lot of it because she helped with the paperwork when Duncan came to get you. And she knows the Calling is a cover story. Now I'm going to tell her the rest."

After an official-sounding knock, Eòran opened the door to announce our anticipated guest. He stepped aside and Analisa sauntered through the door like she was on the runway in Milan. She favored Eòran with a mischievous smile that caused old Mutton Chops to blush. She was smooth — I'd give her that.

But I'd expect no less from someone who made their livelihood by conning others.

She stopped in front of Vee with an amused demi-curtsey. "You called, Your Highness."

Instead of being offended by Ana's mockery, Vee accepted the teasing with a playful reprimand of her own. "What did I tell you about that? It's Vee."

Analisa tucked the long side of her asymmetric bob behind her ear. Even though the platinum was growing out and two inches of black roots were visible, it still managed to look stylish. "As you wish. You're the queen."

"... Who grew up on the wrong side of the tracks in Indiana," Vee amended.

The other girl shrugged. "We all had to grow up somewhere."

She brushed invisible lint on her gray formfitting trousers and straightened her top — which was deep violet and something I suspected she designed herself. The blouse had uneven layers that covered up everything essential while still managing to cling to her form in a sexy way. I hadn't seen anything else like it during my time in Doon.

When Analisa finally finished primping, she asked, "May I sit, then?"

"Please, make yourself at home." Vee gestured to the sitting area. "You *too*, Kenna."

Reluctantly, I perched on the edge of a wingback chair as Vee settled next to Ana on the couch. Vee cleared her throat, shot me a nervous glance, and then began. "I asked you to come because I need your help again. There's a threat to Doon. A curse that's destroying the borders."

Analisa didn't as much as blink in response. "I know."

On the other hand, Vee appeared shocked. "You do? How?"

"Some I heard from Duncan, the rest I put together myself."

She seemed as pleased as the Cheshire Cat, and I couldn't help but wonder if she was as stealthy, too — overhearing all kinds of private things while she hid in plain sight.

Vee rubbed the nape of her neck before her hand twined nervously through her hair. "Do you think anyone else knows about the limbus?"

"Not that I can tell. For a while, I thought Emily might, but I'm quite sure she doesn't." Ana indicated the spell-breaker book. "The book I left you helped, didn't it?"

"You sent this?" Vee snatched it up and held it in front of her. "Where did you find it?"

"Misfiled in the library. It was shelved in the botany section. I couldn't make heads or tails of it, but it looked important." She settled back against the couch. Her body language portrayed a picture of ease and sincerity.

To my critical eye she seemed a bit too rehearsed. "Why didn't you just give it to Vee instead of being sneaky about it?"

"'Cause I'm not part of the Buffy gang, am I? The common folk aren't supposed to have any knowledge that a limbus has us on the brink of extinction. If I trotted up with that book, I'd be met with suspicion. So when I stumbled across it in the library, I figured it would go easier if it came from some other source."

I opened my mouth to fire off another accusation, but Vee silenced me with a glare. She mouthed *Team Doon* before saying to Ana, "Thank you for finding it. It's exactly what we were looking for — in fact, it's the reason I asked you to stop by. According to this book, to break the spell responsible for the limbus, we need a specific weapon. It's down in the castle catacombs."

Ana's eyes narrowed slightly in what was otherwise a perfect poker face. "I heard a thing or two about the catacombs.

They're jam-packed with all kinds of historical trinkets. But the talk is it's nearly impossible to find one's way in those tunnels."

Vee's eyes gleamed as she leaned in. "Ordinarily, yes. But Kenna and I got a private tour. There's a cave that meets up with the chamber where the axe is kept. It's the cave that Jamie and Duncan use as their personal gym."

The girl's eyebrows lifted. "That's convenient now, innit?"

"It would be if there wasn't a locked gate separating the cave from the catacomb. The gate was locked centuries ago and there's no key."

With a slight smirk, Ana said, "I do enjoy a good challenge. Supposing I can pick it, what's the item you want me to pinch?"

Pulling a small sketch from her pocket, Vee replied, "An axe. It's called the Arm o' the Bruce. And it looks like this."

Ana took the drawing and studied it. "Right then. Pick the lock, pinch the axe, and take it where?"

Vee thought for a moment. "My room is too far and we can't risk you bringing it back to the village. We need somewhere secret but not secretive."

"The stables," I said confidently. "Duncan said they have provisions stashed all over the kingdom for their" — *war games* — "training exercises, including at the royal stables. Look for a wooden bench that has weapons and provisions inside. Stash it in there."

"Easy enough." She glanced at the sketch again and then handed it back to Vee. "When do you need it by?"

"We were thinking that you could get it tomorrow night during Fergus and Fiona's wedding reception."

"Good on you," Ana mused. "Very clever. Everyone'll be in the village celebrating. There'll be scant eyes out and about." With a nod, the career criminal agreed to join Team Doon. "I'm in. I'll just need you to show me where the cave is."

"No problem." Vee's eyes flitted to mine and I gave her a nod. Ana already knew so much, might as well tell her the rest. Vee took a breath and exhaled slowly before saying, "One last thing. We need to keep this a secret. From everyone … even Jamie and Duncan."

"If you say so." Ana stood.

Vee followed her lead. "Aren't you even going to ask why it's a secret?"

"I'm sure you have your reasons. We all keep secrets — " She looked at me pointedly. "That's human nature, innit?"

I watched as Vee walked Ana to the door. Just before she left, the girl paused. "A word of advice, *Vee*. The next time you lot have a mind to take a field trip to the witches' cottage, you might want to arrange for a lookout."

With a wink Analisa exited stage left. I still didn't like her — if anything I liked her less now that I'd witnessed how under-handed she could be. "Do you really think we can trust her?"

"Yes." Vee shut the door and turned the key in the lock. "And we don't have a choice."

"I guess not. She knows everything."

"Not quite everything." Vee walked back to the couch looking sheepish. "Yesterday when I touched the Arm o' the Bruce, I had a vision. It was Fergus and Fiona's second wedding night, and I was looking down at the couples dancing in the ballroom. Everyone was together and safe just like we planned."

I had to hand it to Vee, it'd been a stroke of genius to invite all the outlying families to stay at the castle for both wedding night celebrations. That would not only get the people away from danger but also put them under the same roof. Even many of the villagers were staying at the castle after the ball. The rest of Doon would be practically deserted. "What else did you see?"

"My bird's-eye view traveled from the castle, over the village, and through the limbus to the Brig o' Doon. The full moon illuminated the bridge covered in black petunias — they were creeping toward the far side. Then the view shifted and I was standing on the riverbank in front of a Pictish stone. The writing on it matched the spell in the book. You stood next to me and we were both wearing the gowns we'd chosen for the ball. You raised the Arm o' the Bruce over your head and swung. The axe sparked as it made contact, cracking the stone in two."

Goose bumps caused the hair on my arms to stand on end. The room felt freezing cold as I prompted her to continue. "And then?"

"Then I snapped back to the catacombs." She sat on the adjacent couch. "But the vision is pretty clear."

"No offense to your vision, but I've already done the Saving-the-World-in-a-Pretty-Dress thing. It's overrated. If we're going to destroy the limbus spell during the ball, we're stashing sensible clothes along with the axe."

Vee thought about my terms for a second and then nodded. "One more thing … I'm pretty sure you need to destroy the stone by midnight or the limbus will attack Alloway."

Why did it always have to be midnight? Just once I'd like to save the world at high noon like a cowboy. Still, it was a tremendous relief to know everything would be over in two days. Unless we failed, in which case the limbus would creep over into modern Scotland and Alloway would become ground zero for the zombie apocalypse. "What should we tell the others?"

"I'm not sure we should tell them anything. What purpose would it serve? It'll ruin Fiona's celebration."

I agreed there was nothing our friend could do, so worrying about us would only dampen her special event. "What about Jamie and Duncan?"

Vee exhaled like she carried the weight of the world — which I guess she did. "I'm more certain than ever that you and I need to be the ones to go into the limbus and destroy the curse. If Jamie — and Duncan, for that matter — knew what we had to do, they would never go for it. They wouldn't willingly stand on the sidelines while we put our lives in danger."

That was true. Even if Duncan and I had no future, he was too chivalrous to allow me to risk my life. His brother would blow a gasket and then padlock Vee in her chambers. "What about your new understanding with Jamie?"

"We've agreed to trust each other, but this would be too much for him to handle. He'd insist we find another way. But there isn't one." She shook her head, speaking mostly to herself. "I hate keeping things from him, but it's for the sake of Doon. It'll be a lot easier for him to forgive me once the kingdom is safe."

With renewed conviction, Vee reached for my hand and placed her palm against mine so that our rings touched. "It has to be us and it has to be the night after tomorrow."

Fiona had been right about Doon choosing us. From the moment Duncan had shown up in my dressing room, the ending of this story had been predictable. Using the Rings of Aontacht, Vee and I would step into the limbus and break the curse. While not an easy task by any stretch of the imagination, it was pretty straightforward. Thanks to Vee's flash, we now knew how, where, and when. The only thing her vision hadn't supplied — which I felt certain in my gut was lurking just around the bend — was the twist.

CHAPTER 24

Mackenna

In matters of the heart, weddings were the only things more perilous than dances and woods. Bearing witness to others embarking on a sacred union inspired all kinds of fanciful notions — from starry-eyed declarations on balconies to starkly honest, spot-lit moments of confession.

Accompanied by the music of a dozen pipers, I walked next to Duncan in Fergus and Fiona's wedding procession to the old stone church. Today, I planned to keep my wits about me. My eyes would not reflect stars, or moons, or any other marshmallowy shape you would find in a Lucky Charms box. I wouldn't drink to the point where baring my soul seemed like a brilliant idea. Determined to maintain control, I vowed to celebrate in moderation.

The bridal party stopped on the steps of the Auld Kirk. Vee and I peeled left to stand with Fiona while the MacCrae brothers went to Fergus's right. The minister gave a long speech in what I now recognized as Scots, and then Fergus and Fiona replied with, "Aye." The crowd — which seemed to be the entirety of Doon — cheered, and the deed was done.

Or so I thought.

After the applause died down, the minister opened the great wooden doors of the church, and the people filed around us to fill the place to standing room only. While we were waiting for everyone to get settled, I leaned into Vee. "What's going on?"

Other than her eyes shifting briefly in my direction, she gave no indication of hearing me. It was eighth grade study hall all over again. Tugging at her arm, I whispered, "Did they just say their I dos?"

Vee answered using only the side of her mouth closest to me. "That was the first service in traditional Scots. Next is the official service."

"Oh, right," I replied. "The English one."

"Nope. Latin."

Before I could say elp-hay e-may, Fiona's mom ushered me inside. I started forward, and as Duncan regained his place at my side, I wondered what his plan for the evening included. In the past couple days he'd boomeranged from reckless over-sharing to determined aloofness. Ever since our episode of courtyard confessions, he'd kept a deliberate distance. If nothing else, it seemed his drunken drama had served to purge me from his system.

We reached the altar at the front of the church and separated again. I took my place and turned in time to see Vee and Jamie coming up the aisle. For the wedding and reception, the attire was traditional Doonian garb, then dress kilts and gowns for the second-night ball.

Vee looked lovely in her bridesmaid's outfit. She wore a filmy white peasant blouse under a royal blue corset-style vest with a long skirt in the Doonian green and blue plaid. A pin with Doon's crest anchored a plaid sash to her shoulder that draped down her back. Although I wore a matching outfit, and we both had flower garlands in our hair, she wore an understated tiara. Next to her, Jamie beamed like one of the luckiest kilt-wearing guys on the planet — which he was.

Speaking of lucky, Fergus out-grinned Jamie as he strode up the aisle to await his bride. He looked impressive in his traditional MacCrae clan kilt, complete with a sensible blue tam. His favorite Scottish cap, the one with the yellow pom-pom, had been vetoed by the mother of the bride. His pale blond, baby-fine braid hung down his back and swished lightly as he moved.

Behind Fergus, the doors to the Auld Kirk closed as the bagpipes quivered and stopped. Anticipation surged in the ensuing silence until the doors finally reopened to reveal the bride in all her glory. On her father's arm, Fiona, in unmatched radiance, marched slowly down the aisle. Her form-fitting dream dress had a long shimmering train that glided after her just like a mermaid's tail. Strawberry blonde curls that had escaped from her elaborate updo framed her face and neck. Her reverent gaze swept the crowd before settling on her giant husband-to-be.

It was magical ... until the Latin started.

At least from my vantage point at the front I could look at the spectators while their focus was on the bride and groom. Fiona's parents sat directly in front of me in the first row. Mrs. Fairshaw wore a fiercely proud expression that only faltered slightly when she regarded her daughter's choice of dress.

The next two rows were filled with the Rosettis. Mario, who was hosting the reception, had his arm wrapped around his wife Sharron, who softly sniveled into her handkerchief. Their lovely daughters sat off to one side. Gabriella watched the ceremony with rapturous attention while Sofia's pinched face appeared sullen — a word I would have normally never associated with her but which tended to fit more and more. Behind them were an entire row of Rosetti boys. The two sandwiched between their smokin' hot oldest brother and the troublemaker twins were not as notorious as the others but all five looked like heartbreakers in the making.

On the groom's side, Fergus's mom and dad — who were also my distant relations — wept openly. They were surrounded by more Lockharts, all fair blonds or coppery redheads with pale, mottled complexions.

Several rows back, the clump of Destined sat together. Adam, the environmentalist studying the limbus, had returned from the hunting lodge with bleak news. There was nothing he could do to slow it down. He'd promised to be discrete until after the ball, when we'd scheduled a meeting to plan our next steps. Hopefully, that meeting would become unnecessary.

Emily watched the service with a tight, sad expression. Next to her, Analisa was her usual shrewd self. She watched the proceedings with her dark, squinty eyes, frowning as she noted something at the opposite end of the altar. Angling my body slightly downstage, I slowly turned my head to see what had her panties in a bunch, and connected with Duncan's velvet gaze.

The butterflies in residence in my stomach went crazy as I realized Ana had been watching him watch me. My pulse spiked as we stared at one another. From the unassuming expression on his face, it was impossible to know what he was thinking. When I could bear it no longer, I turned my attention back to the congregation.

As the priest droned on and on, I stared at the sea of faces, familiar and foreign, friendly and hostile — even gross Gideon watched from the standing room in the way back. Yet no matter where I let my attention wander, I could still feel Duncan's eyes on me. The skin on my neck tingled with awareness and my cheeks began to overheat. Finally, the minister switched to English for the exchanging of rings, and Duncan's focus shifted to his friends. After reciting traditional vows, the couple was pronounced husband and wife.

When it came time to kiss the bride, Fergus lifted Fiona up to his level. The crowd whooped and hollered while she dangled more than a foot off the ground for the big smooch. The bagpipes began to play and Fergus set his new bride back on her feet so they could follow the pipers down the aisle. The wedding party and all the guests would accompany the happy couple into the village for the reception at Rosetti's Tavern.

As Vee and I passed Analisa, she gave us a discreet nod. Once the reception got into full swing, she would sneak away to the Brother Cave for the Arm o' the Bruce, then stash it and blend back into the party as if she'd never left. Even though I didn't trust her in general, I had no doubt that if anyone could accomplish this task without detection, it would be my criminal-minded nemesis.

"What'll ye have, dearie?"

Feeling totally out of my element, I stared helplessly at the girl behind the counter. Lounging against the bar at Rosetti's Tavern seemed the best way to blend in. I didn't count on there being an actual barmaid at Fergus and Fiona's reception.

"I don't suppose I could get a diet soda?" I asked, flashing her my best disarming smile.

From thin air, Fiona's radiant face materialized next to me. "She'll have ginger wine, if you please. Make that two."

I angled myself toward my friend. "But I'm not drinking." Legal or not, Duncan's recent alcohol-induced shenanigans reaffirmed my love of sobriety. The last thing I wanted was to make a spectacle of myself.

"Relax. There's no actual wine in it." She clasped my arm and turned me around so that I faced the room. "See. Even the bairns like my wee cousin Ewan are drinking it."

I watched dubiously as four-year-old Ewan took a large swallow from a mug and wiped his mouth with his sleeve. Although Doon was a magical, somewhat enlightened place, it was still more medieval than not. I wouldn't be surprised if the wee bairns here were weaned on ale.

Case in point, at the opposite end of the room people were passing around a three-legged bucket called a cog filled with some mysterious concoction "guaranteed ta put hair on yer chest," or so it had been explained to me by Mutton Chops. I watched as Duncan waved the communal cog past without the slightest interest. Good — perhaps we would both keep our wits about us tonight.

"Why don't ye go ask him ta dance?" Fiona asked. Only then did I notice that the music had started back up.

Embarrassed that she'd caught me staring, I stammered something about later. To my great relief the barmaid set two giant mugs next to us. I handed one to Fiona and then raised the other in a toast. "To the new Mrs. Lockhart."

"Fairshaw-Lockhart," she corrected, yelling to be heard over the lively tune. "I quite fancy your modern tradition of hyphenating names." She clinked her mug to mine and took a huge gulp. Following her example, I took a tentative sip of my own drink. It tasted like burnt ginger ale, but without the fizz.

Fiona sighed contentedly. "I do love ginger wine. It brings me back to when I was a young lass. My da would make a batch every Hogmanay."

"Hog-ma-what?"

Her eyes lit up. "I believe you call it New Year's Eve. You're going ta love Hogmanay in Doon. The whole village is lit up with lanterns and we make a procession from the kirk ta the square for the Fire Ceremony. And then Duncan ..." Her explanation dissolved into giggles. "He has ta — visit — every house in the realm ... before sun-up."

"Why?" In order to do what she was suggesting, he'd have to run nearly the entire way.

"It started as a MacCrae brothers wager," she replied with a snort. "Now it's tradition. Oh, Mackenna, there are so many wonderful experiences ahead of ye in Doon."

I considered reminding her that I wasn't really here because of any Calling, but decided it was better to avoid that conversation — especially with the girl who seemed to possess classified information about one's destiny. Instead, I nodded toward the groom milling through the crowd, undoubtedly in search of his bride. "Why aren't *you* dancing?"

Fiona frowned. "I've got something in my shoe."

Without warning she pulled a classic bend and snap. After a moment of digging in her shoe, she shot precariously back up with the offending object pinched between her thumb and index finger.

"Blasted Bawbee!" she complained as she tossed the offending silver piece across the room. It rotated through the tavern in slow motion, striking a middle-aged guy with a beard.

Beardy turned angrily in our direction. His movement jostled a couple of partyers who'd just tipped the cog into the air. The potent punch slopped over the brim of the bucket onto Vee, drenching her bodice. She gasped and at the same instant I recognized Beardy as the ringleader of the mob that attacked us when we first visited Doon.

The room fell silent as Fiona whispered, "Whoops!"

I rushed toward Vee only to be blocked by Duncan who deliberately stepped in my path. As I tried to maneuver around him, he hissed, "Stay back." His hand clamped onto my arm, forcing me to remain behind him.

I peeked around in time to see Fergus take the cog away from the partygoers.

Fergus handed it off as Jamie stepped between his soaked girlfriend and Beardy. His face was as dark as I'd ever seen it. "Apologize to your queen," he ordered.

"She's no' my queen," Beardy sneered.

Jamie balled his hand into a fist and reared back. But before he could throw a punch, Vee grabbed his hand in both of hers and said, "Stop!"

He looked at her in rage and confusion as she calmly lowered his fist. "This is between Mr. MacNally and me," she said quietly. "Give me a chance to handle it before you go all William Wallace."

Jamie hesitated for a fraction of a second before stepping back. "Yes, Yer Highness."

Vee turned to Beardy and addressed his last comment. "I am sorry you feel that way. Should you change your mind, I am here to support you in any way I can. In the meantime, how about we put away our differences to celebrate this wedding. Would you care to dance, Mr. MacNally?"

Beardy's eyes narrowed at Vee and then flitted to the three huge guys — Jamie, Fergus, and Duncan — who had her back. Without even another glance in Vee's direction he stormed out of the tavern followed by a dozen of his cohorts.

Growling something about manners, Jamie started to follow them — until Vee called his name. "Let him go," she pleaded. "They have a right to their opinions. And I'll never win them over if my boyfriend beats them into submission."

Jamie shut his eyes and heaved a frustrated sigh as Vee closed the distance between them. She placed a hand on his bicep and said, "We have an understanding, remember?"

Jamie looked down at her, his fury replaced by remorse. "Sorry, love. Baby steps."

The fiddlers started back up as the prince pulled his queen flush against him. Seconds later, the bagpipes joined in. Once the royal couple whirled across the floor, I realized Duncan still held my arm in a death grip. Raising up on my tip-toes, I shouted above the music, "You can let go now! The scary beard man is gone."

After keeping a polite distance all day, Duncan spun around to grip me with both hands. I gaped in shock as he scowled down at me. Was he remembering our last encounter with Beardy and how he'd cradled me to his chest after coming to my rescue? "What were you thinking rushing up like that?"

"I was *thinking* my best friend was in trouble." I tried to step away, but it was impossible. I wasn't going anywhere until Duncan MacCrae allowed it, or until I screamed bloody murder ... which would kind of blow our whole Calling cover story.

A tray of elegant finger food appeared between us held by Mario Rosetti. Duncan released me to pick up something that looked like a mini meat pie and thanked our host. "*Grazie*, Mario."

"*Di niente*," Mario trilled in his musical Italian accent. He waited until I selected a sliver of bruschetta. "Soon we will be having a party to celebrate your wedding, *si*?"

"*Certamente*."

As soon as Mario moved on, I asked, "How did you answer him?"

"I said certainly." Duncan set his uneaten appetizer on the table and I put mine next to it. "We do have a pretense to keep up."

He was right. I nodded to indicate I was still on board with the plan and then asked, "Would you like to dance?"

"Maybe later." He looked about the room. "Have you seen Ana? I've been looking for her."

I felt heat creep up my neck and prickle my cheeks. She'd been gone for hours, and I was starting to worry that something had gone very wrong. Although I was a fantastic actress, I didn't lie well when I was on the spot, especially to my ex about his new girlfriend. Before I could stammer some excuse, Analisa appeared from thin air with her Cheshire Cat grin.

"You called?" Then, by way of explanation, she shrugged toward the street. "I've been outdoors celebrating with that rowdy lot."

Duncan's gaze leapt from her to me, and as it did she gave me a sly wink. The smile she'd elicited still lingered in his eyes when he said, "Would you please excuse us, Mackenna?"

Was refusing an option? "Sure."

Duncan put his hand on the small of Analisa's back and they disappeared into the crowd. On the far side of the room, Fergus was breaking a piece of shortbread over his new wife's head. The crowd cheered despite the fact that it crumbled into tiny pieces in her hair. Even Fiona herself was laughing at her "good fortune."

There were things about Doon I would never understand. Perhaps these were further confirmations that I was not meant to be here — that I didn't belong.

"This is a celebration. Stop distancing yourself." Vee's gentle voice drifted up from my side. "And before you deny it — I saw you hiding at the bar."

Rather than open myself up to dissection, I decided to change the subject. "Ana's back. I guess everything went okay."

"I saw her. But we were talking about *you*. After we destroy the limbus, you should hang out for a while."

I knew what she was doing. She'd been hinting at every possible opportunity that I should stay in Doon. But the only way that Duncan and I would truly move on is if we never saw each other again. On top of everything else, I couldn't deal with disappointing her. It was too much, and I snapped, "I'm not staying. Once we kill the zombie fungus, I'm out of here. For good. So you better get used to the idea."

I hurried outside and pushed my way through the wedding guests clogging the street until I was far away from Rosetti's Tavern. My stomach felt sick as I contemplated what I'd just done. My second to last night in Doon, and I spent it picking a fight with my best friend.

chapter 25

Veronica

The fact that I lived in a real-life *Once Upon a Time* had never been more apparent. Side by side, our gowns swishing against the cobblestone floors, my BFF and I made our way to the ballroom. And in true fairy-tale fashion, before the night was over we'd enter the evil witch's domain, wield a consecrated weapon, and, if all went as planned, save the day.

Now, if I could just get my knees to stop trembling.

For an added bit of courage, I tucked a hand in the hidden pocket of my skirt and stroked Queen Lynnette's pendant. I ran my fingers over the familiar shape of the heart topped with a crown. The queens of Doon had been doing what was best for their people for generations, because the kingdom *was* their heart.

Tonight, I hoped to prove once and for all that I'd been chosen for this role. I touched the ceremonial tiara perched upon my head, and then ran my hands over the layers of ice-blue silk and tulle floating from my corseted waist. The heart-shaped bodice of the gown was shot through with silver thread, and the skirt scattered with tiny crystals that reflected the flames of each lantern we passed like glints of sun on ocean waves. Fiona had taught me that perception was as important as reality, so I'd given Emily free reign to commission a gown fit for royalty.

"Good thing I insisted we stash a change of clothes. You sparkling like Queen of the Fairies might put a damper on the sneaking part of tonight's festivities."

Recognizing a compliment when I heard one, I tugged on one of my elbow-length silk gloves and glanced at my gorgeous friend. "You look pretty epic yourself." In some lights, the deep blue silk of her gown shimmered into black, creating an illusion of fluidity. The midnight silk was the perfect foil for the spirals of her brilliant hair.

"Why, thank you, my queen." She winked and lifted her skirts in a mock curtsy.

It was meant as a joke, but I wasn't her queen. And I never would be. Kenna was just visiting. Passing through on her way to a life without me. And without the boy who'd been Calling to her for most of her life.

Assuming we didn't die tonight, this might be my last chance to have my say.

As we turned down a deserted back hallway lined with medieval portraits and the occasional kingly bust, I grabbed her hand and pushed her toward a curtained alcove. A place that I was sure had been used for secret assignations and political intrigue for generations.

"Hey! What the —"

I shoved a strategic elbow into her corseted ribcage, and she stumbled into the tiny room. "Quiet. It's my turn to talk." I yanked the drapes closed behind us. The pattern of beads scattered across Kenna's skirt captured and held light, glowing like stars in the dark chamber.

"I can't see you, but I can still ring your stubborn little neck."

"Kenna, can you please listen? Just this once?"

"Fine," she huffed into the dark.

"Do you remember in high school how, despite starring in every theater production, you felt like you never fit in? It should've been the time of your life. You ruled the drama club. But besides me, you didn't connect with anyone. Not even that cute boy who played opposite you in *Beauty and the Beast*."

As my eyes began to adjust, I watched her cross her arms under her chest and turn her face away from me. "He had enormous feet."

"It's always something. Hands too small. Eyes too light. Smile too straight."

She didn't respond, and I could almost hear the realization hit her. The comparisons she'd been making her entire life had been to a certain youthful, dark-eyed prince with a crooked grin — her not-so-imaginary friend.

After several quiet seconds of letting her digest her revelation, I whispered, "At some point, you are going to have to choose to be brave."

"What do you mean, *choose to be brave*? I'm about to face a freakin' zombie fungus." She uncrossed her arms and propped her fists on her hips.

"I mean brave with your feelings. You're going to have to tell him everything. Lay yourself bare, with no assurance that it will make any difference."

"Why on earth would I do that?"

"Because …" I reached out and wrapped my fingers around her upper arms, saying my next words with special care. "If you don't, you will always regret it. You'll always wonder what you missed."

Her eyes had gone wide and moist, the muscles around her mouth contracting as she struggled to hide from me. But it was no use; I'd seen it. She wanted to take the chance. My heart performed a tiny leap.

But then Kenna blinked, lifted her chin, and the emotion fell from her face. "Don't we have somewhere we need to be?"

I let go of her arms and dropped my hands to my sides. There were serious disadvantages to having an actor for a best friend. "At least take the first step and admit the truth to yourself." I met her gaze and refused to break the stare until she nodded.

"Okay." Her eyes shuttered and she stepped back, her next words flippant. "But I seldom follow my own good advice, so don't expect miracles."

That's exactly what I expected, but I didn't push. Knowing what I'd already said was challenge enough, I lifted the curtain and stepped into the torch-lit hallway.

The walk to the ballroom was not far, but it seemed to take an eternity. We moved side by side, in utter silence. Not the kind of silence you could curl up in and read a book; this felt like swimming upstream.

I paused just short of the light spilling from the open doors to the ballroom. "Ken, are you — "

"I'm *fine*." She met my worried gaze with a playful grin. "Time to get our sparkle on. Now go find your handsome prince. He's going to freak when he sees that sweetheart neckline." She waggled her eyebrows.

She wasn't fooling me for a nanosecond with her sudden light mood, but she was right — I desperately needed a dose of courage before facing down the forces of darkness. And I only knew one boy who made me feel like I could save the world.

Sensing she needed a bit more time, I gave her hand a quick squeeze. "Meet you at the stables in two hours?"

At her nod, I lifted my skirts and entered the ballroom. It was like walking into a cloud. Every surface was covered in white, from the snowy flower garlands to the swaths of ivory silk hanging in deep loops from the ceiling. Porcelain vases full of calla lilies, fluffy peonies, and pure white roses were everywhere, their fresh fragrance permeating the air. Even the music was light and airy — a mix of piano and strings.

A heavenly aroma drew my attention to a table laden with a variety of appetizers. A cup of tea and some strawberries were all I'd eaten that day. Suddenly light-headed, I moved toward the food, but was intersected by a flurry of motion.

"Yer Majesty! You look absolutely glorious!" Gabriella Rosetti stopped in front of me and dropped into a low curtsy, her tangerine skirts pooling in a neat circle around her feet.

"Thank yo — "

"Oh, my queen!" One of Gabby's friends rushed to join her. *Melissa? Maria?* It was something beginning with an M, I was sure. "That shade o' blue is exquisite with yer eyes."

Two more girls merged into the ever-growing circle around me, and I noticed every one of them had their hair braided on one side, the strand integrated into their updos. It's how I'd worn my hair on several occasions. Warmth infused my cheeks as the girls spoke over one another, complimenting my hair and makeup and asking about everything from the design of my dress to the color of my nails.

Kenna had painted them in a glittery blue polish called I Have a Herring Problem.

"I — "

But before I could finish, Jamie appeared behind Gabby's shoulder. His warm brown gaze held mine as the hint of a grin tugged at his lips. "Ye'll need to excuse us, lasses, I've a mind to dance with your queen."

The gaggle of girls parted to either side, twittering behind their hands.

Wearing a formal black jacket and dark kilt, the MacCrae tartan draped across one shoulder, Jamie looking more dashing than I'd ever seen him — like a real-life prince. He closed the distance between us, swept into a bow, and extended his hand. "May I have this dance?"

Still bent low, his sandy brows lifted in expectation. I heard at least one girl sigh.

"Always." I grasped his fingers in mine, feeling their warmth through my gloves.

He stood, and I looped my arm through his bent elbow. With a smile and a wave to Gabby and her friends, I let Jamie lead me away. As we moved to the center of the room, I took a rough count of heads. The room was packed, and to my vast relief, it appeared as if the entirety of Doon were in attendance, tucked behind the relative safety of the castle walls.

Jamie swept me into his arms, and horns joined in the song as if trumpeting our arrival on the dance floor. We began to waltz, and I noticed that people milled about, chatting and eating, but we were the only ones dancing.

"Jamie … we're the only people out here." I settled my hand on his hard muscled shoulder.

His eyes twinkled, his perfect lips quirked to one side. "No' for long."

Sure enough, people began to pair off, and we were soon surrounded by a swirling rainbow of couples. Silk, tulle, and velvet glinted in a thousand tiny flames of light. Gabby twirled past in the arms of a red-haired boy I recognized as the daring guy who'd asked me to dance at my first weekly feast. His gaze swept over me and a wide, appreciative grin spread across his face.

"Ye look stunning, by the way," Jamie announced in an overly loud voice, shooting a glare at the cute red-haired boy.

I turned back to him, and caught him staring at my chest before his eyes jerked back to mine. His fingers trailed up from my elbow to the bare skin of my upper arm. It took me a moment to realize it wasn't a loving caress — he was trying to push my tulle-capped sleeve up over my shoulder.

When the fabric wouldn't stay put, he groused, "What good is this blasted thing?"

We circled past the orchestra, the music drowning out my laughter.

Jamie steered me toward the center of the floor. "Are ye laughin' at me?"

"Of course not," I said as another giggle escaped my chest. "You're just so cute when you're jealous."

"I am *not* jealous."

I arched a brow in silent question.

He pulled me closer and whispered against my ear, "All right, perhaps a bit. But when I saw ye tonight, it near took my breath away. And for whatever time we have, I dinna wish to share you."

We'd slowed to a sway, and his earnest gaze locked on my face, the candlelight catching in the flecks of gold in his dark eyes. The room and everyone in it faded away. This was my co-ruler. My soul mate. If these were truly the last hours we had together, could I allow them to be tainted by a lie? My heart gave a quick squeeze.

Is this what Queen Lynnette felt like before making her bargain with the witches? Sure she was doing the right thing for the kingdom, but torn between protecting her secret and begging for King Angus's forgiveness?

I opened my mouth, but the confession locked in my throat. If I told Jamie I planned to enter the deadly limbus and destroy the curse, that Kenna and I were the only ones who could do it ... he'd lock me in the dungeon until he could come up with a better plan. One that didn't risk my life. I couldn't say I'd do anything differently if the tables were turned.

"What?" he prompted, his eyes narrowed in concern.

When I didn't answer, he stopped dancing. "Vee, I know you told me ye have a plan, but if something's gone wrong, you'd tell me, right? Ask for my help?"

"Of course. Everything is fine." But I couldn't stop the shiver that ran through me.

Jamie's expression turned stony. "I canna stand idly by and let you —"

"Shhh!" His raised voice had drawn the attention of several couples dancing around us. I took his arm and steered him into a quiet corner.

Staring up at him, I challenged, "When you told me that you trusted me, did you really mean it?"

"Yes, but —"

"No buts. You can't help me. Not this time."

Jamie crossed his arms and stared down at his feet, his jaw clenching.

I stepped in close and rubbed his flexed forearm. "Can you do it? Can you take this leap of faith with me?"

After several long seconds, he looked up, his eyes stormy, but his voice resolute. "I would follow you anywhere."

I blinked, my vision clouding. His astonishing declaration shocking me to my core.

Never one to handle tears well, Jamie gently gripped my arms. "Why are you crying?"

I swallowed the lump in my throat, and then smiled into his eyes. "I just love you, that's all."

The dimpled grin that spread across his face was so magnificent, it left me speechless.

"Oh well, if tha's all." He wrapped his arm around my waist, and crushed me against his chest, lifting my feet from the floor. "I love you too, my heart. And I do trust you. But no matter what happens to us in this world, we'll always be together." Slowly, he set me on my feet.

I didn't doubt that our Calling could stand the test of time, but right now, we only had this moment. Pulling his head down, I touched my lips to his in a soft kiss. When I leaned back, the intensity of his gaze stirred an urgent need inside me. I didn't want to share him either. Not tonight.

"Follow me." I took his hand and led him through the throng of dancers. I smiled and nodded at their greetings while every nerve in my body was laser focused on the place where my fingers linked with Jamie's. When we reached the hallway, I lifted my skirt in one hand and began to run, tugging my prince behind me. His deep laughter echoed through the empty corridors as we took several turns.

Finally, we reached the curtained alcove I'd been searching for, and, ignoring the judgmental eyes of an immortalized king, pushed through the opening. I let go of Jamie's hand long enough to close the drapes behind us. Then I whirled and pushed him against the wall with a thump, knocking a breath from his lungs. Wrapping my arms around his neck, I stood on my toes and kissed him as if it were the last time.

It only took him a heartbeat to return my affections. Our lips slanted, and it was like I was drowning or falling from a cliff, but I didn't want to be saved. If something went wrong, and I died tonight, there was nothing I would miss more than this — more than him. He ran his hands up and down my back, seeking until one hand wrapped around the back of my neck and the other caressed my bare shoulder.

The touch of his fingers rushed through my nerve endings, lighting me on fire. I pressed against him, unable to get close enough. Jamie grasped my arms, turned us in a circle until my back met the cool stone wall and his heat surrounded me. His lips trailed over my cheek and to my ear as he hooked a finger in the top of my glove and peeled it from my skin. Gently, he sucked my earlobe into his mouth as he removed my other glove. I made an inarticulate sound and entwined my fingers in his hair, my other hand exploring the hard muscles of his chest through the thin layer of his shirt.

His mouth returned to mine, questing. He pushed against me, our bodies perfectly flush. The heavy weight of him had me on the edge, on the precipice of losing control. But as much as I wanted to, I knew we'd both regret it if we didn't stop.

I lifted my hand to his face, pulled my lips from his and murmured, "I don't think we want to do this right now."

Jamie drew back, disoriented, his breath ragged. I caressed his cheek, and he met my gaze before tucking me underneath his chin. We stayed that way for several seconds, and then he stooped and smoothed the layers of my rumpled skirt.

Retrieving my discarded gloves, he straightened and handed them to me before taking a step back. "I'm so verra sorry." He shoved a shaky hand into his hair, and pushed the gold strands off his forehead. "I lost my head a bit. But I've the upmost respect for your virtue."

"I know you do," I whispered with a small smile, his remorse reminding me of the huge gaps between our cultures.

A modern boy would likely accuse me of leading him on after I'd dragged him into a closet and didn't deliver. But not my noble prince.

I took his hand. "We got carried away. It happens."

"No' to me it doesn't."

"What do you mean? It happens to us all the time."

"I mean before you ... before us." He sighed. "I'd kissed plenty of girls."

"Clearly." I held no delusions that I'd been his first.

"But I dinna lose control. It's not who I am." He turned his head, staring past me.

"Jamie, I know exactly who you are. You're one of the strongest, most disciplined people I know." I touched his chin and tilted it so he'd meet my eyes. "But if you didn't lose a *wee* bit of control with me, I'd be insulted." I actually loved that I was the one thing that could make him forget himself.

He stared at me until a slow grin dawned across his face, white teeth flashing in the dark. "Aye."

"Now, we better get back before we're missed, and Fergus forces us to have a shotgun wedding."

As we made our way back to the ball, Jamie asked, "Is a shotgun wedding what I think it is?"

"I'd imagine so." We entered the hallway that lead to the ballroom, and I did a last check of my dress to make sure everything was in its proper place.

"Forced to marry at gunpoint because the couple went too far?"

"That would be it."

Jamie was quiet so long I glanced in his direction.

His ardent gaze captured mine and wouldn't let go. "No one would ever have to coerce me into marrying you, Verronica."

I resisted the urge to fan my suddenly flaming face. This

was a topic I'd avoided like a plague of Stephanie Heartford spray-tanned, cheer clones. Jamie's antiquated value system had a flipside, one that compelled him to higher moral ground than I was ready to consider at the age of eighteen. And especially not tonight.

Seeming to sense my unease, Jamie chuckled and wrapped his arm around my shoulders, pulling me in close. "'Tis true. But we have plenty of time for that, eh?"

"Absolutely," I replied with a decisive nod as we entered the ballroom. A series of chimes drew my attention to the ornate grandfather clock in the corner, and my stomach did a nauseating pirouette. *Less than an hour.*

I glanced up at Jamie's profile. Even if I wasn't ready for wedding bells just yet, his cool assurance that we would have more time after tonight — after the limbus was defeated and everything was back to normal — bolstered my confidence and calmed my nerves.

But then I saw something that stopped me in my tracks — the other looming disaster in our midst.

"What is it?" Jamie asked.

I tilted my head toward where Kenna and Duncan stood on the dance floor, as stiff-armed and fake-smiled as two crash-test dummies. "Their Calling is real, you know."

"I suspected." Jamie steered me toward the buffet table. "But my brother doesna talk to me about anythin' of importance. At least, no' anymore."

I picked up a plate, and selected a few hors d'oeuvres at random. Jamie loaded his plate with at least one of everything and then paused. I followed the direction of his stare to Kenna and Duncan making painful progress around the room. I wondered if their dissention was as obvious to everyone as it was to us. "Neither one of them will ever be happy without the other, will they?"

"Likely no'." He turned to me and tucked a loose curl behind my ear. "But I know another couple who was just as stubborn, not so verra long ago."

"And we found our way to each other."

Jamie's eyes became thoughtful. "Sometimes all one needs is a bit of motivation."

And with that, he set off in the direction of his brother. Knowing Jamie's powers of persuasion first hand, I smiled at the purpose in his stride. Beware anyone who attempted to defy him when he fixed his mind to something.

A wave of dizziness swept over me and I gripped the edge of the table. Remembering that I needed to eat, I popped something into my mouth, but it tasted like glue and sawdust. The music changed tempo, and my eyes were drawn to the middle of the dance floor. Like a mash-up of a hoedown and a Riverdance, Doonian ladies hitched up their skirts and high stepped to the lively fiddle. Men kicked up their heels in abandon and swung their partners in the air. I even spotted a few of the Destined in the mix. Those not participating stopped what they were doing to clap and shout encouragement. Everywhere I looked, I was greeted by broad, carefree grins.

If Kenna and I didn't destroy the limbus tonight, this could all be gone in a matter of days — the glorious melting pot of individuals, the village, the castle, the Auld Kirk, all of it. My eyes burned as they skipped around the room to Jamie's golden head, Duncan's broad back, Kenna, Fiona, Fergus, the Rosettis, and even Emily and Analisa. All the people I cared about were in this room, and all of them were relying on me, as their queen, to keep them safe.

I straightened my spine, set down my plate, and wiped my leaky eyes. I planned on living in this beautiful kingdom with my prince for a very long time. It didn't matter what the limbus threw at us tonight. I reached into my pocket and found the pendant. There was one major difference between Queen Lynnette and myself — I was following the will of Doon's Protector, and therefore, I would not fail.

CHAPTER 26

Mackenna

Many cultures have a version of Cinderella — ours has several. I was a fan of the Rogers and Hammerstein version myself. The fair maiden dressed as a princess makes her big entrance ... the prince looks up ... their eyes meet ... and *Bang! Crash!* ... Instalove, complete with a melodious duet.

In none of those stories does the maiden make such a mess of things that the couple can never recover. Never does she have to stand by while her dream guy waltzes away with some other, more exotic-looking maiden. Maybe the evil stepmother was right all along; love is a childish fancy.

I stepped into the ballroom prepared for the worst, but when the handsome prince's gaze met mine across the crowded room ... *Bang! Crash!* Just like in the fairy tales, we were compelled toward each other. The rest of the world fell away as Duncan's crooked smile reeled me in. He always looked insanely gorgeous, but the sight of him in his dress kilt — gentleman on the top, clan warrior on bottom — stole the air from my lungs.

The admiration on his face made it even harder to breathe

as he said, "I didna think it was possible for you to look any lovelier ... But I was wrong." He took a small step back and continued his appraisal. "I shall have fantasies about how you look in this moment."

With a courtly bow, he reached for my hand and lifted it to his lips. Electric currents rippled from the kiss to fill my whole body with warmth — or was that the beginnings of a blush from his compliment?

After days of estrangement, Duncan was back to his old self. His behavior gave me the strength to harness my voice. "There's something I need you to know — "

"Me first." He continued to hold my hand, the heat of his touch soaking into my skin. "The last time we attended a ball, I asked you not to leave. Do ye remember?"

Of course I remembered. I'd been so tempted to comply with his request. I suspected he was about to give me the opportunity to confess that I really did want to stay. That my heart had developed new dreams that eclipsed Broadway and if he gave me a second chance at happily ever after, I would spend the rest of my days making up for my mistakes.

"This time" — Duncan's sweet smile pierced my consciousness — "I'll ask nothing so foolish. I believe you were called back to Doon to stop the limbus, and that after ye save the kingdom — which'll be soon — you're to return to your own world." His gaze flitted to Analisa as she waltzed by and then refocused somberly on me. "In fact, I'm countin' on it."

I jerked my hand away. "You're counting on me leaving?"

"I know you, Mackenna." His now empty fingers rose to caress my cheek. "You're not of my world. And regardless of the pretty promises that fall from your lips, you'll no' stay where you don't belong."

I was speechless. Duncan's fingertips brushed my jaw as

the hope I'd allowed to grow since Vee's pep talk withered into dust.

His dark eyes glittered with feverish excitement as he leaned closer. "Tonight is about saying good-bye to Doon. It's our last time together in the ballroom — our last ball."

The last midnight ... Kaboom — splat! Giants came crashing down from the sky smashing all my hopes and dreams. And now I was about to get my last and very costly wish. He was leaving me alone.

"What did you need to say?" Duncan blinked at me, waiting.

None of the words that had been on the tip on my tongue moments ago mattered. Pasting what I hoped was a sincere smile on my face, I sputtered, "Just that — uh, you look *a-mazing!*"

He flashed me another grin. The gleam in his eyes made him seem almost maniacal. If we'd been in Chicago, I would've suspected he was on something. He bounced on the balls of his feet, prompting me to ask, "Are you okay?"

"Aye. Just keen to dance is all. Will you do me the honor?" He held out his hand for mine. When I complied, his other hand settled gently yet firmly on my waist. "If this is to be our last time, Mackenna, I'm eager to make it count."

An hour passed in a whirl of crinoline and satin. While Duncan's smile never faltered, something was off with him. He was alternately talkative and silent. For a song or two he'd be all but mute, as if reflecting on some private thought, and then he'd start chatting about random things: some life-changing book he'd read as a child, music lessons at the age of ten that'd not gone so well, the first time he and Jamie had secretly tried ale.

You'd never know by listening that this was a momentous occasion — our last ball together. I tried to look interested, but his stories were all from a long time ago. As I listened to some vaguely familiar tale about the time he'd slipped a frog into the back of his Latin tutor's trousers, inspiration struck.

"I have an idea," I said when he paused between boyhood anecdotes. The musicians were talking a break, except for a classical trio who were in the middle of a slow set. "Let's ask each other one *last* question. Like truth or dare but without the dare."

"So truth or truth?" His eyebrows lifted in question as his head tilted slightly like he was trying to figure out my angle. After a moment of scrutiny, his hesitance melted away. "Ladies first."

This was what I was counting on. In case Vee and I failed to defeat the limbus tonight and I never saw him again — I needed some answers. "Did you know from the moment I appeared in Doon that we'd known each other as children?"

He continued to lead me across the floor, his face neutral, his velvet brown eyes carefully watching. "Aye."

Dancing somehow made the conversion easier. Epic details became small talk. "I don't even get how that works. We weren't kids at the same time."

"Callings are a mystery. They're a divine gift."

"How come you didn't tell me you were Finn? *My Finn*."

"You needed to remember for yourself and decide what significance, if any, it had for our present relationship. As much as I wanted to tell you, I couldna force the information on you."

"That sounds like a cop-out. You should've told me."

He frowned without missing a step. "Cop out?"

"A convenient excuse but not the whole truth."

For at least a minute he was quiet in thought. During that time I was achingly aware of his hand at my waist, how his fingers moved against my hip bone in rhythm with the music. Occasionally his legs would brush mine against my skirts, causing tiny electric jolts to zing through me.

When he finally answered, his words were difficult to hear. "The truth is … I was scared. Scared if I told you, you'd feel even more trapped — like I was taking away your choice. Afraid the truth would give you more reason to run away."

"I didn't run away."

"Didn't ye?"

Totally unfair. I knew Duncan would never be happy in the modern world the way he was in Doon. Still, I deserved to know before I … left him. "You should have told me."

"Aye." The song ended and Duncan stopped moving. While other couples took advantage of the break to eat or get some air, we stood rooted to our spot. Duncan regarded me gravely. "Time for my last question. Tell me this, Mackenna, what would ye have done with it — the knowledge that I was your Finn? Would the knowledge have changed your course?"

Vee's words echoed through my head. If I couldn't be brave with her or Duncan, could I at least be honest with myself?

Would knowledge of Finn have made a difference? Would I have stayed? Or not abandoned him on the bridge? I wanted to tell myself that it would've made all the difference. But some still small voice deep inside told me that it wouldn't have changed anything.

This sudden revelation did not make me want to sing "Kum ba yah." In contrast, my heart pinched, and I wanted to throw something. The truth sucked asphalt!

Duncan and I stood in the middle of the now empty floor. Instead of answering, I replied, "I guess we'll never know. Will we?"

And then I walked away.

Without a clear destination in mind, I found myself near the pastry table. Not that I subconsciously wanted to indulge a sweet tooth — far from it. But the odds of encountering my bestie greatly increased if éclairs were part of the equation. Unfortunately, the only people in the immediate vicinity were the Rosetti twins, who appeared to be competing to see who could stuff the most cream puffs into their mouth at one time.

When I glanced around the room for Vee, I noticed that Duncan had been detained by his brother. Jamie gripped Duncan's arm while he spoke in a quick and determined manner. Although I was too far away to hear what was being said, I could tell from the younger prince's Grumpy Cat expression that the brotherly talk was unwelcomed.

Without warning Duncan hauled off and punched his brother in the mouth. Jamie staggered back in shock as a small trickle of blood glistened in the corner of his lips. Shock quickly morphed into fury when Duncan showed no remorse for his actions.

The entire ballroom fell silent as they watched the sibling drama unfold. With a growl, Jamie launched himself at Duncan and socked him in the eye. Duncan lurched to the side but recovered quickly and drove his fist into Jamie's ribcage, sending him sprawling. Before Jamie could retaliate, Fergus, the older Rosetti boys, and half a dozen other men I recognized but couldn't name were pulling the MacCrae brothers apart.

Duncan shoved at those attempting to restrain him. After knocking four men to the ground, he used a crack-the-whip maneuver on the Rosettis. Turning in quick circles he slingshotted Rosetti boys in all directions. When he was free, he turned and stalked away.

Jamie watched his brother's exit as Fergus hoisted him to his feet. Murmuring "I'm fine," he rubbed at his bleeding lip. Whatever anger his brother's assault had sparked was already gone.

As the room returned to normal, Vee crossed to Jamie. During the fight, Eòran had kept her back out of harm's way. For the first time since my return, I was grateful for Mutton Chops' Inspector Javert-like dedication to his duty.

Vee took Jamie's marred face between her hands and surveyed the damage. Satisfied that he wouldn't be disfigured for life, she gingerly kissed the undamaged side of his mouth. With quiet words and a few more doting kisses, she encouraged him to go off with Doc Benoir.

As soon as Jamie was occupied, Vee scanned the room. Her gaze locked on mine and she gave me a nearly imperceptible nod. The message *"It's time"* whispered through our shared brain. She casually strolled to the doors that led to the gardens. The second Eòran looked away, she slipped outside.

Back in school, when we wanted to meet in the girls' bathroom in secret, she would go first, and after one hundred Mississippis I would follow. I began to count, and as I did I loaded a napkin with tasty treats. If she didn't have the opportunity to visit the dessert table, the least I could do was bring her the most important meal of the day.

Just as I added a mini éclair to the top of my napkin pyramid, Duncan reappeared at the ballroom's main entrance. It was everything I could do to restrain myself from going to him. But I was already at seventy-eight Mississippi. Vee would be expecting me.

"Glad you approve of the pastry selections." Mags Benoir, the doc's wife and Castle MacCrae's head chef, startled me out of my conflicted inner monologue. She regarded me in her disquieting, candid way. "You know, Mackenna, being Called isn't a sacrifice. It's a gift."

My heart thumped out an arrhythmic staccato as I searched

her face, careful to keep my reaction from betraying itself in my eyes. "I know that."

"Do you, child?" I bristled at the moniker but held my tongue as she nodded to Duncan. "Then why did you assume what Duncan would be giving up outweighed what he would gain in his new life with you?"

My neutral expression soured into a frown despite my effort. "When I left him on the bridge, I didn't know we had a Calling."

"Didn't you?" Then just as brusquely as she'd arrived, Mags disappeared, leaving me feeling naked despite layers of fabric.

Grateful that I had other things to focus on other than my train wreck of a love life, I crossed to the French doors and slipped outside. The wide expanse of patio ended in a short flight of stairs that led to the great lawn.

Halfway down the stairs, I hesitated. What if Vee's vision wasn't right? What if in facing the limbus we died or destroyed the kingdom? This might be my last chance to confess everything to my prince. Even if he chose Analisa over me, did I really want to slink away without unburdening my hapless heart?

My Cinderella night had evolved from Rogers and Hammerstein into Sondheim, so that I now found myself stuck in indecision on the steps of the palace. Before I could make up my mind, a small group of Doonians wandered onto the patio at the far end of the landing, and I scurried to cloak myself in the shadows of the garden.

The horse stables, Vee's and my rendezvous spot, was less than five minutes away. Slipping off my shoes, I clutched them in my confection-free hand and started to walk. When I reached the stables, they were darker than Monday in the theater district. Although I knew we needed ninja-like stealth, it didn't make sense that there would be no light.

"Vee," I hissed as I eased myself inside the door. "Are you here?"

I sensed movement directly behind me as a deep, unfamiliar voice replied, "Aye lass. She is."

Chapter 27

Mackenna

Vee's éclairs tumbled to the ground as rough hands dug into my upper arms. With a hiss like angry rattlesnakes, torches blazed to life, revealing about a half dozen men, most of whom I didn't recognize. Off to the side, a trollish soldier stood behind Vee with one hairy arm wrapped around her abdomen and the other covering her mouth. Vee's eyes were huge and imploring, but it was too late to escape. Like her, I'd walked straight into the ambush.

Thrashing away from my captor, I began to scream. A hand that reeked of cabbage clamped over my mouth cutting off my airflow. In one powerful motion, Cabbage Guy's other arm moved from my bicep across my throat to press against my windpipe. I stopped struggling instantly.

As soon as I stilled, my captor motioned for the men to exit the stable and forced me out behind them. Vee and her troll walked just in front of us. As we marched toward the castle, it became clear that something big was going on inside the ballroom. The commotion grew when the French doors flew open, followed by a shout. "This way, fellow Doonians."

The first guests, including Duncan and Jamie, spilled across the patio and down the stairs onto the great lawn. When they saw Vee and me, their bodies went on immediate alert. The man who'd led them to us pulled a knife from his scabbard. Lightning fast, he wrenched Fiona from her groom's side and pressed the blade to her throat. Before Fergus could react, he bellowed, "Halt! Or she dies."

Distracted by the attack on the new bride, the MacCrae brothers failed to notice the other men drawing swords until after they'd taken up strategic places around the perimeter. Vee had told me of the group that opposed her rule forming mobs of six or ten, but this had to be three times that amount. While some of them looked like random farmers, the rest were dressed for the ball, which indicated they'd been spying on us all evening.

"What's the meaning of this?" Jamie demanded. Rather than wait for an answer, he charged the closest traitor. Both men crash to the ground as Fiona yelped in pain. At her cry, Jamie froze. His disheveled head turned in her direction. A small stream of blood rolled down her neck to form a crimson blossom on the bodice of her white gown.

"Fee!" The full horror of the situation shone on Fergus's face as he called to his new wife. Threatening her life was a most effective restraint for the giant of our group. Despite being the size of a redwood and skilled in combat, he was immediately compliant.

"I'm all right," she answered. *For now.*

Duncan must've realized that we were at a tactical disadvantage. He held up his hands in surrender and asked, "What's this about, lads?"

"Treason." The bearded ringleader of Vee's opposition, aka Beardy, stepped from the shadows. Vee's duffel bag, containing spare clothes and the axe, was slung over the guy's shoulder.

With a noise between a scoff and a growl, Jamie replied, "Seems to me, you're the one commitin' treason, Sean MacNally."

Instead of answering the prince, Beardy addressed the multitude of Doonians who now assembled on the great lawn. "I paid a visit ta Gregory Forrester today. At first he was reluctant to speak, but after a little coaxing he told me the most unbelievable story — of black petunias growing along the border and his brother's tragic demise." At the mention of the flowers associated with the Witch of Doon, the crowd began to murmur. "That's right, my fellow Doonians, Drew Forrest was no' killed in any accident. He stepped inta those flowers and became one o' the undead. The Eldritch Limbus is once again ravaging our land!"

The crowd went wild. Many of those present made the sign of the cross and at least one lady fainted. A small gasp drew my attention to the right. Emily stared in disbelief that her true love's death had been no accident and tears started to trickle down her cheeks. As her wounded eyes held mine, she began to sob. Burying her face in her hands, she fled toward the privacy of the castle. I expected Analisa to follow, but she was curiously MIA.

From the opposite side of the great lawn, Mario Rosetti pushed his way forward. "That is a terrifying tale to be sure, *Signore*. But even if the Eldritch Limbus is returned, I fail to see what that has to do with treason. Enlighten us, *per piacere*?"

"Gregory told me that when the queen herself came ta see him after the limbus took his only family and his arm, she asked him ta keep quiet. But I convinced him that the people have a right ta know. Doonians, your foreigner queen deceives you! She has known about the limbus for weeks, and yet she has said naught to you about the impending danger."

Another burst of disbelief erupted from the crowd. Beardy pointed to Vee. "That's right, Doon is perishing inta evil and she does nothing!"

Vee bucked against her captor, her muffled shouts unintelligible. Someone in the crowd yelled to let her speak. Beardy nodded and the hand disappeared from her mouth.

"That's not true!" she countered. "We were trying to stop the limbus. We didn't want to cause a panic."

Beardy stepped toward her. "We, meanin' you and the other American lass?" When Vee nodded, something akin to triumph twinkled in the man's beady eyes. "Then how do ye account for this?"

He pulled the axe from the duffel and hoisted the bag high over his head. "Two changes of modern clothes and shoes, the Rings of Aontacht, and the Arm o' the Bruce, one of Doon's most valuable artifacts. You and yer friend were planning ta cross the bridge, leaving us to perish."

Enough was enough. I bit down on Cabbage Guy's hand. When he pulled it away, I shouted, "We were heading into the limbus to break the curse and save your kingdom, you idiot. That's why I came back to Doon."

"I thought you came back for love, because of your Calling?" I looked through the crowd and found the wounded expression of Gabriela Rosetti staring back at me.

"It was a lie to explain my sudden arrival."

Beardy stepped between us, blocking Gabby from my view as his eyes narrowed critically. "How do ye know the limbus is caused by a curse?"

I froze, my eyes darting to Vee's for help. She sighed in resignation and said, "From the witches' spell book."

Remembering HBO imagery of royal heads on pikes, I inter-jected, "I got it from the witches' cottage. By myself. Alone."

As the crowd reacted to that little confession bomb, Jamie's gaze jumped from Vee to me and back again. I knew we would have more discussion concerning our field trip after we got out of this mess. *If* we got out of this mess.

Handing the axe off to one of his men, Beardy scowled at Vee. "And what did ye learn from the spell book?"

To her credit, Vee didn't try to justify her motives. She just replied calmly, "That the curse is written on a Pictish stone somewhere inside the limbus. To break the stone we needed a weapon blessed by God and sanctified in battle."

Jamie made a small noise of surprise. "Our trip inta the catacombs was about finding the Arm o' the Bruce."

"Yes." Vee's eyes begged Jamie to forgive her for not tell-ing him the whole truth. "When I touched it, I had a vision of us — Kenna and me — leaving the ball and going to the bridge. Kenna needs to strike the Pictish stone containing the curse with the axe. That will break the spell."

The crowd rippled with side conversations so that Vee had to shout to continue. "There's more. In my vision, I saw the Brig o' Doon covered in black petunias. If Kenna and I don't do this now, the limbus will begin to infect the modern world too. Who knows how far it could spread? We've got to go now!"

For a moment, Beardy looked troubled. The evening clearly wasn't going the way he had anticipated. He glared at Vee. "How do we know you're telling the truth? That could be some story you created ta cover up yer grand escape."

Rather than direct her answer to him, Vee implored her people. "You have to trust me. I would *never* abandon Doon. Everything I've done has been to save our kingdom. To save us all!"

Beardy scanned the horrified crowd realizing the tide had turned. Despite Vee's transgressions, she'd regained the support of the people. They wanted to believe her. "Very well," he barked. "If what ye say is true, then we'll let you prove it." He turned to his henchmen. "Get the wagons, lads."

A group of Beardy's men headed back toward the stables. In the hole they left, I saw one of the Queen's Guard being held up by two other soldiers. Eòran. Barely conscious and beaten within an inch of his life, he lurched toward Vee. "Sorry, my queen," he moaned. Then his eyes rolled back in his head as he passed out.

Horrified, Vee turned toward Beardy. "Please," she implored. "Eòran needs a doctor. Let him go."

Beardy nodded and the soldiers carrying Eòran disappeared into the crowd.

"Fiona, too," Vee demanded. "We'll go willingly so you don't need her anymore."

With another nod from the ringleader, the flunky holding Fiona stepped away. Although she'd remained admirably stoic up until this point, as soon as she was free she scrambled to Fergus with a sharp sob of relief. The big man enveloped her until she all but disappeared. Despite the tears that rolled down his mottled cheeks, Fergus was a lethal warrior. Beardy and his henchmen had made a huge mistake by targeting his bride. I'd no doubt that if given the chance, he'd slaughter them without remorse.

As two carts rumbled to a stop on the walking lane, Beardy motioned to a couple of his lackeys. "Seize the princes. Get 'em into the first wagon and bind their hands and feet. They can direct us ta the limbus."

"No." Vee gasped. "The princes stay. You've no quarrel with them."

Beardy shook his head. "You're out of favors, lassie. Besides, they're leverage so ye and yer carrot-headed friend dinna flee."

Harsh. But I'd been called worse.

"Please — " Vee pleaded at the same moment Jamie said, "We'll go."

"Aye," Duncan echoed, stepping forward. "We insist."

Like lambs to the slaughter, Duncan and Jamie climbed into the back of the cart. Once they were settled, they offered their hands and feet to Beardy's men for binding. Vee opened her mouth to protest and then closed it again. She knew they would never let us go off alone with the mob. Even if Duncan didn't care for me the same way Jamie did for Vee, he was honor-bound to protect me.

The man holding the Arm o' the Bruce climbed into the driver's seat of the second cart. Beardy threw the duffel into the back and gestured. "In you go, lassies."

Climbing into the back of a wagon in voluminous skirts was no easy task. Instead of giving us a hand, Beardy watched us struggle and shimmy our way in. As soon as we complied, he climbed up on the running board to look out on the crowd. "If anyone tries to follow, we'll kill both o' Doon's princes. If ye feel you must do somethin', pray that the American queen can deliver us from the witches' death."

With those parting words, Beardy pulled himself up next to our driver, and we rumbled away. The two guards in the wagon with us sat so that their legs dangled over the back edge. Thankfully, they paid us very little attention as we bumped into the night. Once the castle faded into the distance, I scooted over to Vee and whispered, "My hair is coppery, not carroty."

Vee blinked at me. "Does it really matter?"

"Absolutely." When she didn't answer, I asked, "So what's

the deal with the guy in charge, the Beardy dude? What did you do to him?"

"Sean MacNally? Nothing. He's a blacksmith."

"And the leader of the I-hate-Queen-Vee coalition."

She sighed wearily, "I thought he was harmless, mostly. I still don't believe he'd actually have killed Fiona, or Duncan and Jamie."

I noted how she'd conveniently left out Eòran. "You never think badly of anyone … Not your dad for leaving you … Or Eric when he cheated on you with Steph … Not even Janet when she spent the rent money you earned on boxed wine and lotto tickets." Vee's mom had been a poster parent for the reason Child Protective Services existed, and yet my bestie always found a reason to give her another chance.

Vee glanced at the two men. "What's your point, Ken?"

"My point is he'd murder us all — and then sleep like a baby. If the opportunity presents itself, maybe we should think about giving him a shove into the limbus."

She sighed in resignation. "No. We were heading that way anyway. This way you're spared the trauma of riding a horse, and I'm spared from hearing about your horrific horse-riding experience. I'd call that win-win."

Despite her teasing words, she couldn't quite sell her sunny side of the street perspective. But she was right about riding horseback. Remembering my aching thighs from the time we'd galloped to the bridge to save Jamie, I counted the cart as a small blessing. The only horse I wanted to see was the wooden kind used for building scenery.

Grabbing the duffel, I conceded her point by saying, "We should conserve our energy … And change shoes."

Rummaging in the bag, I pulled out two pairs of Nikes and threw the purple size sixes at her. We were too exposed to change out of our gowns, but at least we could face the zombie fungus in sensible footwear.

Before closing the bag, I fished out the rings and handed Vee hers before slipping mine on. That way I would have some warning of the limbus before we drove obliviously into it. I was not about to leave our safety in the hands of Beardy and his half-wit henchmen — discernment was clearly not in their wheelhouse, or they wouldn't have opposed Vee.

For the next hour we bumped along in silence. I had just begun to doze off when a whistle sounded from the first cart. It pulled over to the side of the road, and our vehicle followed. Beardy hopped down and approached us. "The path to the Brig o' Doon is over yon, on the other side of the clearing. We go the rest of the way on foot."

In the first wagon, one of the henchmen raised his sword. With two *thwacks!* he cut the bindings on Duncan's and Jamie's legs. The princes climbed awkwardly from the cart with their hands still tied behind their backs. Several henchmen surrounded them as Cabbage Guy wrenched my arm and commanded, "Walk."

The full moon sat high in the sky — just like in Vee's vision. Pale light bathed the field, making it easier to pick our way across the uneven ground. I could just make out the heavily wooded path to the Brig o' Doon through the trees at the far end of the clearing.

As we approached the forest, the path grew more discernable, as did the narrow line of black petunias that cut across it — and the smell. On the other side of the flowers, I clearly saw the bare-boned trees and dank, oozing moss of the zombie fungus. Only this time, I could glimpse movement and hear creatures rustling in the darkness. Chills crept up my back as I tried not to picture what might be scurrying, scuttling, or even slithering on the other side.

"What is it?" Vee's concern reminded me that for the moment I was safe.

"See the flowers?" I asked.

"Yes. I can see them clearly in the moonlight, but beyond …" She shuddered as if suddenly scared or freezing — maybe both. "Beyond is like there's no moon at all. It's nearly pitch black."

She should've seen it from my angle — but that horror would be her reality soon enough.

One of the henchmen, sent ahead to scout the tree line, called for us to halt. "The mark of the witch is upon the trail," he cried. "Her flowers swallow the path ta the Brig o' Doon in darkness."

Sean MacNally peered into the trees. When he saw the flowers, he crossed himself. Then he took the axe from his henchman and handed it to me. "Time to prove yer loyalty, lassies."

For a moment I fantasized about chopping him in half. My thought must've been obvious, because Beardy clucked at me. He gestured toward his men restraining Duncan at knifepoint. "If you have any regard for Prince MacCrae, ye'll march inta the limbus as ye've been told."

Duncan appeared unafraid despite the variety of blades pointed at him. His right eye — the one that'd taken his brother's fist — was swollen and discolored. I wondered if I would ever see his ridiculously gorgeous, slightly imperfect face again. I didn't even care if I survived as long as I saved him and his beloved kingdom. His image shimmered, and I blinked to clear my glassy vision. I wanted my last memory of him to be a clear one.

Unable to help myself, I slowly crossed to my prince. The men who held him watched me carefully as I approached. As if he could read my thoughts, Duncan growled my name as a warning to keep away.

I shook my head and took another step forward. With his hands tied behind his back and armed men on both sides, he was unable to stop me from fitting my body against his. I pressed my cheek gently against his jaw and whispered, "A night of lasts, remember?"

I didn't care that I was in full view of our captors. They already knew that Duncan MacCrae was my weakness. The only thing that mattered was that he knew it. "I've already said good-bye to Doon." I pulled back to cherish his banged-up face — perfect brows, blackened eye, slightly crooked nose, amazing cheek bones, and lips worth dying for.

"All that's left is to say good-bye to you," I whispered.

"Don't!" His velvet-brown eyes pleaded with me to stop. But it was the last midnight, and we were out of chances. Raising up on my toes, I placed my hands flat against his chest as I angled my mouth over his until we shared the same breath. My eyelids drifted shut. When my lips touched his, he turned to granite. His mouth refused to respond as I tried to steal one last kiss.

Utterly humiliated, I stepped back. "Sorry," I mumbled. "I maybe shouldn't have done that."

"I'll no' kiss you good-bye." He pierced me with his man of steel glare. "You're goin' to come out of this just fine. You were called here to destroy the limbus. As soon as it's done, I'll see you safely back to your chosen life. Just as I promised ye I would."

Duncan was right — a last kiss wasn't in the job description. He'd made it clear all along that I was only here because they needed me to destroy the limbus. I'd let the bleakness of the moment play on my emotions, but now that the whole kingdom knew our Calling was a ruse, we no longer had reason to pretend.

He wanted to move on with Analisa ... And me? Maybe I would start collecting cats. Or better yet audition for *Cats*: the international tour. I could spend night after night lamenting what I'd lost in German until he was purged from my system. But in truth, I suspected I would never get over Duncan. I'd been mourning him since I was twelve years old. And I would never stop.

CHAPTER 28

Veronica

Kenna turned to me, blinking back tears. But her show of emotion wasn't the result of a poignant Austenesque kind of epilogue. In so many words, Duncan had told her to do her duty and get the heck out. I'd been positive he still secretly loved my best friend, but now I doubted those instincts. I moved toward her, the wounded look in her eyes making me want to both comfort her and sucker punch a particular tall, dark, and brooding prince.

But before I could do either, Sean MacNally intercepted me. "This is it, girl." He gave me a rough shove toward the limbus. "If yer really the queen, go fix it!"

I stumbled, caught my balance, and spun on the leader of the mob. I had one more thing to do before I cashed in my ticket to Zombieland. "*Not* until you untie Jamie and let me say good-bye."

He narrowed his eyes, sweat dotting his scarlet cheekbones above his beard. "No."

I lifted my chin and stared him straight in his beady eyes. "I might die saving your sorry hide, Mr. MacNally. But if I don't, I'll still be your queen and you'll wish you'd treated me with more respect."

He blanched. "Ye've got one minute." He gave a curt nod of assent to his goons.

The moment they cut Jamie's bonds, he jerked out of their grasp and sprinted toward me. Picking up my gown, I ran to meet him and threw myself into his arms. He pulled me tight against his chest.

"So this was your brilliant plan? Sacrifice yourself to stop the limbus?"

"I—"

"I canna do this." He drew back and cradled my face in his hands. "I'm not like my brother. I canna watch you walk to your death."

"That's not how this ends." I took his hands and enfolded them in mine. "I've seen it, Jamie. Kenna *will* break the curse. We just have to be brave enough to follow the Protector's will."

"Do ye really think it's going to be that easy?" His brows hunched over his eyes, his grip on my fingers verging on painful. "The limbus is pure malevolence. *Anythin'* could happen in there. Did the vision happen to show you getting out alive?"

I shook my head and my heart stuttered in my chest. The prophecy had ended with us breaking the stone. Was it possible the curse could take us with it? Suck us into its vortex of evil as the limbus drained away? For the first time, I let myself admit that we knew next to nothing about what we were about to face. But I pasted on a smile for Jamie's sake. "No, but the rings will protect us. We'll be—"

"Time's up!"

Jamie's dark gaze intent on my face, he leaned in. Hyperaware this could be our last kiss, I closed my eyes and drank in the whisper of his breath before rough hands yanked me back.

Two men restrained Jamie's arms. Rage contorting his face, he twisted out of their grasp and spun, his fist smashing into a goon's nose with a loud crack. He caught the other one's punch just before it hit his face, countering with an uppercut that snapped the man's head back and dropped him to the ground. The fight was over before I could take a breath.

Jamie turned murderous eyes on the ringleader and rushed him. Duncan, still at knife point, yelped his brother's name. Jamie hesitated mere inches from his target's face. "If we survive this, MacNally, I'm going to take great pleasure in killing you."

Three men jumped Jamie from behind. One subdued him with an arm around his throat, while the other two secured his arms and forced him away from their leader.

Now that Jamie was restrained, Sean followed. "We shall see about that, *my laird*," he spat as he rammed a fist into Jamie's stomach.

Jamie's face paled and the breath whooshed from his lungs.

When Sean reared back to deliver another blow, I leapt forward and grabbed his meaty arm in a death grip. "Stop, you bloody coward!"

MacNally whirled on me with clenched fists, bloodlust gleaming in his eyes. I braced for the impact, determined not to go down. But the hit never came. Instead, he spat, "I granted your request, girl. Now get to it." He gave me a mighty shove in Kenna's direction.

I tripped sideways and bumped into my friend, both of us stumbling over our skirts. Kenna grunted as I grabbed her arm to steady us. With a glare at MacNally, I gained my balance and straightened my dress. I may not allow Jamie to kill the man, but letting him beat the snot out of the jerk was a definite possibility. I turned to Kenna. "All set?"

Her face as white as snow in the moonlight, she held up the Arm o' the Bruce in answer. She glanced over her shoulder at Duncan, who gave her a solemn nod. Then side by side we began to move toward the edge of the forest, the unnatural darkness waiting to swallow us whole. Cold curled in my gut and tingled over my skin.

A visceral touch, like the brush of silent fingers, made me pause. I turned to find my warrior prince tied to a tree, a knife held against his ribs. His searing stare cut across the clearing and our eyes locked, the moment freezing in time.

"Come back to me, love."

Like the first time he'd spoken to me in the parking lot of Bainbridge High, the deep timbre of his voice reverberated deep inside me.

Promises of hope and security and courage flooded my soul as I backed away, holding Jamie's face in my gaze as long as I could. Then, I turned and marched into the forest with renewed resolve.

On the other side of the trees, Kenna took my hand, and the stench of putrefaction radiating from the limbus blasted into me. I gagged and covered my mouth with my free hand. Kenna made a choking sound as we staggered forward.

At the edge of a line of black petunias we stopped. The undulating abyss on the other side was hypnotizing, like staring into the depths of the ocean — fathomless and utterly alien. A shiver ran through me. My stomach rolled and my vision spun. I reached in my pocket and squeezed the pendant until the points of metal pressed into my flesh. This was no time for a migraine.

Taking a deep breath, I asked, "Ready?"

"I guess." Kenna glanced at me and then back to the murky wall. "I just wish I was wearing nicer underwear."

"What?"

"I *really* don't want to die in my granny panties."

"For the last time — we *are not* going to die." I repositioned my hand so it was more firmly in hers. "Come on. Three steps and we're in. Let's count it off together."

We stepped forward, "One …" The rings ignited, and the stench faded into a minor annoyance.

"Two …" The flowers shriveled under our feet.

"… Three!" We stepped into the black hole.

As soon as our feet crossed the border, the blessed Rings of Aontacht blazed, lighting the path before us, but that protection did nothing to block the wind ripping into our hair and tugging at our gowns. Leaning into the gale, we found the narrow path to the bridge. Gnarled trees arched overhead. Their naked limbs linked like a tunnel made of long, spindly fingers. Part of me knew we were safe, but some other more primitive portion of my brain screamed a warning signal. *Run! Get out or die!*

To my right, a rapacious cry rent the air. I jumped and stepped on the hem of Kenna's gown, our shoulders bumping.

"Hey, we're fine." She held up our linked hands, the rings glowing like sparklers on the Fourth of July. "These puppies protect us, remember?"

The desperate caw sounded again, closer. I jerked my eyes up, searching the branches above. There, just beyond the circle of our ring's light, perched the most hideous creature I'd ever laid eyes on. Decomposing flesh peeled from its bones, and only a smattering of feathers peppered its remaining gray skin. The zombified crow cocked its head, voracious red eyes watchful.

When we were directly under it, the bird's desecrated wings

spread wide, and with a bloodcurdling shriek it took flight. I jerked my hands up to cover my head, bringing Kenna's hand with me. The beast circled the glow blazing from our rings. But before I could digest my relief, it dove straight for us.

I screamed, pulled my hand from Kenna's, and everything went black.

Claws dug into my scalp. I spun in a circle, blindly swatting at the creature entangled in my hair. My hand connected with something slimy and wet as a burning pain exploded across my head. With another desperate tug, the crow came loose. I hurled it away with all my strength, and as I turned to flee, I smashed into an invisible tree.

The vision had been wrong, I realized as I lay crumpled on the ground. We were going to die or become zombies. And worse, we were going to fail.

CHAPTER 29

Mackenna

Failure is not an option. So get up before I pull you up by your tiara!"

Vee lay huddled on the ground, babbling nonsense. She was covered in scratches, but safe for the moment. The zombie crow had lurched away, taking a long dark clump of hair with it.

She teetered on the verge of hysteria, and I was right there with her. Ever since I'd first witnessed the undead crow, I'd had nightmares. Turns out my fears were not unfounded. The forest was full of red, beady eyes peering at us. I had to assume they were the limbus's defense system, which meant there'd be more coming.

"Get up!" I shouted.

In an effort to reclaim the path, the fungus had begun to creep its way onto Vee's gown as she thrashed about. Her head whipped one direction and then the other. "Kenna? Where are you?"

"Right here." The zombie crow hadn't pecked out her eyes — to my great relief. Yet she stared sightlessly in my general direction. Why couldn't she see — Of course!

I bent down and slipped my hand into hers. The stench, which had been nearly unbearable, receded as the red and green glow of the Rings of Aontacht blazed to white.

As if touched by Rapunzel's tears, Vee blinked up at my face. She sighed, relief softening her features. Then, suddenly remembering where we were, she started to scramble to her feet. Holding tight to her hand, I helped her up. "You're safe."

With large, haunted eyes, she wildly surveyed her body. Her tiara was hanging off to one side, her hair disheveled, arms scratched, and the limbus had begun to disintegrate the hem of her dress, but all things considered, she was okay. Satisfied that I was telling the truth, she took a calming breath. Her body trembled despite the resolution to be brave.

"The crow?" she croaked.

The cold wind nipped at my exposed skin, causing my teeth to chatter. "It's g-gone — for now. But we need to keep g-going." After an instant of hesitation she nodded vigorously.

In our little bubble of protection, we continued along the path to the riverbank. Mere inches ahead of our feet, the fungus shriveled away only to swallow up the path in our wake. Our heavy skirts were a nightmare in themselves, but as much as I longed to rip away the bottom half of the fabric, I wasn't letting go of Vee for anything.

With each step, unholy things scurried in the underbrush. Every time I glanced behind, the number of beady, red eyes following us multiplied. As the light of the Rings of Aontacht illuminated the way, I caught sight of an undead squirrel. When the light caught the tip of its rotting tail, it shrieked and scampered off the path.

We'd been foolish to go into the limbus without any weapons other than an unwieldy axe. If we'd thought to bring a knife, we could've easily hacked our skirts away — not to mention undead animals. As it stood, we were nearly defenseless and totally dependent on one another.

When we found the Pictish stone, would we have to swing the axe in tandem? I was a whole head taller than my bestie, and although I didn't know much about lumberjacking I knew we wouldn't get an effective swing approaching it like a three-legged race or a bicycle built for two.

The trail narrowed to the width of a deer track. Still gripping my hand, Vee shuffled awkwardly behind me. The rings ensured we were protected from the limbus, but skeletal remains of underbrush snagged our gowns with every step.

The sound of rushing water grew louder. As I led us around a bend, the clearing for the Brig o' Doon became visible through the trees. I gave Vee's hand an encouraging squeeze. "We're nearly there."

Ahead, I could see the bridge. Our side of the riverbank was covered in black slime and little black flowers that'd already made it halfway across. Vee's vision had been dead on. In addition to destroying Doon, the limbus would attack Alloway. We were the modern world's only defense against the zombie apocalypse.

To the left of the bridge stood a four-foot-high tablet of stone protruding from the ground at a crazy angle. Little purple sparks — witch's magic for sure — erupted from the surface. All we had to do to break the curse was chop the stone in half with the axe. For the first time, I felt as if we might come out of this okay.

Rustling at the mouth of the path drew my attention. While the whole forest bristled with zombie critters, whatever made this noise was significantly larger than a bird or a squirrel. It sounded more like an elephant or a bear.

I made a shushing noise and froze in my tracks. From Vee's

blizzard encounter, I knew the occasional grizzly roamed the woods as part of the kingdom's natural border protection. I seriously hoped we wouldn't have to face down a zombie bear to get to the stone.

Vee's free hand dug into my waist as she peered around my side. Mirroring my alarm, she asked in a low voice, "What is it?"

"Can't tell," I whispered as a shiver crawled its way down my spine. "But whatever it is, it's big."

Her fingers tightened ever so slightly. "Maybe we can sneak past it."

Despite the sinking feeling in my chest that said otherwise, it was worth a try. Unwilling to risk another sound, I nodded. Ever so slowly, we began to sneak along the path. The light from our rings provided our protection, but it was also a giant beacon. If it did draw the creature, I hoped the divine force field, or whatever it was, would continue to hold.

The noise grew louder as we crept into the clearing. Just as I stepped free of the woods, Vee gasped. Spinning around, I saw her terror-stricken face first. But then, in the dimness of the limbus, I discerned another face looming just above hers.

Hunks of gray flesh hung from the emaciated face and one eyeball dangled precariously down its cheek. The other lidless eye gaped at Vee like something from the horror movie that'd haunted me since childhood. Its nose and lips were missing, along with its hair. Decomposing skin exposed yellowing bone all over the creature's body. It still wore the tattered remains of pants, which covered most of the hips and thighs, and part of one rotted, flapping boot.

The creature made a guttural sound and reached hesitantly toward Vee with a bony finger. It stopped just short of the light bubble and gurgled again. My stomach heaved as I realized it no longer had a tongue.

Swallowing an agonized squeak, Vee murmured, "It's Drew Forrester."

It took me an instant to connect the zombie in front of us with the boy that'd been Emily's intended. Gripping the axe handle more tightly with my free hand, I quietly asked, "Should we kill it?"

"No!" Vee hissed and then lowered her voice. "We need to try to save him."

This was no baby bird in need of TLC; it was an abomination. I feared Drew was beyond saving, but as Vee stubbornly clenched her jaw, I didn't have the heart to speak the words. He'd been her subject, so of course she'd feel responsible. As gently as possible, I said, "I'm not sure that he can be — "

"We need to try! For Emily's sake." Vee paused to take a shaky breath. "He seems to recognize me ... Maybe he's not completely gone."

Realizing it was useless to argue, I asked, "What do you have in mind?"

"Let's do what we came here to do," she replied. "Let's destroy the Pictish stone. Breaking the curse is his only chance."

Clutching Vee while keeping my eyes fixed on Drew of the Dead, I backed toward the stone. The former Doonian shuffled along behind us like a ghoulish pet. As I glanced over my shoulder to gauge our distance to the bridge, Vee stepped on my skirt. Thrown off balance, we crashed to the ground in a tangle of pretty dresses. On impact, I lost the axe, which clattered across the ground. I reached for it, realizing at the last second that my other hand was also empty.

Vee's scream pierced the night. I turned over to see what was left of Drew on top of her. His bony hands closed around her throat in a superhuman grip. She blindly clawed at him, dislodging little bits of rotten flesh that landed on her neck and shoulders.

Taking up the axe, I struggled to free my legs from my gown and get to my feet. Perhaps Drew could be saved, but as my bestie's eyes bulged out of their sockets my choice was clear. I kicked Drew's shoulder with all my strength. He rolled onto his back, scuttling like a creepy upside-down turtle. Hefting the Arm o' the Bruce over my head, I screamed for Vee to move to her right. As soon as she scrambled away, I lunged forward and let the axe fall.

Blackish blood squirted from Drew's neck. I felt it splatter my face in a cold spray as his severed head rolled away. The putrid stench of decapitated zombie — a thousand times worse than the stink of the limbus — assaulted me. My stomach lurched and I let the axe slip from my hand as I dropped to my knees, retching. The meager contents of my stomach, mostly stomach acid, spewed from my mouth onto wet, blackened ground.

With my eyes clenched shut, I was vaguely aware of Vee clawing her way up my skirts to touch my arm. Patterns danced across my eyelids as we became once again enclosed in the bubble of light. Pulling Vee with me, I collapsed away from the zombie corpse into a tight ball. Had we really been so deluded as to think we could waltz into the limbus and break the curse? I was an actress, not some crackerjack tribute. I was not prepared to battle to the death.

The barren ground against my cheek and arms felt like ice. It seemed to leach away the last of my energy. I could sense the nothingness of oblivion reaching for me, lulling me away from my present reality. Fortunately, Vee's pull was stronger. She rubbed my shoulders, speaking words that sounded like a kindergarten pep talk.

Numb to the core, I opened a heavy eyelid to glare at her. "What?"

"Try, try again." She pointed to the axe lying next to me on the ground. "It's on the handle."

"So?"

"So — Robert the Bruce coined that motto when he was hiding in a cave, nearly defeated. He saw a spider trying to spin a web. After numerous attempts, it finally succeeded. That spider inspired him not to give up — so he tried again and eventually won Scotland's independence."

"What if this is the one we can't win?"

"I believe in my vision. But just because we're sure of the outcome, that doesn't mean it's going to be easy." She touched my cheek. "But we need to have faith that we will win."

"What if I can't?"

"Then I'll have faith enough for both of us." She hoisted me into a sitting position. "We're so close. The stone is right there. All you have to do is finish the job."

My head felt cottony, like I'd taken too much cold medicine. The temptation to go to sleep tugged me toward the ground, but Vee yanked on my arm. "Oh, no you don't! Let's stand up."

She wedged her shoulder into my armpit. Bracing her legs like she was on the bottom of a cheerleading pyramid, she hoisted me to my feet with a roar. Her arm curled around my back and urged me forward. A lifetime of experience told me that resistance was futile. After a few steps of her forced march, my head began to clear.

Less than ten paces ahead, the stone from Vee's vision jutted crookedly from the ground. Violet light curled along the symbols that represented the Pictish curse. Thick black sludge oozed from the base of the stone to form a churning, altar-like pool on the ground. Just above the surface of the pool a purple mist swirled in the opposite direction. The effect gave me a queasy sense of vertigo.

Tendrils of zombie fungus slithered from the pool across the forest floor on their way to suck the life from anything that wasn't already dead — or undead. Vee was right — we had to stop it. According to her vision, I just needed to strike the stone with the Arm o' the — Wait a minute! "The axe!"

"Got it." The certainty in Vee's voice bolstered my courage as she handed me the weapon.

"Thanks." A few more steps and we stopped at the edge of the source of the limbus. The instant our bubble of light pierced the pool, it began to boil. The contents of the pool rose through the mist, forming and reforming as it grew; cadaverous faces, snapping teeth, bulging eyes, claws, snouts, and grasping hands materialized and vanished. Once the thing reached my height it began to hiss as it solidified into a human-like shape.

Sludge dripped away to reveal a pale, skeletal face ravaged by time. With a creaky breath, its eyelids popped open. Vee and I gasped as recognition throat punched us. Clothed in robes of zombie fungus and regarding us with unmistakable fury stood Adelaide Blackmore Cadell, the Witch of Doon.

CHAPTER 30

Mackenna

Just like we'd left her after the last encounter, the Witch of Doon resembled an old, haggish woman. Though now, she looked inhumanly powerful. The shroud of the limbus seemed to suck away most of her remaining color. At certain angles, her bones were just visible beneath her dry, translucent skin. Dirty white hair flapped erratically about her face. Only her emerald eyes, irises sparking with purple magic, contained any trace of life.

My body froze as Addie focused her attention on me. Her creepy leer caused the hairs on my arms to stand on end.

"The plucky sidekick," Addie clucked, her voice as ancient as the stone she guarded. "I thought you'd have run away by now."

Vee squeezed my hand for reassurance as I faced the being that inspired all my worst nightmares. "Not a chance."

"Really, dearie? Because that seems to be your specialty. Face it, you're not heroine material like our little queenie here."

The witch flicked her wrist, and my best friend doubled over in pain.

"Don't let her get into your head," Vee groaned.

"How could you?" The witch's voice had changed, causing me to whip my head back in her direction. But the Addie I recognized was gone. In her place stood Vee in her bedraggled, zombie-gore-encrusted gown.

Her large turquoise eyes brimmed with accusations. "I needed you, Kenna — more than ever when I returned to Doon, but you left me. You didn't just abandon Duncan, you abandoned your best friend. Deep inside, I will never forgive you for not staying."

My heart sank with the weight of her accusation. "I know."

"That's not me!" Vee gripped my hand so hard that pain radiated up my arm. I glanced between my bestie and her doppelganger, trying to get my bearings. "It must be some kind of magical ward to protect the curse. Don't let it confuse you. You have to destroy the stone!"

But I couldn't focus on the stone. The weight of my transgressions against my best friend rooted me to my spot. "I'm so sorry I left you. I wasn't thinking about how hard it would be for you or all the responsibility you would have. I should've been a better friend."

Faux Vee said, "You were only thinking of yourself" at the same moment real Vee said, "I forgive you, Kenna. Now destroy the stone!"

Feeling better, I turned to attack Vee's likeness. But she was gone. In her place stood my beloved aunt. This was not the vibrant, kaftan-wearing relative that shaped my childhood, but a frail, trembling woman in a fungus-stained hospital gown. I blinked, trying to comprehend the image before me. Aunt

Gracie's gray eyes — the same shade as mine — clouded with confusion. "Why didn't you come?"

I gazed at her, unable to say anything. I had no memories of my aunt during this part of her life and had never visited her when she got sick. I only came after ... to the funeral. A spasm racked her feeble body, but she continued in a thin voice, "I called and called for you. I kept holding on — hoping, then praying, for one last moment together. I was in agony, but I couldn't let go. It was my dying wish to see you one last time, but you never came."

Suddenly, I was twelve again and overwhelmed with the terror of losing the most important person in my life. "I was scared to say good-bye."

"So was I."

My vision blurred, but I made no move to wipe the wetness from my eyes. "I thought if I didn't come, you wouldn't leave me."

"You were being selfish, as usual."

The tears that began to flow down my cheeks were warm against my chilled skin. Gracie was right; when she needed me most, I let her down. I was all she had, and I let her face death completely alone.

"Kenna, listen to me!" Vee gripped my shoulder with her free hand, forcing me to look at her. "You were a little girl. Your *real* aunt understood. She loved you and forgave you."

I shook my head, denying Vee's overly kind words. I'd always wondered if Gracie died mad at me for not coming to see her. But the witch couldn't have known that — no one could.

Vee's thumb dug into my armpit as she ordered, "You need to snap out of this! The witch's evil — it exploits our weaknesses. I believed I was worthless and she used it against me. Whatever mistakes you've made, the people who really love you have forgiven you."

"Have they, now?"

I ripped my shoulder free, whirling toward the sound of Finn's voice. He looked exactly as he had the last time I'd seen him, when he was thirteen. As he raked his fingers through his dark hair, his lopsided grin faltered. His wounded eyes regarded me gravely. "Do ye remember what passed between us after your aunt's funeral?"

I nodded. On the Brig o' Doon, Finn had threaded his fingers through mine and lifted our intertwined hands to rest against his heart. With his other hand, he'd cupped my jaw as he pressed his lips to mine in our first kiss. Then I'd looked in his velvet brown eyes and made a promise.

Hurt radiated off of Finn's likeness. "You said ye'd come back."

Before my eyes, Finn grew into a tall, broad-shouldered prince. It wasn't really Duncan — and yet, it felt like him.

"You, Mackenna Reid, break your promises — just like ye break hearts." It was the same accusation he'd made during our recent courtyard encounter. Though I knew in my head the whole thing was a trick, my heart could not deny the truth in his words.

"I'm sorry," I pleaded.

"Save your apology. I trusted you and you betrayed that trust. You destroyed my faith and my heart. You claimed you abandoned me for my own good, but ye know that's not true. Say the truth."

I was vaguely aware of Vee at my side, but I couldn't focus on anything other than the boy whose life I'd ruined. What he said was as horrible as it was accurate. "I ran away. I was afraid it wouldn't work out between us … so I left you before you could leave me. But, if you give me another chance, I'll make it up to you."

Duncan stepped forward to the edge of the sludge pool. "Implore me." I opened my mouth and he pointed to the ground. "On your knees—the way a commoner should petition a prince."

The earth made a muddy, squelching noise as I sunk to my knees. Vaguely aware of Vee gripping my hand, I wrenched it free so I could plead properly. "Please. Give me another chance."

Standing over me, Duncan tipped his head to the side. "Tell me tha' you love me."

"I do. I always have, since we were children. I love you."

"Not good enough." He angled his head from side to side, popping the vertebrae in his neck. "Really convince me."

The words began to pour out of me as I confessed my soul. "I've thought about you every day since I left. Nothing fills that void, not even theater. Being without you is like being trapped in a world without color—I can't hear, taste, smell, or even touch my surroundings ... but it's more—it's missing that spark in the core of my being. I'm half of a duet that has no context or melody without you. And if you can find it in your heart to give me another chance, I'll spend every day making it up to you. I promise."

"Do ye *promise*?" Duncan sneered. His eyes burned with derision as he continued. "You're a coward and a liar. You canna make up for this. You could spend your entire life atoning and it still wouldna make things right between us. I never want to see you again."

"Okay." I closed my eyes against his condemnation as my soul caved in on itself, making it difficult to speak. Even in his rage, Duncan was blameless. I'd earned every terrible, contemptuous word.

"This is exactly what you deserve, wouldn't you agree?"

"Yes," I whispered.

He continued to denounce me without any hint of mercy.

"Because of your choices, you dinna ever get to have your happy ending. You ruined everything and ye've not paid nearly enough."

From a great distance, Vee's voice penetrated my consciousness. She knelt between Duncan's apparition and me, shaking me back and forth. "You deserve to be forgiven for your mistakes!"

"I don't." I opened my eyes to face her. There was no use in hiding anymore; Duncan had ripped me wide open. "I've abandoned everyone I ever loved. I've caused so much pain — I need to suffer for it."

"That's what the witch wants you to believe. But the truth is — the people who love you have already forgiven you. Those apparitions — me, Aunt Gracie, Duncan — they're not us; they're you. Your guilt, your recrimination, your need to suffer; the witch is using your greatest fears against you. You need to let yourself be forgiven."

"I don't know how."

"Stop torturing yourself and just let go. Surrender all the guilt, the pain, everything you've been carrying — leave it all here."

I glanced over Vee's shoulder at Duncan's seething image. Was he really an extension of my own self-loathing? If it was all in my head, could I really banish all those negative thoughts? I had to try — for all of us, but especially myself.

With Vee's help I struggled to my feet. She squeezed my hand as I confronted my own personal demon.

The princely apparition growled in warning. "Ye canna defeat me. You're nothing. Ana's a thousand times the lass you are. That's why I chose to be with her instead o' you."

"Shut up! You're not Duncan. You're not even my subconscious anymore. And I won't believe your lies."

The instant the words left my mouth, the world exploded. The protective bubble created by the rings burst into flames and

I braced myself for searing heat … but it never came. Despite the raging fire, the air was cool and I felt an overwhelming sense of calm, similar to being in the eye of a storm. Vee and I clutched each other tighter as the fire that engulfed us raced across the riverbank, consuming everything in its path.

Addie, whose apparition was once again in witch form, lit up like witch flambé. With a blood curdling shriek, she lunged toward us. Howling and clawing, she flailed against the fiery force-field. The witch and the wildfire burned ever brighter until they reached supernova status. Blinding light flashed as the burning limbus imploded. For an instant I felt an uncontainable burst of power rushing at me from all directions. And then, with a deafening rumble, it was gone.

In the silent aftermath, debris floated through the air, coating my hair and lashes like snowflakes. As far as the eye could see, a fine layer of ash covered the forest and half the bridge. The Pictish stone, while still intact, no longer had any purplish magic coursing through it. The pool of sludge had burned up along with the limbus, leaving only charred earth behind. Even the zombie splatter that'd covered Vee had been burned away.

Vee's awed gaze met mine. "What was that?"

"Forgiveness," I replied with a shrug.

Shielding her eyes from the drifting ashes, Vee surveyed the remains of the forest. "It's done."

Just to be sure, I crossed to the source of the limbus. Lifting the Arm o' the Bruce over my head, I swung at the Pictish stone with all my strength. A single flicker of purple sparked as the cursed rock broke in half with a sharp crack.

With my burdens burned away, I felt lighter than I had in a year — no, in a lifetime. It was a good feeling, one of closure. Dropping the axe, I wrapped my arms around my best friend. "Now, it's done."

ChAPTER 31

Mackenna

A universal truth in acting is that motivation is more important than action. What we do becomes meaningless without the why. Take leaving, for instance. It can be an act of fear, afraid of the unknowable future and what we might have to face if we stay. It can be motivated by a need to control, also fear based, to abandon before being abandoned. Or leaving can be an act of bravery stemming from a heroic heart.

As grim and determined as I'd ever seen him, Duncan hoisted my duffel over his shoulder. With a quick nod to Jamie and Vee, he announced, "I'll be waiting in the courtyard."

I stared at the floor, listening to his receding steps as I groped for the courage to say my good-byes. Jamie stepped forward and placed his hands stiffly on my shoulders. He pulled me into an awkward hug and said in a low voice only meant for me, "Dinna worry. I'll take care of Verranica. She's my everythin'."

After a couple of uncomfortable pats, he let go. Before he stepped away, he said, "Since you left, my brother avoids the loch as much as possible."

Jamie didn't volunteer stuff just for giggles. That bit of information was important, but I failed to grasp the significance. "Why?"

"It's not my reasoning to share. You'll have to ask him."

He stepped away and I followed. "Why are you helping me?"

Stopping at the door, Jamie's gaze flickered to my bestie before settling on me. "I'm not. I'm helping Duncan." Which wasn't an answer. I continued to stare until he added, "He did the same for me once. And I'll say no more about it."

Like the mysterious man from *Into the Woods*, he imparted his cryptic wisdom and then slipped away.

As soon as he was gone, Vee swooped in. Her lovely face furrowed in dismay. "I wish you'd reconsider letting Jamie and me go with you to the bridge."

I shook my head, rapidly putting an end to her request. I didn't have the strength to draw this out. When I'd told her as much last night, she'd urged me to sleep on it. In the clear light of late morning, I wanted to prolong this moment even less. All I had to do was say good-bye, give her a hug, and get out of Dodge — or in this case, get out of Doon.

As much as I tried, I couldn't form words. Instead, I embraced Vee with all the finality in my heavy heart. She hugged me back and was reluctant to let go when I stepped away.

"I've been thinking about something, and I didn't say anything before because I didn't want to freak you out." She nervously cleared her throat in that way she did when she was about to say something I wouldn't like. "If I'd never gone with you to Scotland, then you would've spent the summer alone in Alloway and the Brig o' Doon would've opened normally for the centennial. There's a chance you would've crossed the bridge with the other Destined. But because I came and we found your aunt's stuff, it happened early."

"So? I still would've been the same starry-eyed girl making the mistakes."

"Before the ball, I urged you to be brave with your feelings. Now it's my turn." Moisture trembled in the corner of her eyes as she clenched my hands. "I believe your destiny lies in Doon — that it's the Protector's will for you to be here. So stay. If not for Duncan or yourself, stay for me. Please?" Tears rolled down her cheeks, and my own eyes began to sting in response.

Blinking furiously, I willed myself to get a grip on my own emotions. This parting would be easier for both of us if I didn't dissolve into a blubbering mess. At least this time I could leave with the assurance of her forgiveness. "I can't. Please, this is hard enough already. You have to let me go."

Mournful acceptance radiated from her eyes. She swiped at her cheeks with the palm of her hand, then smiled a tight, wet smile. "Because you feel you have to, I will let you walk away … But, Kenna, I will *never* let you go."

To emphasize her words, she pulled me into one last bear hug. She had the makings of an amazing queen. I had no doubt that the kingdom and the people were in great hands. Squeezing her even tighter, I said, "Promise me you'll continue to defy gravity."

With a noise that was part sob and part chuckle, she replied, "Every chance I get."

Descending the stairs from Vee's chambers, I wondered if she was right about my destiny. Doon was the one place where I felt alive. But in my busted heart, Duncan would always be mine. The only way to set him free was to leave.

Duncan halted the wagon at the path that would lead us to the bridge. Rather than wait for his assistance, I hopped down and began walking. It took less than a dozen steps for him to catch up. Just like when we'd arrived in Doon, he had two mismatched duffels — his and hers, slung over his shoulders.

As he silently matched his pace to mine, I puzzled over Jamie's cryptic lake comment. I vividly remembered the lake from my previous visit. At the funeral for King MacCrae, Duncan had told me about the swans, Romeo and Juliet. Juliet had died, leaving Romeo to glide through life alone. I'd shared the story of my first kiss, never suspecting that under the alter ego of Finn, Duncan had experienced it firsthand.

We moved deeper into the gutted remains of the forest and my thoughts turned darker. In facing down the limbus, I'd confronted my own truth. As much as I'd wanted to believe abandoning my prince had been a noble act, I'd been scared. I didn't believe in forever. Halfway through the woods, everyone leaves you. My philosophy had always been to do the leaving first.

My world revolved around Aunt Gracie until she got sick. When she asked me to come to her bedside, I ignored her dying wish. Not only had I turned my back on her, I'd forsaken Finn, who held equal sway over my heart.

Vee had been my everything first — until Jamie came along. When his love for her eclipsed mine, I knew it was only a matter of time until there was no room for me. I thought it would be better for everyone if I was out of the picture.

And Duncan … leaving him on the bridge meant I would never have to risk him breaking my heart in the future. Because some random day he would've woken up in my world and realized that I was his biggest mistake. At least that was what I believed before the limbus.

If I'd truly forgiven myself — as I believed with my whole being that I had — why could I still feel the wounds from when I was twelve? And why were there fresh ones that made it feel as if something were shredding me from the inside out? In addition to forgiveness, was there something else my heart still needed?

Duncan stopped to slip Vee's ring on the tip of his finger. A puffy, purplish-black circle marred his right eye. After Vee and I had emerged from the limbus, it'd been swollen completely shut. At least now it was partially open. Though every time I looked at it, I had to resist the urge to kiss his boo boo.

With a nod, he said, "The Brig o' Doon's just ahead."

I hadn't planned on replying, but suddenly my mouth opened, and the words that tumbled out surprised me. "Jamie told me you avoid the loch."

Shadows from deep within his soul surfaced to cloak him in darkness despite the shining sun overhead. "Of course he did."

"Why?"

Duncan's focus shifted to something in the distance. "Every time I see that blasted swan, I — "

"You what?"

"I canna stand the sight of Romeo. Lately I've been of a mind that someone should put him out of his misery."

I knew him well enough to know he wasn't suggesting the actual murder of the bird. In his head, he was the swan. And I was his misery. Another little piece of my heart ripped apart.

Duncan and I walked in silence to where the path opened into the clearing. Since the previous evening, rains had washed most of the ash away, but the ground was still barren. Compared to the devastation on our side of the riverbank, the opposite was green and lush. The Pictish stone lay in two pieces next to the cobbled stones of the Brig o' Doon.

Occasionally Sondheim got it wrong. Bad news shouldn't be delivered on the weekend. Partings shouldn't happen at a park, a zoo, or any other special place. It should occur in a time and place that can't be spoiled. Tell me on a Monday morning at the bus stop in the pouring rain, or take me to a garbage dump teaming with flies — someplace that's going to suck regardless.

It shouldn't happen on a bridge ...

The tightness in my chest convinced me that any words of parting to Duncan would cause me to break down. Before he could go any farther, I stopped him by touching his arm. "You don't have to do this."

He exhaled in a huff. "Yes. I do. I told you I'd get ye back to your life, and I aim to do just that."

I was so tired of this destructive song and dance. Sometimes I just wanted to slap him. "I'm letting you off the hook, okay. Just help me open the portal and I won't be your problem anymore."

The incredulity on his face stopped me in my tracks. "You were never my problem, Mackenna."

"Good." Grabbing my canvas bag, I slipped the strap across my torso before he could object. "Then let's get on with our lives. Just stay here and I'll head out to the center."

I turned and determinedly walked across the bridge. It only took me a few steps to hear that Duncan was still following. When I spun around to confront him, he avoided my scowl by looking at his boots.

Holy Schwartz — he was irritating. "Just tell me why. *Why* are you so insistent on seeing me back to Chicago?"

Stubbornly, he said, "I made ye a promise. And I'm bound to see it through."

He was really going overboard with his little object lesson. "I get it! You keep your promises and I break mine. Message received. You're awesome and I — suck." My constricting throat caught the last word so that it squeaked out.

Shaking his head, he continued to stare at his boots. "You

misunderstand. I promised you the first time we met that I would always be there for you. Then after your aunt's funeral, I vowed to wait for you. The following summer I came to the bridge every day. And each day the next summer. Then I started to doubt. When ye finally showed in Doon, I'd all but convinced myself you were a figment o' my imagination. Don't you see? I broke my word to you long before you broke yours to me. I stopped believing in you — in us. When ye abandoned me on the bridge, I realized I'd never repented for that transgression. I'd pressed you for a promise I didna deserve."

Gently, I touched his arm. "Consider your promise fulfilled. You can go home now."

He raised his head to pierce me with his dark, anguished eyes. "I'm trying to — if you'd stop fighting me with every breath."

"Don't be absurd. Chicago's not your home."

"No," he said. "You are."

I did a double take. "But you hate me for what I did."

"Nay. I could never hate you."

My heart began to twirl even though my brain cautioned it not to get ahead of itself. "Really? You've started fantasizing about killing Romeo because of me."

"It's just, every time I see that swan — " His voice cracked. "I just missed you so much. My life fell apart for a wee bit."

From where I stood, that seemed like an understatement. "You stopped going to church ... Did I cause you to lose your faith?"

"Lose it? Nay. I might have misplaced it, but I've since found my way."

"With Analisa?"

"Ah, yes, Ana ..." He had the decency to look away. I prayed he didn't say he'd been doing anything as cold as using her to make me jealous. But when he finally met my gaze, I could see the real and very deep emotion in his eyes.

"Do you love her?" I steeled myself for an answer I wasn't sure I wanted to hear.

"I do care for her deeply." He raked his fingers through his dark hair to form those swoon-worthy chaotic peaks. "I've told her everything about us."

"You have?" His admission stung more than it should have.

"Aye. Ana's been most instructional."

He'd left me to be with her more times than I cared to admit. Although I didn't want to think about all the ways in which she might've instructed him, my mind jumped to the worst possible scenarios. "I'll bet."

He reached into his duffel and pulled out a small leather journal similar to the one Vee had made for him. "Tutoring sessions. Ana's been teaching me many valuable skills for the modern world."

"Why her?"

"She's a friend. Plus, the lass knows how to keep a secret."

Feeling petty and small, I couldn't help myself from asking, "You're really not involved with her?"

"She's Eponine — but of a platonic sort. You're my Cossette."

His confession was so momentous that I couldn't breathe for a sec. That Duncan would see me that way after everything I'd done was inconceivable. When I finally found my voice, it shook. "I thought you gave up on me."

He sniffed, his eyes pleading for my understanding. "I was sorely afraid if I told ye the truth, you'd feel trapped and leave me again. I couldna let that happen."

"So your plan was what? To deliver me to Chicago and then just stay?"

His head bobbed in confirmation. "Our first night in the

royal gardens, I promised I'd give ye my heart and never ask for it back. The last couple months have been so empty." His hands scrubbed his face as if he was trying to pull himself together. When he continued, his voice pitched so low that it sounded like a prayer. "All I'm asking is that you let me dwell near my heart."

Before I could answer, he cut me off. "You don't even have to see me, but if it shouldna work out between you and uh, Weston — should ye ever change your mind — we'll have a fighting chance."

"I tried to tell you a couple different times — he's not my boyfriend." One look at Duncan's face told me that our little misunderstanding had been tearing holes in him. "Wes isn't a nice guy — I don't want anything to do with him."

He blinked at me. "What?"

Fighting the urge to look away, I confessed, "I let you believe he was important to me, but he isn't — "

Without warning, Duncan pulled me against him and his lips crushed mine with a savage desperation. One of his hands wound tightly through my hair while the other dug into my waist as he anchored my body to his. I felt his heart, the one that belonged to me, pounding wildly in his chest. He held me even tighter, kissing me almost too fiercely but as long as he was mine, I didn't care. Just for this moment I would let his spell carry me away until I was brainless.

As abruptly as the kiss started, it ended — over too fast. Duncan jerked away with a gasp. His head dropped and his shadows burst forth. He buried his face against my neck, his tears wetting my skin.

When I thought about how close we'd come to losing each other — again, a sob burst from my lips. My body began to tremble against the weeping boy in my arms. Together at last, we cried, letting our emotions crash over us like giant waves ... until we were clean.

When Duncan finally stilled, he murmured, "I've been so daft. You're my heart, my home, my very soul — please believe the only world I desire is the one where you exist."

Taking his face between my hands, I kissed the tear track on one cheek and then the other, being extra gentle around his blackened eye. "If your heart's been in Chicago, mine's been in Doon. I want to stay — with you. I've loved you every day since I was six years old ..."

Duncan sighed. "From the first moment I laid my eyes on you."

He kissed me again — this time with a tenderness that spoke of the promises of our future life. As I lost myself in him, I could feel the pieces of my heart begin to heal.

When we finally parted, breathless and shaking, I asked for the one thing that would make staying absolutely perfect. "I want to establish a theater in Doon."

Duncan laughed, a deep, genuine sound that infused me with light. "I already told you I'd build ye one."

The right answer earned him a kiss. "And you'll try out for all the plays?"

He answered me with a playful, crooked grin. "Don't push your luck, woman."

"Oh, I'm gonna push." I could say unequivocally, with every fiber of my being, that Duncan MacCrae was leading man material.

"Shall we go tell my brother and the queen?"

When I nodded, Duncan threaded his fingers through mine and lifted my hand to his heart. Although defeating the limbus had been amazing, this was my true miracle — that my deepest desire, something I could scarcely admit wanting, had come to pass.

Now that the consequences of past mistakes had been washed away, Duncan and I could reclaim what we'd lost on the bridge. The happy ending I didn't deserve but wished for with all my heart was mine. And although I knew my wish came at a cost, some still, small voice deep inside assured me that my prince and I had already paid enough.

EPILOGUE

Veronica

The first time I read *Harry Potter and the Deathly Hollows*, I devoured all seven hundred and fifty-nine pages in less than a day. Rumors had been circulating that some of the main characters were going to die, so I couldn't stop reading until I found out if my friends Harry, Ron, and Hermione made it through to the end.

To my everlasting relief—spoiler alert—they all lived. But what I wasn't prepared for was the grief I felt at the end of that beloved book series. There would be no more magical adventures, no more crying over Harry's heartbreaks and triumphs, laughing at Ron's family dramas, or cheering on Hermione as she saved the boys' behinds—again. The series I'd spent half my life immersed in was over.

I told anyone who would listen that it felt like I'd lost my best friend. After losing Kenna for a second time, I knew how incredibly naive that statement had been. It was possible that having a limb amputated would be less painful—and probably easier to live with. I pulled my knees to my chest, and tugged the blanket tighter around my shoulders as another round of shivers racked through me. A cold I couldn't seem to escape.

Jamie closed the door behind him, crossed the room, and then took the three stairs to the solarium in a single bound — all without spilling a drop of my tea. Inside, I smiled at his effortless grace, but couldn't quite summon my lips to move.

"Thank you." I took the cup, wrapped my fingers around its heat, and stared out at the panorama below. Candy-corn-colored leaves rolled like waves in the treetops, dazzling against the background of grassy hills and the sapphire loch. Fall had descended upon Doon — Kenna the Autumn Fairy's favorite time of year.

Jamie sat close and guided my face toward him with a gentle finger on my cheek. "Hey, I know yer sad. But we also have much to celebrate. We're here, together." He leaned in and kissed my lips, warming me all the way to my toes. "And once again, you saved the kingdom. Not even that git MacNally can deny you're the Protector's chosen queen." Jamie's grin told me he'd gotten over my refusal to let him carry out his death threats against the mob leader. Sentencing the man to the dungeons until the next Centennial seemed to satisfy my prince's need for justice.

I rallied a smile, but it faltered as my vision clouded with tears. "She's not coming back this time, is she?"

With a scowl, Jamie took my tea, set it on the table, and lifted me onto his lap. I rested my head on his strong shoulder and bawled.

He let me cry, stroking my hair and my back until the sobs subsided into quiet hiccups. "You never know what the future may hold. I have a feelin' we'll see Mackenna again."

I nodded against his chest, sniffled, and wiped the tears from my cheeks. Jamie set me gently on the settee and then stood. "Be right back."

Perhaps he was right; there was so much to be thankful for. I tugged on the silver chain attached to the pendant resting against my chest. I was a queen, and like the courageous women who sat on the throne before me, self-indulgent pity was not an option.

Letting the cool breeze from the open window dry my face, I inhaled the comforting tang of wood smoke and roasting meat from the kitchens. Those last few terrifying hours in the limbus taught me to take nothing for granted, especially this amazing life I'd been given. I would miss Kenna every single day, but she would always be my sister, and I had to believe our paths would cross again. This was Doon after all, where nothing was ever predictable.

When Jamie returned holding out a handkerchief, I greeted him with a genuine smile.

He hesitated as his dark gold brows lifted in surprise. "Yer better now?"

I nodded, took the hankie, and blew my nose.

"Saints save me from women and their tears!" He flopped down beside me, arms and legs sprawling. "I vow I'll never comprehend them."

"You're doing just fine." I scooted over and snuggled into his big body. His arm went around me, tucking me close.

"If tha's true, then do me a wee favor."

I tilted my head back to meet his gaze. "Anything."

A grin tugged at the corner of his mouth. "Next time you decide to risk your life to save the kingdom, let me in on the plan in advance, aye?"

I arched a single brow and imitated his deep brogue, "Baby steps, love."

His eyes narrowed like a cat's before he pounced, his fingers finding the ticklish spot just below my ribs.

I howled and wiggled, laughing so hard I couldn't breathe. Pillows and blankets flying, Jamie leaned into my ear. "Promise me."

He drew back and I shook my head. "No way."

"That's it!" His dimpled grin faded as he took my face in his hands and lowered his delicious mouth to mine, kissing me with unhurried deliberation.

Soon, I wasn't sure of my own name, let alone what he'd wanted me to promise.

Then, suddenly, Jamie froze. Every muscle in his body on alert, he lifted his head.

"What?" I asked.

He rose to his knees on the bench and stared out the window at the courtyard below. The echo of horses' hooves galloping on stone compelled me to scramble up beside him. Cheers ushered a cart into view, along with the broad form of Duncan and an unmistakable redhead seated on the bench seat beside him.

"Kenna!" With a squeal, I whirled and jumped down the stairs. I was out the door before Jamie caught up to me. *Could it be true?* Had my best friend decided to stay?

I raced down the spiral staircase, Jamie close behind. I tripped down the last three steps, caught myself, and then ran for the doors to the courtyard. Halfway there I had to stop and catch my breath. Jamie looped his arm through mine as he passed. Stars spinning in front of my eyes, I let him tug me through the arched double doors and into the sunlit courtyard, where Duncan was lifting Kenna from the carriage.

Like a slow-motion scene, Kenna turned, her brilliant hair flying out behind her, her lips spreading into a wide smile. But her features blurred as darkness closed in on my periphery. Had I forgotten to eat breakfast again?

I shook my head, but my vision continued to narrow. Icy chills raced over my skin, my heart banging an erratic rhythm against my ribs. This was way more than a skipped meal. The world titled and I lurched forward.

Jamie grabbed me just as my legs gave out. He lowered me to the ground, his beautiful, terror-stricken face hovering above me. His head turned and he began to yell, but I couldn't comprehend his words.

I struggled to slow my breathing, to calm my pulse. My body refused to obey. I grasped Jamie's arms, fighting for air like a drowning person. Shadows crowded in on all sides.

Jamie shook his head, repeating the word "No" over and over, but I needed for him to hear me. Had to make sure he knew. "I ..."

He leaned closer, his warm tears blanketing my face. Unable to get my voice above a whisper, I tried again. "I'll ... always ... lov—"

Agony exploded inside my chest. The ground pulled away beneath me. My entire life narrowed to a single point—Jamie's face as he mouthed the word "love." And the blackness swallowed him.

ACKNOWLEDGMENTS

Co-writing a series is one of the most challenging, fulfilling things either one of us has ever attempted to do. Thankfully, we have wonderful friends who continue to support us on this epic journey that we call Doon.

Thank you to:

Jacque Alberta, for her love for this series, discerning editing eye, and her alter ego, Queen Picky Pants, who pointed out — very rightly — that Highland sheep do not have wool on their legs. Thanks for always watching out for us!

The **Blink** and **Zondervan** teams, for their patient collaboration with two authors who want to have their fingers on every aspect of the process, and for all the amazing work you do.

Agent extraordinaire **Nicole Resciniti**, for being our champion.

Melissa Landers, our critique partner and friend, for being an early reader of *Destined for Doon*, and for occasionally pulling us back from the edge with a much needed girls' night.

Meredith Briski, for helping create the initial vision for Kenna and Duncan's story, and for begging for more sword fights — they're coming, we promise!

The **librarians**, **bloggers**, and dedicated **booksellers**, for advocating *Doon* and supporting these two unknown debut authors.

The **Doon Street Team** — Amber, Amanda C., Jules, Ange, Tracy, Stephanie, Sara, Amanda S., Charity, Debz, Jessica, Rachel, Kathryn, Amber F., and Cameron — for helping us build the Doon brand. Without you we would just be two girls tweeting into oblivion.

Mike Heath, for designing another awe-inspiring, enchanted cover.

Sarah Alsberg, for her social networking genius and infectious *Doon* love!

Our ever-faithful **readers**, for falling in love with Jamie and Duncan, for wanting to be like Vee and Kenna, and for wishing they lived in Doon. Your encouraging messages mean more to us than you could ever comprehend.

The **God** of the universe, our Protector and the Creator of our dreams, without whom our writing would be meaningless.

Lorie would like to thank:

My family and friends, for tirelessly spreading the word about Doon, for being my personal cheering squad, and for occasionally pulling me out of the world of kilts and curses to experience the magic of real life. You know who you are, and I love you all.

Carey would like to thank:

Athena for being the best assistant/theater buddy/daughter that I could ever hope for. Aaron and Harrison, who aren't so bad either! My amazing family and friends for their overwhelming support — especially Autumn Schultz, Karen Powers, Sara Boepple, Mickey Merritt, Graciela Campos, and Shey's girls back in Texas — I love you all bunches! And **Lorie,** whose vision started this challenging and incredible journey; because of you I have been changed for good.

Discussion Questions

1. When Duncan mistakenly believes that Weston is Mackenna's serious boyfriend, Mackenna doesn't correct him. Why do you think she does this? Have you ever decided to let someone believe their misconception was true? Why?

2. Near the beginning of the book, the Rosetti Tavern is set upon by a small mob of dissenters. Veronica wants to talk to them, but Jamie carries her — quite forcibly — out the back door. Was he right to do so? Was this an instance of Jamie being overprotective or was it an appropriate occasion to disobey the queen's commands?

3. Mackenna tells Vee that she left Duncan on the bridge of Doon in order to protect him. Do you think Kenna was successful in this goal? Could there be another reason she returned to Chicago alone?

4. Now that Veronica has become queen, she realizes there is a lot more to the role than crowns and pretty dresses. In fact, much of the job is extremely stressful. What do you think would be the hardest part about being the ruler of a country? What do you think is the hard part for Vee?

5. In order to provide a cover story for Kenna's sudden appearance, she and Duncan have to fake a romance — even though there is a real one simmering just below the surface. How do you think acting out their "fake" feelings influences their true ones?

6. Veronica's father abandoned her, and her mother is more concerned with her boyfriends than her own daughter. How do you think Vee's life back in the States colors the way she sees Doon? How do you think it influences her relationship with Jamie?

7. In Queen Lynette's memoir, Veronica reads, "*Authority, I found, did not make one a queen.*" What do you think that line means?

8. When Duncan catches Mackenna singing in the garden, he admits to her that he watched her Chicago performance. What do you think this means to Mackenna? Why does it catch her off guard?

9. Why do you think Duncan never told Mackenna that he was her imaginary friend, Finn? How might it have changed their relationship if he had?

10. At the end of the book, Mackenna has to face apparitions of Veronica, Aunt Gracie, Finn, and Duncan. What do their words and Mackenna's reactions reveal about Mackenna's secret feelings and fears?

11. Makenna turns out to be wrong about Analise. Were her harsh judgments justified, or should she have done more to understand the true Analise?

12. What is it that enables Mackenna and Duncan to finally admit their true feelings to each other?

Like what you just read? Then check out
this exclusive sneak peak from the third book
in the series, *Shades of Doon*.

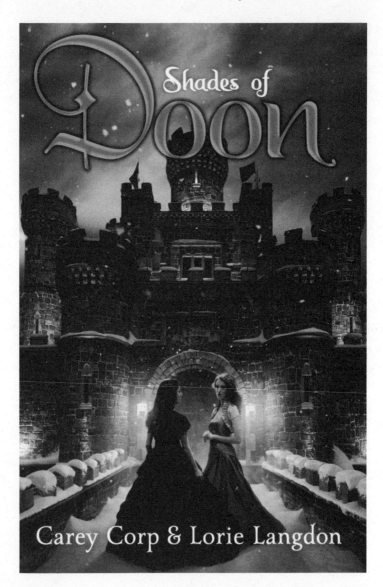

CHAPTER 1

Veronica

Cheating death tends to make you live with your whole heart—to take risks and enjoy each moment, no matter how gritty. I reminded myself of this as all of Doon stood in hushed anticipation of a potential bloodbath. One involving the boy I loved.

A resounding boom split the silence, and a line of drummers emerged from the arched opening at the east end of the arena.

Their leader in full highland regalia, including a headdress over a foot tall, marched into the stadium while brandishing a bronze staff. The drum beats quickened, echoing in time with my heart as they ushered in flag bearers waving standards from every Doon citizen's nation of origin.

Italy, Africa, China, America, India, Australia ... the flags kept coming, their kaleidoscope of colors snapping in the breeze. Everyone in the stadium rose to their feet, and the realization washed over me that this was my kingdom — the beautifully diverse land I was so very privileged to lead.

Sensing my flood of emotion, my best friend, Kenna, wrapped her arm around my shoulders, and we leaned our heads together as the procession filed into rows, and then continued to march in place. The grand marshal twirled his staff and threw it high into the air. The second he caught it, the drums cut off.

Several dozen bagpipers, dressed in traditional kilts, high socks, and matching black tams, streamed in from both sides of the stadium. Their music wove its spell around me, and when the drums joined in, the effect was breathtaking. This dramatic ceremony ushered in the final day of the festival celebrating both our freedom from the evil limbus that had almost destroyed us all and my seemingly miraculous recovery.

The final notes of the song faded away, and the grand marshal gestured for everyone to be seated. I smoothed the fabric of my full-length skirt and adjusted the MacCrae tartan draped across my bodice. Fiona, my ever-wise advisor and friend, had suggested a traditional Doonian dress of celery and forest green stripes. She'd also insisted on fixing my hair herself, plaiting the length into a side braid adorned with silk butterflies and matching ribbons.

The stadium began to shake as two massive war horses, manes and tails flying out behind them, galloped onto the field. Warmth rose in my cheeks at the exhilarating sight of my prince astride his chestnut stallion, Crusoe.

"What are they doing?" Kenna asked, both of us sitting a little straighter as the MacCrae brothers hurtled full speed in our direction.

I glanced down at my schedule of events, but didn't see anything between the closing ceremonies and the big fight. "I have no clue."

The brothers, bare chested and wearing identical kilts in blue and green MacCrae tartan, pulled their mounts to a stop directly in front of the royal box. Duncan, riding his ebony mare, Mabel, quirked a lopsided grin as Jamie dismounted and jogged up the stairs to where we sat in the stands.

Jamie stopped on the stoop in front of us, his gorgeous face a study of contrasts — eyes glinting with mischief while his lips and jaw were set in solemn lines. He bowed with an exaggerated flourish of his hand, drawing giggles from my self-appointed ladies-in-waiting — Gabby Rosetti and her gaggle of girlfriends.

Playing along, I lifted my chin and hiked up my brows, adopting the most royal expression I could manage. But the moment Jamie's dark gaze met mine, my pretense melted into a wide smile. His stare grew warm as he stated his request in a deep, resounding voice. "I fight this day in your honor, my lady queen. And would humbly request a token to take into battle."

The Doonians clapped and hooted their encouragement. I bit my lip. *A token?* Was I supposed to give him a kiss, or something more tangible? I tried to remember what I'd seen in movies.

Kenna tugged on the tip of my braid and instructed, "Give him something he can wear, Highney."

I shot my smart-apple friend a glare at the nickname she'd taken to using recently — a combination of *Highness* and behind. To keep me humble, she claimed. I rolled my eyes at her as I stood and pulled an emerald ribbon from my hair. Getting into the spirit of the moment, I cleared my throat and proclaimed, "Prince James Thomas Kellan MacCrae, my bravest knight, I bestow my favor upon thee!"

There were whoops and applause as Jamie took a knee and

bowed his head over his flexed right arm. I would never get used to the boy who'd been groomed from birth to be king, kneeling to *me*. Hastily, I tugged him to his feet.

With the entire kingdom watching, I brushed my fingers over his sun-warmed skin and wrapped the ribbon around his bulging bicep, just below his tattoo. Even placing it at the indention of his muscles, the ends of the cloth barely met. As I pulled the knot tight, Jamie leaned down and murmured against my ear, "Thank you, my heart."

A shiver ricocheted up my spine, and when he caught my gaze with that wicked spark in his eye, I knew he'd felt my reaction.

I adjusted the band of fabric and whispered, "Try not to get yourself killed. I may require your services later." Jamie grew still and I arched a brow at him, curling up one side of my mouth. "As a chaperone for the festival, of course."

A low chuckle escaped his chest and our eyes met in silent understanding before he turned and jumped off the bleachers. Once on the field, he swung up onto Crusoe's back, took the reins, and wheeled the horse around in one graceful, seamless motion. Then he glanced back over his shoulder to make sure I was watching. *Show off.*

As Duncan guided Mabel away from the stands, Kenna shot to her feet and shouted his name. Just as he turned back, she chucked a dark ball in his direction. Duncan reached up and caught it. Then, to the delight of the crowd, Kenna yelled, "Go get 'em, ogre!"

He gave a salute and then galloped after his brother. Together, they rode to the center of the arena, where the pipers had cleared off and a group of boys were constructing a fighting ring made of ropes and weighted poles.

I glanced at my BFF just as she slipped her pale foot back into her shoe.

"Did you just give Duncan your sock?" I squeaked.

"Yep." She nodded and then turned to me with an impish grin. "I just hope he ties it somewhere far away from his nose."

With a hoot of laughter, I grabbed her hand and pulled her against me. "I love you."

She wrinkled her nose and shrugged. "I know."

Back on the field, Duncan was wisely attaching Kenna's sock to the weapon holster at his waist while Jamie loosened up by rolling his neck from side to side. The brothers' competitors had arrived — Fergus and his only slightly less mountainous cousin, Ewan Lockhart. Fergus tied the length of his strawberry-blond hair back from his face and blew someone in the audience a kiss. I leaned forward and saw Fiona catch it and hold it to her chest, giving her husband a broad wink. They had to be the cutest married couple I'd ever known.

"Esteemed ladies and gents of Doon!" the announcer boomed.

We took our seats and Kenna tilted her head to the side. "The acoustics in here are great. That guy isn't even shouting."

But I was barely listening. I smoothed the hair around my crown, tugged on the sleeves of my blouse, and worked to paste a calm expression on my face. I hated this part.

The announcer continued. "Today, an ancient feud that dates back hundreds of years before the Covenant will be played out before our eyes! The esteemed clan Lockhart versus the noble clan MacCrae!"

The crowd roared, the reverberation of their joined voices and stamping feet signaling the beginning of the fight. Duncan and Fergus exited the ring. Apparently this was a tag team match, and Jamie was up first.

Ewan Lockhart crouched in one corner. With his thick build, shaggy dark hair, and beard, he resembled a Sasquatch ready to pounce. In the diagonal corner, Jamie drew his weapon and bounced on the balls of his feet, my pulse jumping with him. The Doonians had been chattering about this match for weeks, making friendly wagers and trash talking — it was the highlight of the games. Too bad I wasn't going to get to enjoy it.

"Vee, open your eyes," Kenna hissed. "This fight is happening whether you watch it or not."

She had a point. I squinted open one eye and gripped the arms of my chair so hard I broke a fingernail.

The referee gave a signal and the competitors leapt forward. Jamie swung his sword in a forceful arc, the blade angled toward Ewan's head. I leaned forward, both eyes wide as Ewan blocked the blow with a deafening clang. Their swords clashed and they forced each other across the ring and back, neither one of them gaining an advantage, until Ewan's ham-sized fist connected with Jamie's jaw. I cringed as he stumbled back several steps. With a shake of his head, he recovered and charged.

"Don't worry, Vee," Kenna whispered. "It's not real. They're just putting on a good show."

I wasn't so sure about that. I'd seen Jamie and Duncan training in the Brother Cave. They were out for blood. Not to kill or maim, of course, but first blood was a big deal — bragging rights for weeks after. And this was a tournament in front of the entirety of Doon.

Jamie landed a kidney punch just below Ewan's chain mail vest as Duncan and Fergus yelled advice from the sidelines. With a snarl, Ewan lunged, his blade coming within millimeters of my boyfriend's exposed throat. Jamie dodged, but it was way too close for comfort.

Oh yeah, they were taking this seriously. I shot to my feet, but as I yelled, "Stop!" the spectators surged up around me, their screams and applause drowning me out.

Kenna made her way to her feet a moment later. "He knows what he's doing. Have a little faith."

As if to prove her point, Jamie landed a blow to Ewan's back with the flat of his sword, making the giant stagger forward. Kenna clapped in response and shouted, "Whoohoo! Go Surfer Dude!"

I choked on a laugh. *Surfer Dude* was the name she'd given Jamie when we first arrived in Doon, and it in no way described my intense, fiercely protective leader of a prince — other than his longish tawny hair, of course.

A spastic movement down in the front row caught my eye. Lachlan MacPhee, the cute boy who'd first shown me Jamie's playful side with a mock sword-fight in the marketplace, mimicked his royal idol's every move. He rotated his arms in a wide arc, as Jamie's sword smashed against Ewan's with a clang. The other pre-teens surrounding Lachlan shouted and pumped their fists like zealous fans at a professional wrestling event.

Their rapt excitement reminded me that this was supposed to be fun. But as Ewan swung wide and Jamie ducked, avoiding the blade at the last possible second, my attention riveted back on the match. Jamie rose and whirled behind the bigger guy, hooking his arm around Ewan's neck. With a snarl, Ewan flipped Jamie over his head. Jamie landed in the dirt, but didn't even pause. Muscles flexing, he sprang to his feet with powerful grace and the two were back at it, sparring in a complex sequence that had them dancing all over the ring.

"Oh, they're good," Kenna commented, not taking her eyes from the action.

Ewan charged, and one side of Jamie's mouth curled as he climbed the ropes and then jumped and spun, delivering a roundhouse kick to his giant opponent's chest. Ewan teetered back and then fell face-first into the dirt. Jamie, who'd landed on his feet, pumped a fist in the air and the crowd exploded in cheers. My neck and shoulders slumped, the tension breaking free. Ken was right; I needed to trust Jamie. Clearly, he could hold his own.

When Ewan staggered to his feet but couldn't maintain his balance, Duncan and Fergus tagged in. The size discrepancy between Duncan and Fergus was roughly the same as Jamie and his opponent, but the bigger guys moved with less agility and more force. As Duncan and Fergus clashed swords, Kenna stilled beside me. I smirked and opened my mouth to tease her, but bit back the comment when Fergus disarmed Duncan, his sword clanking across the ring.

A hush descended on the audience and my vision went blurry. I rubbed my temples and took a few cleansing breaths before I opened my eyes and — saw a car on the far side of the arena. Not a horse-drawn wagon or a carriage. A freaking modern-day car.

Shimmering like a mirage, the dull red Toyota chugged along and cruised behind the ring. My veins turned to ice as my eyes followed the vehicle until it vanished from view.

Someone to my left gasped, and I twisted to see my assistant, Emily, clapping. Back in the ring, Duncan had regained his sword. My eyes locked on Jamie as he gripped the ropes, shouting at his brother. But it was like I watched him through a window screen. I blinked, desperate to recalibrate my vision, but the walls of the stadium, the people, even the bleachers began to fade around me. The noise of the crowd became muffled, sounding farther and farther away. The floor tilted beneath me. This could not be happening again.

Was Doon disappearing, or was I?

CHAPTER 2

Mackenna

oly Schwartz! I watched the red car disappear down an asphalt lane that had materialized in the center of the coliseum. The ground, which had been flat dirt moments ago, was now covered in gently sloping grass littered with billboards. Duncan, Jamie, and the rest of the Doonians shimmered like ghostly mirages while I grappled with my bearings.

Queasy and coated in a fine sheen of sweat, I dug my nails into the palms of my hands — an old trick for stage fright. The sharp sensation pulled my focus inward and away from the cirque du bizarre happening in the arena. Around me I heard the crowd cheer, but it was muted, as if someone had turned the sound down low.

I took a deep breath as I closed my eyes, and when I opened them again — the road was still there. A blue minicar appeared, following in the red car's path. At the opposite end of the stadium, a flatbed truck barreled toward the tiny car at high speed.

This had to be some sort of sun-induced delusion. Heat

stroke or something. Squinting skyward, I discounted the explanation almost immediately. The early morning sun had not yet crested the stadium bleachers. And the temperatures were fall-like, not scorching.

My surroundings were eerily quiet, and although I could still see the Doonians, my head ached when I tried to focus on them. Beside me, I heard Vee's unmistakable yogic breathing. I glanced in her direction and then followed her wide-eyed stare to the impending collision of the truck and the car.

Without so much as a honk of its horn, the truck smashed into the much smaller vehicle. The sickening crunch of twisting metal filled my ears, along with a strange buzzing noise. The sound surged and became thunderous cheers as Doon snapped back into place. The car accident was gone, leaving me with a discomforting sense of vertigo as I noted Duncan and Jamie standing over their disarmed opponents. They'd won the match.

Fighting the urge to barf, I clapped for Team MacCrae, whom I'd dubbed *Surfer Dude* and the *Amazing Ogre* in honor of Vee's and my first time in Doon. So much had happened since then. My Indiana bestie had defeated the evil witch and, in doing so, became queen of the legendary Scottish kingdom. I'd faced my fears in order to destroy the zombie fungus and gotten a second chance at happily ever after with the boy of my dreams. It was the stuff of fairy tales ... and yet, Cinderella's epilogue had never included delusions of a head-on collision between two horseless carriages.

I glanced at Vee, who was wildly applauding her Charming. She had that manic aspect of someone committed to avoiding their present reality. When she caught my eye, her facade cracked. Her face turned a sickly shade of yellowish-green that mirrored how I felt on the inside.

Jamie, Duncan, Fergus, and Ewan exited at the opposite

end of the arena. Guessing that we would not see them again until they'd cleaned up, I placed my hand under Vee's elbow and lifted her to her feet as I stood. "The queen and I need to use the royal restroom."

Vee's brow furrowed. "No, I don't."

"Well, I do." I tugged at her sleeve. "Are you sure you don't need to tinkle?"

Tinkle was the code word we'd used in junior high when we wanted to chat privately in the girl's room. Vee's eyes widened slightly as she nodded. "Actually, I do need to go."

As she stepped toward the back of the royal box, Emily Roosevelt and Gabriela Rosetti, who'd recently joined the royal entourage as Vee's ladies-in-waiting, moved to follow. Vee stopped them with a wave of her hand. "Thanks, but I think Kenna and I can do this alone."

In tandem, we climbed down the stairs and walked a short distance away from the festivities to a short brick structure. There were several such bathrooms ringing the arena, but only one had a private guard and required a crown to enter. This particular building had two doors, one for the king and another for the queen.

The guard stepped aside and we entered a private sitting room. Divans and oversized ottomans in plush cream fabrics dotted the area. Interspersed tables provided a variety of fruit, sweets, and drinks — all decidedly unappetizing after what I'd just witnessed.

Vee headed straight to a set of sinks at the back of the room, where she turned on the taps and splashed water over her face. One of my first and most favorite discoveries about the kingdom of Doon had been its running water — a pleasant surprise given the medieval kingdom's lack of other modern conveniences like electricity, refrigeration, and microwaves. *Yay for modern plumbing!*

My bestie took her time patting her face dry before speaking. "What's up, Ken?"

She looked so composed that I instantly doubted what I thought I knew. "Uh," I stammered, unsure how to begin. "That was a surprising turn of events out there."

Her brow pinched. "You mean with Jamie and Duncan? 'Cause they were the favorite to win, regardless of Fiona's trash talk."

Though Vee and I shared a brain more often than not, this didn't seem to be one of those times. Rather than fish for confirmation that my hunch about her was correct, I blurted out, "Cars. I saw cars. Actually—two cars and a truck, and they collided with a crunch and I'm pretty sure I'm Coco Puffs."

The corner of Vee's lip twitched, and then her careful composure cracked with a gigantic sigh. "Oh, thank heavens."

"That I'm cuckoo?"

She shook her head as she sank onto a plushy divan. "That you saw it too. I thought it was just me—that I was getting sick again or something."

I sat in the chair opposite her and searched her vibrant blue eyes. "So we're both crazy?"

"No. It means what we saw was real."

Her words were hardly reassuring. "So how come the villagers didn't freak out?"

"Kenna, you really have to stop referring to the other citizens as 'the villagers.' You're one of them now. They're not about to come after you with pitchforks."

No matter how many times Vee said that, I still felt like an outsider. Duncan said to give it time, so I was trying not to obsess about being the new kid on the block. But I was mentally digressing. Returning to the topic of tales from the weird side, I said pointedly, "No one else seemed to see the collision except us."

"I'm not sure why." Vee bit at her lip, signifying she was deep in thought. "None of the other Destined seemed to see it either. Just us ... Maybe it has something to do with our gifts, or our connection to the Rings of Aontacht or the modern world. Or maybe—"

"Or maybe it was PTDS. A post-traumatic Doon stress."

She responded just as I hoped, with a half-hearted chuckle. I'd heard somewhere that a sense of humor meant you hadn't gone completely off your rocker. "I think you mean post-traumatic stress disorder. It's an interesting theory though. We should probably do some research, see what we can find about visions appearing to those called to Doon."

"Okay—let's not do any of that." Vee started to protest, but I rushed on. "Wait. Just hear me out. There's no reason to believe that we'll have more hallucinations. For all we know, it was an isolated thing, like the adrenaline rush bus drivers get when they need to lift a car off a baby. So please don't make a big deal about this."

"But—"

"No buts." The sound of bagpipes drifted in from the coliseum, signaling we were almost out of time. If we didn't hurry back, people would come looking for us. "Let's pretend that nothing happened and enjoy the absence of conflict for once. We've got princes who adore us and a *ka-lay-lee* to go to."

"A *céilidh*." She pronounced it *kay-lee*, like a girl's name. "I'm really looking forward to it."

Fiona had described it as a gathering with traditional folk music and dancing. Apparently the weekly dinner-dances held in the Great Hall of Castle MacCrae were also céilidhs, but the one tonight in the village marketplace, marking the end of the highland games, would be the mother of all gatherings. In addition to dancing, there would be folk art and storytelling — the closest Doon had to a thriving arts scene.

Rummaging through my bag, I pulled out a tube of mango-granate lip gloss and handed it to Vee. "Doesn't a Kaylee party sound better than research?"

Vee contemplated the gloss like it was a horse full of Trojan soldiers before taking it out of my hand. "Besides," I prompted, "what do you think is going to happen if you tell Jamie about this? Do you really want to go on lockdown again?"

Even though Doc Benoir had declared Vee recovered from whatever had caused her to collapse the day that I'd decided to stay in Doon, the cause was still a mystery. And without a reasonable medical explanation, Jamie tended to hover over her like a male version of Mama Rose searching for the slightest hint of a relapse.

"Fine," Vee capitulated, "we can chalk whatever happened out there up to PTSD — for now. But if anything like that happens again — to *either* one of us — we're going to tell our friends immediately and then do everything we can to get to the bottom of it. Deal?"

She held out her hand and we shook on it. "Deal."

After the drama of the Eldritch Limbus, we were entitled to time off for good behavior. In the last couple months we'd rescued Doon not once but twice from evil, and it was high time to enjoy the benefits of saving the world. Her Royal Highney and I had waited long enough for our happily ever afters.

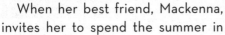

A Doon Novel

Doon

Carey Corp & Lorie Langdon

Veronica doesn't think she's going crazy. But why can't anyone else see the mysterious blond boy who keeps popping up wherever she goes?

When her best friend, Mackenna, invites her to spend the summer in Scotland, Veronica jumps at the opportunity to leave her complicated life behind for a few months. But the Scottish countryside holds other plans. Not only has the imaginary kilted boy followed her to Alloway, she and Mackenna uncover a strange set of rings and a very unnerving letter from Mackenna's great aunt—and when the girls test the instructions Aunt Gracie left behind, they are transported to a land that defies explanation.

Doon seems like a real-life fairy tale, complete with one prince who has eyes for Mackenna and another who looks suspiciously like the boy from Veronica's daydreams. But Doon has a dark underbelly as well. The two girls could have everything they've longed for… or they find themselves in a world that has become a nightmare.

Available in stores and online!

BLINK

Shades of Doon

Carey Corp & Lorie Langdon

After cheating death, Veronica Welling is determined to savor every moment in her idyllic kingdom with both her true love and best friend by her side at last. At the same time, Mackenna Reid is enthusiastically building her new life and a theater with her prince. But just as their dreams of happiness are within reach, the world Vee and Kenna have chosen is ripped away, leaving them to face their most horrific challenge yet—their old lives.

Thrust out of Doon, the best friends are confronted with tormentors from their past and no way to return to their adopted land. When the MacCrae brothers rush to their rescue, the girl's situation turns from nightmare to modern-day fairy tale. But their happiness could be short lived: unbeknownst to them, someone in their closest circle is aiding the witch of Doon in her bid to destroy the kingdom once and for all.

Available in stores and online!

BLINK